The Numen

C. E. Kelly

Dedicated to my mother
Who may, or may not,
have been proud of me
for writing it

How to use this book

This book is a fictional story about a young man making profound discoveries about himself. He is a college student who encounters a strange presence who changes his life. This presence is indicated by chapters marked with a water drop. These chapters are so marked to make it easier should you want to reread any of them.

The story is simple, but the concepts, for some of us, are new. However, this is not a "new age" book, but just a slightly different way of looking at things. Some of it is entirely fantasy, some of it is not. In any case, I hope this is an interesting read, in spite of your beliefs. There isn't anything "channeled" in this book, instead, it represents entirely my own ideas. Writing it was a solitary effort.

Any names, places or references to anyone living or dead, is totally by accident, except, of course, Jesus. He was not an accident.

Love and Light.

CONTENTS

ZIMMER

It was late in the day when the student finally made up his mind to visit this place. He was reluctant and almost sprinted away but another student pushed past him and held the door. He stepped through and looked around. He knew he'd never been here before, even though this place should have been one of his first stops. He would have remembered the old-fashioned blue and green flecked floor tiles and shiny beige walls, and that smell - it was peculiar. It was like a giant hand had mixed flour with Pine Sol and coffee.

He turned down a hall and left behind the natural light coming through the glass of the doors. Tom felt like he was in a place that was damp, only it wasn't. It was just dim. A feeling of doom engulfed him.

The various doors down the hall had numbers, but he was looking for the one door that didn't have a number. At least that's what he'd been told. He'd heard the entire area around the door took on a vague difference that was unmistakable but when he asked his friends they could not explain why or how. They just danced from one leg to the other and looked away.

Yes, the door. It was said to be like all the other doors, made of steel and painted a darker tan with the same silver doorknob. The doors were lining the hall, up and down, all leading to closed rooms, to offices with gray desks, he knew, because the building was like that. All the doors he passed had numbers and neat cards posted in small metal frames listing a title, but that didn't change what was inside. The place was old. The desks were old. Everything about it felt old.

He was about halfway down the hall when he did notice a slight change, a shift in the atmosphere. He shook his head thinking he was mistaken. The smell of pine seemed to have become stronger somehow, but it didn't have the unpleasantness of the cleaner anymore. Now he thought of the freshness of rain hitting pine needles as if he was walking through a forest. When he looked down at the tile it didn't seem so old and hard, but felt like he could be walking on a gentler path. And then it shifted and that feeling of discomfort returned.

He shook his head.

Then he saw what he was looking for - a small table next to a door with a tablet where people had signed their name to go into the room. Anyone signing their name on the simple line had been notified that they were eligible to enter. Some of them had waited a long time for that privilege.

He stood there looking at the roster. He didn't know anybody who had signed in before him. He wasn't quite sure what to do. He looked around, as if somebody was going to show up to tell him what to do, but of course nobody was going to. He printed his name like all the others, signed after it, and momentarily had a strange vision, a kind of day dream. He looked at his hand, but it didn't look like his hand, it was younger - like that of a little kid. He saw himself playing in the woods. He shook his head and stared at the door. Suddenly he was skipping and running off down a landing, heading for an amusement ride, and it was a place of such magical fun that he was laughing in anticipation. Then he was on a roller coaster ride and it was climbing a hill for a great ride. He felt the air going through his hair as he went over the top. He gripped the railing and. . .

He looked down at his hand and dropped the pen that he still held. His hand was burning from gripping it. The dream faded. He stood there stupidly. The laughter had been real. He could hear himself as it died in his throat. Had he been laughing out loud? He was glad nobody was in the hall to have heard the sound because he had no idea why he had uttered such a noise when he really didn't think today was going to be any fun at all. Nobody had said it was going to be fun. He examined his hand. It was red but it didn't hurt anymore.

He knocked, listened, knocked again and still heard nothing. "I don't know what to do," he mumbled.

The door opened by itself.

He entered the room expecting to see the person who had opened the door to be there. It would be somebody saying, "howdy, how are you. . .your turn," or something like that, but whoever had been there, wasn't there now.

The room was empty. . .

Or was it?

Rumor had it that the first student entering this room was a German girl attending the university as a beginning freshman. She had called this place - klassenzimmer (classroom), which was shortened for a time to simply zimmer, even though the building was mostly administration and didn't have classes for students. The name stuck for a long time until a medical student started calling it the Numen room, which some people thought was strange and would correct anyone saying it to: "Oh, you're going to visit Mr. Numen today."

The room wasn't a classroom per se and never did have a number, but then for those lucky enough to find their way into it, they knew what the term really meant and Numen did not mean Mister. "Others liked the term zimmer, and still called it that, which implied more than a room in their minds, because it was foreign after all, since what was in that room was something different. It was an unusual place for each person lucky enough to go through that door.

On this day, it was Tom's turn.

He stood there dumbfounded. The door behind him closed silently on its own and he stepped further into the space still feeling like the roller coaster was under him. He was in a room of light, a sunny comfortable room, not large or small, but the size of a living room. It felt intimate and not at all like a classroom or office. It seemed like it was divided into thirds, but it was difficult for him to imagine its total size since a portion of it was blocked off. There was something very strange about the room. It was unlike any room Tom had ever been in.

At one end, a drape hung from the ceiling and went entirely across the expanse of the space, dividing it lengthwise. It was a flimsy thing that was light and somewhat shear, except it was a deep blue and didn't reveal much. Tom thought about draping he'd seen at the theater, like a scrim, but that was silly, because this was just a room. In front of the drape was a thick velvet cord. It appeared to be suspended, but from what? He couldn't see anything holding it in place. He looked further, walking this way and that, but gave up. The fabric created a visual barrier, one that said "Do not approach the drape."

A voice came from behind the drape.

"Hello," It said, "Welcome."

Tom walked closer and could see a single figure behind the drape. Was he or she sitting? It seemed so. The person spoke again.

"Hello."

"Hello." Tom said uncomfortably, wondering if the Voice was male or female. He couldn't tell. He stood there awkwardly.

There was a polished wood table facing the middle of the drape, in front of where the figure was sitting, which was in the middle of the room. There was a lamp on the table and a roller chair pulled up to it. Along the outside wall of the room was a window, an easy chair and coffee table. There was a picture hanging on the wall and a couple of figurines on stands and another chair in the room. It could have been a side room in a gallery or an art museum. Almost. He thought of a living room. Everything about the room had an elegance. He stood there looking in the direction of the curtain.

"Why are you here?" A neutral voice asked from behind the drape.

Tom coughed nervously through a constricted throat, then laughed as he struggled to frame an answer. "I, uh, I uh, got a call that there was an opening for me. I heard I could learn some things here." He finally said simply.

"Then please sit down and tell me your name."

"My name is Tom." He chose the table.

"You can call me Teacher," a he, or she, said.

"Okay. Alright. I have waited a long time to enter this room," Tom said.

"Why a long time? Was there a line outside?" Teacher asked.

"No, but. . .the room, this here classroom, uh, place, was always taken. Somebody has always been here." He said uncomfortably.

"Always?"

"Well, every time I could. . ."

"Oh. I see . . .and now the time is . . .shall we say. . .right?"

"Yes. The timing for the room is perfect. I am very pleased about it." Tom said, a slight cough escaping. He twirled his fingers nervously waiting to hear something from the figure that had been an "It" and now was "Teacher" and already becoming a "he."

"That means you are ready to learn."

"Where do I start?" Tom asked.

"Start?"

"Yes. . ."

There was an eerie kind of silence. The student could hear himself breathing, so he began to breathe in a shallower manner and strained to hear anything from the Teacher. There was nothing.

"Can I ask a question?" Tom finally asked.

"Yes."

"What am I supposed to be doing?"

"What you are doing." Teacher answered.

"What is that?"

"Asking questions."

"Asking questions?"

"Yes."

"I don't understand. I haven't asked anything yet."

"Yes, you have." Teacher said, "You asked the most important question of all. You asked, 'What am I supposed to be doing?' You are here to try and find the answer to that question. You see, to ask a question is more important than the answer."

"Oh." Tom sat quietly for a while. He knew the experience in this room was going to be different, maybe even life-changing. But he hadn't known how. People who had been in the room never talked about it, but they always seemed to come away with a sense of destiny about them, a way of approaching life had a sense of direction, maybe enlightenment.

"Okay," Tom said quickly, "If I am doing what I am supposed to be doing, getting my homework done and keeping up with my grades, then what am I supposed to be doing here. In this room?"

"Finding your answers," said Teacher.

"To what?"

"To the questions you have not even thought of asking . . .yet. To those things you have been too preoccupied or too scared to ask, maybe too frightened to think about. In this room, you can think about them."

"Oh." Tom thought about this for a minute, then laughed nervously, and said glibly, "Like, like . . .is there a God, or something like that, I suppose?"

"Yes."

"Really. Well . . .is there a God?" He half laughed, half asked, expecting the Teacher to laugh too.

The Teacher did not laugh and in a tone akin to incredulity said. "Well since you asked, you must not know the answer. So, it will take a long time to answer that question to your satisfaction."

Tom abashed, and not meaning offense, blurted, "Well, are you going to say yes or no?"

Tom thought he saw something dart across the top of the room. It went quickly, like a flying insect, but it had a different way of moving and it seemed transparent. He tried to focus on where it had come from but it wasn't obvious. He had a strange feeling of foreboding.

"Would you want me to?" A soft voice was saying. "Would you take MY word for it?" There was a light titter to the Voice, "or do you really want to find the answer? The answer requires getting some understanding about what God is, don't you think? If you know what God is, then you don't need to ask the question. You already know the answer."

Tom looked at his hands, his face turning red. "I didn't mean. . .uh. . .I... uh..." His hand burned again where he had held the pen. He rubbed it.

He wondered if the Teacher could see him. Just because he couldn't clearly see the Teacher didn't mean that the Teacher could not clearly see him.

He fidgeted, and rubbed.

"So, what is your question," the Voice continued. "Is the question: Is there a God? or What is God?"

"I guess the question is, what is God?" Tom answered.

"Where are you going to go to find your answer?" Asked the Teacher, "by looking around, or from me?"

"Well, huh, I'm here," said the student with a tone of resignation. "Uh - you're the Teacher."

"Ah. I see. You are supposing that by calling me Teacher, I am your Teacher, and that Teachers have all the answers? Hmmm. That is not entirely the case. If I give you the answers, I wouldn't be a very good teacher. And maybe that is just a title and nothing more. . ." Teacher's voice trailed off. "Maybe it is better to think of me as a guide? I think you better think of me as a Guide rather than as a Teacher." The Voice paused, but Tom didn't say anything so the Teacher continued. "Where are places you could go for help with answers to your question?"

"I could go to the Bible, I guess."

"Do you think the Bible has the answer you seek?" asked Teacher. "Have you looked in the Bible before, or is that a new book for you?"

Tom suddenly felt sick. He was glad there was a table for his elbows so he could lean his head into his hands. He slumped. "No," he said weakly, "the answer is not in the Bible, and it isn't in the black holes of space either. Science doesn't know. Nobody knows. You don't know. I don't know." His voice became hollow and dark. "That's because there is NO GOD."

Whatever had been flitting around the room became more apparent and even though it didn't have a form and was completely transparent, he knew something was there. It was like it displaced the air around itself and it was coming straight at him. He threw his head down on the table to keep from being hit. What had been a small insect sort of thing before, had now grown in size to that of a mop bucket flying around. He didn't want to know what would happen if it hit him. He could feel the air whoosh as it passed over him. "Ohhh." He gasped turning his face on the table to peer at the curtain. "Uhhh. . .uh. . .what was that. . .?"

The curtain sucked back and forth, as if it was breathing.

Tom became aware of a wet spot against his cheek on the table. He wasn't sure where it was coming from; if it was out of his eyes, his mouth, or his nose, but the goo was coming out of himself. "Ugh..." He struggled upright, and asked the question again. "What was that?"

The curtain calmed down and the Guide, or whatever that thing was, answered.

"That was you."

Tom sat very still. He gazed straight ahead and wondered what it was that had brought him here. He decided he would leave and never come back.

"You've opened the box," the Voice said. "There is no retreat. The cliché about Pandora's box has just happened to you today. You can't go back. . ."

"Oh yes I can." Tom started to get up, but his legs were like rubber and he couldn't stand.

The Guide chuckled.

Tom felt something akin to a scream rising, as he formulated some very loud expletives, but when he tried to speak, nothing came out. Instead, there were more forms dancing around him. He covered his head.

The Voice, he came to think of as his enemy, said softly, "What you are seeing and experiencing will not hurt you. The forms belong to you. It is just that you are seeing them for the first time because you are in this room."

"Oh no."

"Oh yes. I see you really do think there is no God. Your thoughts are quite powerful and large."

Tom squirmed. "Where is God? I don't see God."

"God is in you." The Teacher said.

Tom looked up from his hands at the blue scrim and laughed. "In me? Yeah. . .right! If God is in me, then I would know the answer, I would have always known the answer."

Something in the room seemed to stop. It was as if the air had a movement of its own, like ceiling fans, and suddenly they all had been turned off. The drape was so still it was like a wall. It didn't have a wrinkle or a crease. A person could have projected a movie against it. Tom inspected the drape again, looking this way and that. It was not fastened at the bottom, but hung loosely. Something in the room had stopped. But what? Tom realized it was his thoughts.

"Ask your question again," the Teacher said in a quiet voice, almost as if not to disturb this new atmosphere.

"What is God?" Tom asked.

A voice that sounded very different came from behind the drape. "You will find the answer in you."

"In me?" Asked Tom.

"In you? Yes, of course. And in me too. The answer is in all of us." The Voice emphasized. "You will see God in all of us."

Tom said, "What am I supposed to do with that?"

"Find God. You will find God by looking within, by looking in you."

The room seemed to breathe again.

"But. . .but. . . how will that tell me what God IS?"

"Oh Tom. . .you are going to have to think about this one. . ." the Teacher said.

Tom was angry when he left the room that first day. "What a waste of time," he muttered to himself walking down the hall. It was just a sparring contest between "in You and in Me" and all that. During the time he had spent in the Room he could have been in the Top Shop getting a badly needed haircut.

Later when he saw one of his classmates, Mollie, he told her that the whole experience had been a crazy waste of time. He didn't tell her exactly why or how because it all seemed rather foolish. He sputtered, quietly hitting the toe of his shoe against a crack in the sidewalk "Yeah, hello God." He laughed sarcastically under his breath. "What is God."

Later in his Physics class while he worked out a problem, he said to himself, "yeah, this is where it's at, science. There is no such thing as God. It is a manmade idea to get us through the difficulty of a finite life. We live, we die."

That night as he was falling asleep, he spoke to God, saying, "Goodnight God," and chuckled; then he laughed out loud. "How stupid!" And then, just as he entered that twilight time of half sleep, he felt a twinge of fear. He knew he had to go back to that room, and he didn't want to.

That was the last thing he thought about, about how something was now out of control.

ABOUT TOM

It was the middle of the term and school was dragging out. There weren't any important deadlines and there was nothing much of interest going on. Tom found his mind wandering to questions, all sorts of questions to ask the Teacher. There were voices in his head dancing around like little devils or goblins each wanting to stump his new Teacher with questions that were beyond answers. He amused himself with ideas for his next session. He wondered what the Teacher would say about them. He asked himself why in the world he was going to the Room anyway. He tried to remember what he had heard about it and from whom, but he wasn't able to isolate where the different rumors had started regarding the experience. There had been several.

He didn't have to go there, there was no requirement for him to go. He decided he didn't even like whoever or whatever that Teacher/Guide person was anyhow, although he found it hard to make a judgment on a person he couldn't even see. There wasn't going to be a grade or anything. He was just doing this *thing*. People who had done it talked about the Teacher in awe, like he was Gandhi or some high priest or someone special like that. He'd heard it was the opportunity of a lifetime - if you could actually get a time to go into the Numen - Rooom. He thought about it and in his mind it seemed whoever had talked about it, and he knew he'd heard about it from more than one person, had all emphasized the "oooo" of the term Rooom, like they were saying kangaroo and they were lingering on the "roo." Tom had waited 19 months hoping for a time to go in there, and they'd told him it was futile, that it was impossible, he would never get to go into the room, but then a time, one that really worked for him had opened up unexpectedly. The person who had that time was accepted into a graduate program somewhere else and Tom was given the opportunity to take his time. Suddenly, it was Tom's turn.

Tom thought about the different people he'd heard about that had spent time there. They were all doing interesting things. One guy designed special habitats for poor people and was manufacturing them. He had his own company. One of the women was accepted into the astronaut's program. He had thought there was something special about the Room. But now he was sorry. He didn't feel good about it.

He guessed he would stick it out for a couple of sessions anyway. It was free. It wasn't costing him anything. Later he'd make up his mind. In the meantime, he would just play along with it. It wouldn't hurt anything. It was just a game.

Wasn't it?

Tom thought of himself as an ordinary person. He grew up in middle class America with two loving parents, a sister, and grandparents who were close by and active. He had a dog, a cat, and a hamster named Willy.

He was a good student, but his sister, Camille, Cami for short, outshined him in just about everything except sports, and she would have done better there also, except most of the sports in his school were slanted toward boys, and she didn't care about that kind of thing anyway. Tom did. He dabbled in all of them - football, baseball, basketball and even soccer. He was best at basketball and would have continued there, except he stopped growing. He kept stretching his neck hoping that would somehow help, but he stayed at five foot ten - good enough for high school, and sadly not tall enough for basketball in college. He had a dream about a basketball scholarship, but it was always just a dream. His father always went to the games, but was never overly enthusiastic about Tom's interest in sports.

"Tom," he'd say, "whatever career path you choose, try and make it interesting and flexible for your life. You won't be young forever, you won't be single forever, and your choice won't be forever either. It is nice when you choose something that will give you options later on."

The best example Tom had when growing up was his father. His dad was his best friend, teaching him how to swim and save somebody else if he needed to, how to make repairs with a hammer, mow a lawn, be kind to animals, follow a compass and be a scout.

Mr. Cross was ambitious in his work as a civil engineer but not at the expense of his family. He subscribed to a couple of magazines which he read with interest; they were the kind of reading that helped him to keep up in his field. He supervised some large projects and he often shared some of the details with Tom. "Look at this system, Tom. That lift is designed to bring up a heavy beam. . .and see, look here, that apparatus is there as a safety device. It's important. What if. . ."

Tom wanted to be just like him. His dad cared about so many things.

Tom was not a foolish boy, but he did do something stupid when he was eight, something he never told anybody about.

It was one of those warm summer days and he woke up anxious to be outside and running around before warm turned into blistering hot. He seldom wore a hat, but he pulled on his fishing cap when he dressed that morning. He grabbed a sausage and rolled it into a pancake. "I'm going to meet Abbot," he yelled to his mom as he headed out the door. He had a small pack with his swim trunks that he slung over his shoulder and transferred to his bike. Climbing on, he was glad it was Saturday. School would be out in another week. As he rode down the street where they lived, the school bus came lumbering up the street, just like it did every weekday. He was momentarily confused, but shrugged it off, and continued riding down the street. It was still early.

There weren't any cars on the road. As he rode, he listened for the bus. It always made a loud burping noise through its exhaust when it came back down the street. No bus yet. No cars had come up the street. Just the bus. It was time to cross over. He glanced, but his hat was in the way and so was his pack, which made him a bit off balance. Oh well. He could always hear the bus long before it arrived, so, he took off across the road. He was pedaling and going fast, at an angle, and it was like he was on the wings of an angel. He was absolutely floating. It was exhilarating.

He was to remember the moment forever.

He reached the other side. All was frozen and silent - for a microsecond. It was like one scene was overlaid with another and another - still and clear and perfectly synchronized and in unison. And then his surroundings started to move. He felt a huge whoosh next to his foot and there was a loud honking sound coming from the bus. There hadn't even been time for the driver to swerve or brake.

He turned and saw the shocked expressions on the bus driver and then as it passed, the faces of the kids on board. They were older than him. As the bus continued, he noticed it was a different bus than the usual burping lumbering one that came every school day. Tom dropped his bike. For the first time in his life he felt his heart beating.

He sat down on the side of the road. Everything was quiet and still and clear. The trees and the far-off hills seemed to have a rainbow pattern around them. At that moment he wasn't thinking of anything. He was just feeling something he came to think of as raw fear. He was shocked. He felt something about who he was. His humanness. He realized his own mortality for the first time. It was a bolt of awareness. He had come within an inch of his life!

Linda, his mother, was at home when he returned. He had gone to the river to meet his friend but returned early complaining of a stomach ache. He was grateful she was there, as she usually was. She knew something was different but his explanation of a sick stomach had satisfied her.

She wanted to be at home until her two children were old enough to be unsupervised, although she used to laugh and say "that will never be the day." She was a freelance editor for a book publisher and often worked in the evenings after Tom and his sister were asleep. She said she had the best job in the world doing the final proofs because not only was she getting paid to work, but she was always learning something new. "I've got first dibs on the book! The only thing I don't get to do is be the critic!" Linda had a sunny personality which meant she was frequently in demand by every organization needing a helping hand.

"I wish I could do everything," she would say, "but I can't!" She often passed up helping out with school plays, PTA activities and other functions pressuring parents - but she always asked the Cross kids for guidance before declining; and when she did help out, she wholly devoted herself - with all her enthusiasm. She was in it. "Cami, what is really important to you?" She'd ask. "Is this one of those things you want me to do? Tom, is this an important game? Your dad is going to be there for sure, and I can be there also. . .but. . .you know I have work too. Tell me about this game. Is this one of those important ones, or is it one for the fun? As the years went by, they had an acronym they used. O.F.F. One For the Fun. It meant that this particular function could be OFF, she didn't need to go.

Communication in the Cross family was good.

More often than not, the Cross kids would laugh and say, "This one's OFF." But they did other things not realizing how important their contribution was toward their future. Both of them belonged to various youth groups and were always doing something to help the community clean up, paint up or help the less fortunate. It wasn't until Tom's senior year, that a hiccup appeared, and it came from the unlikeliest place.

It was true that Tom's life as a high school teenager was following a pattern that pleased his parents. He was getting good grades, was alert and interested in his school's activities, his family and community. Most of his friends were boy scouts or basketball players and also were planning on going to college.

Tom took Physics during his senior year because it was a good idea for a youth who was college bound - and his counselor suggested it. Mostly, he'd heard the teacher was funny and interesting and his friend, Abbot, was taking it. It wasn't long into the school year that he and Abbot devised a fun project to do together. That's when things escalated, when the boys truly entered a phase, they referred to later, as being "out of control."

It started with a silly idea. They liked going out onto a lake close-by to fish. They thought it would be nice if they didn't have to work so hard rowing the boat. They wanted something quiet so as not to disturb the fish and the old motor on the back of the boat was too loud so they ended up rowing and like most boys, they thought it was too much work. Their thought was to devise something quiet so they wouldn't have to row the boat.

They called their system the L-W-Glide (for Lake Water Glide). They used what they called bio waste (similar to a compost pile) to make the LW run. There was nothing new or innovative about the bio fuel and in fact, they took that portion of the design directly from another creator and gave him credit regarding it. They wanted the movement of water, even though quite slow, to be quiet - even quieter than if they were rowing the boat themselves. The disturbance of water needed to be something small that had a great ratio for propelling the boat. That was the trick. A fish could move through the water with speed and little upset. Why couldn't they? It was the design of the propeller that would be the trick.

They came up with an innovative solution, one that caused an amount of excitement for their teacher.

"You're going to enter this in the science fair competition, aren't you?" Mr. Thompson pressed the boys.

"Nah." They said flippantly, thinking it just a holiday of laughs. They weren't trying to win anything. That wasn't the point. The two boys only wanted to devise something for their small fishing craft. It was for the fun of it. As Tom explained it later - it was an OFF project!

Preparing the entry would require drafting up the design better, a nice poster, a series of photographs and presenting a model. But they did have the model already, in fact they had about three of their trials, trying to make the system work. Their teacher said the experimental models would be interesting too - that they were part of the solution. Only, they didn't care.

Neither boy wanted to pursue it. But somehow Tom's father learned about it. That's when the OFF became an ON (Only for Now).

The Cross family always had dinner together. So here they were, like so many times before, passing food, visiting about this and that, when Mr. Cross asked the question.

"Did Mr. Thompson help you with your L-W project?" he asked.

Tom's mashed potatoes were in midair. He knew there was no little chit chatty way out of this one. It was like long fingers were throttling his vocal cords into a submissive and weak "yes."

"Well then, it's settled, isn't it?" Mike Cross said pleasantly. We are all proud of you! You must enter your design."

"Wait. Wait. I didn't do this by myself. Abbot won't want to do the science fair. And... and... I don't have all the material. . .and it's lots of work. . .and I have my other classes in school. . .and, I have basketball after school. . .and what about. . ."

Mike Cross roared. It was a sound that didn't start small. It was guttural and loud and short. It was a very big, "HUH???"

The room was silent.

Then again, "Huh? What did you say?" Then more softly, which Tom knew was worse than his father's louder voice, "Did Mr. Thompson help you boys find the machine shop to create your design? Did he help you set up your experiments?"

Tom passed the potatoes, his favorite, without taking any more. "Yes." He said slowly.

"Was he there during your lunch time, your study hall, and whenever you needed him to run your experiments?" Mike's words were going up slightly in tone.

"Yes sir," Tom said, adding the formality to his words. He could feel his face getting red.

"Did he have to do that? Do you have any idea what it might mean to him as a teacher, to your school, to other students to have you enter the fair? What about if you were to get a ribbon? What about if you were to *win*? It reflects on Mr. Thompson you know. You're not being fair to him! It won't be fair to him or to your school if you don't enter. . ."

"To other students. . .?" Tom's words hung in midair.

"Yes. Such a thing sets an e-x-a-m-p-l-e!"

Tom hadn't thought about what it could mean to a teacher's career to have a student win placement in the large science fair.

"But the time. . .the work. . ."

"I'm certain," Mike said patiently, "that the school will give you time from your other classes to prepare your entry, Thomas."

And so, the boys "fun" project turned into a drudge of work. But Mike Cross was there to help. He rented a good camera and took a video of the two boys moving slowly across the water. He worked in the evenings editing it and preparing a continuous loop DVD for the fair.

Lots of people ended up helping the boys. The project was bigger than either of them realized. It was bigger than the two of them together.

It was after they won some money that a happy Mr. Thompson was dancing around the room, almost doing a kind of skip and slam the sidewalk kind of thing, that Tom began to understand.

A few days later, the teacher put an announcement in front of Tom. "Look at this Tom. It's a great scholarship to the university in Physics. There's enough time you can apply. I'm so happy for you! I'm so glad you took my class!"

Tom applied, although he could never tell you why. He worked on the application, and his teacher helped him. He never even told his parents about it; he was so sure he wouldn't get it; and he didn't want to set his father off on some tangent again. The scholarship was huge and he hadn't done anything special to get it, or so he thought. But Tom had good grades and glowing recommendations.

His school principal personally wrote a recommendation, and it included comments about his community work. He was an Eagle Scout, he was a winner in the science fair competition, he was an all-around student involved in school activities - and ALL his teachers were astounded by his performance. "This kid can think." He wrote.

It was a beautiful spring day when the school principal called Tom to his office. Mr. Burger's secretary came personally to get him out of study hall and that was never good. Tom had wondered what had happened and worried about his family. He felt a deep sense of foreboding as he walked down the hall. He walked slowly running his hand over the lockers.

When Tom entered the school office, his Physics teacher, Mr. Thompson was there too, standing and looking very formal and solemn. The principal stood up and Tom figured something big had happened. He was right.

The notification had come to the school. Tom hadn't realized that schools always receive notification about scholarships like this one - not the student or the family, like Tom thought. Such an award reflected on the school and there were ceremonies and the press to be involved. The award was huge. Tom had received a full scholarship - for five years in Physics. Tom was being told about it in advance, but it would be awarded to him at a ceremony during graduation. The school wanted him to know immediately so he could plan the next step in his education, which of course was the university!

The principal cleared his throat, held the letter away from his body and shook it for effect, and then started reading. Tom didn't really hear all the words, except, "Your achievements in Physics have impressed the selection committee, as well as your. . ."

Tom didn't know what to do. He stood there dumbfounded, looking first at his teacher, who was bursting and grinning and then clapping. Then at the principal who nodded, that, yes, it was true.

If Tom had learned anything in his life, it was that moments like these are very important. He could hear his father speaking in his head, saying, reach out and start shaking hands. Keep shaking them, first one then the other. Look happy. Jump up and down. Do something. Be a man. Be a kid. Laugh. Say, "Oh my GOSH!" Pretend you are six years old and it is Christmas. Do this for me.

Tom had mixed feelings. He was not overjoyed. He liked physics, but he hadn't considered the field as his life's choice. In fact, it was near the bottom. Something, somehow, had chosen it for him. But, he obeyed the voice in his head and grabbed his Teacher's hand first, looking him straight in the eyes, and pumped it up and down as if he would never let it go, and then finally released him, saying, "oh thank you, thank you." Then he politely went to his principal and shook his, like an adult.

The two men beamed. Tom's performance had been perfect. The principal gave him a copy of the letter for his parents. "We'll release it to the newspaper right after we present it to you at graduation. Your family should keep it under wraps until then. Please."

Tom knew it was a big deal, a very big deal. He would go to the university and study Physics. He would tell his family that it was what he wanted to do with his life. He would stand up at dinner that evening and ceremoniously open his letter and clear his throat. He would make a very big deal of it. The award amounted to thousands of dollars. It would mean many things to his family. His sister had big dreams for herself, expensive ones for her education. Yes, he would do it. Was he happy about it?

He went to the bathroom, glad that it was empty. He practiced in front of the mirror. He wanted to look overjoyed. He wanted to hear a happy tone in his voice when he told his family, "I was sure I wouldn't get it. I didn't tell you about it. I wanted to try for it on my own. . .to be a surprise if I won it. . .I didn't want you to be disappointed." He took the letter and waved it. "Well surprise!"

Tom never forgot the way each family member looked. His father stood up and came around the table, making himself very tall and very formal and cleared his throat. "I'm proud of you, son." He said, looking levelly in Tom's eyes, like he understood there was something more to the story, and shook his hand. "I have no words to tell you . . .how proud I AM!" He put his other hand on Tom's shoulder, his voice breaking.

His mother stood up too but turned to his sister, did a little dance turning in a circle, and cried.

His sister jumped up and down and screamed.

It was Tom's first sacrifice.

TIME

When Tom entered the room that second week, he expected it to be different. For some reason he thought the drape wouldn't be there, that it was temporary. He also was certain the impressions he had that first time, mostly surrounding that crazy door, were a figment of his imagination.

He remembered his daydream from the last time, how he'd had a feeling of exhilaration just before going through the door, and then the beginning of a roller coaster ride. This time, when he stood at the closed door, the smell of pine changed.

Now he smelled popcorn. For a second he was on his way into the theater with a group of friends to see *Star Wars*. He was carrying a large bucket of buttered popcorn. He smiled and pushed on the door expecting to go through, but he came up against it. He realized he must not have knocked, backed up and knocked, then turned the knob, only it didn't turn and the door stayed in place.

He stood there perplexed, turned in a circle to see if there was something he missed and while so doing, the door became ajar. He went on through thinking the room would be different.

It wasn't.

The blue drape hung there, disturbingly, a lifeless thing, a barrier, something to be faced.

He felt alone and stood looking at that chair, thinking of himself like a person being interrogated in a room with a detective on one of those CIA movies he liked watching.

He smelled the popcorn again, wafting from somewhere, probably being eaten with amusement by the blob behind the curtain as he observed his subjects, his experiments. That's what he was, an experiment. Then he remembered the questions he had prepared for that thing behind the curtain and he ventured further into the room and slapped his paper on the table with authority. "I won't be undone," He thought, sitting down. "Especially by the God thing." He was slightly aware of the shadowy thing that flew by him.

"Good afternoon Teacher Guide," Tom said, flitting his hand up, turning it into a greeting, amazed by the ease of his gesture.

"And what will our lesson be about today Tom?" asked Teacher.

"I have a question about time." Tom said looking at his paper, wondering if he should just get into it, and deciding, why not?

"What is time?" Tom directed to the drape with satisfaction.

"Nothing," came the answer.

Tom coughed to cover the choke building in his throat - a feeling like he had the last time. Then there was silence. He thought the Teacher might say more, but he didn't.

"What do you mean?" Tom finally asked annoyed." Nothing? Time is something. I don't understand the answer. Please explain."

"Go to the window." The Teacher said in a commanding voice. "Describe what you see."

Tom got up reluctantly and went to the window. "Trees." he said. "I see trees and grass, clouds, blue sky. So what?"

"What else?"

"Railroad tracks."

"Do any of those things know time?" Teacher asked.

"No, not exactly," Tom said." But they will deteriorate with time."

He sat back down.

"Do the railroad tracks know what time is?" asked Teacher.

"No." said Tom flatly, not surprised that the Teacher focused on the railroad tracks. The analogy associated with the tracks would be a good one. "I mean they will wear out with time."

"Can they tell time?"

"No."

"But people traveling on the tracks are doing it according to time. Is that right?"

"Well. . .yes, I guess so."

"Yes, let's say for example, they are," said Teacher.

"Like boarding a train or something?"

"Sure. That'll work."

"So, you have a time for boarding the train. According to the way you are looking at time. But let's look at it another way. Anyone can get on and off the train anywhere at the same time, backwards and forwards on the train, or tracks.

"The tracks are not keeping time. Those tracks know nothing about time. Stepping on and off the tracks has nothing to do with time. It has to do with an action. Right?"

Tom looked at the drape with narrowed eyes. "Yes."

"Okay. You know the time you are getting on the train, but the train machine doesn't care, and the tracks, they know nothing about time. We agree. You are the one doing the action. Yes, I understand the train is going to move, but the machine itself is not keeping time."

"Where are we going with this?" Tom asked politely, but annoyed.

You created an imaginary figment to measure a happening of what you are *doing*, of what *you* think is a beginning and an end, but your measurement is not real. There is no such thing as time. You don't have a beginning or an end of anything real, you only have a measurement of an action - your action."

Tom sat in his chair confused. "Yes?"

"The Universe is comprised of ordered chaos," Teacher said, "but that chaos is not governed by time. It is governed by deliberate force. There is a difference. We have become confused by this issue."

"Yes?"

"You are part of that chaos, but you are deliberate, like everything else. Nothing is an accident." Teacher said.

"Oh?" Tom hugged himself and muttered softly to himself, "You could have fooled me."

"We will come back to time." Teacher said. "Why would you think you were an accident?" Asked Teacher. "Now I am asking you a question."

"Well, I wasn't planned," Tom said.

"Oh, you mean your birth," Teacher said. "That's just your birth to particular people, at least they think you were not planned, but you were, weren't you? Otherwise you wouldn't be here. Right?"

"Where is the logic in that?" Tom asked. "Accidents happen every day. My birth was an accident because my parents had a problem with their method of prevention."

"But the Universe did not want to prevent you, Tom." Came the answer. "You might actually think of your birth as a so-called accident, but it wasn't."

Tom looked at the curtain and tried to study the outline of the figure sitting behind it. "Not everything is planned," Tom said measured. "The Universe doesn't go around planning stuff. There are accidents every day. People are hurt, people die. People are shot to death and murdered. That stuff isn't planned. That isn't deliberate."

"That's just the point. The Universe doesn't plan everything and accidents are a part of the norm. What we think of as accidents. But that doesn't mean that everything is not deliberate. Everything IS deliberate. We will come back to that. So, what is your question Tom?"

"If everything is deliberate, why are such things allowed to happen?"

"Allowed to happen by whom?" Asked Teacher. "By God?"

"Yes!"

"Ah yes. . .it all comes back to God." Teacher said quietly, then in a normal voice, "but we are discussing time. You have created the definition of time to understand change."

"Time is more than that."

"Is it? How?

Tom sat there thinking, then said, "It tells us a lot about the origin of things. . ."

"Oh, I see. Hmmm, this is something you understand? Then why are you asking me?"

Tom squirmed, ready to bolt out of the room.

"I'm sorry," Teacher said, and Tom imagined the form behind the drape holding up a friendly hand, "I didn't mean to antagonize you. Time is a complex subject. We use time to measure our very existence but it is not a valid method of measurement. It is fictitious."

Tom made a noise between a snort and a gasp.

The voice of Teacher changed somehow. Now it became almost like a purr. "Let us put ourselves in the position of creator, for a minute, shall we?"

"Okay."

"We are going to create a system, a very simple system." Tom wondered where the Blob was going with this.

"We'll need parameters for things to do what they do, Right?"

"Right."

"Our system is going to be the making of a cake. So, we'll have an oven with heat, cake batter, eggs, water, all the things that go into the making of a cake. How's that?"

"Sounds simple enough."

"Okay. It starts with the cook measuring everything. Anywhere in this system something can be off - it can be a temperature difference, the measurement of ingredients, the size of an egg; the electricity can go off, the flour can be rancid, the timer not exact. There are any number of things that can happen with randomness. Randomness is part of that system. It seems exact, but it isn't. It is created with randomness as an integral part of its nature. Understand? It is precise, but it's not. What we define as chaos is the nature of that system."

Tom thought about it for a moment. He didn't see any chaos in the making of a cake.

"Can we rectify the integral chaos? Think about it. Things happen. Maybe the size of the eggs was off. Or, what about the yeast and the cake didn't rise the way it was supposed to. It could be the temperature wasn't exactly right."

Tom thought back to how his mother had made a cake for his sister's birthday, the warmth of the kitchen and how something had gone wrong. He smelled the cake. . .

The Teacher was continuing. "We didn't like the taste. And so, we say, we will do better with the next cake. The system evolves. Each system evolves. The egg was merely part of a system. In this example, the egg didn't have a consciousness that we are aware of, but everything is connected to everything else, so there is a kind of consciousness we don't know about.

"Yet. Consciousness may equal deliberateness. Everything is part of what IS. Because we are thinking of events as random or chaotic doesn't mean the system is not deliberate. The making of the cake was deliberate."

"What does this have to do with time?" Tom insisted.

"I'm getting to it." Teacher said. "Everything in the universe is changing constantly. It is the same with the cake. The change of the egg within the batter might change at a different rate than the flour or the water. You are changing at your rate. Within your system, your cells change at their rate. You may start to change faster and you will find that you are confused when you try and apply "time" to your existence. Suddenly time may go by at a faster rate. See? The older you get the faster time will become for you. That is because this crazy definition of "time" does not apply. *Change does.*"

When the Teacher said it that way, it was like something had reached into Tom's brain and hit him. It was like he was standing outside of himself and could see his own reaction and it was like a bolt of lightning had hit him. He couldn't hide it. The Teacher could see it.

He smelled the pine again, of being in the forest and how time seemed to relax and go on forever on that childhood day there in the forest. And now time was moving faster.

Tom realized he needed to listen, really listen to this person who had no name.

"The idea of time is working for us in creating universal order within our system - so that all of us know where to be gathered together simultaneously, but that is all. The concept of time has confused you. You associate time with beginning and end, but there is only change, change from one thing to another."

Tom gathered himself and said, "But what about the timer that says . . ."

"The timer, ah yes. The timer. It is important, but it is just a definition, like a book of recipes."

Tom stifled a cough again.

"So okay, you have a foot race. You have set a "time" for it to start. The participants know when to be there according to the sun. This is very important. The runners line up and run. Each has the time that they finished the race. Right? Yes, that is according to your measuring device, but according to the Universe, what actually occurred was this: There was a track. On the track were five people who went through movement on that track. They went from one place to another.

Each person on the track had a change occurring, as well as the wear on the track. It too has a life. It too will change. There is nothing wrong with having time as a definition. It gives us order - in a chaotic system where things change at different rates.

"A recipe gives us order - but the recipe is NOT the cake but a guide for its assembly. It is laughable. The recipe is words, letters written on a page, but it is not flour and water and eggs and the cake. We have assigned time, the concept of time to our very existence, like that recipe, but that isn't the real reality. *Change IS*. The real reality is the change of the participants and their connections one to the other."

Tom felt a chill. Then he said, "But time was applied in order for the cake to change."

"Was it time?" a voice was saying, "or was it how ingredients related one to the other and connected to their environment?"

Tom felt colder and started to shiver.

"Go to the window, the sun is streaming in and will warm you," a female voice said. "When you begin to understand our connections, you may begin to understand a little bit more about God, or at least see God. . ."

Tom wondered why he felt it necessary to sit so still at the table. There was nothing said or implied that he must sit still at the table. He got up and went to the window again.

"You have chosen to enter a system, Tom, and change is being applied all the time, to you and to everything around you. You are connected to everything in this system, just like that egg is connected to everything in that batter in order for the cake to happen. . ."

Tom hugged himself in the sun. He was quiet. The room was absolutely still. He didn't hear anything, not even his own breathing. He listened. He thought he could almost hear the blood running through his veins. He was a system, part of a bigger system, a system within a system and then part of yet other systems and it went on and on. It was too much to think about, really too much. His head begin to hurt. He never, ever thought of himself as being connected to anything, well, except his family and he was connected to them by blood, at least he thought of them that way. He never thought of himself being connected by anything else.

He felt dizzy.

"How can I be connected to an inanimate object?" he asked finally, looking around.

The Teacher laughed, this time with a distinctly male voice. "How can you NOT be? You are part of the system you call Earth. You actually cannot get away from it. When you change even more, you will realize another part of this system, that you have always been part of many things, many that are beyond your present awareness."

"What do you mean, change even more?"

"There is more to this system than you realize. Let me answer this question more fully. You are part of everything within this system, and connected to it." Teacher chuckled like holding back a secret.

Tom wanted to know. "Ohhh?" He inflected questioningly, encouragingly for the Teacher, his Guide, to continue.

"Just like you are connected to inanimate objects, you are connected to what you don't see too!"

Tom looked around the room wondering what that might be, then considered something like the rays of the sun. "Like UV rays and radiation?"

"Yes, like UV rays, and a lot more. You are connected to objects within the system, just like a cake pan to the cake and to objects around you undergoing change too. They are subject to randomness too."

"Yes, I understand, abstractly, but not literally. . ."

"Literally, Tom. Stuff may fall off walls, rust, burn, or move into dust, and that dust may then become clay and may later become ceramic and who knows what? The dust may become nourishment for a tree. You assign time to it, but within the system time is not a factor, change is, and you are part of change, your body becomes part of the change too, of everything. There is a consciousness and deliberateness to everything, make no mistake about this. The pan that holds the cake batter is just as important as the egg in the batter, isn't it? You would not have a cake without it or without some kind of support under the liquid batter. What would you do without support under you?"

"Uh, dunno."

"One thing is connected to another in a stream of deliberateness and we ourselves continue to add to that stream and be part of it."

Tom took a breath. In fact, it was like the whole room took a breath.

He kept his place in the sun. But he wasn't cold anymore. In fact, he felt hot now. He thought about what it would feel like to be the egg in the batter and be put in the oven and turned into a cake - and then be eaten, and then he would change alright, into something really different. Next, he would be in the sewer pipe traveling to a place where they would separate him to clean him from the water and he would probably be fertilizer for a bush somewhere. Maybe he would rather be in the pan, but wouldn't he end up in the same place? Everything into dust? And then he realized, he really was like the cake in the pan. He wasn't that much different.

"Doesn't everything end up as dust? He said more than asked, moving back to the table. Suddenly he felt a whoosh on his cheek, saw the faces on the bus, and he remembered that moment, the exact second when he first realized he would have a physical end to his body and be dust himself. He had been just a child.

A lilting Voice came from behind the curtain. "Well maybe that is the design of this system, that all that you see and know will turn into dust and move into a different part of a larger system."

And now the Voice took on a kind of merriment quality, a kind of happiness, "and what do you think will happen to the system when all the so-called physical attributes you are so used to seeing and knowing move into something else? What kind of system do you think all this will move into?"

"Huh?" He finally said. "It'll all be gone. . ."

"Is that so?" said the Voice. "All to cosmic dust. Eh? But perhaps there is more than one track of change going on. Nothing is gone. Perhaps what we are has more connections than you know about with your current science. There is a momentum, like on the track, a kind of engine, and it goes someplace, and because you don't understand it, you are minimizing it, although the Universe is far from minimal. Maybe even a black hole has properties we don't yet understand? When we think a thought, we don't see it, can't measure it, but it is powerful! - and our thoughts affect change. . ."

Tom realized he had hardly thought about anything in his life. He wondered why not. Being connected to everything meant he wasn't exactly alone in the way he had thought of himself. In fact . .What about the girlfriend he dumped several weeks ago? Was he really connected to her?

Tom didn't want to think. He tried not to. But there it was in the room, just as real as the table and the chair. He could see it, hanging there in the air; his thought about Chelsea. He knew that stuff hanging in the air was all coming from him, *his thoughts*. He tried to bring that particular thought back in, back into himself so the Teacher couldn't see it. He wanted to park it somewhere back into himself, after all it came out of him. He should be able to bring it back, like putting it into a parking garage. He tried, but it moved swiftly around the room. The more he tried, the worse it became, because one thought became several. He reached out his arms and motioned the dancing air parade to come towards himself. But it was futile.

"Once you think a thought, it is out. It has influence and you cannot re-dock it." The Guide said. Amused.

"What about my ex-girlfriend?" Tom blurted uncomfortably, "Am I really connected to her? Will I always be connected to her?"

The figure behind the curtain laughed. And laughed.

THE ELEPHANT IN THE ROOM

Tom lived in a small apartment on Central Avenue just three blocks from the campus. He was in a five-year physics program at the university, and soon into his freshman year, he had realized the need to supplement his educational funds by working. He decided that living in the school dorms wasn't the best option so he added his name to a waiting list for a small apartment located on restaurant row. It had been a two-year wait and he was ecstatic when the call came from student services that an apartment was available so close to campus. The cost was high, but the apartment had a nice parking lot and the savings in parking fees compensated for the difference. He actually had more disposable funds coming from his new location. That probably came from being able to accept a part time job next door. Parking was a premium all around the university.

It was a warm autumn day and Tom walked along at a slow pace. He thought about time and change all the way to his apartment, a thirty-minute walk. He could have ridden his bicycle, as he mostly did, but the weather was nice and he didn't have any books to carry on this day. He liked the way the fallen leaves scudded along on the sidewalk.

Yes, time is a measurement of change, he agreed. Every second of it as those little arms marched around to say the instant position of the sun. Funny, he always thought about it in another way, as a kind of regulator, or maybe as a partner that walked alongside him chanting in his ear "time to do your homework, Tom, time to leave for your appointment."

It wasn't until he took physics at the university that he thought of time as a long arm extending out into space, almost as a visual thing he could see, something that could expand and contract on a beam of light. He started to think of it like a clock that could run a little too fast, or a little too slow. But that really was silly, he knew.

The concepts associated with time were difficult to wrap around, but when he was with the Teacher it hadn't seemed so paradoxical. It seemed to make perfect sense. But now, only minutes later, he wondered why he had thought any of it made sense. He shook his head.

He could see in his mind a clock, ticking away the minutes, marking the movement of the sun, because that is really what a clock did - marked the change of the sun. Then he saw it in relation to all the other things around him making changes - the leaves falling off the trees, the spring flowers blooming, his dog at home asking for his evening meal as soon as the sun disappeared. He thought about his own cells that never saw the sun, how they lived and died according to their own "clock" and all the other little bits and pieces that had their own clocks that regulated their existence and he felt overwhelmed. He was a tiny speck in a huge swarm of moving timepieces, all doing their thing - all deliberate in their own way. How could everything be so random and yet so perfectly harmonious?

When Tom opened the door of his apartment, he lurched. He stood there with the door open and stared, not wanting to go further. It was like he was seeing his place for the first time.

He had a large cushion in the middle of the living room. It was a place where he and his friends could sack out, watch TV and drink. It was a huge bean bag sort of thing, but larger and was filled with a different kind of stuffing. It took over the majority of the living room. His pad was geared toward having a good time, not for studying. There was nothing pretty or pleasant about it. He had a beer sign on the wall and some vampire posters scattered in the living room. In the bedroom he had a *Star Wars* poster, a couple more vampires and a few plastic sci-fi artifacts. He didn't even have a desk. He usually studied on his bed, leaning back on pillows, and if he needed to write something, he pulled over his night stand and used it for his laptop, or went to the library. In his refrigerator he had two six packs of beer, margarita mix, orange juice, bologna, cheese slices, mayonnaise, mustard, old lettuce, left over pizza, and a bottle of Tequila in the freezer.

He looked at that huge bean bag thing in the middle of the floor and said out loud, "I'm connected to you." Then he went in, slamming the door behind him and kicked the bag, laughing hysterically. "Answer me," he said to it, as if the thing was alive. "Answer me and tell me I am connected to you."

Then he threw himself down on it laughing, thinking how stupid he was to believe such a thing, and turned on the television set. "Yeah sure. I'm connected to you and to the ceiling and the walls and all of this crap all around me," he swept his arms widely, "you are affecting my life. . .!" He snickered and promptly fell asleep.

An hour later he woke up with a start. He had been so solidly asleep that he didn't know at first where he was. He looked around for a few seconds and felt like a stranger. Then everything snapped into focus and became normal. Normal? His first thoughts were about the Teacher. What had the "Blob" said about objects? It was quite ludicrous, of course. "I can't be connected to this old thing." he said about the bag under him. "There is no way on earth that this stupid thing is connected to me!"

And then it was like a Voice, something that was not really him, answered in his head. It said, "Of course you are. How many hours have you spent lounging on me, drinking beer and avoiding your studies on me? Yes, you are connected to me. I have changed your life. You even had sex with Chelsea on me and declared to her that you loved her. What a lie! You think you have no connection to me? You stupid liar. LIAR! You think there are no ripple effects that have happened from your lifestyle because I am here, in the middle of your room. . .?"

Tom, who had been laying down, got up on it and stomped his feet. He still had on his shoes and looked at his feet abstractly, but the bag was dirty anyway, so he didn't care, and it didn't care. He started bouncing on it. He jumped. He twirled. He reached for the ceiling. He was eight years old again bouncing on his bed, but the bag's stuffing didn't have enough resistance and it just came up around his feet, engulfing him and making his jumping a pathetic movement on wobbly legs. He cursed "Fuck, fuck, fuck" he said. "This is crazy. You are nothing but an old fucking piece of stuffing. An old big ameba of a thing that I use to be comfortable, to smoke joints and have parties in my living room. You stupid old fucking thing! You are nothing. Nothing!"

He ceased his bouncing, felt his heart pounding in his chest, felt the way he was breathing, saw the light on the ceiling, heard the cars outside, listened to a dog bark, and stopped.

He looked down. The bag was covered with a close-cropped fuzzy tan cloth that had beer and whiskey stains on it. It had a musty smell. It had other stains on it from body fluids as well. "You are a disgusting thing." Tom said loudly. "How can I be connected to you?" Then he thought about the hours he had spent lounging on it instead of studying, the hours watching T.V. - watching sports and drinking. He looked around his living room and started realizing that the space could be a reflection of himself, of the kind of person he was. He was shocked. Was he connected to the room too, to all the things in it? To the walls and the floor and to the ceiling even? Was the room saying something about him? And then he thought of Chelsea again and how he had acted when he broke up with her and then it was like the walls were moving, breathing with a crazy life of their own. He felt dizzy. He reached into his pants and eased onto his back, wishing momentarily that he hadn't been so hasty in breaking off with Chelsea. Now all he had was his hand and this stupid bag and the pulse of his hand jerking himself intently.

"All right." he said. "All right, All right." The bag under him moved easily and nothing else seemed to matter - not the Teacher, not school or the craziness of his day. He added to the mess on the bag, rolled over and was soon asleep again.

This time he didn't sleep so sound. It was a twilight kind of thing. He was wandering and remembering a time during his youth when nothing mattered and he was playing under the big tree behind the house. His dream had a vision-like quality about it. He found himself walking in a circle, round and round and the circle was time and he heard a far-off voice saying. "This is all you have. . .nothing else, just time, a finite amount of time. You don't know how many circles you have! You will change with each circle." He awoke with that thought and considered it something to take to the Teacher. He would say, "We each only have so many minutes, that is different than change, that is a finite amount of time that we have to be alive. So many circles." It is measured by minutes and revolutions of the sun. And then he thought about it and what a minute means and what it measures and he felt almost frantic because he felt like he was bending back against himself.

Change. It is me changing, he thought. Changing and growing older by the minute!

He had never thought about life. Until now. The Teacher. The Teacher was making him think. Why, he thought, am I going to the Room anyway? That stupid Room! That Thing in the room. What was He anyway? A She? An IT? A blob?

It is too late, he thought frantically. I can't go back to what it was like before the Teacher! How can this be happening with just two visits! He got up and paced around the filthy bag, walking around the room, brushing his hand along the wall, thinking how he really didn't need to go back to the Room, to the Teacher. He could say he didn't have the time anymore, that his studies were more demanding now and he had made a mistake. There was no reason why he should go back. He could stop. He would stop. He would never go there again!

But then there was a Voice talking back to him, saying things to him. It said, "of course you will go back, you will return to the Room. You have other questions you want to ask. . ."

Tom put his hands to his head, "Shut up." he said to his thoughts. "Shut up, shut up, shut up!"

Tom looked at the bag - because he had to - there was nothing else to look at. It was a big ugly thing dominating the space - there wasn't anything else in the room. It was awful, everything about the room was awful. It looked bad, it smelled bad and he didn't like it anymore. There was nobody to change it for him. Only himself.

He opened the door and picking up a corner of the bag, tried to drag the bag out of the apartment by himself. "Dammit, Fuck, Piss!" He couldn't do it.

He didn't have a plan, didn't know what he was going to do with it, but he was going to get it out of there. Only, the thing was heavy.

He went around it, kicking it here and there trying to figure out how it got to be so heavy. He sank down, defeated, squeezing a hand around his arm, mumbling, "maybe it isn't so heavy but that I'm weaker than I used to be!

"What the hell. . ."

His wrist alarm went off. "Shit."

Now he had to climb over the bag to get by it to change for work and fetch his keys. He couldn't do anything more about it because, yes - it was time, yes "time" to leave for work. No matter what the Teacher said, the clock regulated his life.

Tom worked at a pizza joint a couple of doors down from where he lived. He had been supremely lucky to find his apartment - and then his job. But it was just a job. He made only enough to get by and there was nothing "fun" about it. He worked at a counter taking pizza orders. He wore a stupid striped shirt and black pants, a kind of uniform required for his simple job.

When he arrived at work that night, he told a couple of co-workers about the monstrosity in his apartment, calling it the "elephant in my living room." They laughed about his "predicament," which was pissing him off, so John, the cook started some of his antics.

John was good at sound effects. He could do cartoon characters and imitate a number of celebrities. He often made noises when a pizza was ready, but the sound he was making now, of a trumpeting elephant, was the funniest of all. He raised his head and made a funny face and snouted his lips and let out a sound that carried through the entire place that sounded like an elephant was charging the place. Every customer in the place doubled up with laughter, but Tom still had a mood on, although it was crumbling.

"Pizza's ready." Tom said unconcerned.

The customer was laughing so hard he couldn't speak. He put a dollar on the counter and begged John to do it again.

"Do it AGAIN. Pleassseee!"

Everything about John's silliness might have been forgotten, except his antics were the funniest of anything he'd ever done and the place was full of customers - and they loved it, all chiming in for him to, "Do it again."

John had the funniest look on his face, just standing there, with his big pizza spatula in front of him, waving it, almost like big ears. He finally said quietly, "When the next pizza is ready. . .I'll do it again!"

The customer, who already had picked up his pizza, waited patiently for the next customer's pizza just so he could hear him "do it again." When John pulled the next one out of the oven, he brought it around for Jake to package it up, and instead of commenting that another pizza was ready, he let out a sound that the entire place would talk about as "the one."

Tom said blithely, "There's an elephant in the room. Our pizzas are the biggest and best!"

The entire room erupted in laughter and claps.

Part of the "funny" was that John was a big guy, really big. He wasn't fat, he was football big. He was tall and square and muscular and a person not to be messed with. He was perfect for handling the pizza oven, because the oven was old fashioned and the dough went into it on a baker's iron that he handled with ease. He didn't need anything modern to help him slide in the pizza. He was strong and preferred his job at the oven. He was good looking, had blond hair, a broad smile, large blue eyes and a square jaw. He wore a white apron tied around his waist, that wasn't really needed but made a nice effect. When children visited the pizza restaurant, he loved doing sound effects from small characters.

He was good at twisting his face around and he didn't mind making himself look funny, which was even more comical since he was so good looking. Only now here he was, making sounds from a big character. He had never done that before. He loved the reaction of his audience, but Tom's "straight man" act added to the funny. The whole thing was hilarious. Jake was at a table cutting the pizza, putting it in a box and labeling it. He stood there wondering what he could do to add to the commotion. He remembered that the first time he had jumped, because he had been so startled. So that's what he did again. John trumpeted and passed him the pizza, so Jake jumped - not a big jump, just a little one (later he added an eyebrow raise), and then he cut and boxed the pizza and gave it to Tom, who declared, like nothing unusual had happened at all, that "there's an elephant in the room because this restaurant has the biggest and best pizza in town."

All three guys had fun doing it and everybody wanted it done again.

It was a couple of nights later, when the restaurant was packed with people after a basketball game, that the owner, Carl, heard the ruckus. None of the guys had told him about it. They were just doing it because it made a boring job fun. Lots of fun. Pizzas were coming out of the oven every few minutes and there was all this noise going on. At first John was silent thinking people would want to visit over their pizza meal. Wrong! First one person put a dollar on the counter, then another, saying, "Where's the elephant in the room? I want to hear the elephant when my pizza is done!"

So, John started trumpeting when each pizza was finished. The whole room erupted in laughter. People laughed and clapped and came up to the counter with dollar bills. By the time the owner came in, John was trumpeting every few minutes.

Instead of people stampeding out of the restaurant, they were stampeding in.

"There's a stampede at Carl's Pizza," Tom declared, just as Carl walked in the door. There were customers backed up, John was trumpeting with every pizza, Jake was jumping, Tom was yapping about the pizza, and people were everywhere.

"What's going on?" Carl asked amazed. "Are you guys crazy?!" But then he looked around and put his hands up and motioned for Tom to continue.

"There's an elephant in the room," Tom said matter of factly in his funny flat tone like there really was an elephant. He was the straight guy.

"Oh, I see," Carl said. "An elephant."

"Yes, and I don't know what I'm going to do about it."

Jake, who was packaging pizzas into the boxes, choked back laughter.

John, who just then took a pizza out of the oven, let out a small trumpet.

"Pizza number 17 is ready," Tom said to the room, and then noticed everybody was waiting. He looked over at John expectantly.

A girl, looking like a student ran up to the counter. "I didn't hear the elephant." she said disappointed, almost like she was going to cry.

John smiled and gave out a really good one. Jake jumped a little, just for effect, and Tom said, "The elephant in the room has spoken because this restaurant has the biggest and best pizza in town."

The customer raised both hands as if she was receiving the Lord and screamed, "YES!" and collected her pizza with a smile, slapped down a dollar for John, stuffed another in the jar for Tom, and left.

Carl stood there and looked at the three boys. "What is going on?"

It was Jake who spoke. "Uh. . .uh. . .Tom's got an elephant in his livin' room an' he doesn't know how to get rid of. . ."

John trumpeted. Another pizza came out of the oven, Jake jumped, Tom declared the pizza to the room and Carl just stood there dumbfounded. Then Tom said to the owner, nodding, in his best straight voice, "There's a stampede at Carl's Pizza, cuz we got the biggest and best pizza in town."

Carl shook his head like something filmy was clinging to it and just then a customer ran up for his pizza saying, "You guys are the best - can't wait to bring my folks here next week!"

Carl turned and looked at the room. It was packed, mostly because of the game letting out, but he had forgotten about that because all he could think about was the three students working there. If a person had been listening very carefully, they might have heard Carl saying something under his breath as he headed back to his office, "*the three stooges. . .*"

Carl had two brothers and for a few summers, when the boys were young, the three of them visited their Uncle Ed's farm. They loved the acreage and often played down by the old mill and stream that was still there, often hiding there because they didn't like helping out detasseling corn. They had a routine of silliness though, and that helped them get through those tight rows of corn. Uncle Ed and Aunt Lydia always teased them about being the "*Three Stooges.*" They had no idea what their relatives were talking about, but then the days of streaming television came along and those crazy stooges from old time T. V. were on a screen during one of the reunions.

Finally, Carl understood. The *Three Stooges* were a silly group of guys bantering through whatever faced them in crazy slapstick comedy. Now, Carl was reminded of those old memories of silliness, but having the comedy in his establishment was something else again. Did his customers really like it? He peered into the restaurant area from the hall again. Yes, they did!

"I don't know what to do with it," Tom said later standing in Carl's office fidgeting as he explained the "elephant" in his living room. "That's how all of this started. It's because I have this awful thing in my living room, this elephant, and I don't want it anymore. It's big and ugly and I only have a car and it takes up my living room and..."

Carl had the night's receipts on his desk. He looked at them. "Do you think my dumpster is big enough?" He got up and opened the rear door and they both peered out at it.

Since the bag was flexible. . .maybe it could be folded into it? The pizza restaurant had a good-sized dumpster unit, and if both sides of the top were opened, maybe they could muscle it into it.

"We can get by for a couple of days until the garbage pick-up," Carl said. "Maybe you could put it in there if you have some help."

Carl went back to his desk and the pile of receipts. "You guys are doing a great job." He said.

A couple of nights later, operation "bag drag" took place after work from Tom's apartment. For Tom, it wasn't soon enough. John and Jake came over and the three of them pulled and tugged the unwieldy thing from his apartment down to the pizzeria by the light of the street lamps, through his parking lot, through the dimly lit alley, and over to Carl's Pizza dumpster. If it had been more like a couch, it would have been easier, but the flexibility of the bag made it difficult. Big John even got underneath it and tried to lift it using his head but it fell to either side like a giant hat that was burying him. They laughed so hard that he let the bag slide to the ground and they tumbled on it screaming in hysterical laughter. It seemed impossible to lift it. The thing had to be scooted. They were like silly drunks trying to stifle their noise, even though they had nothing to drink. It really was comical as they tried to get the filthy old thing discarded.

"How in the world did you ever get this thing into your apartment in the first place?" John asked.

"It wasn't easy," Tom remembered. He and his friends had all been drunk out of their minds when they moved it. But then, he remembered, they added stuffing to the inner foam core after they got it upstairs. It had actually been fun.

"There were more of us," Tom explained. "We put a board underneath it; and we added more stuffing after we got it up to my apartment."

"Well then," John said, adding a trumpet sound, "why didn't you say so! Let's take some stuffing out of it here! Tom, I swear. . ."

They slit it open and scooped out some of the stuffing into boxes. Tom was embarrassed. The stuffing smelled of stale booze and spilled colas, a reason why it was so heavy. The stuffing had absorbed all kinds of spills. It really was disgusting. Nobody said anything. After making it smaller, it still took all three of them to fold it and heave it over the edge of the dumpster.

They were so exhausted from the effort that they lay on the ground, under the streetlight, in the alley, behind the pizza restaurant, wishing they were drunk.

John, the pizza cook, moo-ed and Jake looked at the moon and said, "Hey guys, too bad we threw it away, we could be laying on it now instead of this hard asphalt!"

Eventually they got up and Tom took them to the bar next door, where people had been wondering about the noise, and bought beer. Then he thought about the guys who had helped him and what had just taken place, all because he had made a mental commitment to change his life! Now these fellows were more than co-workers, they had become friends.

When he went home that night, his living room was bare and there was dust and dirt everywhere. Not only had the bag been filthy, but it was dirty underneath it too. Too tired to care, he brushed the dust bunnies with his foot and imagined what he was going to put in the room - and it included a desk.

He went to bed.

TWAC

It was only the third time Tom had walked down that hallway, yet as he measured his steps, it seemed like he had been doing it for weeks. He thought of the short distance now as a "journey." His legs felt heavier with each step towards the "door." What should have taken him seconds was taking him forever. The pine sol smell was nauseating. He thought about the idea of time measuring change and how his journey between the front of the building and the "door" was taking a long time. He considered that maybe he was changing between the outside door and what was going to happen to him when he walked through the "door." He paid more attention to the stinky old hallway and how it would change when he came nearer to the door, an area he hoped was going to become a gentle forest floor. It was weird. Was he imagining it? No, he wasn't.

The hallway was the same, but it wasn't. He wasn't. When it happened, he knew he was at the door and this time, he waited with anticipation to experience what was going to happen next when he touched the knob. He couldn't remember if the vision phenomena occurred after he touched the doorknob, or before. He stood before the door and waited silently considering it.

The door swung open. No, he couldn't remember ever touching the doorknob on his last visits!

He took his first step to go through the door and then it happened. It was a summer's day at the lake. He and Abbot were getting ready to launch their small fishing boat from the shore. He could smell the honeysuckle and the warm sun baking against the landscape. It was a perfect day.

The vision lingered as he continued into the room.

Tom took his place at the table. "Good afternoon Teacher," He said pleasantly, unaware that the Guide was observing his happy thought, which was dancing off to the side of him.

"How are you today?" Teacher asked.

"I've had a good week." Tom said.

"Would you like to chat about it, or do you want to take up where we left off?"

". . .where we left off. . .?" Tom appeared to be confused. "I uh, I uh did come with some questions." He removed a folded paper from his shirt pocket and placed it on the table in front of him. "Where did we leave off. . .?"

"We were discussing time. I think we should get back to that first. There was the example of the cake. May I continue with that?"

"Sure." Tom said, aware that the warmth of the summer day was drifting away.

"Okay, let's continue with the making of that cake."

Tom wasn't ready. It was like he needed to say goodbye to Abbot and the lake and the buzzing of the bees. He could see the outline of the Guide on the other side of the drape. The person was sitting, probably at a table just like the one where Tom sat. Tom's thought about Abbot was replaced by annoyance.

"I believe you are ready," The Guide said observing the shape hovering next to Tom.

Tom was oblivious.

"Let's start at the beginning. The cake started with a thought."

Tom looked straight ahead fascinated as the drape became a kind of screen, exactly like a scrim in a theater that enabled him to see forms moving against it.

"The thought as we know it today," the Teacher/Guide continued," was actually a collection of several methods passed down through generations, an assembly put together that became a recipe. The assembly of the cake, although it seems simple, is all the changes put together to create a better result. True?"

"Yes."

"At one time instructions were verbal as people passed on how to make a cake to each other. Then as written language became more advanced, they wrote down how to make a cake, and the recipe as we know it, was created. But still, the process begins with a thought. 'I am going to make a cake.' Right?"

Tom had to agree. He nodded. This is stupid. He thought to himself.

"So, we have a sequence. Thought - recipe - action - result - consequence (the cake is eaten)."

"Do we always have a recipe?" Tom niggled.

"Well, not exactly, but there is a method. We can call it the Way. There has to be a way of doing something, of how a person learned it. Do you want me to substitute the term, Way?"

"Uh, okay." Tom said, liking that better.

"Okay, we'll call this sequence TWARC. Is that okay with you?"

"I think we can shorten it to TWAC. Thought. Way. Action. Consequence. The result is a consequence." Tom said it like an authority.

"Okay, we can agree, there may be a consequence from the cake that it wasn't cooked enough and the eggs had salmonella and a child became ill and died. The making of the cake was deliberate, the result, or consequence, was random. Consider the power of the original thought - to make a cake. It is unseen, but has the power to change everything that follows it. So, if we apply the idea of time, it is a total picture of the TWAC - the measurement of change, it measures far more than what we can see or feel. You have trouble with this in Physics because you want there to be a beginning and an end. But the measurement of change doesn't work that way. Measuring the TWAC involves the making of a cake, which is more than physical. It is more than a beginning and an end. The so-called end may be a ripple effect that goes on, of course, forever."

Tom sat there stupefied.

"The simple making of the cake includes all the connections that goes into its ultimate creation." The Teacher explained. "It has a multitude of hands and thoughts encompassed in its making. This stream of continuity is extremely important . . . some inventors are able to tap into it. . ."

"I see." Tom said, but he wasn't sure that he could *see* anything at all. He remembered the conversation from the last time. "I'm not certain I fully understand how the cake, or its pan is connected to me. . ."

"As soon as you think about making the cake, you enter into the continuum of deliberateness involved with its creation. Right? You become its creator or not. Okay, so making a cake is not a big deal, but if you were five years old, it would be. So, it is complicated enough to use it as a good example. You assemble the ingredients according to a recipe. You didn't arrive at the ability to make the cake on your own, out of the blue, you needed the help of a roadmap. You cannot put it together without structure. You needed a mixing bowl, a spoon - a pan - heat. Then a process. Altogether, it became a result. It can be a good one or a bad one or somewhere in between. It is judged. Some of the people eating the cake might say, 'Tom sure made a lousy cake!' Or they might say, 'That Tom sure can cook!' Is that about you?' The cake is forever connected to YOU, as well as everything you used to make it. Or what about if you just purchased the cake and ate it? Is that about you?"

Tom squirmed.

"What do you think? What is your thought?" Teacher asked.

"I guess so. . .." Tom whined.

The same Voice, now sounding like a radio commentator said, "we have a responsibility to all that is - all that we encounter. We are always connected to everything, everyone. Especially people."

Tom's vision returned and the room took on the warmth of that summer day with Abbot. He remembered their first conversation about the noisy motor on the boat. It was their first thoughts and silly conversations about wanting to have something quieter on the lake. He could see the thought in front of him that had changed his life, that first thought. . ."

Then he remembered his thoughts about Chelsea on the day he left her. He had compared her to a drink of whiskey that felt good while he was a little high on it, but when he was fully sober from it, he felt "off." He had wondered what he had ever seen in her. She was a student in her fourth year, while he was in his third. She studied regularly for her demanding classes, and while he respected her focus, it meant she wasn't very exciting to him.

Tom hadn't wanted to talk about anything serious, he wanted to find a girl to dance and talk about the current movies and what was happening with the latest singers and just stuff. He didn't want to think about school when he was out having a good time.

He decided to be finished with Chelsea and when he ended his time with her, he was abrupt and cold about it. "I don't want anymore." he had said on that day not so long ago. He meant to say, "I don't want to see you anymore," but it hadn't come out that way and she asked, "You don't want any more of what?" And he answered stupidly, "you."

She had leaned into the bar at the coffee house and put her hand on its edge, like she needed it to steady herself or something. He noticed her swallow. She was thin. It was at that moment he thought of her as truly unattractive. In fact, he wondered how he could have ever had sex with her. He turned his face away because he didn't want her to see his expression of distaste. She was nothing to him, except a glass of whiskey. Now the glass was empty. He got up and left, not even paying for her glass of tea.

Tom thought about her now, and remembered how he had thought of her then.

"Do you think I am connected to an empty glass?" He asked.

The same voice, but booming now, answered. "Of course. You had the benefit of the glass and its contents. Did you break the glass, or return it in the same condition as you received it? Will the next person be able to drink out of the glass? Again, we have a responsibility to everything. Everything. To everyone. This requires a change in the way you think and in the way you act."

Tom glanced at his watch.

"What happens when I don't treat things with responsibility? When I don't realize that I am connected to them?"

"There is cause and effect to everything. The responsibility isn't just to oneself; it is to the entire stream. See?" Tom could see all kinds of things on that curtain that he didn't want to see. He looked away. The Teacher stopped as if mulling it over and then continued more quietly.

"Just imagine how many unwanted babies were created as a consequence. . . of drinking too much. . . liquor. . .Yes. We think we are powerless, but that just isn't true. Is it? Everything we do has a ripple effect. It is as if we are asleep.

"Tonight, put your finger in a pail of water and watch the ripple from your finger. The pail of water is this system and you are the finger, think of it that way. Not that your finger didn't make a difference, like people always like to say. Because it did.

"You caused a ripple effect. You caused some droplets of water to leave the larger pool of water when you pulled your finger out. Moisture was clinging to your finger! You disturbed the water! Good or bad - and by the way - the idea of good and bad is a man-made definition. Good or bad - just like time is a man-made definition. Some things we think of as bad may not be bad at all in terms of the system. It is a definition that requires more exploration, just like time." The Voice changed to the regular simple neuter Voice of the Teacher that Tom was becoming used to, and then it trailed off.

"Maybe this is too much for you. See you when you come again." Teacher said.

Tom looked at his watch. Time had been standing still. He thought it should be getting dark and he had gone overtime, but the day was still bright and he felt stupid. Only a minute had passed. He felt like he did when he was an early teenager being lectured by his parents, but this was different somehow. He was being taught something else, and the Teacher's words made sense. Or did they? Who would ever dream in their wildest that a person would have a responsibility to an inert glass?

Tom didn't want the session to end! Not really. He had so many questions. At first, he thought there were only a few questions. But now there was another big one in the air, about good and bad. He knew the session was over. . .but. . .

"But. . . but, isn't time directional?" Tom asked. "Isn't it always going forwards? I mean, nothing can go backwards and change what has been. . ." He thought about Einstein and time and how it isn't absolute. . . .

"Again Tom, if you are on a circle that you entered, and you are traveling along on that circle, you cannot stop on the particular line or track that you are on, and stay on that track - because you will affect everything else - you are traveling on it at your rate, and you are not allowed to stop because you are always changing and you are going in a direction, as is everything else on that circle, but you can get OFF. Everything else will continue to change without you. Is it going forward? Not exactly, but it is always in motion, as is everything. You can get on again, at any place you want." There was an interesting pause. "Of course when you get off, something will happen to you when you do - you will change to match the condition of what you got off to, your rate of change will alter according to the laws of what you became when you got off. . ."

"What!. . .!?? So, time travel is possible?"

"No Tom, it isn't. There is no such thing as *time*. Is it possible to enter the stream at another place in terms of its change? Of course. You're on a circle and you're not allowed to stop while on it. You have to get OFF. If you stop, then you are off the circle - that particular track. *You're kicked off.* Do you understand what that means?"

"Death?"

"Yes. The laws as you know them right now means death to your physical self, because you enter a different state and that altered state is not the same as this one."

"Your entrance onto the track again will not be as you are now, because you got OFF in order to get on again at another place. You change when you get off. You change when you get on again. It is not a time sequence. It is a change sequence. Right? If you are entering the ocean, you must be able to survive in the ocean. If you are entering another state, as it were, as an ethereal spirit, you must be able to survive in a spiritual dimension. If you are entering the Earth, you must survive in a place of physical dominance as *it* is. I'll use the term "time" for lack of another term, as it is at that time for your entrance - or - the state of its change to accept you. Right? You won't change anything in terms of how other things change, and their rates of change. Only the Universe does that. It is what we call God. It is the force of God - the nature of things."

"Each person is doing their thing, you don't have control of that, but you are connected to them and to everything in this stream of consciousness. What you do can and does affect them. Right? Think of this as the Earth stream." The same Voice, now sounding like a radio commentator said, "We have a responsibility to all that is - all that we encounter. We are always connected to everything.

If you enter the stream again at a different place, of course the stream will accommodate you and nothing will ever be the same again because of you. Does time fold in on itself? No, but change does. You cannot change what is already in the stream, but you can add to what is in the stream. When you get off, you change into the state of what you enter when you get off."

The door swung open slowly on its own, and Tom understood he had to leave. He looked at it expecting to see another student walking through it. But there wasn't anyone.

Tom wasn't ready to leave the Roooom. He had more questions. "Time cannot go back on itself." He said stupidly. "A person cannot go BACK in time. I mean time IS something. It IS directional. Name one thing that doesn't have a time direction."

It was as if Tom hadn't understood anything at all. There was a sigh in the room. The drape sagged.

He looked at the door. "Oh please, I cannot leave yet."

Now the Voice had a tiresome quality to it. "Oh Tom," Teacher said, "You are a physics student. You know this stuff. You can go back, but what is around you won't be what it was per se, and you cannot cause what is around you to change just because you've entered the circle someplace else. You must think in terms of change, not time. Light can go backwards and so can sound but what is around it won't ever be the same. The light itself and the sound will never be the same either - it also depends on what is around it. Yes, you can create an experiment where everything is the "same," but nothing ever is - exactly. Not exactly. Because in the unseen realm of things, it is impossible to recreate an exact condition."

Tom was getting ready to dispute the Teacher. He had done controlled experiments in the Physics lab. Of course, it was possible to re-create things exactly. He could create a vacuum. He could make things the same.

The Guide could read his thoughts. Tom hadn't realized this yet. "The sun will be in a different position," the Teacher said, "with any subsequent experiment. The stars, the great everything will be different. You cannot control THAT in your experiment. Can you?

"We are always connected to everything. The earth stream is connected to the universal stream of ALL that IS. This is what you can measure, what you can see, what you cannot see and what you can see. We are still little humans."

Tom sat very still

"Can you go back to the beginning of your life and do it again, when you have already changed and organically the other ingredients also changed? What about the cake? The change occurred. Can you make a new cake? The cake has to be made from scratch again. Do you understand?"

"The thing about truth, Tom, is that you have intuition. You will feel the rightness of truth - of what you learn. You will have a sensation that tells you, 'Ah this is it, this is the answer I have been seeking. There is truth here.' You must believe what you think you know."

"How will I know?"

"You will learn to recognize the feeling that some call, discernment, but it is more than that. It involves the spiritual essence of our being-ness." And by the tone of the Voice, Tom knew his time was over and that he was clearly being dismissed.

"Infinity has no beginning and end. It is a circle. You understand a circle. In order for infinity to exist, there must be constant change. There can be no stagnation.

"Time's up." The Teacher laughed lightly. "You must go."

The Guide added, "The light in the room has changed, and so have we."

FRIENDS

The next day Tom met two of his classmates before class, Chib and Bruster.

They often talked about areas of their Physics curriculum that seemed "undiscovered." Some of the so-called answers just lead Tom's mind into areas that were gray. His friend, Chib, thought so too, speculating, "There's way more to the Higgs, and when we find it, a whole new dimension will open up in front of our eyes. It will set us back on our heels!"

Chib was always preoccupied with the Higgs and was certain that scientists were looking in all the wrong places, going about it all wrong to find new answers. "We have to think about this in a different way." He would say. "We have to get through a barrier. It's another dimension."

Tom, on the other hand, was more pragmatic. "It's not going to do us a lot of good to discover a bunch of particles we can't even measure or see or cause infinitesimal things to collide or do anything with - that are so small we can't even find them! What's the sense of looking? And now you're saying they are probably in another world, another dimension. What good is that going to do us?" He often would tease Chib about his 'other worldly' ideas.

"How can you say that?" Chib countered. "Every time we find something new, which isn't 'new' at all, it advances science and . . .and . . .lots of great stuff happens as a result! You dumb ass!" Chib always said it affectionately, to which Tom always smiled and answered. "Oh yeah freaky flake, suppose you will find the answer someday and find us a way to communicate without the internet. . ."

"Of course, I will."

It was Friday now and a quiz was soon to happen in Quantum Physics. He, Chib and Bruster sat in the Quad and looked at the material for the quiz. They weren't worried. They knew the stuff.

"Yeah, but it will tell us a lot about the universe, "Chib said, as he once again brought the conversation to his favorite topic - the Higgs. "We don't know squat until we know. It's like saying the world is flat until we discover that it has been round all along. There is another layer out there; I just know it!"

"You'll be the one to find it, Chib, if anyone." Tom encouraged.

It was at this gathering that Tom mentioned the Room to his buddies for the first time.

"I'm going to the Zimmer," Tom said flatly out of nowhere.

"Wha. . .?" Chib uttered almost spitting out his cola.

"An appointment opened up for me."

"Do tell. Have you been already?"

"Yeah."

"You've been holding out on us." Bruster said. "Spill."

"I dunno. It's weird. I mean. . . It's Syfy weird."

Bruster licked the mayo off his lower lip and stared at Tom. "Like how?"

"Yeah, how?" Chib parroted.

Tom started to tell his friends about the room and the figure sitting in there. He wanted to tell them about the crazy drape and the visions walking through the 'door,' but he couldn't. He remembered the times when he asked others about it and he couldn't get any information from them either. He tried to say what was in his mind, to describe the drape and how things changed when he walked in there, but no words came out of his mouth. It was like the words turned into droplets of ice and fell to the floor. He looked wide-eyed at his friends.

"I dunno," he finally said in answer to their expectant expressions. "I can't describe it. But I think you better get your name on the list, Chib. There's information in there that might be helpful to you."

"Yeah?"

"I dunno, it's weird. I think differently after I'm in there." Tom gazed around the room wanting to say more, trying to figure out how to describe the Zimmer. Each time he tried to form words and say them, something else stupid and inane came out. Like, "It's more than a room."

"Like what? Like how?" Both guys were leaning forward trying to eek more words out of Tom, but the words weren't there.

"I can't say. I haven't figured it out. It's a different sort of place. It's. . .uh. . .it's. . .uh. . .a place like no other." That was about all Tom could say.

After the quiz that afternoon, Tom watched Chib hike across the campus. He knew where he was going. Chib was adding his name to the waiting list. Learning was everything to him.

That evening, Tom tried again to describe his experiences in the Room to friends. It was while he was working at the pizza restaurant that kids from his Calculus Two class came in.

"Hey, what's up?" Stu asked, putting in his order.

"I got a spot in the Zimmer," Tom said. "Been going there."

"You lucky bastard. I've been on that list since I got here! How did you swing that? I've never moved up the list. My name just stays there, in the same spot. I check on it too, every couple of weeks." He pointed to the large pizza special. "I think something must be wrong. How long were you on the list?"

A feeling of bravado fell over Tom as he readied to brag about his good fortune. He was going to say that maybe it was his good grades or his attendance record, or about how good he was, but something was happening to his thoughts. He became confused and his words jumbled over each other and it was like there was a sword slashing at his thoughts slicing them into pieces. He looked at his friend confused and said instead, "It's beyond me. I didn't do anything at all. I think they must just select names at random. Maybe you'll be next. I know you're a good candidate. You'll be next for sure!"

Stu smiled. "Thanks Tom. Appreciate the kind words. Maybe I will be next!"

Just then, Big John trumpeted a huge sound, delivered a pizza to Jake, who did his jumping bit, and then it was up to Tom, always the straight man, to say something, which he did, "Another pizza has arrived, hot from the delicious ovens of Carl's Pizza!"

After work, Tom walked to his apartment, like he'd done so many times before, but this time he moved along close to the buildings in the alley. He ran his hand over a brick wall before he came out to his parking lot, and stopped.

A feeling of fear snaked into the pit of his stomach. He looked around as if seeing it for the first time. His old jalopy sat in the first car stall just like he left it and his bicycle was chained to the rack where he'd put it earlier in the day. The streetlight danced shadows from an old newspaper that was dancing in the breeze. It reminded him of something else he had seen in the *Rooom* dancing around like those shadows.

He shuddered and held himself by his upper arms. He wasn't scared of being mugged or of the night. No, he wasn't scared of anything out there around him. He was afraid of what was happening inside himself. There was twice that day he had been out of control; twice his thoughts had not been his own. He had not been allowed to talk about the room. . .and then when he was going to say something to Stu, and he was going to brag about his good fortune to his friend at Carl's Pizza, he had not been allowed to express his thought. In fact, his thought had been destroyed by something, a foreign feeling, something previously unknown to him.

He bent over in that parking lot and held his stomach feeling momentarily sick. And then he stopped thinking about that foreign feeling. He straightened up and went over and picked up the newspaper. Because after all, it needed to be thrown away. Didn't it?

He knew his life had been altered forever, that he had let something enter that would now be part of him forever, that he couldn't put it away, or get rid of it. "What have I done?" He muttered to the night sky.

He threw the newspaper in the apartment dumpster, sat down on the stairs leading to his apartment and looked up at the night sky.

"Oh, dear God, what have I done?"

WHAT ARE YOU (WE?)

"My first question today is about what kind of questions to ask here." Tom began. "That really wasn't very well defined when I was here before and I'm not sure if I should be asking questions involving my schoolwork or something involving my life. . .or. . . just what?"

Toms' vision upon entering the room had been so ridiculous it was easy to dismiss it. He had been a little kid under a Christmas tree. He was looking up at the lights and it was so magical. He turned over and crawled between wrapped presents. There were ribbons and metallic papers that reflected the lights. A voice said, "Santa Claus was here and left you presents, Thomas." It was his mother.

"He doesn't understand yet," His father said. "He is still too little to understand gifts. Give him another year and he'll understand Santa Claus. . ."

"No, he's not," she persisted. "He has to start somewhere and he is starting now to understand how special gifts can be. . ."

"It sounds like you want to know more about me." Teacher said.

"Yes." Tom said eagerly, but Teacher was evasive.

Laughing, Teacher explained," But Tom, this is all about you, not me."

Tom looked at the curtain confused. "I don't get it."

"What do you want to do Tom? Are you here about your schoolwork, or you? What questions do you want to ask?"

"You're not a psychiatrist, are you?" Tom asked.

"Oh, dear sun in the sky and clouds above, No. I'm not."

"Then, what are you?" Tom persisted.

"We are homo sapiens."

Tom clicked his pen rapidly. "That isn't what I meant." He said, his lips tight. "Why can't I see you?"

"It is important not to judge your experience by outward appearances." The Voice said. "Sometimes things are not always what they seem. Too often conclusions are reached on false assumptions.

"What happens in this room is based entirely on you - you direct it, you absorb the information and either appreciate it or discard it. You decide if it has value or not. There won't be anything to interfere with that. You are not reacting to me; you cannot see me. Instead, you are reacting to you, to the information you receive - to how you choose not to receive it."

"I don't know what to do. . ." Tom said his voice trailing off in a whine.

An uncomfortable silence ensued.

"We were talking about time when I was here before." Tom finally said. "About its relationship to speed or rate of change. Do you think it is possible, then, to alter our rate of change to a different speed, thereby we could . . . um. . .um. . ." Tom tried to think of the best way to frame the rest of his question, then blurted, "we could age more slowly?"

But the Teacher seemed unfazed by it and asked in return, "What is it that you think you might change in order for that to happen?"

"Oh my gosh, I wish I had an idea about it - I'd be the richest man on the planet." Tom said warming to the subject and thinking about a science fiction thing he saw recently about a woman drinking an elixir to make herself young again, but it backfired and she turned into a wrinkled old hag. "Do you have any ideas about it, Teacher?"

"Hmmm. I haven't thought about that one. It seems like most of us are ready to go on to something better - if you know what I mean."

"Heaven?" Tom said half answering himself with a long "yeeaah."

There was a sound that came from behind the curtain that Tom swore sounded like a snort and then like something else strange. He was certain that if he could see the Teacher, he would see a face that was scowling at him. But why? What was wrong with heaven? Maybe the snort came from an animal or something. Maybe from a goat. He chuckled at the thought.

The figure behind the drape burst out laughing.

"What. . .?" Tom was embarrassed. That thing behind the drape couldn't have read his mind. . .could it?" Then he noticed an image off to the side and knew for sure that the figure behind the drape could see things from his mind. Tom vowed he would find a way to shield the thoughts in his brain.

"Animals are connected to us, Tom."

What does that make heaven if there are goats in heaven wondered Tom.

The Teacher laughed again. Then a male voice said, "Thinking about this, actually, I would say, it isn't a problem of physical longevity like we think it is. Your question was about longevity, wasn't it? You were wondering if we could elongate our physical existence by altering our change. Theoretically. . .ummm. . . yes. We can slow down our rate of change. Hmm, yes I think such a thing is possible."

"I mean," Tom started, "our organs have a life - they wear out, but what if they are in good shape and we can last longer? If we can slow down our rate of change. . .will we slow down time and live longer?"

"Yes and no. We will slow down time as it relates to us, so maybe, but not as it relates to the sun. The clock measures the rotation of the sun. Yours is not a time question, but a question of change."

"So, if it is more than a physical problem, that means aging has something to do with the earth track. Right?"

"Yes. So far," The Teacher continued, "a track has not been developed that I can jump onto from the one I'm on. I only know how to stay on this one. The one of getting older. If my rate is slowed down, that means I'm slower in relation to everything else around me - they will be faster. I'm not sure I like that. . ."

Tom nodded. What the Teacher was saying made as much sense as anything else on the subject. "But maybe we can figure out a way to jump onto another um track. . . a different track."

"You would want to do that? You made a choice to enter this one."

"Maybe I might want to change my choice. . ."

"When we learn to convert the frequency we are on, we will be able to do this." The Voice said, now matter of factly. But then we won't be like we are now, because we'll be involved with another frequency. . ."

"Convert?" Tom said surprised. The Voice seemed so sure about it.

"Yes. We are able to convert some forms of energy now, such as converting the energy from the sun into power we can use, and other forms. I'm sure you've studied Thermodynamics in your physics curriculum."

"Uh huh." Tom agreed.

"Well, it's like driving a car. Energy is controllable, it's speed can be determined, IF it is accessible. Our speed is not accessible right now."

Tom sat up rigidly. He reached deep into his thoughts. He could alter his physical speed by running and jumping. Why couldn't he alter the speed of his life? "Why can't I alter the speed of my life when I can alter the speed of my physical self?. . .like how I'm running through the air?" He asked the Teacher.

"The speed of your life is comprised of a very complicated system, eh? Everything in your body has to be in sync with the total speed of the system. Your system. You are considering your outward self. I can see that by your thoughts. But you are an entire system.

"It must be," the Teacher said continuing, "that the speed of each of our lives is on an individual track - for each of us, and that it is on an energy level, or frequency we have yet to define. We are not able to understand it yet. It could be something as simple as setting a kind of timer before we enter here. There are certain things that cannot be altered - and unless we can reset the timer itself, then we are stuck with what we originally asked for."

He laughed. "Like a cake in the oven taking a certain amount of time to cook. We cannot change what the maturity is. Think about it. We each have a maturity. It also may be that when we speed up one thing, we slow down another, and vice-a-versa. There is a balance to everything."

"Nah. Not each of us. Some exit too quickly. I don't think that it is all predetermined. Do you?"

"TWAC," The Guide said. "Randomness. . .

"Your original question was about the natural life span, was it not? Not predetermination."

"Why isn't the exit easier then?" Tom asked thinking of the long and arduous death of his grandfather. It was a sadness in his family after his freshman year of college. He went home that first summer to spend it helping his family.

"We are just playing at answers right now, Tom. I wish I knew the answer to that one. Maybe we need to do something to make the transition easier. Perhaps we have abdicated something that is really supposed to be under our control and the Universe is waiting for us to do something and instead we are waiting for the Universe to do it. Huh? Maybe. We certainly have many useful possibilities to make it easier and less painful to exit.

"I don't remember reading anything in the Ten Commandments saying that we should not help ourselves over to the other side. Instead the commandment is:

Thou Shalt Not Kill."

"Well killing ourselves is killing, don't you think?" Tom asked.

"That becomes a matter of language and definition. We don't know how to turn off our individual timers without doing something to ourselves that is not natural. Not yet. Perhaps turning off the timer will never be possible, because doing so may go against universal laws, or laws of nature. It may be that no creature is able to do that, but we do have tools of mercy. Being merciful to oneself. . .well I'm not sure that fits the definition of killing."

"Of course, it does." Tom argued. "So, who do you think wrote the *Ten Commandments*?"

"We have the force of all things, the law that governs and organizes all that IS, and then we have a set of laws that govern and organize how we behave. Do you see a difference?" The Teacher's Voice took on a quality of age that Tom hadn't noticed before. He could almost see the outline of a wise old woman.

Now the image of a goat flashed in Tom's mind again and slowly it changed into an elderly man with a Go-T beard and an elegance of a wise person explaining a thought to him. He shook his head trying to clear the vision. Where in the world had the goat come from anyway?

"Well of course there IS a difference," Tom said. "The force you are describing is science, the other is man's attempt to control themselves."

"Of course. And what is the difference. . .?

"Every species must be able to guide their organization. Our species uses words. Other species use movements, pheromones, and other tools.

"Whether or not Moses, God, or some other entity wrote the Ten Commandments is immaterial to the power of their words. The Commandments are used as an organizational tool for who and what we are. Right? They are no less important." The Teacher's voice became like a beautiful song. "We honor them as part of our God system - because they are."

"I want to know so many things. I want to know who and what I am. I want to know why God has abandoned us and . . ."

"Abandoned you? How can something that is part of you, abandon you. . .? I can see you want to know many things all at once and this is not an easy concept for you." Soft words came from everywhere in the room, not just behind the drape. "But I can help you with your search."

"My search.?"

"Yes. You would not be here, unless on some level you were ready."

"Ready for what?" Tom asked annoyed. "I came here because you had an opening and friends recommended you and I thought. . ."

"That's right. Not to worry. All is as it should be."

Tom became restless. "Okay. If you say so. I don't have any reason to hang around any longer today."

"Have a good week, Tom. Life is more than you think it is. It is like an orchestra playing a wonderful song and you really have no idea about all the different instruments that are playing and how all the various notes are written. There's a new discovery around every corner. Your energy, that field of magnetism that is growing around you, will attract interesting possibilities into your life. Nothing will be by accident . . ."

When Tom got up to leave the room that day, he was glad the session was over. He was frustrated by the whole experience. As he turned to say goodbye, he saw a goat in a green field running. The animal turned, smiled, his teeth crooked and silly. He kicked his hind legs in the air and ran. Tom laughed. He couldn't help it. The vision was funny, and light-hearted.

It was like the joke was on him, only he didn't know what the joke was, but he felt certain he was about to find out.

TOM'S APARTMENT

Tom was breathless. He hadn't been able to do anything about his apartment for a week after getting the bag thing out of his living room. He worked at the pizza joint three nights a week and part time on Saturday and Sunday. He'd had a quiz and homework and he hadn't been motivated.

It was Sunday already and it was turning out to be a long day because it was a game day which meant they were especially busy. Carl wanted him to come in early and stay late.

When he came home that night it was to face his dirty bare room again. Ugh. He made a point of not looking too closely and went straight to his bedroom to study and sleep.

The next morning, a Monday, he had classes, plus he'd agreed to meet with Mollie.

It wasn't until late afternoon that he was finally free of commitments. Actually, the goat trick left him in a good mood. He laughed every couple of minutes at the visualization that somehow kept entering his mind. His mood changed quickly, however, when he walked into his apartment and saw the piles of dirt everywhere. They reminded him that if the floor was filthy like that, then he was filthy. He was the person living like that, not his friends, not anybody else. Him. He couldn't remember the last time he had actually cleaned the place! He kicked up some of the dust, and when he did that, the image of the goat kicking his heels all of a sudden entered his mind again, making him laugh. "This is just dirt" something said in his head.

"Yes," he said to himself. "Dirt can wait." But the thrift store would close at five and there was nothing in the room! He could clean later.

He couldn't find a tape measure, so he used an extra shoelace to see how much space he had along the walls. Then he tucked it into his pocket and headed out to where his old car was parked, but he couldn't leave.

He sat in the car and thought about his apartment upstairs. The thought of coming back to all that dirt bothered him. He pounded the steering wheel lightly with his fist. "What's wrong with me?" he asked himself. "I can clean the place when I come back. . ."

Only he didn't start the car, but instead glanced at his watch and saw he could do some cleaning for a little while before leaving. He ran back up to the apartment and went quickly to work making piles that he picked up with old school papers, because he didn't even have a dust pan.

"What's wrong with me?" He asked himself again as he ran back and forth across the room. "This is awful," he muttered, "really, really awful."

He wanted to do more but it was like a hand pushed him out of the apartment, almost a voice saying, "it's good enough, time for you to go now."

So, he went.

He seldom used the old Buick, but it was a necessity, mostly for driving home for Thanksgiving and going out on dates and stuff like that. He said conversationally to the car, "am I connected to you too ol' girl?"

It was filthy too, with old papers stacked up and even a couple of old beer bottles, but something was pushing him and it kept pushing. He promised the car that he would clean it soon, patting it, grateful for its service, and wondered how come he had started talking to himself. "I love you." he said, starting it. She turned over right away, like she always did.

At the thrift shop he found a small desk with a roll around chair that was perfect. There was also a couch he liked that would fit perfectly in his space so he asked if they would deliver it, but they said they couldn't. He stood there looking longingly at it before giving up. He went over to the chairs thinking he could make a couple of trips for those, and have a few of them around his living room. They would fit in his car. He thought about how nice his living room would look if only he could furnish it normally, but then, he was a poor student and only a desk was really important.

He was at the counter paying for the desk when magic happened. A man standing there collecting a receipt started visiting, as people sometimes do while they wait.

"I don't think the IRS is going to allow me any kind of deduction," he commented to Tom and a lady standing there. "But the receipt for the donation makes me feel like I've done something nice."

"Yeah," Tom said. "It's great you have stuff to bring in. I'm a student and need stuff and it helps me out!"

"Well, I've got more." The man said. "But they can't pick it up right now 'cause their truck is on the fritz so I'm SOL and my wife isn't gonna be very happy with me. . . what a hassle."

The man was turning to leave when Tom added his sad tale. "Yeah, me too. I really wanted to get a couch, but now I can't. All I have is a car and they're not delivering. . . and I don't know anyone with a truck. Now I have to settle for a few chairs."

The man stopped. "That's my problem." He said. "I need to get a couch and chair, OUT of my house. I don't have anybody to help me move 'em right now and I have to work all week and this place can't come out to get 'em and... hey. . .you want to come and help me move them? They're really nice. You can have 'em."

The stranger named Frank waited while Tom loaded his desk and took him to one of the nicer neighborhoods, stopping in front of a brick house. Inside Tom saw a couch and chair that looked new. "You're not giving these away, are you?" Tom asked incredulously. "You can get a lot of money for these. I can pay you something, but not what these are worth!"

"Nah," Frank said. "You can have 'em. My wife is allergic to the fabric. I'm grateful to have your help because it will make my wife so happy to see they're gone when she gets home. Can you and I get them into your place?"

Tom pulled the shoelace out of his pocket. "I think so." He said measuring. He should have been surprised that they were so perfect, but he wasn't. He was just happy.

The two of them loaded the couch and chair and took them to his apartment. Tom thought about his earlier cleaning as he opened the door and breathed out a sigh.

"I have no words to thank you," Tom said, opening his wallet.

Frank just smiled. "Some things are meant to be," he winked, turned and left. As he did, Tom saw the goat again, looking back at him, kicking his heels.
. .

Tom sat on his new couch, felt the woven fabric under his fingers, and squeezed his eyes in pleasure. Only 24 hours had passed and his living space had changed dramatically. Was he connected to it?

He went over to the desk. He had a desk! He got his backpack from the bedroom, pulled his books out, and stacked them neatly. He brought out his laptop, opened it and found the outlet nearby to plug in the charger. He sat down and rolled around in the chair and adjusted the height. "Whoopi-doo," he said delightedly. Then he rolled back to where his books were and opened the one from his physics class. He started doing a problem, but the space was dark. He needed a desk lamp. Tomorrow he would go back to the thrift shop and get a lamp, and maybe a few other things.

Tom looked forward to work later that week, to John and his silly noises, and Jake with his jumps. He was getting to like the job that he once thought of as boring.

When he got there, he noticed the neatly lettered sign still taped on the wall, "Dumpster full until Friday, please collect trash here." He went over and removed the sign thinking about the risk Carl had taken to help him. An inspector would have had a fit about trash being stacked within the facility.

Tom was extra nice to his customers that night, because he felt nice. There was a tip jar on the counter and he never paid much attention to it because it never had much in it. He looked at it and was startled. Sometimes there might be a bill in it, but usually there were a few scattered coins. In all the time he had worked there, it had never been full, but it was full now and his shift wasn't over yet. John was getting tips, but people were laying those on the counter for his "noises." Now he was getting tips too - green tips.

He could not have asked for a better job next to the college! But college kids didn't tip! They didn't have extra money to give to a person working at a pizza counter, only, there was money in the jar - green bills were in it!

What's happening tonight? Tom wondered. He thought about it and then figured there must be some kind of parent orientation going on. He started to notice the people coming in. He was concerned that some of it was meant for John.

At the end of his shift, Tom offered to buy beer again for John and Jake. They both begged off. It was late and Jake was married and had school work pressing him. John said he was behind in his studies and needed to get a paper finished, saying he needed his sleep to finish it in the morning.

Then, on a whim, Tom decided to divide his tips with them. John was getting tips for the first time, but Tom was certain some of the money in the jar was because of him. Jake did all the boxing and labeling, so the contents got to the right people, but he never got a cent.

Why do I deserve all the tips? Tom asked himself. All I do is take the orders at the counter, and tonight, for some unknown reason, there is a huge number of tips. He motioned the two guys to the table in the back room and dumped the jar.

"Hey guys, I got a lot of tips tonight, lots more than usual, and I think you deserve some of this too - lets divide."

The three of them counted out the money and divided the tips. Interestingly, Tom's take was more than what it usually was, and for the other two men, it was a badly needed boost. Jake became emotional, his eyes becoming watery, "Hey pal, you haven't a clue how badly I needed this tonight!" And Big John gave a crazy noise and offered to divide his trumpeting tips with them, but of course, Jake and Tom refused. "Hey, those are just yours, you know? We have absolutely nothing to do with your noises. . . and this tip jar is probably bigger because of you and those noises. Okay?"

Tom squeezed his eyes as he felt a new kind of pleasure and walked slowly to his apartment. When he entered the place, he was startled. It was so different.

He went over to the desk and picked up one of his books and opened it, sat in his new chair, the one matching the couch, and read his assignment. He fell asleep in the chair. Late into the night, or actually early in the morning, he awoke and went to bed. He was repelled by his sheets - they hadn't been washed in weeks and were brown. He vowed that laundry was a priority in the next few days.

He didn't have early classes so he slept in. Then he went to the thrift shop again. He looked around for pictures for his wall. He found a landscape to replace one of his vampires and a set of sheets.

The next time Tom went to work, he noticed the empty dumpster by the pizza restaurant and thought again about his good fortune. He had been relieved that the garbage collectors had taken the bag. That crazy old bag had served to be more than a discard, it facilitated a newly formed bond for the three workers and their boss, which became more apparent as they continued working together. Carl, the owner, started advertising the "stampede" and the elephant in the room continued to trumpet and Tom announced the "biggest and best pizza in town!"

For some reason he wasn't finding the job so boring anymore.

THE SYSTEM

Tom stood there waiting.

He expected the door to swing open.; a feeling of anticipation enveloped him. There had always been a surge of wonder or adrenaline followed by something he liked doing. But nothing happened. He smelled the moss of a forest filled with trees as he danced from foot to foot. He imagined being under a sugar pine. But the door stayed shut.

He reached out and took a hold of the doorknob. He tried turning it, only it didn't turn. It seemed to be locked. He tried moving it back and forth but it stayed fast shut.

He knocked.

Nothing.

He stood there.

What now, he thought.

Oh, I understand, he thought. Somebody else is still in there.

He waited.

Three minutes, became five, and five became ten.

He politely knocked again.

He moved back from the door, took one last look at it and decided to leave, seeing it opening in his minds' eye. He turned to go.

The door swung open.

He stepped across the threshold.

Everything around him turned golden. The forest gave way to harvested fields and brightly colored leaves. Tom and his sister were running behind a wagon filled with big pumpkins. The farmer was bringing in their selections for Halloween. They were laughing and racing. Tom could see a small crowd of kids waiting their turn by the apple cider stop.

The day had been perfect until one of those kids kicked Cami's pumpkin and spattered it all over her new tights. Tom asked him why he'd done that, but he didn't answer and instead tried to kick Tom too, but Tom was bigger and he just grabbed him by his collar and held him high. "You will have to give her YOUR pumpkin now," Tom had said, "and you must apologize."

The kid spit in his face. Tom looked for his parents, but there didn't seem to be any adults around, so he reached for some apple cider and splat it in the kids face.

"I won't spit back on you," Tom had said. "Instead, every time you eat an apple, *it* will spit on you. You will never enjoy an apple again."

"Says you."

"Says the universe." Tom said, dumping another apple cider on him ceremoniously, and chanting, "Everything comes back at you. Every apple you try to chew."

The other kids chimed it, "Everything comes back at you."

"Hello Teacher." He said.

"Hello Student."

Tom sat at the table and stared at the white page in his hand.

Teacher waited.

He fidgeted and fingered the paper. He thought about the news story. He'd seen it on late television, heard it on the radio through his earphones walking to school that morning, and there it was, a huge headline on the Journal Newsstand when he ate his lunch at the Quad.

"Madman Shoots Kids and Self at School. Three Dead."

"There was a horrible shooting yesterday" Tom said. "Did you hear about it?"

"Yes."

"Why do people do such horrible things?" Tom asked.

"They think they are alone." Said the Voice.

"Alone?"

"Yes."

"But they know they are not alone. They know they will be imprisoned. They know they might even be put to death."

"You know that, they don't."

"Of course, they DO!" Tom said exasperated. "They know about prison and punishment and all that."

"People who do these things are not in control. They are being controlled." The Voice said calmly.

"Controlled by what? Satan?"

Then Tom suddenly felt his stomach lurch and a chill formed in his back.

"No. Not Satan. We think of Satan as an entity, separate from ourselves, just like we think of God as being separate. But in truth, Satan is a grouping of that we have created - or a dark cloud that we have put in place - we made it so it controls us, in a kind of paradox. We control it."

"We do?" Tom was lost.

"People who do terrible things ARE being controlled, true, but in a different way than the way we think of Satan - they are controlled by the result of an earlier action of something *we did*. It is a consequence." The Voice emphasized consequence. "Every action has a consequence within the system - our system - and that includes thoughts. You are connected to everything within this system and everything you do has a consequence and every thought and every action has a ripple effect." Teacher raised his hand in a stop motion, but Tom could barely see it, but he did see it. "Yes, I know. You do not want to be connected to this crime, or to the person who did it. But you are. We all are."

Tom gasped. "I guess I am." He said. "Because I feel sick at heart. I'm sick. The parents. . .the teachers. . .the other students…"

"That's true," Teacher said, "Yet, I am speaking about ALL the connections that we have in this system, and there are many . . ."

Tom couldn't imagine what the Teacher was talking about.

"Okay. Let's look again at the cake example. What happens if you blow on the cake? Not much. But what happens if many people blow on the cake? Something happens. It will react. They didn't even know anything would happen. Maybe people were helping a child blow out candles and wax went everywhere. Maybe the cake hadn't been cooked enough and many people were blowing on it and this caused a reaction. Perhaps some people got sick. What if there were people down the street that were using too much power and there was an electrical outage that affected the cooking of the cake?

"Now, let's go to the idea of thought, which is very powerful. Again, thought has power. There might be one person thinking that the cake batter will result in a hard rock and nothing will happen, but if many people believe it will be a bad cake, things happen in the unseen realm of possibilities. The person assembling the cake forgets the water and the cake is a hard rock. The niece says, 'oh I knew Aunt Emma was not going to make a good cake - I just knew it!' Do accidents really happen? Yes. But also, everything within the system is based on randomness of action and consequence. A set of consequences happens from actions you don't even know about. In other words, how do you trace an action that may have occurred from movement within the system before the perpetrator was even born? The movement could have been caused from an action done during World War One - the consequence became an act of violence at a school. It is all **connected**. *Time as you know it is not a factor.* How one thing is connected to another is not based upon your concept of time. Time does not exist. The system will maintain its harmony, even though we don't individually. We are all responsible for everything good and bad within our system. Now listen carefully I am going to give you a very specific example.

"It wasn't up to God to stop the execution of Jesus. Only the members of the system could do that."

The Teacher's statement hung in the air like heavy drops that would not fall because the air was too thick.

Tom was experiencing something slightly new. He thought he recognized having the experience before, but now it was clarified and crystalline. He was having a pure thought. The thought had a kind of vision with it, not exactly a visualization, but something else that he wanted to name. It was a multisensory translation of an idea. He needed to frame a term for his experience so he could make notes about it later.

He struggled about it. Then he decided to call what happened a mun-tra. Yes, that term would be fine.

He found himself thinking, just like he always did: Why did God let such a thing happen? Now Teacher was explaining that God did not allow it to happen. We did.

It was like he was seeing the thought as a flattened landscape and there were all the players going about their business, their lives, the things they do, and then somebody makes a mistake and upsets one of the squares. The landscape corrects itself. He couldn't describe his experience. He could only give it a name. It was somewhere in him. It was a thought, a kind of vision, but not something real, a kind of pattern, something. . . a mun-tra. He could see the truth in it.

He was a tiny figure sitting at the table. He could see himself from above sitting there. He tried to remember what the Teacher had said about God. God is everywhere and is everything the Teacher had said, or had the Teacher said that? No, that wasn't exactly it. Or was it? God is the force, the deliberate force. We are all the God force, he had said, hadn't he? We are all connected, everything, all that IS.

"Is that the system?" he asked, without explaining his thought.

"Mmmm, Tom. Our system is comprised of matter, and atmospheric pressure, and all these creatures that are material, and NOT material - they are ephemeral, or multi-dimensional. . .we cannot see them, but maybe feel them or smell them or perceive them in other ways. . .right? And then there is the vibrational plane, and the one of thought. What I am speaking of, is this system, this system of which you and I are a part. It isn't completely defined. Right? It is this existence that we are experiencing."

"Well, it really is pretty well defined." Tom, the physics student declared, while Tom the young man sitting in the room, looked confused by his own statement.

The Teacher laughed. "It wasn't so long ago that the world of physics declared the atom the smallest unit in the Universe, at least that was until the big split took place into protons, neutrons, and electrons and behold - we have the Quark! What can be smaller than small?"

"Bosons." Tom sniffed, thinking of Chib and the Higgs.

"Maybe. Perhaps we will discover the smallest measurement of all and it may be the most powerful of all. The Teacher paused, taking a breath, "and us silly humans may discover it is the unit of a thought."

The room reacted: thought, thought, thought, thought, thought.

The room was shuddering and displaying a kind of musical disturbance to the light that seemed to be fading in the distance, like an echo almost.

Tom broke the silence by sniffing again.

"For the purpose of our discussions Tom, we'll refer to our world, our surroundings, our existence, as The System. Okay?"

Tom nodded. He understood, although his physics brain wanted to spar with the Teacher, instead, he asked another question.

"Did you say that God doesn't know the difference between good and bad?"

"That's right, Tom. Good and bad as we know it. Good and bad are man-made definitions to describe a cause and effect situation we don't understand. The forces that comprise our system are not morally based, but based on other criteria: action and consequence, male and female, light and dark, wet and dry, backwards and forwards. The concept of good and evil arising from forces outside of our system do not exist. Good and evil exist within our system. It is something we have created. That doesn't mean that good and evil aren't real. It means that good and evil, as we know the condition, didn't arise from outside the system, as a good God entity and as a bad or Devil entity. That doesn't mean these conditions are not part of the God system, everything is, it means that it is balanced *within* our system and we must learn how to manage it as part of what we are. The God force will balance the system when members of the system push the system itself out of balance. There is a balance to everything. Again, God has not imported good and evil into our system. It is our creation. It is important to make this distinction. A God entity does not swoop "down" and control good and bad within our system.

"God could not stop the killing of six million Jews. We must understand this. It is important."

"Why is it important?" asked Tom.

"Because we are evolving and this understanding is crucial." A neutral Voice answered, not male or female and Tom started thinking of the Teacher as "IT" or simply just a "Voice" when this would happen.

"It is crucial to the way we are changing and thinking about ourselves." IT said. "God, as we think of God as an entity, had nothing to do with allowing the harm to six million Jewish people. God is not separate. We must take responsibility for what *we* are and what our connection is to everything."

Tom couldn't imagine what he was trying to learn or why. He sat there in his chair and tried to remember his original question for the day and then it came to him. Oh yes, he remembered, he had wondered why people do such horrible criminal acts? He was still confused. He looked at the paper in his hands. It was shaking. He reread the question to himself.

The Teacher responded, knowing that Tom was confused. "People do such horrible criminal acts because they are connected to a system that is extremely powerful. They are susceptible to an earlier action, perhaps to a collection of thoughts that were waiting to take form. They don't have control over themselves or their thoughts. Thoughts can take form into action, just as action can take form into thoughts. I want to say that again.

"Thoughts can take form into action, just as action can take form into thoughts."

"Huh?" Tom uttered. He was uncomfortable. "My thoughts are my own. They are willy nilly. There's no power to 'em." He laughed, a silly little squeaky thing of a sound that he thought was more animalistic than human. And then he thought about that foreign thought that had entered his mind, that he allowed to come in, or that had taken over when he was talking to Stu, but it had been a "good" thought, one that was better than him! But foreign none-the-less. Did it have power? "No, thoughts are not so powerful. . ." Tom said in even a tinier voice. . ."

"Is that what you believe?"

"Of course. I think all kinds of stuff. It is just junk in my head."

"Do you believe in prayer?" The Teacher asked calmly. "Have you ever prayed?"

Tom fidgeted. He knew where the Teacher was going with this. "That's different." He said.

"Well, you're right, Tom. Prayer is different, because a focused thought is more powerful than noisy junk, but both have power, you know. Take for instance, prayer circles which are focusing prayer for particular individuals that may be needing it, to recover from injury or other happenings in their lives. We don't know how that may be reaching them, but we do know that it is helpful for the person to know that prayers are being said for them. Prayers go into the stream, as all thoughts do, but unfortunately don't direct as easily as we wish they would, so we call on Jesus to help us direct them. We don't understand yet, how to direct prayers through the stream. . ."

"Do you think it is important then to ask Jesus rather than asking God?" Tom asked.

"Of course." The Guide answered. "If you want your prayer to go in a particular direction."

"Why not God?" Tom asked.

"God is the force of everything. God is all the collective thoughts and prayers of everything. So, let us say you are praying for a person who is fighting cancer. There are many such prayers, but if you want a cure, it is more powerful to pray for a solution - to visualize the finding of, well say, a vaccine for a particular kind of cancer. Your thought, your focused prayer, enters the stream and there will be a consequence, a susceptibility, perhaps at Boston University, or at a research facility somewhere, so that a connection, a course of action, takes place as a result of what was put into the stream. In the case of, let's say, Emily, the prayer to help her with cancer entered the stream. Was it directed to Emily? Emily died of cancer. God does not pick and choose. God is the force of the Universe, of All things. But Emily found comfort as she traveled her journey. But when you ask Jesus, He delivers the prayers to her and her caregivers. He made himself into a bridge between our physical plane and the spiritual one."

"What if Emily wasn't a Christian?" Tom asked.

"It doesn't matter," the Guide said." The prayer was made in Jesus' name. It was delivered."

Tom stared at the curtain. He tried to see the person sitting there. "Who are you?" He asked.

"It doesn't matter." The Voice answered. "What matters is who YOU are."

WHO AM I?

The coffee Shop was bustling with students in spite of the early hour. Thomas, a late sleeper since he started working at Carl's Pizza, woke up early and found he'd neglected his coffee supplies. That was the nice thing about living on "restaurant row"- there were many choices close by, including some late-night bars. He liked where he lived.

He ordered a latte and headed into the computer lounge to read the day's headlines.

He opened the science page. The buzz seemed to be about a discovery in a cave system in South Africa. Partial skeletons had been discovered that were causing a huge stir about primitive humans. They named the remains Homo Naledi, saying they could have lived three million years ago. Tom felt a flash of denial.

He read through the material and citations and the references to other articles. He spent the next forty-five minutes reading about it. He always found the evolutionary path interesting, and believed in his own ancestry, but it was still hard to grasp. He far preferred the biblical answer, but understood that was just his ego talking. I don't want to believe I came from such primitive roots, he told himself sniffing. They didn't have much of a presence about them. In fact, the article said their brains were small. My brain is big, Tom thought. But then the vision of an elephant came unbridled into his mind, and he dismissed it immediately.

No sooner had these thoughts formed, then they were followed by stronger ones that didn't seem to be his own. But then Tom was coming to realize that a lot of his thoughts weren't original and weren't his own. In fact, he didn't really know which ones were his and which ones were not anymore. Was there such a thing as an original thought? He wondered. The voice of the thoughts now, he was coming to recognize, had a flavor like the voice of his Teacher.

You are connected to everything. Everything. Silly boy, the thought said. Do you really think the ant, or the bird in the sky, or the ape in the woods is beneath you? Is God beneath you?

Tom, realized the magnitude of the thought, how really egotistical to think that he was "better" than anything else in the world. How had he ever arrived at that thought to begin with, anyway? Oh well, he thought, I'm just floating along, this morning. He curled his toes enjoying the last of his latte.

He gazed out the window and then suddenly, he was somewhere else.

The cave had plant material hanging on the walls. It seemed to be decorative, kind of, and in neat rows. He was carrying an armful of more plant material. The plant had thorns on the stems and aromatic tiny flowers, lots of them. He was happy. He had hunted and gone a great distance to find it. He had given up hope and was walking back when he veered off the path to relieve himself, and there it was. A grouping of the plant he'd been searching for. It was such a happy accident!

They needed this plant for the winter ahead. The tiny person, he was looking at now with such love, was learning to walk upright. She would need it. They all would.

His arrangement for drying worked well but more plants were needed and he would go out again at first light the next day. He examined the west wall and motioned the others to come over. Rivulets of water were still running down the wall from the recent rain. He threw a picture to Little Man, who received the idea warmly and smiled. Yes, he thought it would work.

Little Man trotted out while Tom sat cross legged on his skin picking off the largest of the thorns from his huge bundle. It was dim, the day was late, but he could see enough, because the effect of the light coming in was magnified by the water. The Tom sitting in the coffee shop observing, and being the Tom in the cave, thought it was ingenious, really. How had they known to make a shaft to grab the late sun's rays? At first, he thought it stupid allowing the water to run along the wall, but now he could see there was an area made to capture the water and divert it from their living area. They were using the water. They were using it to magnify the sun's rays and to wash down an area in the cave.

He was making a happy pile of thorns. They would be used to poke holes in a skin to create a type of sieve. His fingers worked fast and sure. Winter was coming upon them. It was never easy, but they had each other. Smile Upon Me, will be so happy, he thought. She would use the sieve to make berry wine. He glanced over at the mound of berries over in the corner. He threw out a thought to her, hunting for her. She was at the rock outcropping, working on a hide. He felt her fingers. They were raw.

There were several of them who lived in this cave.

Tom felt small and insignificant. He had not wanted to be a part of who they were, yet they were loving people, caring and working together and they had something he didn't have. He sat there and struggled with that.

He wanted to go back to the cave, to understand better about it, but the vision was gone forever.

They had a connection to each other that he, Tom, didn't have. They had a sense of who they were.

And then, it was like there was a voice in his head again, talking to him, reminding him, "There is no such thing as time. You are just as connected to them now, as then. . ."

Tom took that thought and threw it against the wall. At least he tried to. That was the first time he had tried to do anything like that, and it didn't work, but he decided he would try it again sometime, because the thought did go away. Real fast.

It sure did. And then he was sorry.

THE DOOR

Tom knew he was obsessing about the door. The last time it didn't open, and then it did.

He stood in front of it to see if it would open on its own. It didn't.

"Open says me." he muttered. Nothing happened.

Then, he gathered his thoughts and threw a blob at the door to open it. He couldn't see the blob, but in his mind, it was a huge thing, a big rock of a thing that had the power of a blast. He stood back. Oh, this is funny, he thought. He aimed it right at the center of the door.

"Boom." The door opened.

Tom laughed, a hysterical kind of laughter. "Is that what this is all about? Me opening the door with my thoughts? Why didn't you say so? He lumbered through the door, oblivious to his vision. Then he realized he had missed it and felt robbed. "Oh," he said. "I missed it."

"That's what happens when you are so self-absorbed." The Teacher said. "You miss the most important things that are happening to you. . ."

"Oh." Then he added, taking the subject off himself, "There are so many horrible things happening all over the world. . ."

"We are bombarded with the thoughts of others all the time. We are bombarded with our own thoughts. Some of them are even spoken out loud or are very focused, without the person even meaning them to be." The Teacher said. "Do you want to continue where we left off?"

"Might as well. I guess." Tom said.

"We were discussing the power of a thought. Right?"

"Right. Are you believing more in that now?"

"Yeah. The demonstration with the door. . .uh... that's really dramatic. Uh. . .Are my thoughts powerful enough to damage it?"

"Let's leave the door for right now, Tom." The Teacher sounded annoyed.

"That was pretty cool." Tom said. "Will I be able to do that again?"

"We'll see. . ."

Tom wanted to get up and go to the door to try it again.

"Tom, forget the door!" It was a command. The Voice coming out of the Teacher was that of a male, a no-nonsense kind of guy.

"But...I..."

"Forget the door."

The happy room turned dark and Tom's arms were pinned by his side, as if he was bound by ropes. He tried to say something more, but he had no voice. He sat there looking straight ahead at the drape. It didn't billow, or sag. It was ridged, like a wall. He couldn't see anything through it now, it was solid, not even like a drape anymore.

But he was still able to think.

He sent out a thought for the first time as a focused communication. He really wasn't sure how to do it, but he copied the thought of the man in the cave. He formed a kind of container, put an emotion in it, a feeling of wanting amends and being sorry, added the color blue and tried to send it to his Teacher, to a place in himself that he thought of as his Teacher. He floated it out and searched with it. It seemed like it was received, but he wasn't sure.

His confinement fell away. Tom received a visualization back. It was clear and understandable.

Tom folded his hands on the table in front him, ready for the days' lesson, realizing he'd already received an impossible lesson that would take weeks to assimilate.

"Take for example a person who is driving a car." The Teacher began describing the driver. Tom could see him.. "He becomes angry because he doesn't like the speed or actions of the person in front of him. He has a fit, alone, in the car behind the other driver. 'You stupid son of a bitch! Who taught you how to drive?! I wish you'd crash your stupid car in the guard rail and get out of my way!' He thinks it. He actually sees it in his mind. He says it out loud, even though nobody is in the car with him. The thought is directed, visualized.

"Nobody ever really taught him the importance of his mind and his thoughts. He is like an innocent child that has never been to school to learn the power he possesses. He does not really mean that he wants the person in front of him to be hurt and to have a terrible accident. No. But he is putting a voice, and great power to his thought none the less. He has made a deliberate thought regarding the driver of a car in front of him, a driver he doesn't even know.

"Now, nothing happens right then, it is only one thought that has been put out into the stream, but think about what happens when you get ten people putting out thoughts against ten driver's - all going into the stream. Into the System.

"There is a collective power that starts building upon the thoughts in the stream. . .and what happens? BOOM an accident happens. Was it an accident involving one of the people who had been one of those driver's that elicited one of the original thoughts? Probably not.

"We do not realize the power of what we are. We don't even know what we are, much less the power of what we can do. That is how we have gone forward with so many things, you know. Collective thought. There is an old saying, 'Be careful what you wish for. . .you might get it.' Well, there is truth in that old adage. Think about it."

Tom was thinking. He knew he would be thinking about today's session for a long time.

The Teacher continued. "There is a stream you cannot see. It exists. Take for example, a situation of many thoughts wishing for an easier way of doing laundry, many thoughts trying to think of a solution for a better way of doing this task, and the power of all those thoughts and wishes begins to take shape, to create a kind of convergence of solutions that can be tapped into. That is why so many like inventions are invented independently by more than one person at different corners of the earth at the same time. This is a proven phenomenon."

"Yes but. . ." Tom started, and stopped. He knew the phenomena was true. He'd read about it.

"Yes, I understand your confusion. You want to know why some people and not others? Why do three people all have the same idea at the same time for an invention and not everybody? Why only their minds? How come they tapped into the stream and not you and I? Ah Tom, we have much to learn. Suffice it to say, right now, that their minds were looking for it during a space when they could receive it.

"Today be satisfied with knowing that thought has power and that it is we who have created the judgment of right and wrong - man has, not God. It is our judgment of right and wrong that can result in what we call heaven and hell and other such manifestations, not the judgment of God. God is a deliberate force, not judgment. Do you understand this?"

"No." He said sadly.

"We have defined good and bad - humankind has. We have defined love and hate and heaven and hell. These definitions are real. God did not do this. God does not judge. We do."

"You mean there is no heaven?" Tom asked sadly. It was a deep sadness, like he had the last time he'd asked the question.

"Of course, there is, Tom. But you must first understand what you are before you have any kind of inkling of what awaits you. . ."

"Do you mean to tell me that there is no hell for the terrible things that people have done?"

"We will talk about that Tom. There is a consequence. It may be more than what you think it is. . ."

Tom was not satisfied.

"The person that committed horrific acts of violence may not even be able to tell you the reason why he or she committed them. We call such things 'mindless' acts, because sometimes it was 'mindless.' But we, society, has increased the number of negative images feeding into our brains by inventing television and other methods of image impression. This has terrible consequences, make no mistake about that. Negative images, messages, thoughts, and actions have power, just like positive ones do."

"But we have the freedom to decide about those messages, about those images!" Tom complained.

"Tell that to six million Jews," a Voice softly answered. "There were thousands, upon thousands of people that could choose to believe the swastika image or not. They could choose to ride along the current or to step off, but they didn't even realize they were on a current."

"What you're talking about is a kind of mind control." Tom said. "We don't do that. I mean Hitler was good at that, I guess. But that was just a situation. A one-time situation. Nobody controls MY mind. We don't go around controlling people's mind with our thoughts and stuff!" He said emphatically.

"Oh, that's what you think!" A booming Voice bellowed. "Most of the time you're walking around in a fog, floating this way and that, your thoughts hardly under your own control, hardly ever thinking an original thought, you know. I can tell you; you know very little about this, and before the day is done, you will look around you and realize that, yes, your thoughts are controlled in so many ways that you cannot even conceive of HOW!"

Tom was pissed. He felt prickly all over. "That's not true! I think for myself!"

"Sure you do, Tom." The Teacher sounded almost gentle now. "Mind control sounds so strong. Let me use softer words. I think I will say today, that as you look around you, you will see that your thoughts are *influenced* by others. I am just substituting the word, influence, for the word control."

"I still don't get it." Tom said. "I don't get how a person can do such awful things. These people are monsters. And I didn't make them that way!"

"Who did?" The Teacher asked. "We are all connected. You are connected to whatever and whoever did contribute to influencing the outcome at the school. I'm not saying that the cause factor was you directly. No. I am saying that we as a collective whole, as something so magnificent, so complete, so part of the force of God, did this - that we have a responsibility in this.

"We have no understanding of what we are, of what we can become - or are becoming. We can be something so much more than what we are. But we are so much less because we do not understand. We refuse to look beyond ourselves, to see that everything is not beyond ourselves - everything. Look around you. Everything around you seems to be beyond YOU but that is a myth. You are more than a participant. You are experiencing everything around you - touching it, tasting it, being a part of it, without understanding it or being part of it. You think you are separate from all of it?" The Teacher tittered in a soft laughter. "What do you think caused a horrible act against those people in this system? Hate, anger, fear, hurt, self-righteousness, ignorance? We could call all of it a huge Disconnect."

There was silence. The room had been active with all kinds of movement. Now all went still and a vision crossed Tom's mind, one that had already been there.

It was of a child's face. It had been splattered with apple cider. Now Tom was sitting at a table in a cafeteria. The lunch tray was sitting in front of him. There were sliced apples in one of the compartments.

"Can I have your apples?" A friend asked the young man. Tom was him, but he wasn't him.

"Yes," the young man answered. "You can have them. I don't eat apples."

A thought form hung in the room in front of Tom. It turned into long tentacles which became like ice and then fell onto the table in front of him.

Tom jumped to his feet.

"What is this place?!" He screamed. "I'm leaving! That kid deserved what he got!"

Tom tried to turn for the door, tried to lift his feet, tried to move his body, but it was like he was frozen in space, frozen to the spot. He spoke again, but only the words were in his mind and they didn't come out of his mouth. "I want to leave. I don't like what is happening here!"

The room started to breathe. It was like everything in it was alive. The more Tom tried to escape his confines, the more it was like he was in the middle of a maelstrom. The angrier he became, the more the room responded.

Finally, the figure, the Guide, the Voice, The Teacher, whatever SHE was - The She Wolf, yes, something other worldly and he didn't like her or him or whatever IT was, raised a hand. He could see her, he thought he could, and she was standing there shining and radiant and both her hands were raised as she stood there behind the curtain. Soft rain drops of a silky essence began to fall. He was surrounded by a feminine something that immediately dissipated everything, his thoughts, his emotions, the activity of the room - everything. He thought of wildflowers, like the shooting stars growing under the Manzanita bushes where he used to play and explore as a child. He loved those sweet plants.

He was back on that day again. His mother was there. "Tom, you must buy that little boy an ice cream. You must follow the punishment you gave him with something positive. You cannot leave him like that. You must enable him, make it easier for him to apologize to Cami."

"No, I won't." Tom said.

"Yes, you will."

"I won't." Tom dug in. But his mother won and Tom went and got the ice cream and softened his interaction with the boy.

"It was a hard lesson," the boy continued in the lunch room. "I've never been able to touch apples since the day I did something so mean that a kid cursed me. But luckily he was a nice person who taught me a lesson. . ."

Tom could move now. He would always associate shooting stars with his mother.

"It is always uncomfortable to learn something new," the Teacher was saying, but Tom's mind was still under the bushes where he played as a kid.

"Sit down Tom." The Voice commanded. "We will continue with our lesson."

"What causes a person to do such horrible things, you ask? Disconnectedness. Yes. You can use the argument that the perpetrator is connected to others that are also of the same criminal minds. His friends are murderers and rapists and robbers. So, in that sense he or she is connected, but to others of the same kind? Was that true with the Germans - being connected to other Germans? Did all those Germans hate the Jewish people? It was a very large membership group.

"We can govern ourselves into being what we want to be. We are what allows this to happen. We teach others. We allow such groups to exist. Sometimes we even worship them in our movies and programs. It is we who allow it. But we can be examples. Like your mother was to you. You do not know what would have happened to that kid if you hadn't bought him that ice cream. . ."

Tom wasn't really listening. The events in the room had been troubling. He felt out of control. "There's no way out of here?" He questioned.

"Tom, do you want there to be a God in heaven?"

"Yes," Tom answered in a feeble voice," of course. But according to what you say, there won't be."

"What do you think heaven is?"

"I haven't really thought about it."

"Yes, you have."

"It's a peaceful place, I guess. A place where we stop living. A place where we are judged."

"By who?"

By God, of course." Tom was tired. He didn't want to talk about it. "There is no God. I don't want to talk about it."

"Tom, do you want there to be a God here on Earth?"

"Yes, of course."

"Well, when we all take responsibility for the God that is in us, then we are a part of God, then we can have a God of love. That is the lesson. Love for us is action. It isn't a pretend love. Do you understand what I am saying?"

"Not exactly." Tom gave a lonely reply.

"Do you think Jesus loved you?

"Yes, I guess so.

"Why do you think so?"

"Because the Bible tells me so?"

"No Tom. . .Why do you think so?"

"Because He gave His life for me?"

"Do you know of any other person who gave their life for you, or who would give their life for you?

"Yes."

"Well Tom, then you have seen a God of Love, haven't you?" The Teacher said. "Seen, felt, touched, known, because you are connected to those who are part of being a God of Love. Yes? And you are a part of being a God of Love. Do you think there is some purpose in that?"

Thomas started to cry. He was so tired. He just wanted to leave.

There was no deity up in the sky, no far-off judgment day, no separate spirit that was going to make himself known to him and say, 'I am God and welcome to heaven.'

He felt that special intuitive rise in his body, that kind of vibration that was almost a sound that the Teacher had told him about, that happening that he was beginning to recognize, that certain something that was telling him this was the truth. He was part of something grand and wonderful and miraculous and beyond the reach of human thought. He could feel it and it came from the heart and maybe from the soul of being.

"God is everywhere and is everything. It is we who are creating a God of love." The Voice reverberated from the entire room. It was everywhere, in the walls, off the walls, inside himself, outside himself. Everywhere.

Tom found himself in a space where there was no time, and acknowledged, that he, Tom, was part of God and he could be that part that practiced Love. He became like a giant, a huge being looking down on all the different aspects that comprised the earth - the waters and the rocks and the mountains and the trees and the little insects and the flowers and the food that is grown. He saw the people striving to make their way along all the different paths crisscrossing the landscape. He could see their struggles and how little they knew about themselves or the world around them or the other people they would encounter in their lives.

It was like they were sleeping and trudging along in a dream, trying to make sense of their dreamscape. He looked down on all of this with a new kind of understanding that was huge, enormous and all encompassing. And then the balloon popped and suddenly he came down to size, and he was just Tom sitting in a small room at a table. A twenty-one-year-old college student with tears staining his cheeks, sitting at a table, thinking foolishly that he was part of God! What foolishness!

"How can you NOT be!" A Voice that was huge and booming filled every crevice and corner and every tiny bit of his being. It threw him back against his chair. "Look at those hands that once belonged to a baby, that can now play the piano. How can you pick up a wrench and turn a bolt tighter, how can you write a report or lift a heavy bag of cement, or wipe the tears away from the face of a child and not be part of God? Look at those hands and tell me about the Force that was responsible for the creation of them; tell me that those hands are not part of something truly magnificent; tell me that the mind sitting in this room has no purpose and was created to just be born and die away as if there was nothing deliberate in his existence at ALL. How can you tell me that your cat and your wonderful little hamster are not ALL part of God, just like you?" The Voice demanded, "or those trees or those mountains?"

"Who are YOU?" Tom asked. "WHAT ARE YOU?" Tom demanded.

"I am part of God. I always was, I always will be, in whatever form I am in. I am the same as you." And her Voice was like the ripples of the creek where Tom had gone for picnics as a child. Her Voice was like the Voice of his Mother, or the wind as it came away from the cliffs on a soft summer's day. He knew that Voice. He had met her somewhere in a dream.

"Some say Jesus was God. Some say, most say, the Bible is the Word of God." Tom said lamely.

"Of course," The Teacher said. "Jesus understood. And the Bible will tell you many things if you ponder the words, because of course, words in the Bible came from beings of God, like us - as you are learning about what *we are*. But, given the light of what you are learning, Jesus could not introduce you to the laws as you know them now. We were not advanced scientifically to have an understanding at that time. We didn't even have an understanding of the rotation of our Earth or of the various species depending upon this place we are in, this place called Earth. The laws of nature and God's laws are one in the same."

"Hah! Do you believe that Jesus was the result of a virgin birth?" Tom asked pointedly.

"Yes, of course. But not in the way you understand it. There is an important point being made." The Teacher said. "But not in the way you think. Why does it matter?" The Teacher asked. "The important question to ask oneself is, why should that matter? Should any religion - and its basis of belief - be based on whether a man and woman have sex or not? The laws of nature are perfect. Are they not? Why would we question such a thing?"

The room filled again with that glorious essence.

"Should we not base our beliefs on the miracle of what we are? Perhaps THAT is the point, to look beyond the surface of what something seems, to what it actually IS. We are the result of a deliberate Force and that is the miracle of our existence. None of this is an accident - and the birth of Jesus was NOT an accident. *His birth was deliberate.* THAT is the point being made. We must learn to honor not only His birth, but our own and that of each other, to honor birth beyond what it seems."

Tom ran his hand through his hair. "Yes," he said. "I can understand that. I can. I do." He got up from his chair to leave. "I guess."

He paced. He sat back down. The Guide was not finished.

"We are all born beautiful innocent beings," her lilting Voice was saying, "beautiful beings coming here for various reasons from different places. We are all on a track - all moving on our own necessary speeds of change. . . all moving according to our destiny, all a part of this amazing system. . .and so. . .we say. . .Welcome. Welcome to that virgin being that each of us are, that innocent virgin being that has entered this circle to be with us. We are ALL virgin beings."

"Huh?"

"Do you understand that? Tom. We are ALL virgin beings. We all come here as virgin beings." She emphasized. "We come here new and innocent, as spirits who are acclimating to a plane of physical dominance. We are babies with no knowledge or care about sex. Do you understand? We are innocent. All babies are. That's what being a virgin means. Jesus was born a virgin being. That is the point. Somehow that point got distorted, was changed into a different kind of story, trying to describe the importance of Jesus. The point was about Jesus, not about his mother."

Tom, who had started to pace again, stopped, his hand suspended in space.

It was about Jesus.

How come nobody had ever told him that? It was one of the reasons he had a problem with the Bible. The virgin birth. . .

It was about babies. It wasn't about him or sex or anything. . . except what it means to be a spirit and enter here. It was about innocence.

Tom would never think of the Virgin Birth again in the same way. Every birth was a virgin birth. Every birth IS a virgin birth. *Every creature arrives here innocent.* The wonder of that revelation stunned him.

Every being was coming into our existence as a virgin being, an innocent creature, here for a reason, here as part of a deliberate force that was beyond all human concept of our dimension. All with innocence, all new. How had he missed that point? It seemed so much had gotten wrapped up over the conception of Jesus rather than Jesus himself.

Tom held his breath. He stood up. He sat on the floor. He exhaled. "My birth was a virgin birth?"

"Of course. You came here not knowing anything. You were as innocent as anything can be, Tom, and that is what virgin means. The story, if you want to call it a story, is about Jesus. . ." The being on the other side of the curtain expelled a huge sigh. "The story is about Jesus," She repeated, "not his mother. When we realize that, we will create a kinder more loving existence for women in the Christian world. The laws of nature are perfect and beautiful and right. They are necessary for the physical dominance of our world."

"Scholars may have made some alterations here and there to celebrate the life of Jesus," the Teacher continued, "because He was so special and they wanted nothing to minimize Him. We must forgive them. They didn't understand. We will never know why they said such a thing. But it doesn't matter. Does it? What matters is that we have a marvelous system here, a physical system and we should celebrate it, not condemn it. We should understand our own innocence, our own journey and the things we need to learn as we mature and grow here."

Tom could feel the release when it happened. It was like a grip had been loosened. He knew he could leave.

"You will come back," the Teacher said. "It is not me that has brought you here. It is you."

Tom left the room feeling drained. As he stepped into the hall, he thought about Chelsea. He wondered how he could have thought the things he had thought. How could he have been so cold and unfeeling as to compare her to an empty whiskey glass? He didn't like the taste he was detecting about himself, it was like the real taste of whiskey, in fact he tasted like stale whiskey even though he hadn't had anything to drink for a week.

He deliberately made up his mind that he wouldn't think like that again. This was very clear in his mind. "I don't have to think thoughts like that." He said to himself. "I will not think like that again about another human being." As he said this to himself, it was like his inner voice reminded him of his Teacher. Then he repeated it. He was surprised how clear and focused his thinking was, instead of flitting around like a flying insect - the way his thoughts usually were.

He walked along thinking about reality and even though he knew he couldn't hang onto all the moments from the room, he could tap into the room gently now and again, seeing the experience in a cloud, or in the wings of a butterfly, or in a drop of rain.

Or in the happiness of a silly goat.

Tom understood he had let something in, and maybe it wasn't so bad after all.

FAMILY

That afternoon Tom had time after class to fuss around his apartment. He cleaned the kitchen, scrubbing the counters and wiping down the refrigerator. He wanted to have some real food and made a list. Then on a whim, he picked up the phone and called his parents.

His mother answered. Tom could see her smiling as she always did when she answered the phone.

She had been in the kitchen wiping down the counter and her hands were still wet. "Why Tom," She said happily, "I was just thinking about you. You must have heard my thoughts across the wavelengths or something!"

It was true, she really had been thinking about him and had been wondering how his studies were going. It was a long time since he'd called. They had a chitty chatty sort of call, but Tom, with a new sense of pride in his apartment, invited them to come for a visit, which was surprising. "I can sleep on the couch," he said, "and you and dad can sleep in my bed. You can stay the night and we can go to one of the games or the spring festival. What do you think?"

"I think he has a girlfriend, that's what I think," she said to Tom's father snapping her apron when she hung up the phone. "He has invited us for a weekend. Fancy that, Mike - that's a first." She hung over the big man looking at him in her wide-eyed way.

He'd been reading the newspaper but when she leaned over him, he let the paper drop to the floor and circled her with his massive arms. "Oh boy, oh boy," he said, "tell me all about it Mrs. Cross, and I'll drive you all the way there to find out, but not before we relive our own foolish ways. . ."

"What do you mean re-live?" she chided in a husky voice. "We never let go of any of 'em. In fact, we've added a lot of new *foolishments*." She tugged on his collar and twirled playfully with a few of his chest hairs that showed near it. Then she lowered on top of his lap and a kind of fire dance started in their eyes as they looked at one another. An outsider would have thought the heat of their romance could only come from new love, but their feelings deepened and reached new heights with each passing year.

This was something Tom had observed in his parents and he didn't want to settle for anything less in a relationship of his own. That was the problem with Chelsea, the fire had gone out very quickly between them. Sex had become routine, a Friday night affair - like an obligatory glass of whiskey.

His parents were never in a hurry either, although sometimes that annoyed the Cross kids. Tom's father always said, "Tom, it is important to hurry when you are at your job, at least for most employers. They are paying you a wage, money out of somebody's pocket. Right? Just figure, it is out of your boss's pocket, like his own money, even though it might be his boss's, but the money comes from somebody's pocket, and they need to know you care about that and you will give them a full measure of yourself. So, don't lolly-gag around. Not at work. When you take your break, always come back just a little bit early, just a little bit. Now, it is just the opposite when you come home. When you leave that work place and you walk in the door, it is to smell the roses, to enjoy your wife and your great kids, to spend quality time with them. You cannot rush that. So, when you walk in the place where you live, you give a nice kiss, not some fast thing, but a sweet kiss, and you give full hugs to your kids. Something might happen and they might not be around tomorrow. And Tom, when you tell your sweetheart that you love her, you really tell her, every time, - with your hands, with your eyes, your voice and your consideration - and you tell her with your time. Don't be in a hurry. Hurry is for work, not for home."

Tom's father didn't have many philosophies or a lot of teachings that he wanted to pass on to his son, save this one. He said that if a man were to live an honest and honorable life and were to follow this guideline with how he divided his time, that he couldn't go wrong. When Tom saw other families, and how they spent their time and then compared his own, he realized how happy his family was. He found himself agreeing with his father more as he grew older. "A simple life with simple rules," his father always said.

Tom thought about them as he hung up the phone and kicked himself for being so selfish that he hadn't called for months. His mother had left messages, but he hadn't bothered to call her back. What had he been thinking? That was the problem - he hadn't been thinking. He sat down at his desk and thought about them now.

Tom's parents never said anything among themselves about how long it had been since they heard from him. They were just happy that today was the day.

"Tom reminded me that we've never seen the apartment he now has on Central Avenue, nor have we seen the place where he works. He says it is just a common ol' pizza joint, but he likes it and he has a couple of nice friends that work there. He said he has his place fixed up and he'd like us to see it." Linda chatted.

"Uh. . .- he's got a girl alright." Mike said. "Tom's a pig. He never gave a horse's behind about what his place looked like before. He could care less."

That week, Tom spent his tip money for a few things for his apartment instead of spending it on liquor. He had poured a shot from the almost empty pint one night, but it hadn't tasted very good, in fact he wondered why he ever drank that stuff to begin with. "It tastes vile," he thought. He decided not to buy another pint and spent the money on a welcome mat. A welcome mat?

His buddies, Don and Bobby stopped by with two six packs on Tom's night off and were all ready to plop down on the bag to vegetate. "Hey, no shit, look what you gone and done." Don said. But Bobby came right in and started to put his feet up on the couch, took one look at Tom, thought better of it, and took his shoes off. "Yeah, guess I better take these off." He said.

It wasn't the same. There weren't the shots of whiskey to be chased with the beer, and there wasn't the bag to lounge all over and creep up on and hick all over. It just didn't feel the same. Something had changed.

"Hey dude, what's with you anyway?" Bobby asked through a fog of downed beers. "You ain't the same."

"I'm just getting ready for my folks to visit," Tom said lamely, not really sure what to say.

Tom chose to sit at his desk and twirled two newly sharpened pencils. He was considering questions to ask and wasn't paying much attention to the guys. In fact, he really wanted them to leave.

"Reincarnation?" He wrote it down.

"What are you doing buddy?" Don asked annoyed. "Pull your chair over here, or better yet, pull your body over and sit yourself on a cushion on the floor. Shit Tom, you look funny perched on that chair."

"Have you ever wondered if you lived before?" Tom asked.

"Yeah, every time Lulu looks at my cock." Bobby laughed, making a loud slurping noise on his beer can," That girl makes me KNOW that I have lived before, and that I'm living again!"

"Oh, Fuck Bob, why can't I meet a girl like Lulu? All I can find are stupid scholars that tell me," Don exhaled and raising his beer, said in a high squeaky voice, "maybe when I get to know you better honey."

"You gotta stop trolling the library stupid," Bob said. "Get off your bicycle, ditch your glasses and go downtown. You are a stupid son of a bitch, Don."

"And you are a cunt sniffing, hound dog," and they clicked their beers together, motioning for Tom to be part of that exchange. When he wasn't, Don raised his eyebrows.

"What's with you, ass hole? Are you sick or something?"

"Mollie won't have any of it," Tom said. "I dumped Chelsea."

"So, what's up? Feeling sorry for yerself?" Bob asked. "Why did you dump Chelsea, you dumb fuck! She was putting out. You said so. When did you do that?"

"It's been awhile. Then I started up with Mollie. I thought she liked me, and she tells me she does, but she doesn't let me below her waste. I'm getting tired of trying." He raised his beer with a resigned shrug.

"So that's what's going on," Don sighed, "You're beating yourself in the shower, like me. It takes a man's ego and smashes it - it hurts when all he can do is watch himself going down the drain and into the sewer like he ain't good enough to be between some fine girls' legs. Oh shit," he burped loudly, "I am so fucking tired of the game. I just want to bury myself to the hilt. . ." He put his hand to his crotch.

"Oh, shut up," Bob burped back. "Talk is cheap. Come on, let's go out and find you a real woman down at Flan's. Tom doesn't have any hard liquor anyway." The two of them were on their feet, crunching the cans and cussing about there not being any joints around to smoke either. Tom had always been good for a puff or two, but clearly, he wasn't having any of it tonight. "Hey friend, you wanna come along? Maybe you can score. . ."

Tom walked them to the door, clearly preoccupied and obviously not interested. "I got school stuff," he lied. "You have one for me, and you Don, find yourself a woman!"

Tom looked at his friends as they were leaving. They looked seedy and unkempt. He didn't think they had a chance of meeting anyone. Tom looked down at himself and realized he looked like that too. He went into the bathroom after they left and surveyed the image looking back. He needed a haircut. He hadn't shaved for a few days, but that was the style anyway. But his beard was too uneven. He could go a day or two and the stubble looked sexy, but more than that and he just looked lazy and dirty. His dad always told him," Be clean shaven. It doesn't matter what others do; it only matters what you do. If you look clean and orderly, you are, and others are attracted to you, even if you are not completely in style, they sense you are an orderly person." Tom had scoffed at his father. But how did he, Tom, think about himself? He looked at himself more closely. Am I an orderly person? Am I a nice person? Am I a smart, caring, nice person? He realized he hadn't really thought much about himself and now looking in the mirror it was clear - he needed to clean up his act. He picked up his razor and shaved. "I am an orderly person." He said out loud. "I am a thinking, aspiring individual, who cares about other people."

He went back to his desk and added to a list he was making. "Get a haircut."

Then he wrote:

Have we lived before?

Tom thought about his questions all week. He kept hearing about Allah and Islam in the news, about terrorist zealots doing their evil deeds in the name of their God. Their God? But then, he thought, the Bible is filled with much of the same in the old testament.

Their God? My God? Whose God?

GOD?

CONSEQUENCES

Tom had a dream. He couldn't remember which night it actually started, but he had it again another night. There was this big dark pit and it was filled with movement. He was looking down into it and hearing horrible screams coming out of it. Tom understood that it was hell. By the time he visited the Room again, he had had the dream a third time. It was the same each time: a pit of darkness so deep that the entities in it could not see out of it nor get out, and he could hear screams of horror, "help me, help me."

Tom stood at the door. Ah, the door. He took one last sniff of the pine forest, gathered his thoughts together, and stepped back. This time he visualized that the door led into a vault that held vast records of knowledge and he must use care opening it. He visualized a huge keyhole lock, the kind that takes a skeleton key. He saw a key in his hand, a golden key. He placed it in the lock and turned it. Voila! The door opened and this time Tom stepped across the threshold in such a way that he hoped he would experience a vision.

He wasn't disappointed.

The sign said he was entering Chetham's Library in Manchester, England, one of the oldest libraries in the world. The smell of polished wood and leather greeted him as he walked into a breathtaking chamber of books. He had never been in such a beautiful place. The domed ceiling spoke to him of artistry and craftsmanship. He stopped in this room and was looking at it all. . .and then suddenly he was in another room, also polished and beautiful and he was taking a seat at a table. He was to wait. This he understood.

I am a scholar he whispered to himself, sitting at a reading table, waiting for the delivery of an important book. He felt anticipation sitting there, waiting to see what the book contained, knowing it was going to be something special and wonderful . . .. . ."

As the vision dissipated, Tom was shocked to realize he wasn't standing at the door anymore at all, but was actually sitting at the table where he usually sat. Waiting.

The Teacher greeted him cheerfully in a feminine voice, like his mother used to use when waking him up in the morning, at least it seemed that way. "Well hello, Tom. How's everything?"

"Weelll, good, I guess. Been having a disturbing dream, and you know, I never dream." He began. He had been all set to ask about reincarnation, but the questions nagging him from his dream wouldn't go away.

She spoke to him softly. "Where do you want to start?"

Tom wanted to tell her things he hadn't mentioned before - about his apartment changes and his friends at work; but his dream was so troubling that it stopped him from going there.

"Teacher," he said thoughtfully, "what do you think the consequences are for bad people? We talked about hell and you said there were consequences and I have to believe there ARE consequences, like hell. Do you believe in hell? You said before that Satan was of our making. I'm not sure I understand this."

"Tom," She said, "I think you are asking at least four different questions here. Could you be more specific about what you are asking?"

Tom asked sadly, "What is hell? Is there a hell?"

"Oh. Yes." Her voice was thoughtful, even though she'd only said two words. "I'll try and give you an acceptable answer."

Tom looked at his hands and imagined what her answer might be. He could hear those voices, "Help me. . .help me."

"Hell is something we've created, like we talked about." she said simply, then continued. "But it isn't as simple as what you might think. Hateful actions, and an entire bucketful of things we find unacceptable, must have punishment, and because we loathe dealing with such issues, because of course they lead to confrontation and war, we have. . .created. . .hell.

"We have taken the deeds, the actions that cause us the most pain in this system and we hope another part of our system metes out the punishment. She was silent. Tom wondered if it was for effect or because she didn't know what she wanted to say.

"We can't do that." She said emphatically.

Tom's confusion was so blatant that he could see it forming. He reached up a hand and tried to wipe the dancing air away, like so many insects.

"This is like saying, I am going to beat you and starve you when, one, you have no physical body to beat, and two, no need to eat. What is done in this system stays in this system. Sorry. We innately understand that all actions have consequences. True enough, but it doesn't transfer out of the system for which it belongs. We are worried that once a person exits the physical system, then they are no longer accountable. So, we have created hell so they will be accountable, so they will be punished.

"Let's say that there is a crime committed in one country, and so the criminal exits to another country where the punishment would not be as severe, or not at all for the crime, because it was not committed there. It is the same principle. Right?"

Tom heard what was being said, "Yes, okay." Then he shook his head meaning that it wasn't okay. "But, aren't we accountable for what we do in this life?" He finally screeched. "We don't just get away without answering for our . . .um. . .our. . . our sins! We can't just go around killing people and doing bad things!"

"Well, it's like this." She said, "The idea, or the concept of heaven and hell is a concept created here - one of our making. . ."

"Yes, you make that point, "He said with exasperation, "So if there is no hell, what happens to a person like Hitler? Or the person who killed those kids?"

"If he is out of balance from this system, then the next system, rejects him."

"So where would Hitler go if he didn't go to hell?!!" Tom yelled.

A measured voice answered, a voice he had not heard before. "Hitler's consequence must take place in the Earth system, attached to the physical system. His crimes were against people. We are talking about two things here. There is the consequence of a horrible war brought about by people following an influence. There were many factors involved with that influence.

"All the individuals themselves that perpetuated terrible acts upon a group of people - and that group of people, by the way, has been persecuted for centuries, because they are part of a system that is allowing it to be so. People continue to say it, think it, and for whatever reason keep a hold of it! That is a discussion for another day because the world must become one world, and we are not. The world itself is suffering for its wrongs."

Tom took a breath. "I used to think of the world as such a big place. Now when I think about being connected to everything it seems to become smaller somehow. . ."

"Yes." Teacher said. "That's because now everything is personal. It belongs to you. So, then there was Hitler himself who was at the helm of all of this. Today we are discussing Hitler alone." The Teacher stopped again momentarily.

Tom said, "Yes. I want to know what happens to somebody as heinous and horrible as Hitler!"

"You want to know if he went to a place we think of as Hell. You want to know what his personal consequence may be for hate, murder, torture, and acts against the system in which he was a part, but of course he didn't realize his connection to all those he hurt.

"He was, and continues to be, connected to all the people he hurt. Just because he is no longer Hitler physically doesn't mean he is not still connected to the system for which he belonged. What he did means he is connected to it until it is resolved, reconciled and completed. He was, and still is connected to all of what he did, to **everything** until balance is achieved."

"Huh?"

"Since Hitler is no longer part of this physical system, or it may seem so, the system that extended matter to his being, our world, may include his identity in the stream where it (his identity) experiences the full impact of his actions. His identity is trapped in our stream - no longer limited by what we call matter but still trapped by us, still part of our world. He caused himself to be trapped by what he did. What he did continues to be part of our, and his experience. It is very real. This unseen stream is connected to us and is part of our world." Again, the Teacher waited, realizing She had introduced a new concept, one that would set Tom's physics mind in a new thinking direction.

"We do make our own hell, Tom." She continued. "It is not a punishment meted out to us. It is our own personal consequence. Action - re-action." Her Voice changed and started speaking as a man. "There is no pit that we are thrown into - no fire and brimstone, no knives that cut into us. However, every knife that we cut into another, and every person we burned, we are free now to experience *it as it was experienced.* And every person whose heart was broken by our action – of what we did, we experience. We do not escape the consequence of our actions. What we are, we take with us. We keep our identity for all eternity and consequence is the price that comes with this law, God's law. We can travel around and experience being many things, a cat, a this and a that, but you are still you and I am still me and we are still connected in this unimaginable soup of ALL creation. There is truth in these words, 'What you sow, you shall reap.' There is a stream that is connected to our beautiful Earth containing a soup of all the vibrational things connected to the Earth and we cannot escape it, because we are part of it, until an exit can occur. It should not be thought of as spirits haunting a place or roaming around. No, not like that, not like that at all. It is much more than that. All the agony that was as a result of Hitler, and all the love and forgiveness that may have occurred as well, and all that occurs in the future, because of Hitler, is and will be in that stream. That ripple effect that Hitler caused is forever in the stream, a cause and effect. Hitler's consciousness became free of its material boundaries and thus connected to it in its entirety, to experience in full awareness and consciousness all that he did - as it was experienced."

"Oh my God." Tom whispered. "But, I heard people in my dream, in a deep pit crying out words, "help me, help me. That had to be hell!"

"The identity of Hitler must reconcile the Earth experience before continuing elsewhere." She continued. "It is a very sad reality that people were thrown into pits and now the perpetrators are experiencing those pits. . . as they were experienced.

Tom sucked in his breath.

"This is a hell that is vastly different than the one punished by an outside force." A powerful Voice continued. "It is the one we each create and it is so much more in its scope than we can imagine. The stream is a force - it picks up everything. Good and bad. There is no escape."

Tom, always so personal in his thinking, had now jumped back in this mind to the break up with Chelsea in the Coffee House. "Do you mean that I will experience how Chelsea felt as a result of my mean behavior in breaking up with her?"

"Oh Tom. Of course." A light laughter started from behind the curtain, then it spread out, as if the laughter itself were threads of gold and soon it filled the room with an essence that lifted Tom with its buoyancy. He didn't see the smile, but he felt it and it surrounded him. It was large and all-knowing and comfortable.

He snuggled into it.

"Consequences are not necessarily all bad." Laughter again. "Maybe you have already experienced the consequences." Laughter again.

"We will talk about the power of love and forgiveness another time. Also about the power of what her thoughts about you might have been. . . ."

Tom sat bolt upright. He had not thought about THAT.

"Also, about guilt and the negative consequences of that." The laughter stopped, not abruptly but with a softness and understanding.

"Intent, action, thought, etc. - it all has its ripple effect. Hitler is still part of the system, in one form or another. The consequences for actions are not clearly known by the perpetrator in this system until ALL ripple effects are known, which they will be. None of us escapes what we are or what we do."

"Some consequences affect the entire system. For instance, there is a consequence to the creation of the internet and the entire system adjusts in relation to its advantages and disadvantages. In relation to bad deeds and criminal actions, we look for consequences to the perpetrators and there is, absolutely, a system of right and wrong. First, there is the punishment, or reward we have created within the physical, or the seen system of which we belong.

"For instance, you belong to the system of democracy in the USA, so you have that system. The bigger system then, is the one of perhaps, the physical system of Earth, of which we are all connected, and then the bigger system of which we are a part - The Universe.

"If we take a look at the crime of the twin towers, for instance, we see a ripple effect that has affected the world and literally millions of people and is still going on today. The negative effects have not been countered with positive effects because we have not known how to do that. In fact, the negative effects have continued to blow up larger. It is like a fire that is out of control. It feeds upon itself. Those negative effects go into the stream and affect us.

"We are a physically dominated dimension." She explained. "The consequences are here. There is no time involved, but rather the involvement determined by those affected, or of how the needs of the system must be balanced. The consequences may take place a century from now. It can be very scary indeed. There is a stream and it is like the very air we breathe.

"Hitler. He was/is connected to everything, right? In this system - this dimension. Do you understand what that truly means? It means that Hitler is/was connected to everyone that experienced everything that he did - all the pain and sorrow, direct and indirect - all the ripple effects. He just didn't realize he was connected. Everything he did to them; he did to himself. He was not alone in this - what about the many that were connected to him? - That allowed all of what happened to occur? That means those who worked for him, who were complaisant, who knew. This is a very big concept, so it is hard for our minds to wrap around. We are individuals, and yet we are not. It is this thought of being individuals that causes us loneliness, we feel this sense of separation, but that is an illusion that comes from our physical bodies, but it isn't real. The physical body is separated, yes, but that is all. And it isn't really separate either - it is connected too, in its way, but it is self-directed and has autonomy. We fear the loss of identity. We fear the loss of "self." We fear the loss of our personality and who we are. It is almost an unreasonable, sinking darkness - in a part of our being that says such a thing could happen to us. That we will lose who we are, our identity. Well, such a thing cannot happen to us. We change, but we are always ourselves. You are always you. I am always me. I may not have the physical body of a cat, or a human, or whatever I was while in a physical dimension, but I will always be "me" in the universal order of things. There can be no other way.

Tom shook his hands. He brought them around his face and trembled. "I can't. . ." He started. Then he noticed there was an old book sitting on the table in front of him. It was bound in beautiful leather, open to a page that was written in calligraphy with black ink and gold accents.

He was in the library again. He felt the comfort of the old room and the stacks of books. He heard the voice of the Teacher at a distance.

"There is a universal order to everything - a deliberate, chaotic movement of absolutely everything. It is in that chaos that we find our individuality. It is this chaos that gives it to us."

Tom nodded, understanding the principle of chaos.

"Good." She said, "When everything is in a perfect row it is all alike. Do you see my point? We are not all alike, not all in a perfect row. That is why accidents can happen and do happen. That is why everything is not predetermined. That is why there can be pain and accidents and things that are not the way you think they should be, because they cannot be if you are to BE you and if I am to BE me. Chaos in the Universe is necessary. But everything really is ordered. Light and dark. Yin and yang. The principal applied to everything. To us in our limited brains, we may see many things as imperfection when it is just the opposite. It is the perfect way." The Teacher stopped abruptly, again.

Tom turned a page in the book. He looked at the cover and the title. "TWAC."

"I'm sorry," a masculine Voice now said. "I went on a kind of tirade, I think. I do get a little passionate about this. So many of my students have difficulty with the concept. But you are a physics student, and I forgot that for a little bit.

"It is important to understand time doesn't apply. Do you see that now?"

Tom leaned back in his chair. He blinked, and blinked again, not saying anything at all. The book had said something important. He tried to find the page again.

"Yes, you can blame God for an accident, for not preventing it." Teacher said, "You can blame God for being God. And where does that get you? You are still part of God and God is still God and the tree out there is still a tree, and you can cut down the tree and it will change its physical character into something else, but you cannot destroy what the essence was/is, the life force of the tree. That is an illusion - you think you can, because you have rendered it dead here, but it is still part of the God force. Your loved one who was in that accident is too. Nothing stays the same, your pain will transform, although maybe not for what seems a long time. But there is no time. God is God and there is nothing you can do to change any of that and all you know is within the force of God and will continually change.

"Hitler's crimes are a deep chasm that should never, ever be forgotten, but how these crimes are remembered, how we speak about them, how we as a collective whole choose to embark on a future *without including the negative effects* they represent, is what is important to us. We must not hate. To hate will perpetuate such a crime again. **It gives power to the condition of hate.**"

Yes, that was the page that Tom had seen. It was about the power of hate.

"I hate Hitler. Don't tell me not to hate Hitler!" Tom spit.

"We must understand that all those terrible things, those awful deeds were partly a condition of other, listen very carefully, other, deeds, that occurred within the system. Hitler and others with him were susceptible. It gave power to Hitler's deeds.

"We must be very careful. This is where the idea of Satan arose from. Do you understand this? It is us giving power through our own hate to past heinous deeds. Out of the hate we have created a thought form - or a condition that scholars put a name to. They called it, Satan. But it really is a thought, the power of a thought, coupled with emotion and visualization."

"He was vile, and his cronies were vile!" Tom said in an elevated voice. "I certainly will hate him!"

"What is hate, Tom?"

"Why it's, it's, total non-acceptance. It's . . . it's a feeling of distaste that is strong and. . .and"

"Tom, if Hitler were to walk into this room right now, would you pick up a knife and kill him?"

"Uh. . . uh. . ." Tom faltered. "No, I don't think I could just do that, unless he threatened me. Then I could."

"Would you take pleasure in it?"

"No. I wouldn't take pleasure in hurting or killing anything." Tom said honestly. "I just, I just. . ."

"Then you don't hate Hitler and it would be good not to say it. You must own what you think and feel. You have a great and deep sorrow for the things that were done to hurt the Jewish people. Your deep sorrow is a kind of love that can be directed to a group of people in a positive way. Your emotional response coupled with directed thought and perhaps by some sort of action can have tremendous power, the kind of power that counteracts a negative stream towards these people. Do you understand? Non acceptance is not hating.

"The identity of Hitler experiences everything that was wrought by his doing, not just at the time, but also the ripple effect. . . You cannot affect the action and consequence of what he owns. There was action, and as a result, consequence. You cannot add or take away from the history of that. What you can add or take away, and you have to be careful about that, because THAT belongs to you. . . is what is existing now - what you are adding to the stream, what may be a result of your thoughts and actions. It is actionable."

"You mean it is up to us to change the negative effects of Hitler? You mean he goes on his merry way while we are left with the ugliness and horror of what he was? What he did?" Tom was screeching. He rose half out of his seat, an anger rising in him. He wanted to tear down the curtain, to see the person behind it, to say, "There is fire and brimstone for all eternity and Hitler will be screaming forever in a soup called, Hell."

"Sit down Tom," a calm Voice commanded.

"Who else is left with the negative effects of Hitler, Tom?" The Voice asked. "Who else, what else, can change the effects, except those of you who are living with the consequences now? Who else, Tom?!?"

At that moment, Tom's stomach rolled. He thought he was going to be sick.

"This, this stream, - it sounds like the dark side," Tom blurted, "like some kind of science fiction sort of thing, like it is the Satan realm itself, like it's some kind of scary shit that affects us and makes horrible things happen to us from the past! You're describing another dimension here with us. That's what!"

"No, not like that," the Teacher responded. "Stay with me. I want to give you a better example, a better understanding. Words have gotten in the way of describing something that has not been defined and has no words. This stream isn't a force outside of us, it is part of us - it is what we create. It is our memory. It is a collection of what we are. Everything - good and bad. It is our Earth consciousness, our physical and spiritual reconciliation of what occurs on this plane. It is Earth memory. It is a holding place and a stream that can draw information to it - like a magnet. It is a bridge to the next dimension and we reconcile our physical life within it, and the memory of it will be in that holding place forever. It is the memory of the Earth/world. Our identity cannot go on - to the next place - until reconciliation occurs. As long as effects hold us, we are in the stream experiencing the effects."

"Do you think we have the ability to change the effects?" Tom asked, as a hypothetical question.

"We cannot change what has occurred. What is done, is done. The effects are based on that. There is a reconciliation. Sometimes we have help with that. We can affect the ripples. . ."

"So, you think Hitler is trapped in the stream? What about people who do good things, are they trapped too, watching, or experiencing the effects of the good things they did?"

"Yes." But you must not think of this in terms of "time" but in terms of change. Right? All the changes that occur because of Hitler, Hitler experiences."

"Do you mean then, that all the changes that occur because of Jesus, Jesus experiences?"

"Yes."

"Do you mean that He is trapped too?"

"Well yes and no. If a balance, or reconciliation occurred, which probably did, then Jesus is free from our stream. But Jesus IS in the stream. . ."

"Why is Jesus in the stream?" Tom asked. "It doesn't sound like our stream is a place of . . .uh. . .choice."

"Many things happen in the name of Jesus," He answered.

"That isn't good." Tom said thoughtfully.

"It isn't bad," Tom. "It was His choice. Jesus chose to be a bridge for us. He gave His life - - and more - - for us."

"Yes, but please explain. I'm not understanding. . ."

"It is the law of cause and effect. Sometimes things are not what they seem to be. . ." a sad Voice said softly from the other side of the curtain.

"It's because of what we do. . ." Tom said.

"Yes. We are mindless beings. We are learning. Our change is slow and painful, I think,"

"I didn't realize we could hurt Jesus. . ."

"Yes, He is here with us. There has been no greater gift. . ."

"So, when we call on Him, He is right here with us." Tom said. "And when we speak of Hitler, he is too - right here with us?"

"Yes."

"This stream, can we control it?"

"In a way. We can send loving and helpful thoughts to those within it or we can send punishments. We don't yet know how to control this. Sometimes we cause an essence to be bound in the stream, bound to us because we cannot forgive, or we don't want to let them go. . .and by doing this, we cause ourselves to be bound." The Teacher paused, and there was one of those silences.

Tom waited.

"It is the consciousness of our system. It is what we are. Within that record are many things. It is a collective whole and all of our history; all of our accomplishments are within it. Sometimes we can tap into it."

"After we leave the stream," Tom said in a small voice, "do we then go to heaven or hell?"

"Oh Tom." The Teacher said sadly.

It was like something in the room was falling. There was a sense of sinking down and the vibrancy of all colors in the room was turning brown. Tom tried to get out of his chair, but it was like he was inside of a radio tuner and somebody had turned the knob on it controlling the gravity and even though he wasn't heavier, the air around him was. He couldn't get out of his chair.

His head started to hurt and the clarity of his thoughts became more murky than usual. He was floating in something, and then whatever it was snapped, like a huge rubber band, and everything became clear, like the outline of the trees after the rain on a clear day and he knew. He knew that he was part of everything and there was no city in the sky, no dungeon down below, but a sea of something so beyond his comprehension, that he would just have to accept his part in it. He would never have a choice. He just was and would always be. The room had been disappointed in him, but forgave him and showed him, in his foolish childish mind, that there was an order to everything.

"Thank you, Teacher," he said.

Tom was shaking when he left the Room that day. He was so cold. He had felt the chill of truth so many times. Of course, he hated Hitler. He had always hated Hitler.

He sat down on a cement wall near the hedge by the square where they raised the flag every morning. He looked at the flag and thought about how free he had always been to express his thoughts, of how he had heard ideas that very day he would not have heard if he was living someplace else. He could not imagine what would be required to change the negative effects produced by Hitler.

How does a person change the world? He asked himself.

A tiny Voice answered, one he had actually hadn't heard coming from inside himself before. It said:

"One drop at a time."

SCHOOL

When Tom sat down to read his email, he read on his homepage about another archaeological discovery. An area had been discovered that was being called a Prehistoric Picnic Spot, that the artifacts discovered were dated to half a million years ago. They found advanced flint tools indicating "hominids developed modern thought patterns." It was said to have been reported in Archaeology Magazine, a reputable source. He cross-referenced it because many things on the internet were so much hype. When he did, he discovered several stunning finds. He couldn't believe the things he was reading.

Tom, like many other students, was concerned about global warming, but he hadn't considered the implications regarding archeological finds. He came across an article about receding ice patches that were causing many artifacts to surface everywhere and archaeologists were challenged by the tasks of locating, documenting and preserving the finds before they were destroyed. Suddenly the profession of Archeology didn't seem so foolish to Tom, but it wasn't something he wanted to do. Of course, physics wasn't either.

When he went to class later that day, he mentioned it, asking if other students had been following the announcements.

"Do you think we evolved from the apes and went through those stages to get to where we are?" He asked as they discussed the articles while they worked on experiments in the lab.

"I think it's a reasonable conclusion," Chib said. "Mr. bones," referring to a mountain man discovery, "wasn't so pretty to look at by our standards, but that doesn't mean he was stupid, or that he didn't care about his world or know things we haven't even discovered yet." He mused.

"Yeah, his genes are very much in line with ours." Tom said.

"I don't know what the big hoopla is," Shannon furrowed her forehead, "I mean, why are people so concerned about whether or not we came from the apes anyway?"

"I think it's about the Bible - that we were created in seven days, and the idea of evolution might make it false and many people want every single word to be exactly true . . ." Tom said leaving it hanging in the air.

"Well what do you think the meaning is in the Bible? How do you think the world was created in seven days?" Shannon challenged.

Tom loved these discussions with her because she too spent time in the Room, in fact Tom later realized she was one of the people who told him he should put himself on the list to meet with the soothsayer, or more literally truthsayer. Interestingly, her perspective was always a little different than his so she must have asked different questions than those he asked. Perhaps she had never asked the person in the room about evolution before, because she thought she knew what the answer would be.

Tom could just hear the Voice saying, 'Of course we evolved. . .and we are still evolving, because we must. Change is happening with every breath, movement is inevitable. It is the nature of the Universe. It is what infinity is. . .What eternity is.' That's what He'd say, always talking about change.

"Well," Tom said, "Time does not exist. . . only change. So, the Bible is defining a change - that the process of creating the system here, that we are part of, happened according to a plan. As the Teacher would say - a recipe. Do you believe that?"

"Yes. I do. Do you?"

"Yes. And that the ingredients of the recipe were in place pretty much from its beginning."

"Uh huh."

"Well, we know that Adam did not exist without Eve or vice a versa. It is timing that confuses us, the process of creation, the gene mapping - all those things we have yet to understand. But one thing we do know," he paused sweeping his hand around him, "is that all this is one melting pot, is one unit of possibility, is one system together, and is all God. Everything."

"And parts of this were created in seven days," she laughed, "according to a time that does not exist." She laughed again. She looked at Tom with wondrous eyes and continued, "and what we are is far more than this," she pinched her flesh, "and so we rebel when we think we were created in seven days."

Other students in the room stopped working and stared.

"That is because we cannot conceive of what we were before, or what we will be. . ." Tom said oblivious to their effect on everybody else.

They both laughed.

"I'm going to ask the Teacher anyway." Shannon said. "I want to hear what She has to say about it."

Chib sniffed. "Who is this person you guys are always talking about anyway? How come you think he knows so much?"

"Because he/she does," They both said it at once which elicited uproarious laughter in the room.

Tom wagged his finger, "There is no such thing as Time. People have gotten all hung up on the seven-day thing."

Chib looked at them closely, narrowing his eyes. He decided they really believed it. "Did this come from Numen?"

"Numen?" Tom asked. "Who is that?" But the conversation was already continuing. They both nodded.

"I thought so." Chib scribbled a note to himself, but they both knew he didn't need to write anything down. They wondered what he was writing. He was the best student in the class!

"I don't know why there is anything troubling about evolution," Chib said. "There is so much evidence to point to our origins. What difference does it make?"

"Some people think it means . . .well. . .if you believe in evolution. . .that you don't believe in God." A guy at the other table said.

Chib looked at him with disdain and said flippantly, "Well, do you?"

"Don't know why I should." He said, but when Tom thought about the comment he realized the guy hadn't really said one way or another. The other student sitting next to him piped in, "I'm with Hawking. There is no God. God is a construct by a superstitious society."

"Yeah, we're still in the dark ages," Chib sighed.

Shannon's eyes met Tom's and they both nodded. "Perhaps," she said, "It isn't up to science to prove that God exists. How do you prove something that is a foregone conclusion? It is like saying there is no sun."

Shannon had super good hearing. Tom's was pretty good too. They both heard the whispered comment between the two other students.

"Aw, she's just a stupid girl." One said to the other.

"Yeahhh."

REINCARNATION

Tom's questions were neatly folded in his pocket when he got on his bike, but something strange happened to him along the way. He stopped at the mini market to buy a soda and a man in front of him paused on the way out, looking at him.

"Hey," he said. "I know you."

"Yeah," Tom said scrutinizing the fellow. "Yeah. Sure." They stood there for ten minutes going over the possibilities, but finally gave up. It was funny because the feeling was mutual and was so strong that they exchanged information.

Tom couldn't shake the feeling, so by the time he arrived at the Room, he had changed his mind about his questions - at least his first question. His first question was going to be about evolution, but then reincarnation didn't seem so different from that.

"What are your views about reincarnation?" He asked innocently, thinking he would go on with his other questions, but then he should have known better, because every question had deep implications and required him to think and then think some more and one question always let to others.

"You are wondering if you lived before, or if people in general have lived before?" the Teacher asked. "You mean here on Earth, or someplace else?"

Tom was startled, his thoughts dancing through space. "Um. . .Um. . .Yes - to everything you said. I wonder what you have to say about reincarnation - about me, about everybody."

"Well, I think yes and no." The Voice said. "Your movement continues all the time - for everything here. It must. But let's talk about you. You move from one condition into another. Change is always occurring, and it has always involved you."

"What was I before I was born?" Tom asked.

"You." The Guide said.

"Me?"

"Yes. You."

"But what was I before I became this?" Tom was exasperated. "What was I being? Doing what? Did I live before?"

"Only you know that," The Voice said. "I don't know that. All I know is that you were you. You have always been you. If you were living in another physical system, or this one, only you know that. . . I don't."

"How can I know THAT?" Tom said with irritation. "I don't know that. I have no idea."

"Well, you were something," the Teacher said patiently. "Let us explore the possibilities. You went through a change to enter this system. You had to be part of another system, or dimension before you entered this one. True enough?"

"No, I don't think I was part of anything. I think I was created from a seed being fertilized."

There was laughter on the other side of the curtain. "Is that what you think about all this randomness around you! Is that what you *still* think?? The creation of the world, its atmosphere, its system and all that's in it?" A soft laughter filled the room and every crevice in it. The sound didn't die away, but just continued as the Voice spoke over it. "And the ingredients of the cake just magically appeared . . . and the cake came together and was baked and came out without any creation and there it was and we just continue to take it for granted and that it is all an *accident* and who is stupid here. Us or the Universe? . . . and how can we separate one from the other. . . ummmm? We just think the cake happens and nobody makes it?"

The Teacher continued patiently. "Change. Eternity cannot exist without constant change. You are part of eternity. That means you were always part of eternity. You always were, you always will be. . ."

The laughter continued until it became like liquid drops of softness falling from the ceiling on Tom and engulfing him, until he saw how absurd everything was except the words that held truth. He was being held within those words and the truth was in them.

He had that special feeling, or sound within him that he was getting to know, that he associated with a kind of identification, a kinship with the Teacher's words. It was a deep place that was saying, yes, he had been something before, if only a speck of light, but something, yes, something else before he had been born into this something, that made him what he is now.

"You asked a question before being born," the Teacher said. "and you were instantly brought into this system as an answer to your question. During your life, you will discover what your question was/is. . ."

Tom stopped breathing. What was my question, he asked himself, looking around the room, trying to think of what it could have been? What was my question. . .

Who or what was this person on the other side of the curtain? Whatever was this about? Tom stood. He took a deep breath. What was my question? What was my question? He kept asking himself looking around, almost frantically. "This is crazy. CRAZY." He whispered, turning in a circle.

"Is it now?" Teacher whispered, so low Tom almost couldn't make it out.

"Huh?"

"Okay, you are saying the concept is crazy, but you were either liquid, or light, or a see-through substance, or a thought, or dust of some sort, or living matter in another system, or what we call spirit. . . Right? Is that right enough? You were a spark of something. Right?"

"It would seem so." Tom said, very hesitantly, stopping his circling and beginning to pace methodically.

"Whatever it was, you entered this system innocently, as a baby, learning everything you needed to know to exist in a physical dimension - here from the beginning. Not everybody does that, you know."

"What do you mean?"

"There have been children with memories of prior living. Did you have any of those memories?"

"Oh. No. I didn't have any childhood memories of anything."

"Everything was new. It was like opening up a book for the first time for you?" The Teacher asked.

"Yes."

"At least you think so. Is that how you remember your childhood?"

"Yeah."

"Some people came from this same system and were born again immediately, and these individuals seem to know that. They have a far memory of it, but I don't think that is the case with you. Only you know that." Teacher said, "So we must surmise that you came from another system, or dimension. We all are in another dimension before coming here, anyway. Aren't we?"

"Uh."

"We must. And when we leave here, we give up our physical bodies. Don't we? We go through a change. Yes?"

"Uhhh. Guess so."

"Guess? You *guess*. . .?

"Well, you didn't bring a physical body with you from someplace else, Tom. You acquired it here. But you did arrive with a certain amount of knowledge, or *knowing*. As your life continued, you had some sort of knowing. True? At least you became aware of your knowingness."

"Knowing what? What do you mean? No, I don't think so. I didn't know anything."

"You have always known you were something more than protoplasm, or you worried that you weren't. That comes with awareness. Yes?"

Tom, the ever-confused Tom, nodded.

"You may have had trouble believing that, but you have always known that you might have been something more. You have had an awareness, a consciousness, a hope. A worry." The guide laughed.

"We think we are the only beings that have this, but in reality, all creatures have a knowing of what they are, but they don't worry about it like we do." The Guide laughed again. "We are all part of something beyond our physical selves. . . we are part of the Everything. . . .

"About the question of reincarnation Tom. It is possible. If you lived before in this system, you would have a knowing of it. Some people say reincarnation is not possible because look at all the people who are living now. We have a huge population and if we lived before, then how come there are so many of us now?" The Voice stopped for a minute to laugh again, but softly. "That is only if we apply the concept of time. Tom, remember, the Universe does not know time. There is no time. It doesn't mean we didn't live in a condition that you consider to be the future. It doesn't mean we didn't also live a different life that somebody else is living right now during the same period of time."

"What!" Tom saw a huge form come out of his head and jettison itself toward the drape.

The Teacher laughed. Tom wondered how come he thought of the voices differently - The Teacher, The Guide, The IT, The Voice - all these different Voices. He decided the room was a supernatural place. . .

"Well, many things change when you give up the silly concept of time. Huh? Seems like you were still hanging on to it. Eh?

"Do you understand?" The Teacher asked. "And what about the future? Remember, there is a balance that must be achieved. It may take many in order for that to occur - maybe many from the so-called future, to rectify the so-called past. . ."

"What? No, I don't understand." But Tom did have an idea of what the Teacher/Guide was saying. When the element of time, and a linear construct was removed, it meant he had a different way of thinking.

"For example, you are in a library and you pick up a book and you read it. It is in your hands. It is your story to read. You become the character in the book. But - there may be more than one copy of that same book.

The Voice was substituted by the Numen. "Then you put it back. Somebody else takes it out. You go and take out a different book at the same time and you read it. . . the story is not governed by time.

"You have already read the story, now you are reading another story while somebody else is reading the same story you just read. The story you just read is not governed by time. The story was under your control - while you read it. The story was only your story while it was in your hands, and then it is in the hands of the identity of whoever is reading it, and now you are part of another story. You both went through a change while you read the story - the same story. Kind of. Get it?"

"Oh my gosh, NO! This is a slightly different concept than reincarnation." Tom said.

"Is it now. . .? Why did you ever think reincarnation was consecutive or linear in a time sequence? Are you saying that if you lived before that it had to be in the way you view the past?

"That is according to your definition of what the past is, not that of the Universe. Reincarnation is a physical concept. It is a concept of your identity being in this place - in a physical place similar to Earth. Right? Such a thing is not according to time because linear reincarnation only exists by human definition, not a spiritual one."

Tom had always considered the concept of reincarnation to be according to a timeline. The Teacher's words had a totally different viewpoint on it. He sagged. He never considered that a life could be - lived over and over again, or that his identity could skip around to different time periods - according to the "balance" concept like what the Teacher, or was it the Numen, was describing. What about his freedom of choice?

"What about my freedom of choice?" Tom asked, as if the Teacher could follow his thoughts and would know what he was talking about.

The Teacher did know. "Perhaps there are some paragraphs in your story, or a page here and there that allows for freedom of choice, because there is that element of chaos and random events. Right?"

Tom breathed a sigh of relief. "Yes. Right!"

"But there probably are certain events that are pivotal and are supposed to happen. Not that they always do, but that they are set forth in your story. We call that destiny."

"Destiny?

"Yes. Fate." Teacher said, "There is an illusion in the story that there is freedom, which there is to a degree, but there is fate too. Combine fate with the ingredient of randomness, which allows for change, and the Universe adjusts for the occupant in the story. . .for whoever is occupying. . .shall we say - the recipe? Just like the making of the cake. . ."

Tom was beginning to think he should have left the Room by now. He was wishing that he had. This line of thinking was more than he wanted. Tom decided he didn't want to talk about time or reincarnation anymore. He didn't like the idea that somebody else had lived his life before him or that somebody would live it after him. Maybe.

"Which God is right?" He asked.

"What!? What do you mean?" The Teacher was obviously irritated, but was patient at the same time, then inquired. "What do you mean, Which God is right? What are you talking about?"

"Well," Tom said, "There are all these religions, and they are all based on there being a God, but each one describes God differently. Which one is right?"

There was a soft laugh coming again from around the room. It seemed to be a day of laughter. But this was an indulgent laugh. And then, "You are serious, aren't you?"

Tom squirmed. "Yes." He said in a wee voice.

The laughter in the room died abruptly. An entire crowd of voices answered him. Every voice that he had heard before in the room was present. There was a roar of sound as they discussed between them what they may have missed in their instruction to Tom. They answered together.

"All the various descriptions of God don't mean anything in terms of what God really is. Silly." The Chorus said. Then one voice said, like a solo singer, "Do they?"

"Those religions are trying to describe what YOU are in relation to what God is. Right?" The Chorus continued. "God is Everything that IS. Everything that IS. You are connected to everything that is. Religion cannot change what God IS. Religion only has the power to change YOU, to modify your perception. God just IS, has always been IS and always will be the almighty IS."

"But Christians say God is love. . ."

"Tom!" The Soloist exclaimed with some amount of exasperation. "You must think about what has already been said here! Who and what is feeling the love? You."

Tom thought about it for a minute and then answered, as truthfully as he could, by saying, "I don't know. I have tried to think about it."

"That's right. You don't know. We are in a vessel experiencing certain things. We must define what those things are, and then maybe, maybe, we can experience a measure of what God IS. At this point, we don't even realize our own magnificence. We don't even comprehend the kind of love we want to assign to ourselves or how to experience the God Force, do we? Please think again about what has been said here. We must comprehend love within ourselves. Love is just one facet of what everything IS, and God is everything, ALL that is, including love, and hate. ALL that IS, IS God. . ."

Tom never thought of himself as being magnificent. He touched his foot that had come out of a cast the year before. It was a stupid injury because he had been drinking too much when he took a wrong step off a curb. He fell halfway, twisting his ankle hard and fracturing a small bone in his foot.

It was the same foot that had set an animal trap when he was a kid. He was at first elated when he had come back the next day and saw he had caught a creature in the trap, but then he saw how it had struggled for its freedom before finally dying and he sat lonely in the woods and thought about what he had done. Perhaps it was the first time he realized what compassion was. He was so sorry. He cried. The tears were not for him - it was for the animal he had harmed. It was a lesson his father wanted him to learn.

He rubbed his foot slightly thinking. It was the same foot that had kicked Eric Shoemaker's shin when he refused to share his pizza pie. Eric had screamed and Tom had laughed loudly wanting other kids to hear his bravado. That foot. It was part of him. It was connected to him. He felt it burning. A strange sensation, there under the table.

"How can we humans say anything about God when we have such disrespect for what has been created in ourselves and the world around us? We disrespect everything, but Everything IS God."

A slightly different voice explained to Tom. "That means we, meaning we humans, have no respect for God. Pretty awful, huh?"

"Religion doesn't have the power to create God, it only has the power to try and control YOU - to create how *you* perceive God, - The God in you: your beliefs, and what you do and how you thinketh. It only does what you let it do. It can try to tell you how to believe. It can even cause you to kill people in the name of God! It can, actually cause you to believe that God is separate from you. God is not separate from anything. God is Everything. Love is not invisible and inert. Love is complete acceptance, forgiveness, kindness, compassion and all the things that fill us with nourishment that feeds who we are, and that doesn't happen through nothingness. It happens through everything, and through actions. It happens when a person receives an answer to a prayer about a sick child needing a heart transplant. It comes through an action. It happens in our physical system, though our connections. We are developing what we want, and have termed, the Love of God. Thought has power. Prayer is thought. We are connecting with the Everything that is God. Make no mistake about this. God does not know love or hate or kindness or compassion. God is the almighty Force of our Universe and we are a part of the Force and it is we who are creating this facet because it is something we want, and we will evolve and enlighten and create this condition. The condition of unconditional Love.

"We want a God of Love and we have had a very important and enlightened being showing us the way. One thing He tried to tell us, is that it is through being connected, as we all are, that this will happen - it is not through our separateness. That doesn't necessarily mean religion per se. Religion does try to control us and I don't think that is the message He came to give us."

"How? What?" Tom asked agitated. "What is the message"

"He said, 'For where two or three have gathered together in My name, I am there in their midst.' It is a lesson not of organized religion, but of organized thought."

"Oh, I see."

"This is an important lesson, Tom. We will have to wait until another time. Enlightenment is a path that cannot be abdicated to a religion. It is a way of being."

"Do you really think somebody lived my life, exactly like me before me, and might live it after me?" Tom asked.

"Why not?" Said Teacher. "You are not your body. You are having the privilege of being Tom and experiencing his story. You should honor and respect him and realize the difficulties of being him. It is not easy being in the human condition, even though it is only for such a short time of change."

Tom blinked. He blinked again. He breathed. He moved as if in a dream. He got up like he was a robot.

"What was my question? What brought me here. I mean to Earth? If this is an answer to a question, I asked. . .What did I ask?"

"You will know, Tom. That is something, you will know."

"I did have another question for today. It was about evolution. Did we evolve from the apes? What do you think?" He asked.

"No," said the Teacher. "I don't think we evolved from Neanderthal Man."

Tom thought he was going to fall through the floor.

"No? . . . No? Why not?"

"It isn't a problem if we did," said the Teacher. "It is truly beautiful to think of one species evolving into another, or morphing into something else . . .superior." The Numen spat out the word 'Superior,' saying it with scorn.

Tom had never heard the Teacher use such a tone before. He reacted with surprise.

"We have such an ego; we like to think we are superior to everything else! We really are such specks in the scheme of things!"

Tom's eyes remained wide.

"Yes, there were others who lived differently than us, but that does not make them a part of our evolutionary path. We are connected to them, not superior to them. There is a difference. We are evolving now - what we are - and we are recognizing it. Perhaps that is something important in the mix. Recognition."

Tom's face fell in a look of disappointment.

The Teacher moved behind the curtain and it fluttered. "Tom, because two dogs are bred together to produce a third dog puppy, one with droopy ears and a larger size, it doesn't mean that they have evolved. It means that they had sex together and mixed their genes. It does not mean that they evolved or were meant to do so. Perhaps Neanderthal man was more loving than we ever thought of being. . ."

Tom went to the door and almost forgot to say "Thank you." He turned back to say thank you but he knew the room was no longer occupied. The emptiness of the space without the personage behind that drape was shocking.

It was just a room now, an ordinary room.

THE ANIMALS

When Tom got home that afternoon, he was exhausted. It was his day off from work and he was oh so glad. He decided he wasn't going to do anything. He was tired of school, tired of thinking, satisfied enough with his half-clean apartment, and he just wanted to chill out.

Mollie sent him a text. "You home?"

He didn't answer. He turned the T.V. on. His remote was on the fritz and he meant to get a new one at Walmart, but forgot. It hadn't been on his radar with all the other things he'd been doing. He hadn't been watching T.V. for a while. In fact, he couldn't remember the last time. A commercial was on, as usual. He sat down and waited.

A nature program came on about Zebras in Africa. He was going to change the channel but was too tired to get up to do it. So, he just sat there sipping on a soda watching it until he discovered that he was interested in it. The program said the zebras migrate a great distance every year to the same place – a location where the rains come. They feed on the grass, then they always migrate back. The show was about that, with film crews set up along the beginning of their migration path, but nothing was happening! The animals had barely enough to eat and little water and still they hadn't started their migration. The herds continued to stay! Day after day, they stayed. The animals weren't moving.

Part of the crew went forward to where the Zebras always go on their trek, and found it was in drought, which would change when the rains started, hopefully soon. The water holes were hard dried earth. There was no water there at all. Days passed and none of the expected rains came. Back where the zebras were congregated at their starting point, although their food supply had dwindled to almost nothing, they still had a little water. Now, the migration season was coming to a close and still the zebras had not moved. It was unprecedented. The time for their migration was essentially over!

Then one day, like a signal on demand, they all started on their path. It took many days, and the film crew knew they would die when they reached their destination.

They had just enough hydration in their bodies to make it, but the film crew knew it would all be for nothing. There was no water at their destination! The big surprise was. . . the day they arrived - it rained. The question was, how had they known?

The comment in the program was, "The animals somehow communicated with their environment, in ways that even we cannot do. How had they known exactly how long to postpone their migration?"

Tom checked his mail before he went to bed. There was an article on his Facebook from the *Washington Post* about an Orca Whale carrying her dead baby on her back for many days. Some people thought was an act of mourning! It said that whales were dying off because humans had netted their food supply, polluted their waters and ran ships through their hunting lanes. The funeral procession of 75 whales and her act of mourning, it said, was watched by the world. Some said they thought the whale was obviously communicating her sorrow - - to us.

Tom shook his head sadly, then wrote a short email to his folks, a quick text on his phone saying goodnight to Mollie, and went to bed. He entered a deep sleep.

"Hurry, you must load the plants and seedlings, "The man above yelled down to him. "We will grow them into larger plants on the roof. Hurry, hurry."

Tom was loading as fast as he could. There wasn't much time. He felt the urgency, even though there was bright sunshine outside. It was crazy to think a storm was coming.

The animals were arriving in pairs, greeting him as they came on board. He could hear them. No, he couldn't, not the conventional way, but he could understand them - each and every one of them. He greeted them back, in the same way. "Welcome," he said.

"We must hurry," they kept saying to him, "The storms are coming. Soon." They were pushing each other to hurry. Some were galloping.

The group kept coming in a long line, steady and fast.

"Do you think the ramp will hold?" Tom yelled up.

"Tell them to space out. If they feel it move under their feet, they must space wider." He yelled down.

Tom relayed the message. It was a kind of visualization of the ramp and its movement and how they must react to it. It was a different way of thinking and communicating, but quick and clear. It was like the thoughts he had when he lived in the cave so long ago with his family.

They told him they understood - they had already understood the man above him.

A lion leapt up lightly alongside him and he froze, but their eyes met and Tom relaxed. The animal licked him with a huge tongue across his cheek, and continued further into the confines of the ship.

"You mustn't hurt any of those coming aboard. "He said after him. We have food set aside for you. It is important those coming aboard be preserved - that you not hurt them"

"I know." He said. "Thank you. Have you seen my mate?"

"She's not here yet." He could feel his worry.

"Do they all know?" Tom asked Noah. "Are they all aware of what's going to happen?

"They are the ones who told us." He said," They all know. It is they who asked for our help. We are all communicating together. . .it is a God thing."

The pace was frantic. Tom was an observer and a participant at the same time. Then the picture speeded up, like a movie on fast forward, and the next thing in his movie/dream was bringing up the huge ramp, which needed to be pulled in with a system of pulleys and ropes. First, they were frantically adding a tree paste to the wood that would seal the doors. Next, bringing up the ramp to seal against it. The ramp was huge and heavy.

Tom could see black clouds sweeping the landscape and coming towards them in the distance.

They were still working on sealing openings when the first storm arrived.

"Not to worry. It will take some hours before the landscape floods." A chorus said to him.

The rain began in large drops.

Two elephants appeared just as Tom's strength gave out. "I can't pull the ropes. . . .the rain. . .it is beating against the ramp. . .everything is so slippery. . .and. . ."

The female wound her trunk around one rope and the male around the other. Together they brought the largest of the ramps into position and the men lashed the findings into place. There were big wooden turn screws that brought the unit tight against the paste. There were several of these to turn. Two creatures similar to raccoons were helping to turn the smaller ones and a large baboon was going along and doing the last turn.

The bottom half of the vessel was closed.

The rain was like a solid sheet of water when it arrived. The sky opened and there was nothing except the water! It rained and rained and the very earth was being swallowed by water.

The huge vessel began to move in a skid like a giant sled in too deep snow. Tom worried about trees and rocks and debris that could hurt them.

"Don't worry," Noah yelled over the din, "We have built this to withstand the storm!"

Then the landscape turned into a lake and their vessel started to float. There was a current, but it didn't affect them much. They started to move toward the distant mountain. In not so many days, they lodged against the side of it where they were better able to weather the horror outside.

A directed shoot of water came in for the animals to drink and another to clean waste out. It was ingenious how the system worked. It was like nothing he could have ever imagined.

He noticed, on occasion, there would be a bit of sun peeking through, and the rivulets of water would magnify the light.

Tom realized he was asleep and started to come out of it, when he heard, or felt, another animals' voice.

It was a cry coming from the water. "Help us. Help us. We are dying. Your species no longer hears us. . . you don't care about us. . . you are flooding the earth. You are the torrent that is squelching out our existence."

"I cannot help you," Tom said, half asleep. "I am only one person."

"That's too bad, because we are all connected. When we go - you do too."

Tom felt a stabbing pain.

He heard a high whine. The cry rippled through the water and against the mountain and rocked the inside of his head. It was a terrible sound coming from a mother whale. She should have been able to weather the flood he thought confused. It was the sound of agony.

He woke up and turned on the light. It was 2:30 a.m.

His dream was so real, that when he stood up, his legs buckled as if they were sea legs - like when he'd been on the lake for many hours and the boating had been rough. He shook his head trying to free himself of the horrible feelings from his dream. He walked around his small bedroom. One of the posters of a vampire was still on the wall. He tore it off and ripped it to shreds.

He heard something fall during his tirade. The bedroom was carpeted, yet there was the sound of something falling to the floor. What had he seen in that poster anyway? He had liked the image of the dripping blood. . . He remembered that. Then he recalled something had fallen. But how could there be something hitting the floor when there had only been that awful poster and falling paper? It wouldn't make a noise on the carpet, would it? He dropped to his hands and knees and looked under the bed. He saw something flicker. He ran his hand on the carpet and felt it more than saw it. He brought it out. There it was, a tiny giraffe. He had gotten it when he was at the zoo so many years ago, when he had fed a giraffe and the attendant gave him the charm. "Here," he said. "This is for you, because you love the animals - and they love you."

Tom sat on the floor and held the flat little charm. He hadn't seen it since he was a child.

He had wondered what had happened to it. . .

And then it was like a voice, almost, just like the one in his dream - an idea imprinting itself on his brain:

"I've been right here with you. All the time. I've never left."

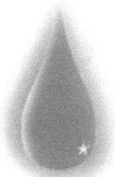

MEETING SUSAN

Tom's next meeting time for the Room changed to Thursday. He had been concerned because of conflicts in the new term's schedule. But the Teacher accommodated him seamlessly.

He arrived too early. He was concerned about the new day thinking he better wait a while outside - he wanted to be sure the person in the room before him was finished, but nobody came out, so he checked the sign-in sheet and saw the line was blank. He thought that was strange. The sign-in sheets were always full. He didn't know why this day should be any different than when he came before. He knocked anyway, then stood back and projected a thought towards the door. It opened.

He stepped through and entered an area of fluorescent light, strangely cold. He took a step back. This wasn't the kind of vision he was used to having. . . although there was still an emotional quality to it that sent his heart racing. He thought of a hospital. The room smelled of antiseptic and sickness. He continued into it, but the environment was too foreign for him to stay there. He was glad when it dissipated.

"Is it okay for me to come in?" he asked. "I'm a little early - I was waiting, but then I looked and saw there wasn't anybody signed in. . ."

"Yes. Come in." Replied the Teacher, but he sounded different.

"I waited," he said again, raising his voice questioningly and gesturing a hand toward the door. "What happened to the person before me?"

"I don't know," But there was a feeling of unrest in the room.

Tom thought that was strange - that there was something the Teacher didn't know. He looked at the drape and the color wasn't normal. It had changed from a pleasant middle azure blue to a brownish hue of blue. Funny, he had never noticed before that the drape actually changed color.

"The sign-in sheet has always been full," Tom said. "Was there supposed to be somebody coming in before me?" Tom asked.

"Yes. A regular." The Voice said, concerned.

"I can look at the sign in sheet from last week, and see whose name is there and try to find out what happened. Do you want me to do that?" He offered.

"Yes. Please do that." The Teacher said. "She has always been here. There is something not right about it."

"Okay," Tom said. "I will look and see, then maybe I can figure out what happened."

"It is your time now," The Voice said. "I don't want you to lose your time."

"It's okay," Tom said. "I'll look." He bounced out of the room and leafed through the sign-in sheets hoping that last week's was still in the pile. It was.

Her name was Susan Finley. Her cell phone number was neatly printed after her name as was the custom for all of them. He wrote it down and went back into the room. He stood by the window and keyed in the number, but it went immediately to her voicemail, like her phone was off or full. Strange, he thought. Students never, ever, missed their time in the Room.

"I sent her a text," he said, and sat down.

"Good afternoon," he was apologetic, pulling at his notebook to find his questions.

Tom felt different, as if a connection was lost between him and the Teacher and he wasn't sure what to do about it. He just felt it. In the future, when Tom thought back upon that day, he would say it was the only "traditional" conversation he ever had with the Teacher. It was more a chit/chatty sort of thing, instead of the seek and find questioning that he had become accustomed to. In fact, the session gave him insight to the Teacher that was normal - that maybe the figure behind the drape was human after all. Before that day, Tom had even considered that the thing behind the drape was some kind of spirit entity. It used to bother him.

They discussed Tom's studies and his family. They talked about the university and his job. It was the only occasion that the Teacher learned anything about his personal life. Off and on, Tom checked to see if Susan had answered his text.

"Maybe she had a test or something like that," Tom offered, "and she had to turn her phone off." But there was a feeling that crawled up his back - a feeling that said something wasn't right, even though he had never met her.

When Tom left the room, he stopped and sat on the rock wall and pulled out his computer tablet. He called up the student body and her name. Actually, it was a kind of email address system that the university had, and she was there, a senior, majoring in Nutrition. He wasn't able to see an address for her, but he could see her student email address.

He sent her a note. Then he closed his computer tablet and went to the Quad where he met Mollie for lunch. From there he went straight to work at Carl's Pizza, never very busy on Thursday nights, but now becoming busier because of John's antics.

When he rounded the corner, he couldn't believe it. The place was packed. He checked the campus schedule on his phone thinking he must have missed something, but he didn't see anything.

When Tom got off at the usual 1:00 am, he went to his apartment and checked first thing to see if Susan had answered his email. Nothing. It didn't feel right. Something was wrong. "It's none of my business," he said to himself. But it was. He'd told the Teacher he would find out about it. How was he going to do that? He didn't even know her.

He sat quietly in his living room and listened to himself think. What if something had happened to her and she needed help? All kinds of 'what ifs' filled his brain. He finally picked up his phone and called the hospital on campus. He asked if Susan Findley had been admitted in the last five days. Since he seemed to know who he was asking about, they didn't have a problem giving him information. No, they said, they didn't think so, but they had him describe her. No, they didn't have anyone of that description, nobody named, Susan.

Then he called the two hospitals in the local city. One of them said, "maybe" which he thought was a strange answer. Either she was there, or not - no maybe.

He gave them her name again, along with the age he thought she'd be - and maybe turned into a "yes" she had been admitted. Was he a family member? NO, he said he wasn't. Did he know of a family member? No, he didn't. Then, they said, get lost. That seemed strange to him. Why was it important that he be a family member?

He couldn't sleep and got up early that Friday morning. He drove his old car to the hospital, a place he'd never been, and thinking himself quite the busy-body, went in to find this girl named, Susan. What am I doing? He asked himself, but only in passing. He was determined.

The hospital had that strange feeling, like in his vision. It wasn't hard to find her room, after all he had her name, and he was a legitimate visitor during regular visiting hours. A nice woman at the desk told him she'd been moved to a regular room that very morning from critical care, so he would be able to see her. He grabbed a newspaper, so he wouldn't be entering her room empty-handed and headed to the 4th floor. What he found there shook him up. Susan was beautiful. She was sitting up with a tray of untouched food when he walked in.

When she saw him, she reached up and touched her hair, as if it hadn't been combed, but it had. Some of it had been parted and was pulled back with a barrette. Her face turned red and she looked down at her tray.

"Hi," he said. "I brought you today's newspaper," as if he was some kind of volunteer, only she already had the paper.

She looked up at him with the greenest eyes he'd ever seen. "Thank you," she said. "I feel like I've lost a year out of my life instead of only a couple of days!" She managed a laugh, then winced.

"How are you feeling?" He asked.

"Well, they had me up and walking the halls this morning and told me I can go home soon, except. . ." She laughed nervously, "except I can't go home because I don't have anybody there to watch over me." Then she realized she'd said too much, and had revealed to this strange man, that she lived alone. "I, um, I uh," she put a hand to her mouth, "don't have anybody there until tomorrow, that is." She flushed again and put her other hand to the top of her hospital gown, checking its closure.

"I'm Tom." he said in a friendly voice. "I'm the student that comes after you - to meet with the guy in the Room. I searched for you because the Teacher and I... uh. . .we were worried about you. Are you okay? What happened?"

She clapped her hands in delight, pushing her tray away. "I am so pleased you guys care about me, I feel a whole lot better now," she said, no longer wary of her visitor. "Honestly, this has been awful, but I'm really very lucky. I was downtown when I collapsed. I hadn't been feeling well, you know kind of cramp-y and I vomited. I thought it was some bad food I got a hold of and that it was a monthly thing, you know? I don't like to make a fuss. Well, it was my appendix. It burst. Yes. That's what happened to me. I was in town, doing a little shopping. I had parked my bike in the rack. Oh, I hope it is still there! I felt so sick!" She stopped, realized she was talking very fast. "Oh."

Tom smiled, nodded. "It's okay. I want to know."

"I had a sack of some peaches I bought. I thought they might settle my stomach. That is the last thing I remember until I woke up and there was this doctor asking me for my name. I guess it was pretty bad. I have been really sick with it. He asked me if I could give permission for surgery. I said sure, told him to do what they had to do - and I was so lucky. I had my student I.D. card with me and my proof of insurance so he could go ahead. It was just by accident that I had it! He wanted my next of kin, but I didn't want to tell him, so I just closed my eyes - pretending. I didn't want to tell my mom. My mother is fighting breast cancer and I didn't want to trouble her. After all, I have my own student insurance and she lives a long distance from here. I guess I was a big mess. They scooped me out!" She laughed, doubling over in pain, then coughed. "They told me it is good for me to cough," she said. "I was really a mess."

Tom sat with her that morning and learned she was considering graduate school. She gave him a key to her apartment so he could bring clean clothes for her. "I wasn't sure what I was going to do," she said.

"I have friends, but my cell phone is dead and I don't have a charger here and I don't know their phone numbers, they are all in my phone! I know I should be thinking more about these things, but I really have been just trying to feel better. I think the nurses will fix me up with a charger and I'll ask someone, and actually I was going to . . .just at the time you showed up!"

"Not to worry, I can help you." Tom smiled.

The things she had on when she was brought to the hospital were a mess from the peaches, which had cushioned her fall. She told him how she had been carrying them in a paper bag when she fell on them. She didn't remember it happening, but the nurse told her that her clothes were a mess from the soiled peaches - and she took a look at them when she was up that morning. They were in a bag in the closet and somebody really should have gotten them out of there and to a laundry. "They're pretty bad," she said.

Susan was embarrassed by having this strange boy do her laundry, but he said he was doing his anyway and his building had machines. She was still too tired to care and was grateful for a solution, one that had happened automatically. Besides, he wasn't really a stranger, was he? He was going to the Room too. That made him somebody special.

Tom left with the sack of her clothes and promised to return with clean ones from her apartment and her phone's charger.

He found the key to her bicycle lock in the pocket of her jeans along with some loose change when he loaded the washer. She hadn't said where she was when all this happened, but she wouldn't have been very far since she had felt so sick, so he went out on his own bicycle to see where she might have been. He found her bicycle and went back for it with his car.

Later that day, Tom came back with fresh clothes. The next morning, he took her home. She lived in an apartment a couple of blocks from his. He had put a few groceries in her refrigerator, had picked up her mail, and chained her bicycle outside her door. He half carried her inside. He had told the hospital personnel that she would not be alone - a half truth, but she had promised him she would call friends to be with her in shifts, and he was close-by, only a phone call away.

It was Sunday and his work started in the afternoon. It was a day most people called in their pizza orders for delivery. They watched games on TV or had friends over. He surprised Susan by having home delivery take her a pizza that evening. He was off at 8 o'clock and went directly to her apartment. She had two girls with her and he could see they had eaten the pizza he'd sent. One of her friends promised to stay the night.

Monday was crazy, but he found a few minutes to check on Susan.

"I didn't know how poorly I had been feeling," she told him. "I feel so much better, I'll be able to go to class later this week." He could see she was worried about starting the term. It would be bad to miss the beginning of a class.

"I'll pick you up and take you," He said. You shouldn't ride your bike yet."

"I don't even know you," she exclaimed, "Yet here you are when I need you! A friend for life!"

Tom remembered his promise and took Susan to her class later in the week. He had finally cleaned up his car, taking it to one of those do-it-yourself places where he ran the wand over it to wash the dirt off, but more importantly, used their vacuums. He'd done that before picking Susan up from the hospital and giving her a ride home. His life had changed in every way he could imagine. His car, his apartment, and now, this girl. What about this girl?

CHURCH

It had been a long time since Tom had been in a church. Chelsea had tried to get him to go with her, but he'd laughed about it, saying to her, "Church isn't going to help me with my sins, Chelsea. A person has to repent for 'em and not keep doin' em!"

She hadn't thought he was very funny.

But Tom was thinking about attending a service. In truth, he had never gone to church on his own without his parents. When he first came to the campus, he had learned about the youth groups during orientation. Chelsea went to one of them, but he couldn't remember which one, and although she'd encouraged him to go with her, he remembered saying, "over my sinful naked body. . ." And he meant it too.

He walked along an area of the campus that students called, Hi-lo Row, because of its elevation difference and because it was always called that. It was a wide path that had campus buildings along one side and a mixture of frat houses and light businesses on the other. It was late morning and he had no idea if any if the churches along the street side still had any services scheduled, and then he saw a small white church with its doors open and a few people going in. He hoped it wasn't the church where Chelsea went. He circled around to the front and heard the crunch of the frost under his shoes. He wanted to get a glimpse inside before committing himself, but it was impossible. A couple of students saw him.

"Come in with us. We'd love to have you join us."

The morning was brisk and cold as winter was still hanging on. The sun was already bright, promising it could get better but he was eager to get into someplace warm. Their sign listed services beginning at 11:00 - in five minutes.

He nodded gratefully and went in with them. Another student shook his hand and pressed a program into it saying, "Welcome. You're going to want this."

He separated himself and sat in the back. It felt right.

Soon a choir began to sing. They were mostly students his age singing to bongo drums. He didn't recognize the language, but when he looked at the paper in his hands, he saw they were singing in Swahili. The song was called, Good Morning Jesus.

"Good morning Jesus," he whispered, when it was time for the congregation to sing their part in English, and then with a singing voice, "Thank you for coming." He sang. "We needed you to help us." The choir sang some words again in Swahili and the drums played back and forth. Then it was his turn again. "Show us the way." He believed these words, like he had never believed them before, yet weren't they contradictory to what the Teacher said? No, they weren't. The Teacher told me, he said to himself, there were no contradictions in the life of Jesus.

He reminded himself that He came to help us understand we are all connected to Him - and to each other. He wanted to impress upon us that forgiveness is the most important thing of all - compassion and forgiveness. He stopped animal sacrifices and showed us by living example not to hold on to grudges, that our beliefs about ourselves makes us who we are and forgiveness is key in our lives.

Tom shook his head. The concepts were simple, yet difficult. Perhaps religion had methods he could use on a daily basis; he could combine his inner knowledge with this outer reality of methodology. Wasn't everything in life a compromise? Wasn't it up to him to find an inner balance?

The pastor prayed for peace.

"All thought has power," the Teacher has said. Tom bowed his head and said fervently in his head, "Lord bring peace to the world." And then he shook his shoulders, as if to shake off a cold chill. Who was Lord? Who was this Lord? Who was he asking for Peace? How was he to focus? The Teacher had said to call upon Jesus. Yes, that was how he should focus his prayer. "Jesus, help us to bring peace to the world. . ."

When he looked up, he saw the cross. He looked at it and asked again for peace. Maybe people should pray with their eyes open, he thought.

He remembered words the Teacher had said: "If I have helped one person better understand their reason for being here, then I have fulfilled my reason for being here."

"What's my reason for being here?" he asked himself. Again. For the hundredth time. "Why am I alive?" Obviously, the Teacher knew his reason, Jesus knew his reason, perhaps his parents even knew their reason; but why me? He looked at all the different symbols in the church. He looked at the flowers by the pew. He looked at the statue of Jesus, and all the things placed around the altar area. He looked at all the stained-glass images that were in the windows. Some of them had sayings written under the scenes that were in the glass. "Love one another," one of them said.

He didn't hear much of what the pastor said. There was some kind of lesson about "being ready."

After church there was a coffee time in the foyer. Tom tried to escape, but there was no getting around the groups of people reaching out to him with welcoming hands. He heard a discussion that got his attention, one that he'd heard before, about end times and "chosen one" and how a number of people would be chosen ones. He wondered about it. It was another one of those things that never seemed to make sense.

Tom didn't recognize any of the students, but then he didn't know why he should. It was a large university, and the student population numbered in the thousands. The university offered everything in their graduate schools - dentistry, veterinary medicine, medical school and more, including the arts.

"What are you majoring in?" A friendly student with a name tag saying Richard (Rich), was asking him.

"Oh, uh. . .physics," Tom answered.

"Really?" Rich wasn't asking a question of him, but the meaning was surprise. "Hey Ash, come over here and meet Tom." He gestured to a girl standing loosely by a small group of women. Clearly, she was grateful for the diversion, and came immediately.

"Tom is studying physics. This is Ashly, my wife. She's a student teaching at Central, and I'm at Boyd & Johnson interning until I take my CPA test."

"I'm a fourth year," Tom said. "Will graduate next year."

"Oh my gosh," she said, "Physics. Guess you don't believe Steven Hawking. . . or do you?"

"Well, some of us don't. Some of us do. It's pretty much like Hawking's ideas are everywhere, aren't they? Not just us in Physics." Tom said somewhat defensively.

"Oh, didn't mean it that way," Rich said. "It's just a surprise, that's all. Honestly, you're right, there's so many atheists out there. We hope you come again."

By the time Tom left the church, the landscape had warmed more. He decided to continue walking along the path. He'd never been to that part of the campus before. Sometimes he'd considered riding his bike on this part of the path, but he was always on his way to class and never had the time. Now he looked at it with a different eye; he was thinking it would be a nice ride for him and Susan to take.

He surprised himself, that he was thinking about her so much.

He spied a coffee shop on the corner and he could take her there. He never wanted to go to the place where he broke up with Chelsea again.

That week Tom prepared more than he had for other sessions with the Teacher. He sat on the couch with his notebook making his list of questions. He had lots of them - mostly stemming from his time at the church. He wrote down questions about being an atheist, chosen ones and more. He prioritized them.

His first one, and one that always had bothered him, had actually turned him away from any teachings in the Bible, and that was, how the world was created. The business about the seven days was laughable! And then there was Adam and Eve. Yes, there were many things left unanswered.

Tom put his notebook away. The questions would have to wait. Right now, he had his parents coming for a visit and an apartment to clean. They would be surprised. Yes. He was looking forward to their visit. He would take them in to have pizza and hear the funny noises. He might even take them to the little church - they would love the walk on the path. He would show them around the campus and to where he went for his classes. He hoped his mother would help him select something from the thrift shop for his wall. They had lots of pictures lined up along the walls in the thrift store. Every one of them was less than five dollars.

It was time to decorate.

THE BIBLE TELLS ME SO

Tom came in with several questions hoping to get through two of them. Most of them came from the short time he was in church, which really was a reminder of things he'd been taught for most of his life.

The first had always bothered him, and actually had turned him away from the Bible - and that was how the world was created in seven days!

But when he asked the question, one that he was certain had no logical answer, it was like so many other questions he asked.

"Let's go back to our lessons about time," the Teacher said. "Can we agree that time is constructed and imagined by man to organize ourselves?"

"Umm, guess so, but it really does organize the Universe."

"According to?

"Uh. Science."

The drape reacted.

"Uh. Sorry."

"Did you look at your watch before coming here? Did you notice what time it was so you could be here for our meeting?"

"Yes, of course."

"So, we agree. Time organized *you*. Can we further agree that the basis of the system is our orbit around the sun? The process of telling time, is categorized in relation to the sun. Right? Now, we are talking about the clock system of telling time."

"Right."

"And that is the one that bothers you about the Bible. Probably.

"Okay. One day is how the earth rotates. It is almost 24 hours. That involves the rotation of the Earth. And then we come back to the sun, and the Earth orbits around the sun, which takes a year. It is all in relation to the sun. So, we have a year broken into units of 24-hour days, minutes, and seconds all based on the sun. It would really be interesting if we based it on . . .say. . .Saturn. wouldn't it?" The Teacher chuckled.

"Yes, of course," although the science major in Tom wanted to qualify it further, wanted to discuss the precise criteria, but then he didn't want to bog the Teacher down with something that they both knew.

So, if you wanted to measure everything going on in the Universe, and you wanted to find a constant to measure against, you would need to find a universal truth. Would it be the largest thing? The smallest? How do you find a constant when everything is changing?

"How fast do you think the dust turned when it was forming? Do you have any scientific figures that may give you an idea about that?

"Four times faster," Tom said.

"Yes, just like when you were a child. You grew faster but time was slower.

"If you were writing a document to speak to everyone, through ALL the ages, at a time when there wasn't any science at all. . . I wonder what kinds of things you might say?"

"I dunno. . ."

"And for us now, we must take a leap perhaps to catch up to it.. . . ummm?"

"To catch up? But it is archaic!" Tom sputtered.

"Is it now."

"YES!"

"Because it has things to say that you cannot yet prove scientifically you are just discounting what it has to say?"

". . .but. . .but. . .seven days. . .the heavens and the earth. . ."

"What are the Heavens? And what is the Earth?"

Tom felt his face turning red. "I think. . ."

A wise old man now took over the voice that had been the Teacher. He started talking in a strange low sing song, "I thinnnnnk we discussed what Heaven is. and. . . what Earth is. . ."

The ceiling of the room disappeared. It was just gone. The sun had been streaming in the window, but that was replaced by sky. The sky turned dark. Tom felt dizzy as he looked up into a black sky, and as he did, a million stars started to twinkle. Then the walls of the room and the table and the floor disappeared and he was floating in his chair in the middle of all those stars. He hung on to the arms of his chair with white knuckles. His heart was beating wildly, like the first time he entered the room and he felt like he was about to go on a roller coaster ride. "Oooo" He exclaimed.

And then, the stars disappeared and all kinds of filmy things started appearing and going about doing all kinds of things in a strange sort of way that Tom could not explain. It was like he was in the middle of some sort of dream, one that was comprised of light and sound and very ethereal color. And then slowly, he saw a landscape being built. It was like a marvelous painting. There were mountains and trees and tropical plants and oceans and. . .and. . .

"OH." Tom said. It was like he was watching the creation of a wonderful painting.

"It will take millenniums to add all the details to this painting, Tom." An old lady said.

"Yes. Oh."

Then an old man said. "Heaven and Earth may not refer to the creation of the planet, Tom. The Bible does *NOT* pretend to be a scientific document, in other words, it cannot tell you *how* the planet was created, but it does give you instruction about *YOU*."

"Could the Bible be describing the separation of the physical from the spiritual dimension? May it have taken only a short measurement of change by our standards . . .? How long do you think it took to separate *YOU* from *YOUR* other dimension to bring you here. . .? *Hmmm*?"

"Uh. . .uh. . .I have to read the passage again," Tom said. As soon as he said it, a Bible book appeared on his table.

He opened it.

Thomas read the passage in Genesis. He applied what he'd learned about the physical dominance of the human dimension, and what he had learned about a dimension he knew so little about. He understood from the passage that there existed a substance that could be called our planet at the time of genesis and that everything about it was of God. Everything. The teaching was clear.

"Well, it's kind of a fairytale," Tom said with resignation.

"Oh, it is?" The question hung in the air, in the night sky Tom had been part of, in the very air he breathed, in the sunshine coming in the window.

"Again, there are measurements of time, and then there are not. You can measure it by a beam of light. . .and now there are discoveries that there are measurements even faster, or you can measure it by our sun. What measurement do you want, Tom? God's? Would you confine the Bible to your measurement?"

Tom sat there quietly.

"Well, what about the Adam and Eve thing" Tom broke the silence." um. . . that whole stupid Garden of Eden story?"

"One of the important things to realize about our beautiful world is that many dangers are present here. It is our freedom. God did not make good and evil. We did and it isn't the so-called snake."

The Teacher paused to laugh. The laugh spread outward until the entire room was breathing and laughing.

"Yes, of course, there are dangers that can hurt us. Snakes, insects and many other creatures - they inhabit the world with us. This place is teaming with life! First, I want to say that the snake is not a lowly creature, but a creature that struggles in its life cycle of survival as we do. We have a complete and harmonious system and it is important for us to come together, as a species, to understand it. Imagine, if we were to have eradicated the spider, we would not have its wonderful web. We are now learning from the miracle of its fiber!

"Secondly, we must learn to live in balance in this world - with the snake and all that it is. For whatever reason, we have not been doing that since day one. We can assign blame "OH, it is her fault, she listened to the snake, and some say, 'but he didn't have to follow' and the argument will go on and on as we continue to hurt one another and our Earth.

"At one time, we could hear the snake. . ."

"What happened? Why can't we hear the snake anymore?"

"Is there a lesson here? Yes, we have been given knowledge, but we sleep. The Bible tells us we were given knowledge from the very beginning but still we sleep. We know good and evil. According to the story, Eve wanted to know God, or, didn't understand from the very beginning that she was already part of God. By identifying with the physical (eating the forbidden fruit), Eve would know both good and evil of this physical world. She would become entirely physical, the body she would occupy would die. But she would gain something."

"What?"

"The answer to a question."

"What question?" Tom asked

"WHAT IS GOD?"

Tom just sat there. He was a bump. He was just nothing more than an unthinking lump.

The room was filled with sunshine. Then it clouded over and the room was filled with thunder and lightning and then a breeze came through and fluttered Tom's hair and the drape shook and danced and there was a strange rustling noise. Then all was quiet again. And still he just sat there. He had no sense of time. There was no time. There was only the feeling of . . .something else.

He didn't speak.

"The story of Adam and Eve is about virginity, in the truest sense. It is about innocent beings coming into a physical world. They had left all they had known in order to gain something special - regarding God. By coming into a dimension of physical dominance, of matter, that is Earth, they ate from the tree, and yes, it was physical, and yes, they gained knowledge, but with it came responsibility. They turned their backs and left a place of security and serenity. By choice. It was their choice. It has always been about free will, temptation, and all the things that comprise the existence here. **The physical dimension**. It was designed to be this way.

Some may call it "a fall from the garden" as indeed it may seem like that - a fall from someplace else into this container, but for each of us, there is a reason. We do not exist in both dimensions simultaneously. We must follow a series of laws. . ." The room chuckled as if holding back a great secret.

"If you wanted to know all that God is, what more could show it to you! The story is as true today as when the Bible was written. Don't you think?"

Tom thought of himself. He thought about Chelsea. He considered himself better than her. He thought about the whiskey glass and how he had used her and. . .and. . .

"I'm going to be sick," he said, getting up to leave.

Only, he couldn't move. It was like he was against an invisible wall or something.

"Sit Down!" A booming Voice exploded. "What right do you have to perpetuate the negativity you brought in here today? You are the one who wanted to know about Genesis. You knew it already - in your bones - in your very genes, and you came in here thinking you could walk out of here and not own any of this? No, you can't. You can only own the best in yourself now. You have learned too much. You must leave here with what you really ARE!"

Tom sat down. He didn't have a choice. He was so ashamed.

The room was silent. It stayed that way.

Finally, what seemed forever, Tom said, "I'm not better than any other living creature. I don't want to be. I want to learn to love all the creatures I share this planet with. I don't even know the "old" Tom anymore. I used to know him, but I don't think like him anymore and I don't act like him anymore and I don't even know where he went. Sometimes I'm afraid that I'm going crazy or something. I don't even like that person, the one I used to be, and. . .and ." Tom had a faraway look in his eyes as he gazed across the room. "And I'm saddened by the things I did. My priorities have changed."

"Yes, I know," Teacher said kindly. "You must believe in yourself and who you are now. It may be necessary for you to 'right' something that is plaguing you. There's more than one way to say 'you're sorry.' You may need to find it. Start to visualize an action that will result in a good outcome - the one that will give you peace."

"I don't understand, though, if we're all connected and everything, why are there references to the 'chosen ones.' Religion keeps making interpretations about that - they even have a number, like two-hundred and forty thousand and things like that. I went to this little church on Sunday and heard people talking about it. . .

"Who are the chosen ones?"

"Chosen ones?" the Teacher asked in return.

"Yes," Tom said "The people who are chosen by God during the end times."

"Oh, I see, "the Voice said lightly, in a way Tom was beginning to recognize. "Chosen by God? How is God going to do that? Will God be like a giant hand that's going to swoop out of the sky and say: you and you and YOU?"

"No." Tom answered in a small voice. Then in a very tiny voice he said, "Maybe."

The Teacher chuckled. "Oh, I see. Well, we always have free will, Tom. So, when it comes to matters like this, Tom, *we choose ourselves*. Since God is not separate. . .well . . . I guess we just must choose ourselves, mustn't we? There isn't a God that is going to do that for us. Do you understand that?"

"Well. . .I'm not sure." Tom finally said, hesitantly. "Oh, I don't know. I mean, if God is not separate, and is in each of us, then that means we can't go around asking. . . God . . I guess."

"Yes, you are thinking about it" Teacher said softly. And then after a few minutes of silence,

"What does it mean to choose yourself?" Teacher asked.

Tom could hear his breath; it was raspy and tight. "What does it mean to choose myself?" he whispered under his breath to himself, at himself. He rubbed his fingers over the table top, as he often did, and for an instant he shut his eyes and remembered sitting at another table not so long ago, when he was sitting with his father. "It is your choice," his father had said. "No one else can make this choice for you. You have to decide . . ."

Decisions were difficult for Tom. When he did make them, he felt uncomfortable and always told himself they were just "temporary"- he could always go back, always do something else. He searched for a way out in his mind.

"Ministers speak about being 'called' he said simply. So, I think there must be something beyond ourselves that chooses us," he concluded.

And then something very strange happened again in the room. There was a subtle shift. Everything was just as it had always been, yet it wasn't, somehow the room's contents seemed newer, fresher. The Teacher spoke but the Voice took on a familiar quality and reminded him of somebody else. He thought he heard The Teacher, the "It" part of the Teacher say something, but he wasn't exactly sure.

The Voice sounded so much like his Mother from years before that he jumped. They were living on the acreage on Maple Way. He could hear her calling from the distance of the house, "Tommy, Tommy, come to dinner."

He was on a wooden platform his father had built up in a tree and he was fastening cardboard from a box around a branch that he had colored brightly. She was calling, but he didn't want to come. He heard her voice coming closer, "Tommy, where are you? Are you up there?" He remembered flattening himself on the wood floor boards, and then making a decision, "Yes, Mom, I am up here," he called down. "I am coming."

Tom sat very straight now at the table. "Do we always choose ourselves?" he asked the Teacher.

"It isn't an easy question to answer," The Teacher said conversationally. "Leaders are often chosen by election, but they have to decide first, and there are occasions of people being selected to do things against their will, but by and large, when we are discussing life's spiritual matters, the things we think of as 'God's choice', then yes, we choose ourselves. We are listening to the God in us - The God connection."

"But don't you think God chose Jesus to do a task, that perhaps Jesus didn't want to do?" Tom asked.

"Does a child want to come in from play to eat their dinner or to clean their room?" The Teacher asked conversationally, almost knowing the thought that Tom had been thinking - of being up in the tree. It startled him, as so many things did in this room.

"Jesus most certainly did choose himself. He didn't want to and wrestled with that choice, one that he knew was coming. He wanted, as any of us would have wanted, to be 'delivered' from such an agonizing, painful and difficult experience. Jesus was in tune with His destiny."

"Oh, I seeee." Tom said, not yet wanting to give up, so he persisted again asking, "what about this number. . .this number of 240,000 Chosen Ones, I've heard that, at least I think that is supposed to be the number."

"Ah, is that what is troubling you?" The Voice asked. "The World would be well served if there could be that many individuals who do choose themselves to follow a courageous path of enlightenment and love. Perhaps such a prophecy might be true given the number of beings we have living on the Earth today; and what do you think these Chosen Ones would do?"

"Well, uh, um, I don't know. I guess they would be the ones to have everlasting life." Tom said. "Oh uh, guess that isn't right. . . guess they will be the ones to lead us into a new World . . a new way of living. and thinking. . .a new life, so to speak. I mean they say. . .the End Times."

"The End of What? The Earth as we know it? Humankind as we know it? Ignorance? Don't you suppose, if we really were to have 240,000 people who choose themselves, and they actually recognize the God within, and they recognize God in Everything - in ALL that IS; and that they do realize that they are connected to ALL things, that the world would be a vastly different place?"

"Yes, I guess it would be," Tom said thoughtfully. "Do you think it would be difficult for them to lead us into that way of thinking?" Tom picked at an imaginary something on the table top. "Teacher, what do you think the End Times means?"

"Maybe it means an end to ignorance. Maybe it means an end to so much foolishness. What do you think it means Tom?"

That seemed so ridiculous and so simple, especially in a university setting that Tom began to laugh hysterically.

Then the Teacher broke in and said, in a very level sounding tone, "We are all going to walk to the edge of the Earth and hold hands and jump off, because the World really is flat, you know."

They both laughed hysterically. Then the room laughed too. It seemed like the whole world was laughing. And then it stopped abruptly, so they did too.

The room became so quiet, in fact he had never heard what quiet really was before this. This was quiet. He couldn't even hear his heart beating or his lunch churning in his stomach. There was no traffic noise, or students outside walking. His own breath seemed to freeze against a wall of truth. The Teacher had said something so simple to impress upon him that we are doing things for no reason. All reason had gone to the edge of the Earth and mankind was engaged in so much silliness.

"We think we know something about God and the Universe, but we know nothing." Tom blurted. "We hurt each other and run around in a state of stupidity for which we have no ideas at all. Why? We don't know why. We ask why all the time." The silence had broken like glass tittering to the floor.

"Yes. . ." The Voice said softly.

"We have to recognize that God is in us. We have to stop asking God to do everything FOR us. We must realize that God is not outside of us, but part of us. We must become accountable for what we are and that we are all connected. . ."

"Right." The Teacher said.

"Then the choice becomes ours. . ." Tom lifted his head and widened his eyes.

"Some might say, it is people helping people, spirits helping spirits, the magic of the Universe, a God thing," the Teacher explained. "When more than one chooses, then the goal becomes very reachable and powerful. We understand, in the universal order of things, that time doesn't exist, right? Then, we understand that there are no beginnings or endings, except in our own perceptions.

Who or what is to bring about this change? Those who choose to bring it about. Does it stand to reason that change will occur? It is the law of the Universe. Everything, everything is in a state of change, always. Our system will change, of course. There is no conflict here. Only the truth."

"Why is Jesus' way the only way?"

"Because His way is the only one accessible to our narrow and limited minds right now. The spirit was visible in Jesus, co-existing as was generally impossible for us to realize, and came through to this physical dimension to be visible to us. Imagine a step in one dimension and a step in another to give us proof of the physical system and the spiritual one at the same time. He did that for us. Not only could we see the spiritual dimension, but by so doing, we could see the presence of God in Him. He was the only one we know about that actually could do that. But even more than that, He gave us lessons on how to nourish the next system, which is important to everything we do because we are connected to here and now and what is to follow. Heaven? What if there is so much more than our limited view of what we think heaven is? It is just like being locked in a room your whole life and then somebody opens the door and you walk outside and voila! - There is an entire world of stars and sunshine and trees and valleys and people and animals. You've seen nothing yet! There is so much to look forward to. And listen, listen to your heart. Look and listen. There is so much ahead. Stop and look around. We are taking all this for granted, and can you imagine how much we looked forward to this experience right here, right now? To the trees and valleys and all this wonder? Just one flower is amazing. This system is incredible! Try and appreciate it and live each day in a state of wonder because you are here! Appreciate this, and you will appreciate what the next system is too."

"Other prophets have said there is a God." Tom said simply, not wanting to let go.

"Yes, they did, and they were right, of course. But any prophet that said God was an entity, a separate, apart entity, was really not thinking. Clearly. Imagine all those sacrifices and pagan things that people used to do! Horrible! God is the Heaven and the Earth and is everything that IS. Period. What can be any clearer than that? Hmmm? We were in First Grade. Now we are in Fifth Grade. One of these days we will be in Junior High. It will really be different after folk's graduate.

People of this Earth will see things in an entirely different way, and the words in the Bible in a new light. Many of those words will still apply.

"If Jesus lives through you, what are you connected to? What are you part of? If Jesus lives through the person next to you, what is that person connected to? How are you both connected? Sometimes it helps to have a facilitator, mmm? It takes two to be connected and when it is all new, and there's learning taking place, it takes a line, a cord, something that passes between the two places to help the connection to occur, doesn't it?

"There is no conflict, no conflict Tom."

"Then why do Christians shun Science?"

"There is something in it they are not understanding. There is a human ego question that is getting in the way. They do not understand that Everything is God. They think of themselves as separate because of their ego and they are afraid of losing their identity." Tom felt the Voice smile. "They think they are better than the possum or the fox, but they are the same."

Tom grunted.

The Voice continued. "This is ALL one system. ONE. The idea of evolution, or being connected to other creatures seems to be repugnant to a lot of people. Why? Why would something of God's design be repugnant? Because they don't see it as God's design. Because they think they are better than God. They see themselves as something separate from God. Tom, think about this. Better than God! Separate from God? Better than ALL that IS? Better than ALL of creation that made the design of everything?

"WE are evolving. Everything is changing. Everything must change all the time in order for infinity to exist. There must be change. Everything evolves, or changes. . . ."

Silence stretched in the room. It stretched until the room seemed to be elongated and then it snapped back on itself and Tom realized he'd just been sitting there, a lone figure in a room with a person behind a curtain. It really was bazaar, the whole thing on this crazy day, but was it? He put his head in his hands.

"We are not alone." The Voice said. "Ever. Never. We just think we are."

Tom started to cry softly.

"Why are you crying?" The Teacher asked softly.

"Because. . . because. . .I realize I thought I was alone, and it hurt. It hurt to be alone. I am crying because there was a hurt I didn't know I had. I had a sore and I didn't know about it, like my foot was an open sore and I didn't know about it until I tried to walk on it and then when I took a step it hurt and a pain shot up through my leg. I didn't know I had this wound. I am crying because I have to hear these reminders, because I have to hear you keep saying all this, again and again. I don't understand why.

"I am crying because I am giving up who I thought I was."

CARL AND MARSHA

"What are you going to do with a History degree? Nobody is going to want you! You won't be able to find a job." Carl's father said to the young man sitting at the end of the table for the tenth time. His mother was next to him nodding in agreement and patting his hand.

"If we don't know where we've been," Carl said to his father - and the other family members gathered together on that Sunday afternoon for dinner, "then how will we know where to go in the future?"

"That's a lame argument. That quote has been used by everybody; I think it is even in Star Wars!" His young cousin piped up, and was hushed by his Aunt June.

"Besides," Carl said, ignoring him, "History is a required course in High School and I can always teach."

"Teachers make lousy pay," his brother said.

"Money isn't everything." Carl used the argument more than once. "I want to like what I do." He scowled at his brother, inferring that his brother didn't like what he was doing.

Carl's mother ended the discussion by clearing the table and saying, "Carl is going to do what he wants anyway. Besides, he has plenty of time to decide his major. He's just starting college. He won't need to decide for another two years. This conversation is really premature. Let him be a kid."

Carl lived at home and was going to the local state college. He was taking required courses that every student has to take. He loved history. His family harped on him the entire time, but his advisor at school encouraged him. Carl somehow didn't realize that the department desperately needed students like Carl - he really was just a number, a warm body needed to keep the history department alive.

Shortly after he finished his undergraduate degree, he soon understood the truth about his degree. Nobody wanted a history major. But somebody did want him. So, he joined the military and it didn't matter; it was just like he'd heard - the military had a way of putting a person into entirely new career fields, especially if they had a history degree.

Carl ended up as an officer in the kitchen. He couldn't think of anything more distant than what he had studied. He had NO experience with food, or food service. His brother loved to rub it in.

"Yeah Bro, you got yourself in deep this time. Heh? Ha ha ha. You're in there slopping around with the pigs, ain't ya?"

But officers, even new ones, didn't slop. Carl was involved with paperwork. The cooks liked to cook. Nobody in the kitchen wanted to do the paperwork and there were miles of it - the ordering - the types and quantities of food - and especially the stocking of food before a ship leaves the harbor. Carl had a mentor that helped him understand the importance of his job, something he had never considered before.

He told his mom that his history background made his military career interesting. He studied how entire voyages had failed because of scurvy and the lack of nutritional needs. He looked into many historical aspects of food on voyages. He liked his job.

One day, by accident, he came upon a supplier of cinnamon roll dough, a chance thing really, that made him a hit. The dough could be frozen and literally thrown in the oven rock hard and it came out great every time. Everybody loved those cinnamon rolls, because they had lots of cinnamon and their interior had been infused with real butter. He learned something about nutrition from Jimmy, an officer who was also working in food management. "The cinnamon has good value," he told Carl. "None of us will get enough of it to make much of a difference health wise, but what the heck. It sure isn't bad for us. If we have two rolls in the morning, it may help keep colds and bronchitis away. It hasn't been studied. A lot of things haven't. We use it on our horses; we lace their apples with it, and they love it and they are healthier because of it! I swear they are!" And so, Carl became interested in how seasonings and foods could be beneficial in many ways. He even gave mini seminars to the cooks and introduced seasonings. They seemed to like him for it.

He introduced those rolls onto every ship that came into the shipyards where he was stationed. But like the Japanese say, if you are the nail that stands out, somebody will come along and pound you down. Carl got pounded with orders to Iraq. He thought he might be sent to the Middle East, but on a ship, not to a land assignment. His assignment wasn't on a ship, but to a military base. Food and water are the number one priority in all areas where the military are assigned, water being the first priority. An excellent contractor had bid on supplying the food for the bases in Iraq and it would be Carl's job to coordinate local operations. There were pluses and minuses to the assignment. He hated the heat, but he liked learning the food business from one of the world's great providers. Plus, the assignment had made him eligible for additional scholarship money upon his return.

Carl had thought he could get his teacher's credential while in the military, but soon realized it was impossible - the needed credential was based upon the state where he would be employed. So, he settled for a master's degree, which he received part time while being in the Navy. He liked the military. Actually, a lot. He could take courses at the various locations, all from the same university - and the tuition was essentially free. He could even study while he was on board a ship, which happened to him now and again.

Carl thought of himself as a lucky person. He'd seen many of the places he had only read about in books: Japan, The Philippine Islands, and even a couple of days in Australia. Some didn't think he was so lucky because of his Middle East assignment, but he even liked that. He found the food service operations amazing. The quality of the food that the contractor provided was first rate and it kept up morale. Carl learned more about the marriage of food to history than he ever thought possible. Battles were lost because of food supplies!

Now he was down to his last six months, and he was stationed at Portsmouth Naval Shipyard, only 85 miles from his hometown! Life was good.

It was a hot summer's day, only four months before being discharged, that he met Marsha. They were on a few days of leave from the ship. His friend, Jimmy, also from New Hampshire, wanted to show the guys a special horse his family would start racing soon. The horse was training at his family's farm along the route they had selected for the day's drive.

They arrived in the morning at the farm, which was really a horse ranch, in time to see Angel Feet Twosome trotting around a well-groomed dirt track. They stood at the fence and watched her for a time, but were grateful when Jimmy's family had them in for coffee before continuing on to Dartmouth. Andrew and Toby wanted to see the campus there, one of the loveliest and one of the most expensive, in the country – "just to see it." Andrew and Toby weren't from New Hampshire and thought Carl was crazy for wanting to go there, but were game to go "along for the ride" in their rented BMW. Both Andrew and Carl had just finished a deployment in Iraq and scholarships were available - on top of their GI benefits. "Yeah, I think the funds will cover most of it. . .and why not go to the best, when we can? Eh?" Andrew wasn't from the East Coast and was looking forward to either entering the job market or continuing with school.

They were walking the campus when they noticed the Hanover Inn, a historic hotel and restaurant. It fit in well with the grace and charm of the old and well-preserved university.

The four of them were dressed moderately well - to meet Jimmy's folks and for the campus visit, so they decided to go there for lunch. It wasn't the kind of place for four college students - but they weren't college students - were they? They were all officers. They had been around the world and were educated. Why not?

"We're officer's and we're gentlemen!" Andrew said laughingly. "We fit well in these digs!"

It was popular because there was a job fair going on, and Miss Marsha Jones had just finished an interview at one of the tables. She was wearing a classy skirt and heels with a casual flowing cover that doubled as a jacket, but had a slightly less formal air about it.

She positioned herself in line behind the four young men and pulled out her phone, apologizing for being momentarily rude. "Just seeing if my friends are finished and can have lunch with me," she said. She mumbled that she apparently missed them.

"I want to go here," Carl announced to the others. "All I need is my teaching credential - and having one from here will look good. This is a great pl. . !" He gestured turning. . . and that's when he saw her standing directly behind him. "Uh. . .uh. . ." he uttered embarrassed and dumbstruck by her long reddish-brown hair and hazel eyes.

She was blasé as she gazed at him, "Yes, you can't do better." She smiled, pretending to be part of the great institution, although she was from the state university down the road in Manchester. Briefcase in hand, she was at a career fair where she hoped to land a job as a trainee in hospitality management.

There were others she knew from school who planned to be at the fair too, but it was crowded in the room. She wished she and her friends had set up some kind of informal lunch meeting, but a person didn't keep a phone on in such a restaurant, so she immediately turned it off again.

"I'm just on the lookout for some of my friends. I'm not sure they are going to be here," She apologized, looking around.

Carl took the bait. He was good at making decisions. His father told him it was a talent - that is, to be able to make a clear decision and stick to it living with the consequences. "That's the sign of a good leader," he told him. "A person who can make decisions without hemming and hawing around - none of this waffling all over the place. Nobody likes that and those kinds of people waste everybody's time. But you Carl, you think quickly and you go with your choice - good or bad. Best of all, you take responsibility for it. I wish I could take the credit for teaching you these things, but it really is something that is ingrained - it's a personality issue and you've got it."

Carl made a decision. "Why look for your friends," he said smiling at the beautiful Marsha, "when you can have lunch with four handsome gentlemen, one of which is me." He gave a small bow at the waste, almost like a butler. It was done in jest and seemed appropriate for the upscale surroundings. Before she could answer or protest, it was their turn to be seated and he corrected the number to "five."

The lunchroom boasted a buffet, and although somewhat formal, it also had a warmth about it that made conversation easy. She was raised in a town almost next door to Carl's hometown; and after some very animated conversation, they found out that they'd been both raised Methodists, although Carl could not have said how they got on that part of the conversation. She tried being polite every now and then by including the other men in her conversation, but Carl always tried to bring her back to just him, although she especially tried to converse with Jimmy, who was by nature shy, so that didn't work very well.

Carl was sure only a few minutes had passed when Marsha told him she needed to return to the job fair. "It's my reason for being here." She said simply. "I'm graduating and I'll need a job."

He didn't know how she managed to eat so fast, but her plate was empty and he couldn't think of a way to keep her there, so he asked her for a date the following Saturday.

The next four days were filled with thoughts of her. "I can't get her out of my head." he told Jimmy, half singing the lyrics to a song. "I go to sleep thinking about her, I dream about her. I wake up thinking about her."

"Love at first sight." Jimmy said chuckling.

"Yes, I guess so."

Only it wasn't that way for Marsha. When she got back that evening, she did a background check on Carl and his family. She wasn't going to get involved with a near-do-well. She looked at the family's home on Google satellite and perused the neighborhood where they lived using its 3-D view. They lived in a nice part of town, but they weren't wealthy. Carl's father made a modest income and his mother also worked. Not bad, but not great. Their home was paid for.

Then she did a background check on Jimmy. She was interested in him from the beginning - not Carl. But Carl kept getting in the way. A few times she managed to bat her eyes at the other young man, but he acted like he didn't notice, especially when he started a conversation about his girlfriend, Sarah, who was "waiting" for him to get out of the service. He was from New Hampshire too, and as far as Marsha was concerned, fair game. It wasn't like he was married to Sarah yet. The guys talked enough about their morning visit to his family's horse ranch so she was able to view his family's place on the computer too.

They were wealthy, like she suspected. They had to be, to race a horse. She smelled it from the beginning. It was the way he carried himself, the way he ate his meal and inserted polite comments in the conversation. Slightly older than Carl, Jimmy had completed more years in the Navy. She wondered why; but then discovered he was a graduate of the Naval Academy at Annapolis. She wasn't surprised. She didn't know what he had studied but she guessed his future was set out before him.

The only way she was going to get to Jimmy was going to be through Carl.

She had agreed to go out with Carl and now she was glad she had.

As time would have it, Marsha discovered Jimmy's relationship with Sarah was more than casual and a wedding was being planned. But when she saw Sarah, she thought she had a chance, because in her opinion, Sarah wasn't much competition.

Marsha suggested activities that included Carl's friends. She arranged the rental of a party boat for an outing on the lake, but the minimum needed was six people. "Would any of your friends like to join us?" She asked Carl innocently. And when Jimmy and Sarah were included, she wasn't surprised. She was careful how she came on to Jimmy, careful how little things happened that made Sarah look foolish, and then she came to the rescue appearing like a particularly thoughtful person. She even had an extra set of concert tickets, and of course, invited Jimmy and Sarah.

Later down the road Jimmy tried to warn his friend, saying, "You're not seriously considering marrying her, are you? You can do better, Carl. . ." But Carl could not think straight when it came to Marsha, and Jimmy didn't want to tell his friend about the night at Murphy's when Marsha seductively got in his car and said in a husky voice, "I can't stop thinking about you, Jimmy, maybe we can go someplace and just talk." She looked at him with bedroom eyes.

At first, Jimmy thought she must have had too much to drink, but none of them were drinkers, including Marsha. She hated booze - and boozers. He also never knew her to do any kind of drugs. There was pot around, but their group of friends agreed to wait until they left the military before sampling any part of the local scene. It was too risky with the drug testing program going on in the military.

Jimmy tried to laugh it off that night in the car. "What are you doing, Marsha? You know I care about somebody - and you know my best friend really, really likes you!"

"Oh, do you really think Carl likes me?" she pretended, recovering. "I didn't think I was that important to him, and sometimes I get really sad about it." She feigned a pout.

Jimmy looked at her with an understanding that was not about her words, but about her game. He was playing back. He knew what she was, he hadn't missed the come-on's she'd been making when Sarah and Carl weren't around, but he went along with the game, giving her a soulful look. "No. He really does. I know he does. You're all he talks about."

"Really? I don't hear from him very often and I've gotten the impression he must have somebody else and. . ."

Not wanting to perpetuate the game and clearly wanting her out of his car, he reached across her and opened the passenger door. "I'm very sorry to hear that. I wish I could be more understanding," and gestured to her to get out.

The next time Jimmy saw Carl, Carl was cold to him - and then Jimmy really did understand. Marsha was poison.

Some months later, Carl proposed to Marsha. He'd wanted to ask Jimmy to be his best man, but after the things he'd done, he couldn't have him stand up at his wedding. He understood that Jimmy's Sarah was a plain girl and not gorgeous like Marsha, but he really thought the other man would have had more restraint than to come on to Marsha the way he had. It was that night, in the parking lot at Murphy's, that Julie, a fellow officer, observed Marsha buttoning up her blouse. "She jumped out of the car and ran to her car and it looked like she was sobbing. I thought I should check on her so I did. She said nothing happened, but he tried. She said he wanted one last fling before tying the knot."

"What was she doing in his car?" Carl asked innocently.

"She said she wanted to share a secret with Jimmy. She wanted him to know that she always dreamed of having an engagement ring designed by her uncle - just in case you really liked her. . . and were going to ask the big question."

Later, when Carl was snooping around for a ring, Marsha's mother suspected, and told him he should drop into her brother's jewelry shop - that he designed jewelry." Don't tell her I told you." She said. "Let it be a surprise."

Marsha had covered her tracks, and the fallout was Carl's best friend.

The beautiful Marsha married an ecstatic Carl. He was beside himself with joy.

Carl did get into Dartmouth, and he did have a great scholarship, but Marsha got a job somewhere else with a wonderful hotel group. So Carl gave up his Dartmouth dream.

He knew he could make history come alive for his students in ways his teachers had not done for him, and there was a major university in the city where they were going, so he could go there instead.

But Marsha had other ideas. First, there was a house to buy. She said it was because rents were too high and it would be a good investment. That logic seemed premature to Carl, but he wanted to please her. He explained, going to school was only for a year and they could find some student housing in the meantime, but she wasn't listening. He said it would be difficult until he finished and maybe they'd need to relocate in order for him to find a teaching job, but again, Marsha would have none of it. She didn't want to feel temporary in her new job, she said.

He asked her, "How can we buy a house if I don't have a job?" But they looked anyway while she tried to convince him to go to work. Only finding a job in a college town wasn't so easy, especially with a history degree.

Then he saw the pizza restaurant for sale. He knew he could make a go of it. Carl had learned a lot about food management, a lot about what young people liked, and about waste. He knew that having too much of the wrong inventory on hand, could kill a restaurant. The price was unbelievably low and the location was perfect. He could see why the previous owner had failed. He wouldn't make the same mistakes.

Marsha was lukewarm but they would be able to buy a small home on his veterans' loan and his dad was going to help him with the pizza place and Marsha's job made everything possible.

Marsha had studied the economics of small business ownership while in college - a big reason why she never wanted to own one. She never thought such a thing would be on the horizon for Carl's future when she met him. He'd talked about teaching, and that was bad enough, but a restaurant? Such an idea was abhorrent. She had believed with encouragement from her, that he would get a job or continue on for an advanced degree and choose the university arena for his teaching career. That's what he'd always talked about. She could be quite comfortable being the wife of a professor. Carl already had his master's degree and had served with honor in the military. It was beside the point that she wasn't in love with him. They could have a good life together.

The only problem was, shortly after they were married and getting settled, Carl changed.

"The military gave me a wonderful food service education," he told her. "I can do this. Just think, we can own our own place!"

She was blown over. He had been so excited about it that nothing she said made any difference. She pleaded, she coerced, she manipulated. She did everything she could think of to block such a move, but Carl was blinded by enthusiasm. The good life she had imagined, the summer vacations, the nice salary stream, the house on Blueberry Hill, were all smashed to smithereens.

"I'll have no part of this!" Marsha said, not lukewarm anymore, knowing from the very beginning to steer clear of the place, otherwise she would be drowning in pizza and hours of no-win drudgery. The pizzeria wasn't her dream and she didn't care much about him. He had misrepresented himself!

The few happy weeks at the beginning of their marriage were over and daily routines took over. Marsha was pissed and she stayed that way. At first, Carl was too much in love with her to notice. He was out there, making his mark, hanging on to the gorgeous woman he wanted, while she went to work building her career, telling herself she had made a bad mistake.

She remembered how she had sat at the table, tears streaming down her face, but Carl was so excited about it that he couldn't see her hurt and anger, which most often exhibited itself in devious and silent mannerisms. She told herself, she would keep her feelings to herself. The bastard wasn't worth it.

They agreed it would be "temporary." Marsha couldn't see owning a pizza restaurant for the rest of their life and in reality, he couldn't either.

"There's no money in it, Carl!"

Time came and went. It was a living. Carl was a good manager. The location was perfect and business was steady. He knew how to balance his inventory, and gradually he paid off his father. He was proud to have full ownership at five years. But nothing seemed to satisfy Marsha and she increasingly moaned about wanting a better house. Carl took out a small second mortgage and added a room to the house and a sun porch. His brother came over and helped him on weekends and he did most of the work himself. The pizza restaurant couldn't afford to give her a new kitchen and other things she wanted, but Carl hoped the bright new rooms would add to her happiness.

But they didn't. Nothing did.

COLLECTIVE THOUGHT

The vision couldn't have been stronger or more complete. Tom had stepped into the magic of the theater. He realized his dream visions were all of places he'd either already been or probably would visit sometime in the near future. They were magical, yet they were real. There was all the anticipation he had looking at the curtain and the wonderful image he saw there. Why, it was the Cat in the Hat! Well, not exactly. There was the red hat with the stripes on the curtain and Tom knew when the curtain came up, he would see the cat on the stage. He was very excited.

He was walking silly, reciting some of the lines when he came to the table.

"Imagine that," he said.

"Hello Tom," The Teacher/Guide said amicably.

Tom was glad for the vision and how it had lightened his mood, but the feelings dissipated when he looked at his questions.

"What's up?" There was a note of concern in The Guide's voice.

"Oh, I have so many questions," Tom said," I don't know where to start. Last time left me with more questions than answers. I just kept thinking and dreaming the whole time without any peace."

"Maybe your question is about thought?"

"Yes. My question is about thought. You always know what I am thinking. You keep talking about the power of thought and about not hating. How am I supposed to do that? Not hate?" He asked.

"There is a huge power to collective thought, like it says in the Bible: "When more than one person is gathered in my name.""

"How did you know. . .?" Tom was still thinking about his visit to the church. It seemed like whatever, whoever the Guide, or Teacher or whatever, whoever was there in the room with him, knew everything. Didn't he have any privacy?"

"Human beings are social creatures. We like to be in the company of others who believe as we do. We like to belong. Have you ever been in a small group of friends who like to drink as you do? Maybe a shot of whiskey or two. . .?"

Tom nodded. This was something he could understand.

"The Bill Gates' think tank, or brainstorming sessions, were like that - they were groups of like-minded creative people gathered together with a common goal. Many wonderful, and horrible things happen as a result of like-minded people gathered together.

"You combine this truth with a visual focus, and the power increases a hundred-fold. There is a synergism that comes from a group working together, focusing their creativity and throwing out ideas for the other members to build upon. Creative think tanks use the technique for problem solving or to create new products or systems. Right?"

Tom could readily agree with the example. Just recently he had read about the creation of the Apple computer by a group of guys in a student's garage.

"My question is, what is expected of me in the Universal order of things to be a good person?"

A light ray came out of the center of the blue curtain. "There is more than one set of rules, Tom."

"What do you mean?"

"The Universe has many dimensions, of which we understand very little. You are living in one of them. The Force of God has only a few rules that I can identify. You have been introduced to them."

"What are they? Can you tell me again?"

"Sure.

God is the Force of the Universe.

God is Everything

God is infinite.

Everything is always changing.

Everything is connected."

"That's it?"

"Yes. That's it!"

"Well. . .What does it mean to be a good person?"

"I think you are asking what the rules are for your physical dimension? Do you want to know those? We've covered those too."

"Yes, Please."

"Okay, here are those:

Exist

Learn

Observe

Connect

Act

Respect

Preserve"

"In this physical dimension, you first Exist, then you Learn and you Observe. You look at everything from behind your eyes. Sometimes you realize that, and mostly you don't. You Connect with your world, and if you can, you Connect with Everything. Your Actions impact everything, the ripple effect. Once you understand that, then you realize how important it is that you Respect all things. When you do that, then you will Preserve this world."

"Is that's what it means to be a good person?"

"That's the **rules** for this dimension. Then you have the rules you set forth to govern yourselves as *human beings*, of what you want to accomplish by being here. Right? Then you have rules for the country you live in, etc."

"Oh."

"Can you give me an example of a person who lives by the rules we set forth as human beings?"

"Yes. You have the Ten Commandments, you have what Jesus taught, and one of my favorites was a simple rule that Albert Schweitzer lived by. He had a **reverence for all life.**"

"I will read about him," Tom promised.

"You don't have to Love all things in order to achieve balance in the stream of things, but to **love one another** is something we strive to do here. If you practice the Golden Rule, **Do unto others as you would have them do unto you,** you can hardly go wrong. Also, as you connect, you realize that **Forgiveness** is very important. . ."

"If we focus on visual symbols, especially at the same time, the power of our rules is tremendous.

"I will give you two symbols as examples of power - this will help you in our discussion. The first example, since we have been talking about Hitler, is the swastika. What a strong symbol! This is a symbol people looked at. It was placed everywhere. Consider what it was that people did while looking at the symbol. That power was amazing. Imagine raising an arm, looking at that, and then also yelling, 'Heil Hitler.' The swastika, combined with physical input (raising the arm), sound input (heil Hitler) combined with a sense of belonging to a group, created a huge power, one that some might say even controlled minds. Strong color, red, with that symbol was put into play as well.

"Every group has their powerful images - those that you focus on seeing, and those that you focus on doing. In the Christian religion, there is the symbol of the cross. This is usually at the front of the church."

The Guide stopped long enough for Tom to remember his time in the church, of looking at the cross.

"The cross appears on Bibles, around people's necks, etc. And what is the one that people do? Can you think of movements that are action symbols that people do, that are Christian? Maybe even ones that involve taste?"

Tom realized the Teacher was asking him, because there was silence and he was obviously waiting for a response. He thought about it for only a few seconds before answering. "Well, there are three, actually," he said. "The one that everybody knows is putting your hands together in prayer. Like this." Tom raised his hands and held them against each other, and placed them under his chin in the familiar reverent posture. "Then there is kneeling with the head bowed. Then there is the sign of the cross made by Catholics - a sign in front of their bodies. Like this: Father, Son, and Holy Ghost." He demonstrated the action.

"Yes," The Teacher said. "That wasn't created by accident." The Teacher said. "And that's often coupled by words, the same words each time."

Tom nodded.

"Some scholars felt the symbols were not enough to identify their group and added the stylized fish. You see it here and there on cars and places of business so you know you are encountering a like-minded person. . ."

"What about other religions? Do they have action symbols too? Can you think of some?"

The heat rose in Tom's face as he thought about the images he had seen in National Geographic and on television of people in prayer in the Middle East. "There are visual images of minarets in Islamic countries." he spoke low, as if there were others in the room to hear his comments. "And the way people pray on their rugs, and wash their hands." He said, realizing the power of what they were doing. "The women constantly wear reminders to everybody what their religion is. Their prayer is ritualized and repetitive."

"Yes," said the Teacher. "They belong to a group. The rituals make their faith stronger." That power will kill another six million people."

The Teacher was silent for a moment. Then the Voice said simply. "What do you think of the power you have invited into your living room?"

"What do you mean?" Tom asked. "My living room?"

"Do you think a gun is a powerful image?"

Tom squirmed. "I guess so.

"Well now," said the Teacher, "If I were to just draw a silhouette of a hand holding a handgun, would you know what the intent of that image meant?"

"Yes, pretty much."

"What?" asked the Teacher. "I can't hear you. Yes or no."

"Yes."

"What does the symbol mean, Tom?" The Teacher wanted more specifics.

"Authority. Threatening. To kill, I guess."

"You unthinkingly watch images every day, and in most cultures, we are exposing our children to them unconsciously. Then we wonder why they commit unspeakable crimes? Do you think the crime of gassing Jewish people was unspeakable?"

"Yes."

"What is the difference between Hitler and what we invite into our homes? We are responsible one to another. We can say it is for the sake of entertainment or for protection. Hitler said it was for the sake of the economy. We can make all kinds of excuses for our lack of responsibility, for our aloneness, but the true reality is - we are all connected on this planet Earth. We can say it is for the sake of religion. We can say it is for the sake of God. But it all comes down to one thing.

"It is what is in you. You are responsible for you, and what you do. What you watch, what you say, what you perpetuate. What you allow, unthinkingly, allow into your mind and how you involve others."

Tom got up and went to the window. He shook his head. "No" he said. "No. It's different."

"How is it different?" The Teacher asked.

"Well, we don't mean for our movies and TV to hurt anybody."

"We don't mean it?"

"That's right. Everybody knows it is play acting. It doesn't mean anything." Tom said.

"Does a four-year-old understand that? Does a mind that is floating along really understand that? Or does it just take it in, unthinkingly. . ."

"Well," Tom said, holding his position, "we must explain that it isn't real, that what we are doing isn't meant to harm anyone."

"Oh, like the yellow star wasn't meant to harm a Jewish person?" The Voice asked.

"That's not the same," Tom said.

"No, you're right, it's not the same," Said the Voice. The yellow Star required an action, it wasn't passive. Oh, but turning on the television isn't the same - it's passive. Changing the channel - that doesn't require an action. Making the movie and thinking about all the bad things that went into making that "play" into the story, that required creative thought. . . oh well. . . that didn't require anything - no action at all, right? It was all just passive.

"Thought has power." The Teacher said. "The TV program started with a thought, don't you think? - a creative one at that. And then had to be written down and said and shared - and then even acting out. Passive?

"The next thing was communicating it and putting music to it. Right? All of that creative, powerful work, before it ever got to you, and you were connected to all that goings on, although maybe not in a way that was very strong, you say, . . - and then you invited the whole thing into your home, into your brain, or worse yet, into that of your child."

"It is too big a burden." Tom finally said.

There was silence in the room. Finally, Tom realized he needed to frame a question. "Why is this revelation such a burden?" he asked.

"Because it makes each of us responsible. It was okay when you could blame the criminal, or his mother, or somebody else, but each of us plays a part in this system. We all have a responsibility and every responsibility carries a burden. Some burdens are heavy, some are light. Most of us think we cannot make a difference. Again, there is the saying that implies this: Put your hand in a pail of water and you raise the level of the water, remove your hand, and the level will go back to where it was. The implication is you *can't* make a difference. But you did. The big picture may be too much to comprehend, consider a picture that involves drops instead of oceans, and your part may be better understood. The drops that cling to your hand, because you put your hand in the water, are so very important. You had an effect. Put your hand in the water! The level will never be the same again. The cleanliness of the water will not be the same. Once you realize that you are not the ocean, but you are the drops in the ocean, your burden becomes light, instead of heavy, but you also become more accountable."

"Oh, I see." Tom said, feeling shivers up and down his spine. He remembered his thought by the flag, about being a drop of water. He shook off the chill, it was the feeling of truth that he was getting to know and he wished it wasn't.

"But. . .but. . .we like stories, we like to tell them and to watch them and to win against the bad guys. . .and. . .and. . ."

"Yes," The Guide said sadly," We opened Pandora's Box, didn't we? It is entertainment. And for this, there is a price. We have not understood the terrible price we are paying. It is okay, but it is out of balance. We need to bring balance into our lives, into the minds of our children, into our living rooms. It is crucial. . ."

"There is seldom an apology at the end of a movie, or storybook, for the awful things depicted. An apology would help to negate the terrible result of what has been created. In fact, I cannot ever remember seeing such an apology. Instead, people feed on the horror!

"I will think about this," Tom said rising out of his chair. Then on a whim, as a last thought, he turned and asked, "Is there such a thing as evil? Real evil?"

"Of course," the Teacher answered. "but sometimes evil isn't exactly what you might think it is. It can be something more, or less. Pure deliberate acts against a system may be categorized as forces akin to annihilation. One person can have a thought you might categorize as evil, but when there is collective thought that manifests itself into an entity that has a force of creative, destructive power, that can upset stability, then we might coin the term antichrist, because it is so powerful. In order to understand this unified force, one must understand all that is within it. Evil is but a part. Some might think it is the devil whispering to us to watch television. . ."

"Sometimes something that you view as evil might be nothing more than a traffic signal telling you to go somewhere else. It is signaling a direction that must be taken. It is taking the element of choice away. Because you suddenly did not have a choice anymore, you called it "evil" but in the stream, it was a "direction." There's an important distinction here.

"Was Judas evil?. . or. . .was he just doing something he was compelled to do?"

"Hitler was evil," Tom said simply, then he added.

"So was Judas!"

PLANS

Tom's parents had planned to visit during spring break, but those plans changed - in a happy way; although somewhat melancholy for Tom. His father had a week's vacation from work and his mother planned her freelance work activities around the trip. But their postponement was actually Tom's fault.

It had all started during Christmas when Tom gave simple gifts. He gave his sister Cami a scarf, and his mom and dad an assortment of scratch cards from the state lottery in a Christmas card. Linda opened the Christmas card that had the tickets inside and was pleased with her son's remembrance, but was distracted by Tom's gift to the dog, which was really a gift to his father, because Tom knew his dad would love playing with the dog.

It was a great day. The weather was cold but good enough that they all went outside to play with the dog before coming inside and continuing with the holiday. Tom's parents forgot about the scratch tickets inside the card. The family sat at the table playing games, eating snacks and having a great time for the day and a couple of days afterwards. Then Tom loaded his gifts, (a couple of sweaters, a book bag and a car organizer), into the old Buick and headed back to school.

It was two months later when Linda was straightening papers on Mike's desk that she came across the scratch cards. She opened the Christmas card thinking to read it a last time before trashing it when she saw the lottery cards! She sat down at the desk and scratched off the coverings. At first, she had trouble going back and forth to the winnings list to realize that she really had the hopeful winnings. She had the combination, but then there was an "extra" box yet to be scraped clean and that's when she fell off the chair.

They had won some money with the rows, and also the Grand Prize. A Cruise!

She was in her car in a flash to verify the truth. It was true. The simple had turned into the incredible and the best time of year to go was coming up; and they had the time off already! The dates were synchronized. It was like magic.

It was beside the point that Tom had only given them a simple scratch card. Linda was on the phone with all her friends telling them that her son, Tom, had given them a cruise vacation! Which, technically, he had.

Tom was sitting in the Quad cafeteria eating a hamburger with Chib when he got her call. His mother was so excited she could barely talk so he had trouble understanding her. She had music going in the background and her voice was elevated. He had never heard her so excited or so happy. In truth, he had forgotten all about the lotto tickets and for a short time could not connect with what his mother was saying.

"I'm dancing around the room!" She said, "I've been dancing to surfin USA 'cause we're going on a cruise and I'm going to be snorkeling and swimming in the ocean! And it's all your fault!" She took a breath. "Oh Tommy, thank you, thank you, thank you! You're the best son any mother ever had!"

"Uh, you're welcome." He said.

"I'm sorry." She said contritely," I hope you won't mind too much, but we won't be visiting you just yet." She sang in sing-song style, "We're going on a cruise, we're going on a cruise. - and it's all. . . your . . .fault."

Tom started laughing. He couldn't imagine what she was babbling about, but he was happy for her.

"What did I do?" He finally broke in.

"The scratch card lottery tickets you gave us for Christmas! One of them hit the jackpot - the grand prize, Tom! We forgot about them and I just scratched them off and one of them was the *grand prize*. I just took it in and verified it. Honest!"

"Oh my Gosh!" Tom swallowed, dropping his hamburger on the paper. "I don't believe it!"

"Yes. Yes. They have a ship leaving at exactly the same time as we planned our trip. Oh Tom. The prize is for a suite on a glorious cruise and money too. It's like a honeymoon. It's just right for your dad and me! And it's our 25th anniversary year! Can you believe it? I'm so happy!!"

Tom hung up the phone in disbelief.

Chib hit him lightly on his shoulder. "Well, are you gonna tell me? What's going on?"

"Yeah. I gave my folks a lotto ticket for Christmas, you know, a scratch card, and it hit the jackpot for a cruise vacation. No joke!

"They're not coming for the break?"

"No. They're going to go on a cruise vacation instead." He laughed unbelievingly.

"Soooo, we ought to figure out something to do," Chib said. "I'm not doing anything."

Chib pulled out his computer and set it in the middle of the table expectantly.

Tom, with mixed feelings, picked up his hamburger and started eating again. "Yeah, okay, yeah, guess so."

Chib was the best student in the department, maybe in the whole university. He was Tom's lab partner. At first Tom was put off by Chib and his abrupt mannerisms, which after a while Tom attributed to a cultural difference.

Tom and Chib started chatting about the Teacher as soon as Chib got his time in the zimmer. His discussions with Chib were almost as interesting as those he had in the room. "Where's your evidence?" Chib would challenge. "You have to have evidence."

Tom would say glibly, "Look around." Or he might say "It's up to us to get the evidence. We're the next generation of brains."

They would play a game about what they would be called. "We're going to broaden human understanding like no other. We're the next generation! "We're going to synthesize all of it together. Maybe they'll call us the synthesizers. Ha ha ha!"

"Yeah. We'll bring together genetics and DNA and the big bangs and mini micro dams and other good stuff. huh?"

"Or maybe they'll call us the mobilizers - for moving humanity to where it needs to be!"

Other students would look at them and wonder what all the fun was about, but the jokes were just between Chib and Tom.

"But really, Chib, you can't do anything, be a star, until you believe the guru in the roooom," Tom chided. "He - or maybe she . . ."

"You don't know?"

"No, I don't know."

"Anyway, like I was saying, he, or maybe she, or maybe IT, will turn your comfortable little world upside down," Tom would say.

"Nah, I'll turn his world upside down. He won't know what hit him!" Chib would exclaim. "He's seen nuthin' yet!"

Chib picked up a glass beaker, cupped his hands around it and blew into it. It fogged up for a second. "See. . . there's something in it," he said, "hot air."

"You stupid fucker."

And the two of them would laugh themselves silly while the rest of the room wondered what could be fun about a boring experiment. But Tom and Chib, so different, were alike too. They both liked a challenge.

Tom had been so happy when Chib got a time with the Teacher. It made things between them interesting! He had two meetings just before the spring break.

Chib started calling the Teacher "It" until he could figure him/her out; and the "It" gave the two of them great conversations.

Plans being what they were, subject to change, the two of them would be hanging around during spring break. Chib would have been around anyway, with nothing to do, and Tom would have invited him to meet his parents, but that hardly filled the time for a foreign student.

"You know," Tom said, pulling Chib's computer closer," I was on the bike path - the Hi-lo path a couple of weeks ago, and I thought it would be nice to go on a bike ride. We could go for a ride, do an overnight somewhere, find a cheap place to stay - maybe a bed and breakfast place?"

Both boys had good bicycles. They were on a budget and that kind of trip wouldn't cost much. And so, the planning began.

Chib, always meticulous, printed out their maps. They would ride 70 miles each day, stay over two nights and be back on the third day. They called their trip the Mobilizer Champs en Tour. They divided their duties. The plan was in place. They'd leave after a couple of days into the break.

But right now, they still had finals to worry about.

MARSHA

Marsha made one of her sharp comments again. It wasn't that she wanted to quit working. She didn't. She only made comments like that to Carl so he'd appreciate her. He was taking her more and more for granted, as if her monthly deposits into their joint checking account was more of an expectation rather than a joint effort coming from the two of them. It was true that Carl put in his share, but he never wanted to talk about how they were moving towards a joint goal, nor did he ever celebrate her abilities. Her end of the year bonus was twice the amount she expected and actually much more than the amounts given to other employees, she was certain about that, but Carl had barely even noticed the large check she had proudly put on the dining table back in January.

"Aren't you going to deposit that?" he'd asked.

"Yes, of course. But I wanted you to see it first." She said proudly. "To see my bonus."

"Oh my gosh." He said, kissing her. "That's great." Then he continued into the kitchen, going straight for the freezer where he reached in for a popsicle. "You want one?"

"No thanks. It's too cold out to be eating a popsicle."

"They're still good, and no calories to speak of." He started licking the popsicle, which she found annoying. "What did you do today? Anything interesting?" He asked, sitting at the table.

"I landed the Baldwin contract." She said.

"That's good, baby. I hope they appreciate you! You've been bringing in the business regularly. I swear, you bring it in every week!"

Marsha blinked. Her bonus check was for five thousand dollars. Maybe Carl hadn't really seen it, or the amount of the check, although the $5000.00 was in big red letters. She considered the check to be very appreciative.

"Carl," she said softly. "Of course, they do. Look at this." She picked up her check and ran her fingers over the amount, showing him. "This is enough for us to have a very nice vacation don't you think?"

"Yes. Yes, it is." He said, embarrassed. He had misread the check for fifty dollars and now he was flabbergasted to see the real amount. "You're worth every penny. . .and more." He exclaimed. "I'll be curious to see what you decide to do with it."

"Wha. .? Yeah. . ." she said, "yeah," realizing that something was different about Carl. His normal attitude of watching every penny was sounding different. It wasn't like him to be so free about money. It wasn't that he was grasping, that wasn't it. He watched the ebb and flow of cash in relation to his business - much of which was dependent upon the university schedule of events. She continued to be pissed about the direction Carl took with his "career" and the satisfaction he seemed to derive from it.

The problem of the pizzeria and his decision shortly after they married and his "once in a lifetime" opportunity still hung in the air.

"The military gave me a wonderful food service education," Carl liked to remind her. "I can do this. Just think, we can own our own place!"

He had been so excited about it that nothing she ever said made any difference. The good life she had imagined, the summer vacations, the nice salary stream, the trips to Hawaii, had never materialized.

Marsha kept the promise she'd made to herself to steer clear of the place, to never be drawn into its intrigue. The pizzeria wasn't her dream.

There was something about the conversation that left her empty, but her marriage had always been like that. At first, Carl was too much in love with her to notice her ambivalence. When he asked her about her work, she never believed he was very sincere. He was always fooling around with the receipts from the restaurant.

The last year had been a good year for them both. Marsha's vacation time had been increased now that she had more than five years in with the company and her sales team were bringing in high-end clients. Not only did she receive an end-of-the year bonus, but she was getting regular commissions each month, something she wasn't sharing with Carl.

As for Carl, his business was booming. His three "star" employees were bringing in more customers than he had ever imagined. So far, he hadn't rewarded them in any way, and they didn't seem to need it. They were bringing in a boatload of tips. They seemed happy enough and actually were somewhat oblivious to how valuable they'd become to Carl.

It would not be a problem at all giving the "Stooges" time off during spring break. The town would be dead, business would be slow.

Or so he thought.

SIXTH SENSE

Tom felt the wind come up as he trotted briskly trying to beat the rain. He and Chib were waiting for the storm to pass before starting on their bike trip.

Tom didn't understand a thing about the door. When he'd discussed the phenomena with Chib, thinking his friend was experiencing it too, Chib had looked at him like he was crazy.

"You're losing it Dude," Chib had said eying Tom like he was some kind of freak.

"Well, how do you get in the room?" Tom had persisted.

"I open the door. I knock first, open the door, and walk in."

"How do you open it?"

"What do you mean? I turn the knob, dumb ass, how do you think?"

"Do you have visions, though, when you first enter the room?" Tom persisted.

Chib just hung his mouth open. "You're one strange Dude, Tom. I mean there is that crazy drape thing, but that's about it."

It was clear their experiences were different, very different.

Tom stood once again in front of the door. He knocked politely and tried the knob. Nope. It was fast shut.

He didn't like what he was feeling. His face smarted. Why was it up to him to open the door in such a strange way? He wondered.

He looked around. Nobody was in the hall.

What am I? Somebody with special powers, or something? He knew better. The only time he could do anything unusual was with this door. He had tried to open the bathroom door in his apartment where nobody could see him. He spent minutes upon minute trying to make it open with his mind. Of course, nothing happened! And the vision thing - that was weird too.

Tom never had visions before coming to the room or powerful dreams either.

He kept standing at the door, and then it was like a voice was talking to him in his head saying," Well aren't you going to come in?"

Tom wondered if he could make something really big happen if he tried really hard. He looked up and down the hall again. Nobody. He stood far away this time. He visualized a car speeding down the hall and careening into the door and smashing out the door and some of the wall with it. WHOOSH!

There was no noise. He hadn't thought about a noise, only the car and the hole. It seemed funny to see a hole without a noise. There should have been a huge crash.

There was no crash, but the aftermath was huge. It was just as if a car had smashed through the door and wall!

It happened! He wasn't imagining it!

He daintily tiptoed through the hole, acting silly about it and noticing the gap was disappearing behind him.

"Oh yeah," he exclaimed with pride. And then no sooner had he uttered those words than a vision was upon him.

He was drifting over a parched landscape. He was in a kind of balloon-type contraception that was floating low to the landscape. He was with Chib who was at a control panel, like some sort of wizard, his black hair long and flowing this way and that. He turned to Tom grinning. "WhooHoo," Chib exclaimed. "It's working!" The two of them were having the time of their lives, but this was clearly Chib's show and Tom was along for the ride. . .

There was a kind of electricity in the air, almost an ozone sort of smell and Tom could hear a huffing kind of noise. It was strange, like the opposite of Twenty Leagues Under the Sea.

He was still breathing hard from the exhilaration he felt in the balloon thing when he came over to the table. The room was different somehow. He looked around and then peered through the window trying to see if there were openings between the clouds. There were none. The sky was densely clouded over. He was distracted.

The room had a shimmering quality to it. It felt like the entire room was breathing - huffing, like in his vision. He couldn't figure out where it was coming from, couldn't seem to find a source, yet it seemed so natural. He shook it off and took a seat.

"Hello Teacher," he said. "It seems different here today."

"Good afternoon Tom, "The Voice said good naturedly. "I was wondering when you would notice."

"When?"

"Yes. Actually, I think having a darker day was necessary for you to see it."

"Oh." Tom said lifting his voice questioningly." I certainly do see something. It shimmers, actually."

"Yes, it does." Teacher said," All energy, be it light or audio, or a person's energy, has movement. Humans haven't developed the sense to detect it very well. I think we can feel it, but we haven't defined that sense yet. We have only just defined the basic surface senses so far."

Tom didn't know where he was going with this, but knew, like all things in the Room, the Teacher would have words that contained a revelation.

"How many senses do you think we have?" Tom asked.

"Several, but right now, we are limited by three things," the conversation started. "First, we are limited by the perceptions of our physical body, - we have been taught about this since we were toddlers - 'don't touch that - it will burn you!' Yet, make no mistake, we are more than we think we are. We have our spiritual or psyche self that resides in the shell of our physical body. Strangely, we are not teaching ourselves about the various parts of what we are, which includes far more than just our physical body - we need to learn to perceive more to our existence. We don't even know how to teach it, because we don't even understand what we are! If we were able to reach beyond words and demonstrate to each other how energy translates within our fields of energy, how our colors intersect and what can happen with areas of our knowledge merging - which of course we don't even know about, it would be phenomenal. We would learn things instantly and be able to give knowledge to our children with immediateness."

"Do you mean we wouldn't need to speak audibly anymore?"

"Maybe. We are still very physical Tom. We are in a dimension ruled by matter. But, we simply could add another marker - one that says we are residing in this dimension while being part way in another. . . to our. . .um. . .place mark. . . so, to speak. Our voices might become like a homing beacon or maybe a guidance system that say, for example, could function like the energy of electrical currents or the hot stove, and then it would become energy intersecting energy, before ever reaching our physical bodies.

"We could impart knowledge in another sense yet unknown to us, but still one that is very real. Do you understand? I'm talking about energy to energy, like a wave length an instant before it is heard. Sometimes you may have noticed a disturbance to the very air, the clear air, by heat, and how it disturbs that air, but we usually shrug it off. Or sometimes we will observe an after image of somebody after they have left the room, or where the place was where they were occupying a space before, again for only the slightest of a microsecond. These observations are somewhat visual and physical but they give you an idea of what I'm talking about. Sometimes it is a memory thing, sometimes it is something else. On occasion we call it Deja-vu because we don't know what it is. So, of course we are limited by our physical beingness.

"Second, we are limited by a lack of measuring devices to prove the theory. We can prove how much a person hears, sees, smells, tastes or what their sensory acuity is, as with a pin prick, but as yet, we haven't determined a way to measure some of the other senses. So, a definition is lacking for some of the other things we sense.

"Third, we are severely limited by something I call bombardment. It is like a person who is twenty years old and hears for the first time. They are bombarded with sound, with noise coming from all directions, from everything all at once. The brain has to learn to prioritize. We don't even think about this, because our brain has learned to do this from the time we were born. We have been prioritizing everything involved with our senses from our first encounter with life here, and education has helped us do that. We learn to see a series of marks on a page, that to the untrained eye are unintelligible marks, and we put them together to learn to read. We translate sounds into language and music. We develop preferences for taste and smell, but it takes experience and repetition. But, because we lack the conscious awareness of senses beyond the big five, our prioritization needs some help. We need more education, like everything else. Who or what is helping us?"

Tom could "feel" the Teacher looking at him and sat up straighter. "Some people can see things," he mumbled.

"Yes, I know." She remarked. "I am not speaking about what we call psychic ability or other things people see. That puts us back into the sense of sight. It's the same with hallucinations. There is a very big difference between hallucinations and what I am speaking of. Hallucinations are things people think are real but aren't." Tom could actually perceive her smiling, "The detection of fields of energy are things people perceive but think they are not real but they are real." She laughed softly, and the laughter became like pearls of water cascading around the room and making the shimmer effect more apparent. She cleared her throat gently and continued. "People perceive God a million ways every day but think God is NOT real, but of course there is nothing more real than the God presence all around us and in us. Some members of our animal kingdom know the reality of God better than we do."

Tom was quiet. He could sense her smiling and thought to himself, "the Teacher is on a roll today." And then he wondered how. . .how could he sense that she was smiling?

The instruction continued. "We have a term also, to explain the phenomena when there is truth and the circumstances and actions seem to come out of someplace, we cannot explain. We call it intuition. We think it is supernatural or something. How crazy is that? That is just as crazy as hallucinations.

Many people have saved themselves from harm because they felt the hackles rise on the back of their neck. They felt fear. They didn't see fear. They didn't hear fear and they didn't actually feel fear. It was something else. What they felt intersected their existence and they paid attention to it. Intuition is a term we all know, but we really don't consciously know how to bring it into play. It is just with us. Hmm? It just kind of happens to us."

Tom studied the single painting on the wall and thought about the few times he attributed an action to his intuition. There was once when he was eleven that he knew there was danger. He and the Miller brothers were playing at Johnson's Bar, a water hole down at the river by the bridge. It was a hot summer's day and the boys had gone down there for a swim, just as they had done many times before. There was nothing dangerous about the area. It was called a river, but it was really only a creek in the summertime. There was little current and the deepest place was only waist high, but it was fun and cool.

All three boys were in the water on their inner tubes when Tom got something, he called it a "hunch." Without even thinking, he yelled out to his friends, "We have to get out now - hurry." There was no reason for it but there was something about his tone that made them act quickly and they scrambled out of the water. Seconds later, a car came careening around the curve leading to the bridge and the car didn't make it and landed in the water squarely where the boys had been. The frightened driver climbed out of the car and was okay, just shaken up a bit as he explained that his brakes had failed.

Tom was remembering it now, as he had many times since. The Miller boys told their parents that Tom had saved their lives. But that was crazy, it had just been luck. Just luck? Now the Teacher was describing an event that he'd never been able to explain. The boys would have been badly hurt, perhaps even killed if they hadn't acted on Tom's "hunch."

"Yes," Tom said strongly, "I do know what you are describing."

"Well, this thing, intuition. . . it does just kind of happen to us, doesn't it? Like our other senses that happen to us, such as the smell in a room. Maybe that is part of the definition of what a sense is - is that it just happens to us. But with the main senses - those we have defined; we have an amount of control over them. Right?

Well, Tom was thinking now. "Yes," he said. "But I'm not sure what you mean. Control?"

"We can shut our eyes. Right? Or we can block our sense of smell by plugging our nose. We can numb our mouths so we don't feel pain. . ., etc.

"Now let's go further into this." The Teacher said. "Think about this now, Tom. When we satisfy one of our senses, it brings about great pleasure, or it can bring about great discomfort! Right?"

The room had one of those silences Tom had come to know so well. It was always silent while he thought about something. Now, he was thinking, in a very male way, about the sense of touch. Yep, there was great pleasure associated with that one. But then a person can really get hurt too. Next, he thought about taste. Yes, that could go both ways too, from the body rebelling having tasted something awful, to the pleasure of candy. Sight was the same way. He was enjoying the glow of the room, yet, if he looked directly at the sun, it would be painful. And of course, hearing would be at the head of the list with the new music releases. But it could be really bad if the volume was up too loud or standing next to a chainsaw. A person could even lose their hearing! Then he thought about intuition. . .What was the test of good and bad? Yin and yang? He couldn't think of one, except that intuition could be true or false, he guessed. Maybe that's why people didn't believe it half the time.

"Teacher, I see your point. But I don't see a yin and yang to intuition. How would a person measure intuition? We could call this a sense, but it is kind of inert. You know?

"Precisely." There was a satisfying sharpness to the Teacher's retort.

There was silence again. It was as if the Teacher was waiting for something. She was.

It went on for a very long time, until the Teacher finally said, "What is there about the detection of energy that could be yin and yang, Tom? Let us say intuition is based on a type of energy. . ."

Tom didn't know. He didn't answer.

"What if a person was placed in a vacuum and positive energy was applied, not the kind to make a person's skin crawl, but something pleasant. Like the energy we might perceive as love. I don't mean touching, I mean just a loving condition, or atmosphere, by way of lack of words. And then what would happen if an energy were to be applied akin to hate? Do you think a person would have a reaction to that?"

"I don't know." Tom answered. "I don't know that such a study has ever been done. I don't know. I don't know. . ." He said lamely trailing off.

"Do you think the condition of loneliness would be inert?" The Voice insisted.

"NO."

"There's been studies of that." the Teacher chided. "People die sooner. . .much younger when they are lonely. Why do you think that is?"

Tom thought about that." Everybody needs love and companionship."

"Yes."

"Our physical senses serve to keep us alive," the Teacher continued, not letting up. "Our sense of thirst, hunger, smell for food safety, hearing as in danger, sight to find food etcetera, perhaps to find a mate; touch, again for safety as in whether or not something is too hot. But there is something else we have yet to define, and it is very important. We may call it a sense of longing, because we don't know what else to say. If we can find this, it will help unlock a key, one of unspoken communication, one that will help us recognize God around us, one that will calm our questioning soul. It is the one that lets us know we are far more than just this physical shell. Perhaps, Tom, you will be the medical professional that will measure this sense, define it and give us a way of enlarging upon it? It is the one that reaches out and connects us to Everything."

"And so, what is that. . .this sense that connects us to everything?" Tom said, tired of the Teacher saying everything again and again. In an effort to steer away from it, he said, "this thing about longing is very real. We keep trying to make contact with alien beings in the Universe - hoping we are not alone." Tom mused. "I guess that is why we do that. . ."

The Teacher laughed abruptly. Then the entire room seemed to change into a jumping cacophony of silliness beyond description. The uproar wasn't just sound, but also images and tilts and Tom thought he was going to fall off his chair. He couldn't help himself as he hung onto the table's edge. He joined the fun. He was laughing too. He couldn't help it, the laugher was contagious.

As it died down, he waited, certain the Teacher would explain, but this time, it wasn't the Teacher, it was a movie in his head that seemed to provide the answer as to why the room had reacted.

In the movie there were many creatures, all from Tom's life. There was his dog and then a stray cat that came to the door for a handout. He saw the birds on the wire outside his window. and the little jumping spider that he'd put out the door. He could see a kind of glow that connected all of them with him. He could perceive a kind of vibration that he was sending and using to communicate with each one and actually experience them - and them with him. He understood that it didn't involve sight, or sound, or anything he had known.

The vision disappeared.

Tom sat very still.

"It is absurd for us, the way we are trying to communicate in such a slow process with other beings," the Teacher said. "When we understand what we are and what they are, the process is instantaneous. We do not have to use the speed of light, or sound, unless we have a need to be audible. As you know, the way we communicate has its flaws.

"Here we are, reaching out trying to communicate into the galaxy instead of right here with all these wonderful beings that we share the planet with! Once we start unraveling more, then we will have less isolation!" He laughed, suddenly in a more companion-like way, instead of the Teacher's formality.

Tom realized he had been holding his breath. He thought about his vision and chalked it up to wishful thinking.

"Tom." Then again, "TOM!" Another Voice appeared, an It, and the new voice was irritated. "Put your ego self aside please!"

"No, you don't know everything." Tom pouted. "You can't."

"Listen. Your grandfather used Morse code. He used it for the fun of it to communicate with other ham radio operators throughout the world. Think about it. A series of dots and dashes. People were so proud of the accomplishment - then. And after that came the telephone with wires. And what have we graduated to now? Antennas. We now have cell phones we carry with us.

"What makes you think you are anywhere close to understanding how everything, everything, works?

"Just imagine some of the science fiction books that were written about clones. That wasn't so long ago. What did you think when you read about that when you were ten years old? Huh?"

Tom smiled remembering the book he'd read, sitting in his tree house, fantasizing about a kinky science that could never exist. He gazed at the drape. There was something behind there that knew he had read that book. He wondered what it was. Whatever was back there, it could reach into his mind, read it, feel his emotions, know his secret thoughts, even when Tom himself had forgotten about them. He shuddered but at the same time he didn't feel afraid.

"Everything we are," That new Voice continued, "all that is, has a place mark, an identity. We are temporarily limited by our physicality - our brains. We are as the ocean, poured into a tea cup. When we leave our physical dimension and enter into the next one, that part of our address changes. Ha ha ha. A forwarding address."

Although there were instants that Tom had felt uncomfortable in the room, he liked the way he felt sitting in it. He liked the things he learned by being here. There was a feeling of comfort it contained, which today he attributed to the light, although there was something almost unseen about it. That thing called atmosphere. . .maybe he would add that term to intuition.

It was time for him to leave so he rose from his chair and looked out the window. The day was still gray and overcast. He had forgotten that. He looked back around the room, his eyes wide in a very childlike way. It was still light and airy, almost sunny, yet no lights were on.

Tom thought again about the yin and the yang of the other senses, whatever they were. His thought enlarged, and he went deeper into his thoughts. He was like a dog following a scent. What were these other senses? He wanted to know. What was the yin and yang involved with them? He could understand intuition; but what were the two sides of it? He stood there trying to think. "Why is it hard to think sometimes?" he said out loud, although he didn't mean to. And then he realized the other senses he was trying to discover were not really involved with his brain.

He took a deep breath and went inside himself and tried to move his brain aside, tried to stop thinking, tried to become fluid. He visually pushed his eyes going inside himself to his braincase and pushing the area where his brain was kept. He pushed and made himself quiet, and quieter. He slowed his breathing. The yin and yang startled him when it came. There was a fullness, like he was a vessel, and there was an essence occupying every crevice of his being. He felt it. And then something so strange happened; he had an awareness of having no borders, no boundaries. He was everything.

And then he felt a boundary.

And then. . .Intuition.

And then a boundary again.

And then intuition. . .and he realized intuition had *no boundary.*

He understood he could not call it up at will, but something could reach out and communicate it with him. If he let it. He understood the yin and yang of it – boundary and no boundary.

"Do we have Guardian Angels?" He asked.

"Of course."

All of his experience disappeared and he was normal, just standing there gazing out the window. He turned away from the grayness of the day, back toward the glow of the room.

"What does our discussion have to do with the light in the room?" He asked, because that is where it all started on this chilly dark day. "Why is the room so light? Where is it coming from?"

"Why Tom," The Voice said softly, "the light is coming from YOU."

INTUITION AND SUSAN

Susan didn't answer Tom's call that afternoon. He thought she might be on a voice call so he sent her a text, and when that didn't get an answer, he assumed she was on her bicycle. It wasn't unusual, especially since spring break had just begun.

Susan had told him she was going to catch up on "all the things that had slid into the never-ending pile under the laundry."

He hadn't been able to go over to her place, between work, tests and getting ready for his parents' visit, but everything was different now that his parents weren't coming. He had called her right away to tell her about his folks' big win, but hadn't gotten an answer. He wanted to ask her for a real evening date. His job had been interfering with things he wanted to do with her, like asking her to a concert or a movie.

A feeling he had trouble describing started to nag him. He had his own chores to do, a few things to get ready for with the bicycle trip and his own pile of laundry, but as he collected his belongings, something akin to a bothersome itch began to dance across his neck area. He reached up and rubbed his neck laughing. Then it spread wide, across his shoulders, almost like a chill. He ignored it and sat at his desk for a few minutes looking at Chib's map, but the feeling persisted. He shrugged it away.

He carried his laundry downstairs, and then on a whim he'd never be able to explain, set the stuff in his car and rode his bike over to Susan's apartment. She wasn't there. He stood there stupidly. But then he had that feeling again and it reminded him of the earlier discussion with the Teacher, about when people had "hackles rising on the back of their neck." It was like that. He stood still and felt it, trying to listen to what it was, trying to ascertain what was creating a disturbance in him, or on him or through him. He wasn't sure what. He felt the little hairs on his neck, along with the bigger ones on his head. They weren't normal. Susan wasn't there. But where was she?

Her place felt deserted, abandoned somehow. He could see her things through the window and everything seemed normal. But then he saw her bicycle. So what? She often walked instead of riding her bike, and if she was doing laundry, she would have carried it to the next block Laundromat.

He pounded on her door. Nothing. He went to the neighbor's and pounded on their door. Out popped a kid of about eight years old who seemed to be living there, which was surprising since most of those apartment places didn't allow children. "Hey junior," he said to the boy, "What's up?"

The kid, irritated at being called "Junior," looked at him and blinked.

"Hey," Tom said, wagging his finger threateningly, "where are your parents? Are you here alone?"

The boy tried to close the door, saying nothing.

Tom quickly stopped it from closing with his foot. "I'm okay," he said. "I'm not going to try and come in."

"Get Away! You can't come in here!" The boy raised his voice louder, screaming, "Get out, Get away, HELP!"

He knew he was scaring the kid and held up both his hands but kept his foot in the door while the kid kept slamming the door against it, trying to get him to remove it.

"Hey, you better talk to me kid." He said forcibly, but with a convincing tone. "Might start by telling me what's up with you."

The kid dropped his insolent air. "Nothing's up. I'm just hanging out at my brother's place. What do you want?"

"I'm looking for your neighbor." He said, removing his foot. "Have you seen her around?"

"Nope. Haven't." He said slamming the door in his face. "Haven't seen her for days." He yelled through the shut door.

Tom tried Susan's door again, wishing he had kept her key. "Susan," he called out. "Hey Suz." Then he dialed her phone. No answer. Again. He looked around to see if that kid was watching. He knew how to open a door with a credit card, and although Sue's door looked a little more secure than that, he gave it a try. Nothing. It was secured with a dead bolt. He started to walk away, then turned back, and said, "Oh okay," as if he was talking to her. He leaned in close to the door and pretended to be apologizing to her about something the night before, in case people were watching, and focused his thoughts on the door. Nothing.

He understood his thoughts were divided and he needed to think only about the door. He tried again. He focused, mentally seeing the door coming unlocked and slightly ajar. The door sprung open and he was in.

He sprinted to the bedroom. Susan was unconscious on the floor, her cell phone in her hand. As he ran to her, he thought at first, she was dead, but then it registered to him that she probably had too much color for a dead person, at least that's how it seemed. He picked up her arm and it was lifeless, but there was a slight pulse and he could feel some breath on his hand. "Oh Sue, what's happened to you?"

He called 9-1-1 on his phone. He always had the impression that things happened very fast on a 9-1-1 call. Wrong! He kept saying to himself, "hurry up, hurry up. She's dying!" It seemed to him that the call was slow and laborious. The person on the other end wanted to know details and he didn't know anything. "Just come, Please. Just get here. Help.

"I don't know," he kept saying, and "Please . . . and. . .Oh please."

There wasn't anything that Tom knew to do, except position her so she could breathe easier. Her breathing was so shallow!

He tried to remember when it was exactly that he'd last spoken with her. It was during the week sometime. She said she was going to the library to study - that the neighbor's music was bothering her and she needed quiet to prepare for a final. She still had one to take.

He hoped the two of them would hit it off, but they were slow in moving forward. It felt right.

Finally, two men and a woman showed up. They were carrying gear and moving fast.

"How long has she been unresponsive? When did you discover her?"

They quickly placed her on a gurney and moved her out.

Tom was next to her, at least trying to be, trying to hold onto her lifeless hand, but they scooted him out of their way. "Sir, let us do our job."

"Sir?" He said under his breath, and then realized they said that to everyone.

"Can I ride with her?"

"Are you family?" One of the men asked.

"Almost," he answered. "I'm her boyfriend."

They hesitated and then motioned him to get in. "He'll know something about her," one paramedic said to the other. "We should let him come along." The University hospital was only a mile away.

"Is she diabetic?"

"No." Tom answered. "Not that I know of. But she had surgery a few weeks ago."

"What for?"

"A burst appendix."

"OH!" It was like something they needed to know had been answered. They were looking at her abdomen. Whatever seemed on slow motion now was on fast forward.

They were on the radio, calling in an emergency. Speech was urgent and clipped. Tom heard it and he didn't. It was crackling and he wondered why they weren't just using a cell phone instead of a radio, because of course they all had cell phones and the reception was probably clearer and easier on a phone. Tom glanced down at the phone still in his hand.

"Not secure." A voice said. ". . .a cell phone is not secure."

The comment didn't register or make sense to Tom. The only thing that made sense to Tom was that Susan was unconscious and he was sitting in a screaming vehicle and then he thought it might be kind of hard to use a cell phone with all that noise from the siren and how would a person know if they had someone on the other end and. . .and. . .Tom did understand one of the things being said on that radio. . it was a word, the one thing he could get from craning to understand their terms - it was the word, *infection.*

Tom realized the enormousness of Susan's situation as soon as the ambulance doors were thrown open. There was an urgency to every move. There was none of this waiting in the E.R.

Nobody asked Tom who he was. Nobody cared. The only thing they cared about was what he knew. "Where did she have her surgery? How long ago? Did her wound open up with aftercare?"

Tom remembered she did take a spill on her bicycle a few days ago. No. He couldn't remember how long ago.

"Where is her family? What are their names?"

"No, I don't know." He answered. "Well, yes, I am her boyfriend." He only told them that to assist in the process, but he really wasn't her boyfriend. He hardly knew Susan. He came by to check on her healing process, to help her and see how she was doing and just to be friendly.

Tom thought of himself as a friend, although he could see something more looming in their future. She'd only said something about her family that one time in the hospital, when he first went to her room - that she hadn't wanted to trouble them.

Tom felt helpless - inadequate. "Is she going to die?" He asked.

"Maybe. We hope not. If you hadn't found her, she would have died. Soon. Has she been sick? Vomiting? For how long?"

"Yes." Tom said. "She thought she had the flu a couple of days ago and told me to stay away - she didn't want to give it to me.

"Does she have the flu?" Tom asked.

"No." The examining doctor said. "That's a symptom of her infection. Her wound is red. She probably thought it was from an injury from her bike fall. She's critical. It's a miracle she's still alive. . .but. . ." the doctor's voice trailed off as she looked at Tom. It was the look that scared him.

"There's nothing you can do," they said. "We're opening up the wound area. . . it has to drain. She's on I.V. antibiotics. It would be good if you can obtain information to contact her family." Tom could see her abdomen now - it was distended.

Tom had never been in a hospital with a sick person before - except when he visited Susan's room. But he didn't see her sick. She was perky and, on the mend, when he met her before. This was different. Here, in this place, he was seeing an area where people were being treated. He was behind the scenes, and now, they wanted him to leave.

"You shouldn't be in here," a nurse was saying. "Come with me."

He sat in one of the waiting areas and pulled Susan's cell phone from his pocket. Maybe he could find some information about her family in it, but it was dead. He was shaking it, like it could come back alive, when a nurse came up to him. "Not to worry," she said. "We found family information in the university records. I've contacted her mother. You've been so much help. Do you realize we would not have known who she was without you? We were able to contact Mercy and that saved time getting her history and other information from them because of what you knew."

They told him there was nothing he could do, and since he wasn't family, he couldn't stay in the room with her and they couldn't give him updates on her condition, so he'd just be sitting out there with nothing to do and feeling stupid. Something about the HIPAA Privacy.

He left the hospital and stopped for a beer on the way home not wanting to be alone. One of the nurses gave him a tip on how he could get information about her. "Ask for her 'location' in the hospital, that you want to visit," she told him. "If they say they can't tell you that, then it is time to worry, but if they tell you, then she is better. It means you can visit her. We can give you that information - it isn't about her health."

Tom sat at the bar. He considered ordering something to eat because he hadn't eaten since that morning, but he decided he couldn't. Even though Susan was not really his "girlfriend" yet, something in him knew, positively knew,

. . . she was the "one."

WHEN I DIE

Tom decided to keep his appointed time for the room, even though they were leaving on their trip in the morning. They'd postponed it by a couple of days because of Susan's illness. In fact, Tom didn't want to go on the trip anymore and wanted to cancel it, but when he saw the disappointment on Chib's face he quickly changed his mind, saying it wasn't the trip he wanted to postpone, but the ride itself because he was in such "bad shape." This caused Chib to go on a long harangue about the merits of going on the trip to get in better shape and that the two of them should lengthen it by another day. There wasn't anything more he could do for Susan anyway and the ride would do him good. Susan was on the mend and he didn't need to worry anymore that she was going to die.

"Hey good buddy, she's going to be okay. Let's go." Chib said convincingly.

Tom stared at the ever persistent "door." He cleared his throat and said words this time along with his thought. "Open," he said. There was no response. Aggravated, he said it again, "Door, I command you to OPEN."

Nothing.

Tom stood there feeling stupid, his usual feeling when standing in front of the door. He decided to try the knob just in case. It never moved and today was no exception.

"Damn you," He said to it.

The door turned an angry orange, as if it was mocking him. Pissed, he tried the knob again. It was hot and almost burned him.

"This whole thing is straight out of a science fiction movie," he said, blowing on his hand. "This makes me cr-a-zy." But he looked around, saw another student and waited until she disappeared through one of the doors. Then he stood back, and audibly said, "Clear."

He concentrated. "I'm gonna blast you to smithereens." He muttered and saw a stream of fire coming from his solar plexus.

The door ignited, but that wasn't all. The fire alarms in the building all went off. People streamed out of offices. Tom ignored it, knowing it wasn't real and stood waiting for the fire to go down so he could step into the room.

"False Alarm," he said to a couple of students hurrying by. They glanced at the door and he wondered if they could see the dying flames, but they didn't seem concerned.

"Oh," they said, slowing.

Tom stepped through.

He was instantly at the top of a hill with Abbot. They were on their bikes.

"The first one to the bottom gets to light the fire."

At the bottom of the long hill was a culvert. The race always ended by veering off to the side and hitting the edge of the pipe with either the bike's tire or a foot.

The wind raised Tom's hair and he felt exhilarated as the bike gained speed.

Later, he and Abbot rode into the campground at the local park and rode up to a fire pit. "I've got hot dogs and potato chips." Abbot had said earlier. "Can you bring the buns and other stuff?"

Abbot was Tom's best friend. He'd received a scholarship too, but not as good as Tom's, but it hadn't mattered, since Abbott wasn't interested in Physics anyway. Abbot's scholarship was a general one that he could use anywhere and he'd opted to stay at home and go to State. Abbot was interested in computers and information management.

Tom's destruction of the door using fire had probably prompted his vision with Abbot. He was still lingering by their camp fire roasting marshmallows as he stepped further into the room.

Tom knew exactly his question for the day.

"What happens to us when we die?" Tom blurted, more than asked.

"Hmm, I was wondering when you would ask that one." The Teacher/Guide mused. "I think you have skirted around it actually." The Teacher paused, then said. "Not a lot."

"Not a lot?!"

"We will still be who we are." The Voice said. "Is that what you really want to know?"

"How so? How do you figure that?" Tom asked.

"Just because you leave your body behind doesn't mean you are not you anymore. When you changed your clothes last night, did you stop being you? No. You might have changed how you related to your environment, because you changed from school clothes to pajamas, but you were still you. So, when you die, you will see things differently, experience things a little differently. That's all."

"Duh." Tom said sarcastically, then, "yeah, that's for sure. . .a . . little differently. Do expound on that one!" Tom could hear himself, almost like an echo coming back, and he hadn't sounded very nice. "Oh, I'm sorry - I'm not being very nice, just a little upset right now. . .but I really do want you to explain."

There was a space of silence, like there often was, but it was more than that. There was just enough time to allow for change to happen, for something in the air to dissipate - to disappear, so the words of the teacher could then fill the space and be understood. Tom began to think of it in colors. The space between the colors was neutral and important. The colors of the words swirled and needed to disappear and fully dissipate so there would be a purity to the next set of colors - otherwise there could be a mixture that would be muddy, and that might influence the colors of the next thought. He understood the space. He told himself he would remember this principle during a disagreement. He believed it would be the only way for both sides to be fully appreciated - to allow that space.

When the space was over, a lyrical Voice, one that he hadn't heard before, began. "We all exist on a vibrational level, for lack of any other way to explain it." This new Voice said. "We're not sure, on this plane, how to measure ourselves on the next plane since we are used to measuring individuality physically. We have made some strides with Pheromones. But mostly, we've looked for physical evidence of who we are, like fingerprints, retina scans, voice recognitions, and such, but in reality there are other ways that more closely resemble who we are, that are not physical - such as our wavelength, for lack of a better description, that is unique to each of us - and this is absolute. It is a combination form.

"I will give you an example. I'll start with the sound of middle C. Keep in mind, I'm giving you an example only." The Voice stopped talking for an instant, then said. "Do you want me to continue with this?"

Tom was interested. "Yes. Yes. Please continue!" He sat up straight.

"Okay, so let's start with the sound vibration of middle C. It is the easiest to relate to since we all seem to be able to register that sound and hear it in our mind, but I'll make the sound anyway." The Voice made a hum of Middle C. Tom understood the reason for the lyrical Voice. It could sing. "Then let us pretend we are describing a person we shall call, Vincent, and Vincent has an overtone of B-flat 3, which is the black key, a flat, immediately below middle C." He sang the C with the B-flat together. "That isn't our favorite, but when it modulates, it isn't bad. Like this." Then the Voice added the B-flat in a modulation and it became more interesting.

Tom wondered how a Voice could make that sound. He recalled going to a performance of a visiting troupe from the Japanese Kabuki Theatre. They could do very interesting things like that with their voice.

"Now, listen to what happens when we apply volume, and intensity, like this:" The Voice demonstrated. "Then we must add something like an E-flat 3, which is lower, slightly off-center flat, entering and modulating at a recurring speed of 3/5ths times the basic tone."

The Voice demonstrated something that Tom had never, ever, heard before and he knew that no human voice could ever make that sound! He wanted to say something, ask something, like, "How are you doing that? No human voice can do that!" He wanted to ask again, what are you? But he knew, this was not the time to say anything, but to listen.

The Teacher waited for Tom to synthesize what he was hearing, then continued.

"Add to this a light frequency, that takes into account where you belong – your "home" in the Universe along with an intensity factor that has to do with your rate of change and it too may modulate. The atmosphere in the room changed slightly. There was a time when Tom couldn't have perceived it, but now he could feel it . .see it even.

"Finally, there is another factor that is added to this mix - and that has to do with Vincent's physical plane right now. Let's say Vincent is on Earth, and so we can assign an "E" to the mix for the physical attributes that are assigned to Earth's matter, but this is not your identity, only your plane of existence right now, like where you are on a step ladder - it places you into this system. That "E" modulates and has intensity factors too and it has given Vincent his right to exist at this address called Earth. That "E" is temporary and is not Vincent's identity, but is more like a costume. The tone receded and seemed to dance against the walls.

"It is almost like. . .well, it is hard to explain. . .but maybe think of it as almost like. . .um. . .gravity."

There was a knock on the door and a student stared into the room.

"Vincent, it's not your time yet," The Teacher said," You'll need to wait in the hall."

"But. . ."

"Yes. I know There's a mix up, thirty minutes off. Very sorry. Thank you for understanding. Come back in thirty minutes."

"Uh, Okay." Vincent backed out of the room quietly, "I'm so sorry."

"Don't be," Tom said sucking in air, lots and lots of air. "No worries at all."

Tom sat there, and sat there, and sat there.

The more familiar Voice of the Teacher interrupted his space.

"Let's continue with your lesson. Okay?"

"Okay." He said shakily.

"It is just like being a cell in a body, that cell cannot be in another body, it can only be in Vincent's body, although we are learning how to change its marker. It has a marker that tells what kind of cell it is, what body it belongs to and how it functions. The fact that the same kind of cell is in everybody's body doesn't change its identity. It is in Vincent's body - it's address belongs to him. It is a particular kind of cell, belonging to Vincent.

"Okay, let's make this something we all know and understand, shall we? We each have our marker, our V (Vibrational level), I (Individual overtone, or tone modulation), B (Belonging - place), E (eternal change factor, in this case, Earth). That is what we are. Our VIBE. It is what you are, what I am, what your dog is, what the birds in the sky are. You can die Tom, but it doesn't change what you are, or what I am. It doesn't change your VIBE. Your connection with God remains the same, has always been the same, will always be the same. This is where we have such difficulty with "after" life experiences. We are trying to measure what a person is by two different standards, instead of ONE. The only thing that changes is something akin to taking off a pair of jeans. *You can't measure change where change does not exist.* So, let's say you die. YOU didn't change. Your pair of jeans did. It is easy to see what happened to them!"

The Voice paused for effect. The color was a bright yellow-orange and it didn't change until both Tom and the Voice laughed. Their laughter turned the color lighter and lighter until it merged with the regular atmosphere of the room and became as nothing. "Yeah, nothing." Tom said.

"Your physical body, that I have compared to jeans, changed. It died. End of story. You left the physical body that you are wearing. Using the analogy of jeans, trying to measure a pair of jeans in comparison to one's identity is a bit lame don't you think? That is how our scientific community has been trying to measure afterlife. Comical, isn't it? Right now, that is what we are trying to do. We are using the pair of jeans as our baseline, when in reality, it is the other way around. We just don't know how to measure the real you - yet. When we do figure that out, then it will be very easy to prove after life. Maybe too easy. It might be that a lot of us will want to bail out, but there was a reason we put on this pair of "jeans." The Teacher stopped, and then added (with an amount of speculation that had not been present before),"It may be necessary for us to utilize the physical plane as a tool to assist with the change factor that is necessary for us on the other plane, like eating is to survive here.. . . so, we have no choice, our VIBE undergoes some amount of change during our life, a natural growth. . .for the next plane. . ."

Tom's physical life: Tom=VIBE/m   Tom after death=VIBE (the matter, that was his body, is removed) but the "E" remains until it is replaced with something else, like "S" for Saturn, or some address like that. . . .

"So, your question right now was/is," the Teacher continued, "What is going to happen to you when you die? Right? Well, you are already connected to your place in the Universe, of where you belong. Right? So, you are already here." The Teacher was smiling and Tom could feel it. He smiled back.

Tom waited. He wanted the space, waited for the space - to be. Just to be. He understood the necessity for it.

It was all too interesting to say a word. He needed to absorb.

After the space, he started scribbling in his notebook as fast as he could.

"So, I could say we are going to go back home, except we are already connected to home." The Teacher said. "What happens to you when you die is you take off your physical clothes and you become more aware of you - your home and of yourself. That's all. That's it. That's what happens to everything else around you too. It's no big deal."

"Do you really think that?" Tom said almost hysterically. "NO BIG DEAL??!!!"

It was the words, "No big deal" that brought on Tom's sudden reaction. It was a very big deal when his dog died and it would be a very big deal if Susan died, and someday when his parents would die - no matter how natural that might be - that will be a huge BIG DEAL!!!

"No Big DEAL?!! It is too. It is. It IS TOOoo!"

Tom raised his arms up to his head and ran his fingers through his hair and scratched his scalp while the silence of the room registered his outrage.

It took a while before calm was restored.

"I see," came the methodical answer." There is a difference Tom, between loss and what happens when we die." The Teacher, who had been a **he**, now became a **she**, and she reached out to him and hugged him with her words. "The loss is not permanent." She said with an infinite kindness. "It is not forever, and the change is smaller than you think."

"We are all connected to God and each other. All things. Your dog and you. . ."

Tom interrupted again. "How did you know. . .uh. . .what I was thinking. . .? About my dog. . .?"

The Teacher ignored him and continued. "We're part of what God is. . . always have been, always will be. We belong in a way that we don't see, understand or perceive right now. I don't know why we don't know it. But nothing is going to change what we are. I can't tell you why this is hidden from us, except whoever thought that a pair of jeans was advanced enough to know these things? Really now. We put on a pair of jeans to wear for a while. So what? What did we expect from them? To last forever? How come we expect the pair of jeans to know all this?"

"What happens when we die?" Teacher asked. "Nothing. I don't mean you are nothing, I mean you continue. That's it. That's all. Nothing happens. Your jeans will fall off of you. Where you go first, will be determined by what you did. You have to be in balance before you go to the next place. We talked about that. There is a stream connected to our physical, material dimension that is a bridge dimension that balances all connections with this material one. Once there is balance then you'll go somewhere else."

"If you did something stupid in Upstate New York, you might be detained before you return to your address of home, Eh?" The Teacher explained.

Tom felt as though his chair was melting into the floor.

Finally, Tom felt righted again and managed another question. "So, what is heaven then?"

"Heaven is simply a term assigned to a dimension that does not have the physical properties of this one, which means, it does not have our perception of evil, which also means our perception of good. Since good and bad as we know it, have been of our making, our human making, then it is safe to assume the condition of good and our perception of heaven, exists here. However, there may be reasons to visit other planes of existence, and a whole new set of rules will exist there. Good and bad as we know it here may be different somewhere else."

Tom decided he didn't want to think about that one. "I guess there is no answer for that, is there?"

"Jesus gave us some guidance about what to expect." The Teacher said.

"Oh. My understanding from the Bible is that heaven is going to be physical and we resurrect and all that. . ."

"Well, you can put on another pair of jeans, Tom, and it might be an upgrade. You may graduate to another physical plane for a time, but be assured, that will change too. Whatever you think your state might be in heaven, it won't be permanent. Eternity cannot exist in stagnation. Neither can you."

Tom's head hurt as he tried to think about all this.

The Teacher continued. "So, you are connected to your home place while at the same time you are physically living breathing and conducting yourself in this system, the physical dimension. It is just like you get in your car and you go for a visit to another city. You are still connected to your home in the city where you belong - to your address where you have decided to live, even though you are presently visiting upstate New York. You return to your address where you live when you are finished with your visit. You take it for granted. If you have an accident and something displaces you, you may not get back for a while, but you still have a home, that is, if all things are in order.

"If everything is not in order, you may take a detour (such as being jailed for drunk driving). I'm just using this as an example. We're not talking about other things like homelessness here, etc. - only the principle of leaving a place and returning to it or having an address. I cannot give you a demonstration of that, because to do so would be extremely dangerous. It is physical in character. You are connected to your home place through a vibration that doesn't let go of you. Ever.

So, together, this is your "fingerprint" your marker that says where and what you are in the Universe, it says how each of us belongs in our particular place. Nothing can change or alter this. However, we can take a detour before getting back to it. Like I said, there is a balance that must be reached. . . Right? Hitler must be accountable to those he wronged. He will balance out the consequences experienced by every one of those people he touched. Is that hell? There is no such thing as "escaping," Tom. We always, always, must balance what we have done."

"That means," Tom said thoughtfully, "that we must balance the extraordinarily good things we do too, doesn't it? Just like the bad things?"

"Of course. Your experience includes everything, good and bad - everything from your existence that caused a ripple effect. You will experience the ripple affects you created.

"We make our own hell, Tom, and that may be far worse than anything imagined, because it isn't a punishment meted out or handed down - it is the one we have made unto ourselves. Likewise, heaven is too. Those things that have rippled out from us to effect change, to bring about a positive condition, we experience too."

Tom gasped. "What about being sa. . . . .uh. . .being. . .saved." He had trouble getting the word out loud. It had taken on a sudden importance to him so he could hardly say it.

"Saved. . .Saved from what?"

"Saved from our sins." Tom said.

"Oh, you mean when Jesus saves us, in a church?"

"Yes."

"Well, Tom. I believe I can tell you what it doesn't mean. It doesn't mean that the things you have already done disappear, or vanish from the world of consequences. The action and consequence from whatever the sin you did has already occurred. You may not have experienced all the consequences of your actions - all the ripple effects of what you caused - because you yourself were constantly changing. You couldn't see the big picture. You were busy being you. However, during the space that occurs after your life here - that breath of space - you will then understand - do you know what I am talking about. . . ?" The Teacher merged into yet another Voice and paused.

Tom nodded. He had come to understand the space concept, or the silent, pause concept.

The Voice continued. "Well, during the space, or limbo, that is when the actions and consequences of a person's life are experienced."

"But. . .but. . .what about being saved?"

"I was getting to that."

"Okay. Sorry."

"What does it mean. . .saved?"

"For some, Tom, it means a limit of the physical realm of the "E" of our address and an assistance in how balance occurs. The law of action and consequence cannot be escaped, but the human definition of good and evil, of course, belongs to the "E" and we can and do leave it. Jesus gave us help, a formula for rectification, or balance so we are not caught here - experiencing it again and again. We are able to lean on him and accept our shortcomings and forgive ourselves so we can do better. Forgiveness cancels or helps put our life in balance so we can go on. . . Right? Forgiveness does that."

"Yes. So, it is important to be saved."

"Hmmm. Yes and no. It depends on the person. It is important to understand the power of forgiveness, of love and compassion. Jesus can perform the act of forgiveness when we, or others cannot."

"Forgiveness. . . .?" Tom looked at his hands and a strange pall hung over the room as he tried to think about what was being said about forgiveness. He thought he knew. Had Chelsea forgiven him?

"Oh Tom, what about forgiveness? Forgiveness does not absolve any of us from the deep sadness of what we have done to hurt another. It doesn't change the ripple effect, or the hurt that we initially caused.

"Being saved is mostly about the perpetrator. Forgiveness is mostly about the victim. When a victim forgives, or moves on, and no longer harbors ill will toward the perpetrator, then a limit has been placed upon the consequence. We call that grace. Real grace. A perpetrator can try and save themselves from a consequence, but they really cannot do that. It is the victim, or the forgiver, that does that. Action and consequence. Jesus steps in and forgives when a perpetrator asks for it, or asks to be saved from the consequence of their action, and this assistance will help us in the balancing, but all of us will experience the ripple effect of what we have done in our lives."

"Have you learned the answer you sought?" The Teacher asked.

"Somewhat. I am not going anywhere when I die except to where I have always been." Tom said.

"Not exactly," the Voice said." Ha ha ha. Who knows where you will go next? It is a grand adventure! What I said was - you will always be you."

"Why am I so afraid?" Tom asked.

"We have our sense of fear precisely because we think there should be a big change upon death and we are very fearful there won't be. This gets a little complicated, so follow me with this. I have been talking about the knowingness that we all have, Right? That knowingness has been telling you that your identity will NOT be changing. Yes, it will have changed - have learned, we are always growing, of course, but not like other aspects of ourselves - I am talking about identity. Id. You. Understand?"

"Yes." Tom said.

"Our physical, logical brain is telling us there must be a change, a BIG change because for our brain, there will be. It will cease to exist. The computer will no longer exist. There won't be a need for it.

"We are really scared nothing is going to happen - that we will be annihilated along with our brain and physical body. Wrong. Something does happen. We just leave the physical behind – our brain. *Nothing happens to us.* But our brain ceases to exist. Our physical brain doesn't realize that our identity merely continues. Our continuance is the opposite of nothing (what pair of jeans would know this?). Oh my gosh, we say to ourselves, nothing is going to happen to me and that means . . .the end to the me I have known while I experienced the physical me . . . and *I thought that was the real me.*" The Teacher chuckled. "See? Your physical self wasn't the real you! Yes, I know, it was, but it wasn't!"

The silence tingled.

"Nothing means everything????"

"Yes." The Teacher said in a whisper, ever so softly, "you think you are going down with the jeans, but that is only your physical brain telling you that it is going to do that! Not you! On the identity level you know you will still have your identity, you have always known that, you were born knowing that, and that is the reason why you have fear. That is why you are so scared about death. Because nothing is going to happen. You are scared nothing is going to happen and you want there to be all kinds of things to happen, bells and whistles to save you. But you don't need that to happen - you are just going to drop off your jeans! What will happen is like this. . .you have an ocean, and then you have a paper cup of ocean water bobbing in the ocean and after a while the paper cup dissolves. . .and then the water in the cup becomes part of the ocean again, like it always was. Kind of. You just don't remember where home is, that's all, because you are still connected to the jeans, still identifying with them. You have to quietly realize that you are not your physical brain, and that right now the part of you that is perceiving this system does not perceive the real one. You just left the real one temporarily, for this experience."

Tom nodded, but he still couldn't grasp the full meaning of what the Voice was saying. "But my brain is me," he whined.

"You really think that?" The Teacher laughed cynically.

"The brain learns from its environment. But you, the You of You, have brought something more into your physical existence - into this system, so you must realize it is up to you to teach your brain about you."

"Teach my brain?" Tom said too loudly, then again moderating his volume," Teach my brain?"

"Yes. There is a part of you that can teach your brain about who you are. Some call it the soul." She smiled, then continued.

"So, you have your identity marker - You, yourself, are YOU. You always will be. You continue to be you and you will experience more of the real you than you did when you were covered up here as a human wearing your jeans. Right? So, that's what death is. Nothing. It is nothing. You do not die. Silly. We are scared that nothing is going to happen, that we will be nothing, instead of saying hallelujah nothing is going to happen!"

"Oh shit, oh shit." Tom said softly. "My brain is going to die and I thought there was going to be an end to me!"

"Nope. Your identity knows more than your brain, because you'll be tapping into all that is and you'll know so much more. The physical plane is limited. Ha ha ha."

The room filled with the softest of laughter and it was like the tinkling of many bells, all ringing together beautifully and in perfect harmony. There was a shimmering in the room again, but different than any Tom had seen before, and it matched the sound of his laughter with that of his Teacher's and a million tiny rainbows filled the space and he was being supported and carried along on a magnificent silver wave. He knew he had learned the truth. He lost the feeling of time and space and there was no room anymore, no Teacher, no question. There was only the answer and he was part of that answer. How long he floated like that he could not say because it was something he could never be able to put words to, it was something beyond description.

Slowly, and ever so gradually, Tom became more aware of his surroundings. He was able to feel the table under his hands and the chair under his body. He could see the blue curtain with the figure on the other side and the windows as they had always been. There was the campus with the sun starting to peer in between scattered clouds of a mostly overcast day. He saw some students walking between the buildings and he felt connected to them, really connected for the first time.

He took up his paper, smiled and said. "Thank you, Teacher." He held the notebook closely to his chest. He didn't remember leaving the room, but recalled greeting Vincent in the hall. He remembered how hard he hugged the notebook, and felt it become moist with his sweat as he walked along thinking about death. What death?

He would remember that day, it would be in his dreams, it would walk with him and remind him that he truly did possess a "soul" and that his soul was something a little different than he thought it was and now he understood what some philosophers were trying to describe. The soul of him was truly him, his identity, his ID, his Everything, his connection to all that IS. His brain was not him, his brain would be his tool, to control to think with, to use. Nothing would control his brain again, except him. He would learn to control his thoughts and to control that brain in his head because now he fully did understand that his brain was not who he was/is but was his body's computer, his physical self's modulator. He, Tom, was occupying a physical body that would die, but he would never die. Death was a myth. Death was something that only applied to his physical self - not HIM! He laughed again softly and then with a mystery to the sound. It was one of the best days of his life. Yes, his life.

He went home, to his apartment and marked that day on his calendar. That day became a new kind of birthday for him, a date he would always remember as a special day - a day that he truly was born, not "born again" that was not an idea he subscribed to anymore, but the day that he found himself, he found out who and what he truly was - and yes, the Teacher had been right all along. God is Everywhere, is Everything and I am part of God and God is within ME.

He would never be afraid of the cloak of death again. He would never see an animal as a "lesser" creature again. Now he understood that he was an identity merely wearing a "cover" similar to a pair of jeans for whatever reason. That cat or dog or ape or whatever it was having its experience, was just like him, wearing a cover of something, and they too were connected to everything, just like him.

He would never have to be afraid again. Of anything.

He skipped and hopped and danced.

He would forever see the world in an entirely new way.

Yes, he would.

SUSAN'S BOYFRIEND

Tom stopped at the hospital on his way to work that evening. Susan was out of critical care and had been moved to a regular room making it easier for him to wander in and say hello. He didn't need to explain himself - that he was the "boyfriend," which he wasn't, or try to pretend that he was a family member, or something akin to that. He was just Tom, a friend.

Her door was ajar and there was a woman sitting in a chair by the window with a magazine on her lap. Both of them were asleep. He thought about quietly backing away when one of the hall doors closed, ever so quietly, but it still brought the lady by the window to full alert. He guessed she had been waiting for a doctor.

She looked at Tom and quickly surmised that he wasn't the person she'd been waiting for and her body slackened.

Tom put a finger to his mouth in the universal language for quiet and backed into the hallway. She glanced at Susan and tiptoed over to the door and both of them moved out and down the hall to where they could make introductions. The woman introduced herself as Judy, Susan's mother.

Her first words were, "thank you."

He in turn found himself hugging her and saying, "I'm just so glad, so glad. . .it could have been. . .awful. I think she is going to be alright now."

She leaned back. "Is she?"

"Yes. She is going to be fine."

"Tom?"

"Yes."

"You saved her life!"

And just like that, the ice was broken, but there never was any ice, just two relieved people.

From that time onward, Tom was always going to be Susan's "boyfriend." It was like a destiny thing and there was nobody and nothing that could be done about it. It was just going to be.

When Tom went to work that night, he was more subdued than usual. The conversation with Susan's mother, though not long, had been thoughtful and sympathetic. They had gone to the cafeteria but they talked mostly about Tom, because he hadn't felt very comfortable talking about Susan without her being there.

Sometimes her mother started veering off, sharing events from Susan's childhood, but Tom always managed to bring the conversation back around to the university. She seemed confused that Susan and Tom were not really in a relationship - yet. To everybody else, the two of them were bound to one another.

Tom stopped by the hospital again the next morning on his way to meet Chib. It was 6:45 am, but morning rounds at a hospital were always early so he knew Susan would be awake. Even so, he was careful when entering her room in case she was able to sleep through the morning noise. He peered around the door and saw she was sitting up drinking a cup of coffee.

"Is that real coffee?" He asked good naturedly, marching into her room with a newspaper, much like he did the first time they met. "Don't you know caffeine is not good for you right now?"

They both laughed. She was feeling better.

"Hey, where can I get a cup of that brew?"

"There's a coffee station in the visitor's lounge down the hall." She said.

"Did you sneak down there for it?"

"In plain view."

"Chib and I are going to do it." He said.

"You will positively freeze to death!" She eyed his outfit. He wore elasticized pants and a long-sleeved T-shirt.

"No worries. I have a fleece with me. Besides, real men don't cry." He glanced down. "I have my bike shoes downstairs. I'm taking these too, for when I'm not riding." His second pair of shoes were one of the few luxuries he had in his small pack.

"Call me. Send me photos along the way - every day. Please." She begged.

Tom kissed her. That was all that had ever been between them, and this kiss was like the others. There was no romance to it, no fever, but it had another ingredient, something very special.

"You know, it's like I've known you forever," She said. "I've never felt so comfortable with another human being."

Her room smelled of antiseptic, a smell that seemed to permeate the entire hospital. It was familiar to Tom and he didn't know why.

"You know it's funny," he said, walking around the room, "I feel comfortable here, like I belong here or something. . ."

There was a plastic sleeve at the base of her bed that had a chart in it and he pulled it out. He looked at it, reading. "I can't understand it, but the act of pulling it out was familiar." He shook it off. "You know, a kind of deja-vu thing. . ."

"The Teacher says there are no accidents," She said smiling. "You just saved my life."

"I'm glad they finally have you in a regular room," he said embarrassed, changing the subject.

"I better go. Chib is meeting me on the path by the Quad. I'm happy your mother is here. I hope she likes me."

"Of course, she does. You saved my life." She repeated.

"Gotta go." He smiled backing out of the room waving, and turned to walk briskly down the hall.

"Thank you," she called out, "for saving me. . ."

Chib was sitting next to his bicycle, a metal coffee cup in his hand. It was clear he could fit the cylinder into his bottle holder on his bike. He was using it to warm his hands.

"It's a cold one," Tom remarked.

"Won't be, once we're working our bodies on our bikes."

The bike path went alongside the campus and then veered away from it, crossing through town and then by the river. It was created from an abandoned railroad route. Organizers raised money and paved it for thirty miles. The two boys rode alongside the first ten miles, until it narrowed. At nineteen miles, they got off the path and went to country roads leading to their first destination.

Tom had bike shorts under his pants that gave him extra padding for his seat, and he'd added a gel-top to his seat. Still, the hurt of a bike seat had him half standing already by lunch time. He was grateful for their first break. The two of them sat gingerly at a fast food table, and howled. "Ouw, ouw, owuwee."

Tom pulled out his phone and snapped a photo of Chib, then one of himself. He sent Susan a text with his photo. "having lunch."

They stopped to rest along the way, hoping to see something of interest, but there wasn't much. They searched around an old cemetery where a person might find arrowheads and they stopped along the river bed and scouted for agates but came up empty handed at both places.

They finished their first day's ride before 4:00 pm.

Tom had reserved a cheap motel in a small town. The place wasn't a booming spot for travelers but it did have a small cafe and a gas station where they bought a six pack of beer. Exhausted, they ordered take out, drank a couple of the beers, watched T.V. and fell asleep before 8:00 pm that evening.

It was sometime during the early morning that he knew he was dreaming, but it seemed so real.

There was a line of people waiting outside and they were all so sick.

"You can't come in here," he said to a bald man pushing a cart with a person lying in it under a light drape. "You have to wait outside."

The pusher said, "I must bring him to you. You are the only one that can help him." He gestured to the cart.

Tom turned to a bowl of water that had been filled from a pail. He didn't have any running water. His hands and wrists hurt from washing so many times in the chlorine water and pulling gloves on and off that were too tight. They hadn't been able to get gloves that fit his large hands.

"There are many sick people ahead of you," he said kindly.

The bald man nodded, stood his ground. "He is your reason for being here." He said in a soft voice. "There are no accidents in your life."

Tom pulled the drape back and woke up.

His hands and wrists hurt. It was still dark outside. He turned to see the clock and saw two eyes looking back at him.

"You're awake too."

"Yeah," Chib said." I just had a dream that woke me up."

"So, did I. It's that damn beer. Gets to ya every time." Tom said getting up.

"I'm so sore. I don't want to move." Chib said mournfully. "Would you bring over that plastic trash can so I can pee in it?"

"Lazy ass." Tom muttered hobbling to the bathroom. "Too lazy to piss. I always knew that about you."

"Not just me. . .you're too weak and feeble . . .and selfish. . .to bring over that trash can. Fucker."

As Tom finished peeing, he could see the outline of Chib in his bed. He leapt on top of his bed and started bouncing over his friend exclaiming, "Bale out, bale out, bale out," until Chib finally slithered to the floor.

Chib was laughing so hard he could barely cuss, but he did, a whole stream of expletives. "You shitting fucking ass hole piece of used toilet tissue. . .

Tom, who had also arrived on the floor in the jostle, said in his straight-man style, "I thought you had to go pee. I was just helping you out."

"Break my bones is more like it." He said hobbling away grunting and groaning to the bathroom. "It hurts to move."

"It was your idea." Tom commented.

"No it wasn't. You're the ass hole idiot that talked about the bike path."

And so it went. They laughed for another hour before getting back to their dreams. "Do you remember your dream?" Tom asked.

"Hell yes! I was like a space cadet. Had on a uniform and everything." Chib giggled. "I was driving a huge dirigible, you know, kinda like a blimp, and I was over an arid region, like a desert, maybe Ethiopia. It was hot and sunny. The blimp thingy was hanging in the air, moving a little bit, floating there in the sunshine. You were there too." He snickered. "Though you weren't doing a damn thing. I swear, you are a lazy ass, even in the dream! You were just looking out the window while I was doing all the work!"

"Do tell more, Chib!" Tom encouraged, extremely interested.

The top of the thing was covered in solar film, collecting power from the sun and the interior of it was busy converting the power, you know, a bunch of thermodynamic shit, and guess what it was doing?"

"Sucking in air! And huffing and puffing!" Tom said.

"What!? How in the hell do you know THAT! It was MY dream!" Chib made a huge sucking noise and Tom doubled in his bed laughing.

"That's ALL I do know," Tom said. "What's the rest of it?"

"And then, and then, that blimp was compressing and squeezing air like some kind of living fruit, into high pressure, and then, and then . . ." Chib made some kind of huffing noise that made the two boys howl even more.

"and then. . . and then . . .what?" Tom asked through tears. "Did it fart or something?"

"Sure did. The big machine farted all kinds of baby farts through a zillion, jillion jets out into the air! Nasty liquid farts!"

Tom stopped laughing.

"I was sprinkling the fields in Ethiopia with water." Chib said choking hysterically. "The process squeezed moisture out of the air. It compressed the moisture out of the air. Ha ha ha ha."

Tom laughed over the mental image of Chib driving the huge machine in the sky, but the laugh was different this time.

"I was this crazy scientist rain-maker just sauntering along in my rain-maker machine, sprinkling the fields. Ha ha ha. But what I was doing was huge and it made a lot of water. And. . . and the water was clean. Really, really clean. Ha ha ha. The machine took the pollution out of the water. Ha ha ha!"

There was silence there in the dark. For a minute, Chib thought Tom had gone back to sleep, but Tom was floating somewhere and he wasn't asleep.

"What was your dream Tom?" Chib finally asked.

"Well first, let me say, I saw your blimp thing in a vision in the room." Tom said, a chill going through his entire system as he lay there.

"I think in principle, it can work." Chib said. "I've been working out the energy conversion process, and it stands to reason that all air holds moisture. The problem is simple, It IS a matter of squeezing moisture out of the air. A person doesn't have to have clouds to do that."

Thomas had always thought Chib was a genius.

"What was your dream?" Chib asked, "But you ought to know that I never have any visions in the room."

"Mine wasn't any fun at all, Chib. I was in a place like Ethiopia too. I was a doctor and I didn't have any running water and I was washing my hands in an awful bowl of chlorine and putting them in tight gloves that didn't fit!" Tom started laughing and Chib too. Now that the dream was over, it seemed hilarious, especially after the one that Chib had. "I woke up on top of my sore hands and wrists, from riding yesterday. . ."

"Yeo-ohhh, mine hurt too! My butt hurts, my balls will never produce a baby, my back is on fire and I can never finish an experiment at a bench again, and it is all your fault Tom!"

Tom farted.

The next night, Chib asked Tom," Do you think you might want to study medicine? You have to go to graduate school in any event. You'll never get a job with an undergraduate Physics degree. You could apply and see what happens."

"Nah, my grades aren't good enough," he answered. "Besides, I haven't taken any of the pre-med stuff."

"You have one more year. You could take something this summer. Wouldn't hurt. You have four years. They'll let you take graduate stuff during the summer, I bet."

Tom ignored him. "Where do you think you'll try and go, Chib?"

"Harvard."

"What?! But that's not the best place for an advanced degree in Physics! You know that. Why are you talking like that?" Tom asked.

"In my country, having a degree from Harvard is everything. I didn't get in as an undergrad, so maybe I can get into their graduate school. I'm so ashamed."

"You are talking foolishly, my friend. You're the best student in the whole university! You can get in anywhere. You can get a wonderful fellowship. You can go to a program that is doing great stuff and Harvard isn't the place - not in Physics. You have to follow your dream - of what you want to do. Harvard is a wonderful school but not for a rainmaker!"

On the third day of their ride, the landscape warmed under a sunny sky. It seemed like wild flowers were popping out of the ground in minutes. There wasn't any traffic on the back-country road and it was rolling with gentle hills and their ride was glorious. The soreness of their bodies seemed to vanish into a gentle wind. It was exhilarating.

When they arrived at their stay for the night, it was at a small family-owned place that had a restaurant with four rooms attached. The owners were friendly and welcomed the students. It was the perfect ending for a perfect trip.

The owner's daughter, Cece, shyly served the boys and asked about their studies. Chib, who never talked to anybody except Tom, warmed immediately. "My friend here," he said, "is going to be a medical doctor; and I'm going to work on some of the world's problems with water."

Cece smiled at Chib and said, "I have a special interest in water too, I studied hydrology at the university, but I had trouble getting a job. I thought I could get a job with the Forest Service, but it hasn't happened yet. So, I'm helping my parents out right now."

"Really?" Chib was interested.

Tom slunk down in his seat. He'd never seen his friend interested in any girl before. Tom soon excused himself saying, "I hope you don't mind, but I'm going to photograph the flowers and send some photos to my girl. She's been in the hospital and I want to cheer her up."

And with that, Tom disappeared.

Later, when Chib entered the room, the two boys talked about futures that included more than career goals. Chib wanted a career woman, a person with interests similar to his, a woman interested in traveling the world.

Tom just wanted Susan.

WHY?

Tom met a few more students who attended sessions in the room. He already knew Vincent, Susan, and Chib. When they talked, he always asked carefully about their experiences upon entering the room, but none of the others seemed to have any involvement with the door, or any strange visions. They were always interested in hearing from Tom, but he never revealed the true extent of his experience.

He was troubled by the door. He knew of no other way to get into the room, except through that door. He had to apply a thought process to the barrier. Every time he asked the Teacher about it he got the same answer.

"Because it is important for you."

Tom understood it had been crucial when he needed to help Susan, but he never revealed to anyone what had actually happened.

On this day, Tom felt defeated. He didn't want to try and open the door with unconventional means anymore. He just wanted it to open gently, like a normal door. But when he tried it, it wouldn't open. So, he sucked in some air and puffed it out nice and easy, thinking about the huffing of Chib's contraption.

The door obliged.

Tom relieved, walked through, half expecting that the vision experience would bypass him.

It did.

Then he was sorry. The visions were usually nice.

Tom thought of himself as a methodical person. He could sit still in one place and just think. But today any observer would think of him as an agitated person. He walked first in one direction and then another, pacing and fooling with his fingers like a squirrel peeling peanuts. He didn't sit down at the table or by the window or even at the end of the room. Finally, he just leaned against the wall.

"What's going on?" The Teacher asked concerned. "Are you going to be sick?"

"Going to be. . .going to be?" He said, raising his tone. "I already am!"

"You can call it off for today." The Teacher said calmly. "It isn't required that you be here. It's okay."

"It isn't that. I'm not that kind of sick. I couldn't sleep at all last night. Every time I try to sleep, I wake up again thinking about the futility of it all. Honestly, there is no answer." He bounced his head against the wall, making his point, and then let it rest there. "I'm so tired - tired of thinking. There is no way out. We are all rats on little wheels running on two feet instead of four, going around and round and we cannot stop and get off, we just keep going around and round. . . that circle you are always talking about!" He paused, sputtered, and continued half spitting his words. "I guess I should have said treadmill? Yeah. That's a better choice because we are human after all. Aren't we? Aren't we lucky?"

"Tom. . ." Teacher gasped at his sarcasm.

"Why." He said simply, not even making the word into a question, just a long and exhausted, "Whhyyyy." trailing off into silence.

"You're a physics major," Teacher started saying softly, "you know that some things cannot be answered - that 'why' is not the question."

There was silence in the room now. As the silence grew larger the room became smaller. Tom felt like the room itself had a breath and it had stopped breathing and now it was closing in on itself, and him, like in an Edgar Allen Poe story. He put his hands against the wall thinking it must be moving, and he wanted it to stop, and it wasn't going to stop, because it wasn't the room at all. The effect was coming from Tom.

He looked at the ceiling and was surprised because he had never looked at it so closely before. It was quite lovely and appeared to open into something else. Tom tried to see where, but he couldn't quite focus on it. He became dizzy and thought maybe it was an illusion and he vowed he would check it out once he sat down. He pushed harder against the wall; then he bent slightly and brought his hands to his head and leaned into them like he was cradling himself with a headache.

"Why?" He asked again, looking now at his feet. "That IS the question!"

"That is the big question for you, isn't it?" The Teacher said.

"For everyone! Isn't it?"

"Not for everyone, Tom. Some people just accept the why, and they wonder about other things."

"Like what?" He looked up.

Tom's face was red from looking up and down. He was red too from lots of sun on his bike trip. His hair had grown longer than usual because the haircut he'd planned hadn't happened - he'd been too busy - and he didn't care anyway. But he had listened to the teaching of his father that morning - and shaved.

"Why are we all here overpopulating the Earth. . .?" He demanded. "None of it makes any sense!"

"You are asking questions you cannot answer. When you are doing an experiment, you answer the question for THAT experiment - not for ALL the experiments in the book. You must answer the question of why YOU are here. You cannot answer the question of why somebody else is here." The Teacher said patiently. "You cannot know that. That is for that person to answer. NOT YOU!"

"But. . .but . . .what do you think the purpose is for this physical system?" Tom asked the question, couching it with "think" instead of the way he'd been asking questions in the past. He would have asked before: "What IS the purpose," but with this question he wondered how the Teacher was supposed to know *that*? Nobody really knew that. Nobody ever had any idea about it. It was the BIG question, wasn't it?

"Sit down Tom, take a breath and consider your surroundings.

"Everything derives energy from something else until we are down to so-called nothing. But there is no such thing as nothing when God is Everything. Is there? Our concept of nothing does not exist. The idea of nothing is a human construct, a fantasy. Even deep space has a few protons, doesn't it?

"Is there anything, *anything*, that does not have a rate of change? The very rocks change, even the soil and even the atmosphere. Everything does. What would happen if there was something that didn't? Here we are, on a circular path, part of a process with an artist we call God. You are on a path, I am on a path, we are together, generating energy."

"Energy?"

"Well, we are, aren't we?"

"I guess."

"Well, let's go to an energy source you understand. Light. Light is energy. Right? Such as photons that last Quintillion years. . .right? That is, if you're considering time. There's light from the sun, from waves. . ." The Teacher paused. "Do we agree?"

"Weeeeelll."

"The Universe is based on laws that we call science."

Tom agreed. He could not think of an instance that light just happened for no apparent reason at all.

"Just because we don't yet understand the spiritual dimension in this dimension, it doesn't mean other dimensions don't get their energy from someplace too." The Teacher said lightly, continuing the hypothesis she started. "What did we think there was before we discovered photons?"

"We say there is no such thing as 'perpetual motion' for the creation of energy, because we don't understand that there may be an answer that we have not yet discovered - that it reaches into another dimension.

"Draw a circle. That circle is a track. Going around the track are all the things that are moving, that movement is the engine of eternity, it is the motion of force, of deliberateness. We don't leave here and just sit on a cloud somewhere and never move and never change. . .do we? Our movement is energy."

"We are off to the next adventure. So, we are presently in this system. This system is a kind of engine driving around a circle. We are part of that. When we leave this system, we go to another one that is also in motion and is changing. Why? Because it is the law of eternity. It is God's law. It IS, what it IS. You can't cease. Nothing is allowed to cease. It may just be that simple.

"There are dimensions we don't perceive and they must have energy too." Teacher said. "We may give a certain type of energy - - and we get another type of energy back. Other forms have to have energy for their change too, whether it be to be born again into this dimension - or another one. It is the way the universe works. Our place in the Universe gets energy from a number of sources, and the next place does too."

"Wha. . .?" Tom knew by the Teacher's tone that something important has just been said. It was like the Teacher has given him the step to an experiment that should not be left out. But the Teacher had said this before. Hadn't He/She? Wasn't it just being said in a different way?

Tom looked at the curtain wishing he could see the figure behind the drape for the hundredth time. Often, he visualized a person with a smile. Sometimes it was a wise old man with a long beard. Other times he was a she, like today with her lilting voice and the face of a beautiful woman, almost Cinderella-like and ethereal, like a fairy-being that was on tiptoes ready to take off into the cosmos. On other occasions, the Teacher or Voice or whatever IT was, said something so profound that there seemed to be an effect that came over the room, a color, or a sound, or even a feeling, that the form - whatever it was - seemed to evaporate and cause everything to become peculiar. When this occurred, he could only describe his observations as a feeling, an aroma that permeated the room with a loveliness and a rightness that always settled his questioning mind.

He adored the presence and sometimes longed for it. When this happened, he thought of the presence as divine. He was thinking about that now as he contemplated what could possibly be the purpose for the energy created by a human, or an animal or any living thing. He was thinking about energy as he observed the drape and realized the Teacher was explaining a connection he had not considered before and it was important.

"Numen." He whispered looking at the drape.

The form behind the gauze stirred, casting a slight shadow around the fringes. "We keep asking ourselves the question why? instead of what?" The form was saying in a Voice that splayed out from everywhere, from every direction.

The sound had no origin from behind the drape but from the very air surrounding everything in the room. ". . .because if we understand the what is" Numen continued, "then we begin to understand we must have an important role, because we are beginning to see what we are, like the example I am going to give you of a watermelon.

"It is not such a common question to ask ourselves why is there such a thing as a watermelon, but instead, we answer the question, **what** is a watermelon? It is a delicious, nourishing fruit meant to be eaten. Everything gets its energy from something else. Right? It is the way the system is. The watermelon from the soil, from the sun, from the decaying bugs in the soil. Then you from the food of the melon. That is **what**."

. . .and the silence in the room was suspended in the air waiting. . .

. . .waiting for more.

"That is what - it is the **what** that is important to us. Right? We don't ask why. We understand why. The purpose of the melon is to eat. The energy cycle charges itself with everything that is needed, like a battery. How amazing is amazing.

"So, what about the cake we sometimes talk about? In this case, we go beyond the what and answer the question of why most of the time. We often bake a cake to celebrate a birthday, or as a finish for a meal, or to celebrate friends or a holiday. We do it in answer to our question of why. Why do we make the cake? We are the maker, the one putting the ingredients together, so we have a view of the why. We know why.

"The ingredients of our world would be clear if we were the maker with the overview, but right now, we are not in that position. We are in the position of what, not why. We are the watermelon."

Tom tried to remember the various things Hawking had to say. He remembered the deflating and flat comments from him: "There is no God." Everybody in the Physics department, the labs, the classes, everyone he was used to being around, none of them believed there was a God, but truly how did all this happen anyway?

"How terrible it was when he had actually believed there was no God, no reason, no direction or purpose. He had felt so lonely and sick inside. He had felt alone.

"There is no God." He had parroted and perpetuated. "Steven Hawking says there is no God!" Tom blurted without thinking.

All the physics students had talked about Hawking and his proclamation like they had known it all along. No God. But something about it had never rung true. Something about it had always seemed off.

"Steven Hawking says there is no God." he said quietly again, to the room incredulously, not meaning to, but thinking out loud at the absurdity. Why had he said it? But the Teacher responded anyway.

"Just because somebody says something doesn't make it true, you know that. At one time, scholars thought the earth was flat and everybody believed them - but that didn't make it so! Hawking believed his hypothesis to be true, and he brought about a dialog, which was important. Wasn't it? You brought his words into the room today. His conjecture was not without value. Perhaps he was really saying that there is no God in the terms we have defined God - or the terms he used to define God."

"There is no definition for any of this." Tom said with a sweeping motion.

"Let us go to the concept of the circle again. If you take one small string and wrap it in a circle, it cannot create an entire ball, it is only one strand. It takes many strands bound together to create a ball. An infinite number of stands. You would not say that your human body was made of only one cell, would you? You cannot say that about God. What is God? God is in you, every fiber of you, every cell of you, and in everything you do or ever thought of being, and in your every thought. You are connected to all that is.

"Well, to repeat myself. . .If we understand that God is the force of the Universe, then it helps us to realize why bad things happen to good people. God is not looking at everybody with love. God is everybody and everything we do, and all those things we do not know, and all the things we do know and all that we think and all the things that we believe are not perfect. And why should our system be perfect anyway? Maybe we were created not to be perfect. At least not according to our view, our understanding, our feeble definition. We were created with deliberate randomness."

"Entropy." Tom said quietly.

"That's right. We are learning, as children. We are like six-year old's. We understand that one plus one equals two. As we grow a little, we'll be able to multiply four times six. And then we'll be able, with time to do fractions! We don't learn everything all at once. Our brains are limited.

"God doesn't love some people more than others, some animals more than others. God just is . . . everything. Just IS. The little bitty baby and the old person and the tree and the clouds and the droplets of water. It isn't a matter of love, is it? Break it down. We are part of a system; we call it the Earthly system. We are part of Earth. As such, we have defined our system. WE have. Jesus helped us. Others too. Many have helped us along the way. At the same time, we have been discovering the laws that define us, that govern us, laws such as how we keep our air clean, what are germs, etc. Science IS important."

"Why was Earth created?" Tom mused, going back to the why of it. . .

"Now that is a big question, isn't it? Ask Da Vinci why he painted the Mona Lisa. Earth is a planet, like other planets. It may be difficult to isolate ourselves as a solitary unit, but each system is unique, just like the example of the cake. Each cake that is baked is unique, isn't it? So, let us assume that planet Earth is a solitary system unlike any other, although there may be many other planets similar that exist for the same reason. First, consider the concept of eternity and all that is within it; we must look at the Universe as a whole, of what we can. The Universe is chaotic, but not without direction. Everything within it has a direction, has focus, has motion.

"Presently we have planet Earth happily orbiting around the sun. The planet came out of something else and will turn into something else. Time is not a factor. It is presently needed by us as a system, and as those needs change, it will change and so will we. What is Earth fueling? Something - seen or unseen. We do know it is sustaining a number of creatures while they are changing."

The Teacher hummed a little tune about a caterpillar changing into a butterfly. Then continued.

"We must be very careful about our planet Earth because we don't understand its purpose and how we are connected to it. Yet.

"We must soon gain more understanding because we are harming it."

"You speak about it as if it were living." Tom chuckled.

"It is! Everything about it is living, Tom." The Teacher said.

"Well, what is our purpose for being here? I sure can't see any reason for humans to be walking around harming the earth, can you?"

"Does everything have to have a reason the way you think of it? You must go beyond your own thoughts of reason. Think about you and your own experiments. Do all of them come out the way you had hoped or is there some trial and error involved?

"Sometimes, is there a result that is a wonderful surprise? I find it completely amusing that we all, yes all of us, seem to think that all of this must have a reason that we can see and understand while we are going through the experiment, or that God is all perfect, when what we do is not! Does that make any sense?

"We are part of the God system. We are proof, absolute, irrefutable proof, that everything in the God system is NOT perfect." The Teacher laughed.

"I think this is the most futile experiment ever!" Tom commented.

"You are a physics student, Tom." The Teacher's voice took over. "Is any experiment ever futile?"

Tom was stunned. He worked his mouth to say something, but nothing came out.

"Maybe you have answered your own question of why you are here, Tom. Maybe you have a part in an experiment." The Teacher reasoned. "Maybe when all is said and done none of this should be preserved? hmmm?"

All lightness, all laughter disappeared. What the Teacher was saying were words that brought fear to the room. It hung in the air. Tom realized he had been thinking that. That none of this was worthwhile. . .

"But every experiment is. . .worthwhile. . . Tom," Numen said. "When I make a chocolate cake, it is because I like chocolate. Not all of us have the same reason for being here. But we seem to think that there is one big reason for all humankind. I find that strange. Why would we think that? Have you been thinking that, Tom?"

Tom looked at his left hand and saw that his forefinger was lightly drumming on the arm of the chair. His whole body was moving in that same rhythm - his left leg going up and down as if there was a little tune being played by his leg.

"Why are there cats and dogs?" Teacher asked. "They are all part of our same system. The human race is part of it. Maybe, for some, it was a good place to park and slow down and smell the roses. Think about it. The spiritual system that doesn't contain matter is probably moving pretty fast." Teacher said.

"I guess that depends on whether or not we are aligned with lightness or darkness." Thomas, the physics student said.

The Teacher laughed and laughed. "Glad to know you are thinking about this.

"For others this may be a meeting place, like for lunch. Or, it may be to learn something, like going to school, or just a great experience. Imagine! Look at this place! It really is something magical, isn't it? Well there is a list of reasons, aren't there?"

"What question could this possibly answer?" Tom asked looking around the room. He sat there thinking about the reasons why there were people, all these different reasons. And then the Teacher said something that caused Tom to slip off his chair.

"Maybe the spiritual you, wherever, whatever you were, asked a question you were seeking. . ."

"What could I have possibly asked?" Tom inquired innocently.

"What is GOD?" Boomed the question. It was the second time the Teacher asked that question, but this time it quite affected Tom.

Tom immediately shrunk down to the size of a pea. He felt so tiny in the room. He heard himself parrot the question in his tiny little voice as he picked himself up from where he was half off the chair and perched precariously holding onto the table rim.

"What is God?" He said repeatedly in a voice so tiny that he could hardly hear it himself. "What is God? What is GOD? What is God? What is God? What is God?" He sat down on the floor, then laid flat and looked at the ceiling.

"That is the question you may be answering, that may be the reason why you came here," He said in a matter of fact tone. "You may have asked that question, and because you did, you were born here on Earth from wherever or whatever you were before you came here. What is GOD? And this just may be the perfect answer for that question.

"Or maybe you are here to help others answer that question. . ."

Tom was dumbfounded. He wrinkled his brow in confusion, laying there on that carpet, gazing at the ceiling. "How. . .could. . .?"

"Yes." Numen answered in a huge gesture.

Tom envisioned that the Teacher/Numen, whatever the creature was, had made a sweeping gesture with the "yes," although he couldn't actually see it, he felt the air move and he knew it had moved. He knew it wasn't his imagination.

He turned trying to peer under the drape from his place on the floor.

"Yes." He said again sweepingly, taking in everything: the sky, the earth, the students outside, everything.

The room tilted and opened into a beautiful landscape and there was a lilting Voice that was a song. "Of course, Tom. Everything is God and here you can really experience many things, many various aspects of creation.

Tom was dizzy and he shut his eyes briefly. The room was heavy, but not in the same way as it had been heavy once before. The gravity in the room was stronger, heavier, holding him to the floor while at the same time he was lighter in relation to it. How was that possible? He had the sensation of floating. He was up near the ceiling looking down upon himself, upon that body that was glued to the floor!

He tried to look over the top of the drape at that figure behind the drape, and the feeling of floating vanished.

He was sorry he'd done that!

The room began to twirl slowly and he grew larger and larger and there was a slow rotation going on around him and he could see lights and colors within it. Then suddenly everything became the right size in relation to him and he was back to being himself.

"Oh," was all he could manage. He breathed deeply.

"Yes Tom," Numen said with a sweetness, a kindness, a fullness, he would always remember, "This is God. You are seeing, hearing and experiencing God. For some of us, being here may be the answer to a question asked. We just forgot the question!"

Tom breathed. He had been holding his breath. The silence in the room became a shimmer of the colors of truth again. The room became a container around him making him see clearly his world. A new kind of classroom. It held him in a kind of hush, a whisper.

"God is the deliberate Force of free will." Teacher continued. "Everything has its own way. The tree can grow in its own way and the rock can fall off the mountain. The star in the sky can implode and a comet can come directly our way and harm us. Everything in the Universe has its own way and its own Deliberate Force - that is what God is.

"God is the Universe and the guarantee, the absoluteness guarantee of freedom, to be. You can destroy what you are, and hurt others within this system because you are deliberately free, governed by God's law of freedom to exist.

"There is no conflict between science and God - to think so is the real heresy. God is science. God created all that is and all the direction that governs all that is. Of course. That is what God is. Everything, everything that always was and everything that always will be.

"The puzzle is so miraculous, so amazing, so beyond any concept of human thought that it is impossible for us to envision how we even fit into all of it. But we do."

Tom started to cry, soft tears.

"Why do I have to keep going through this to comprehend it?" Tom asked feebly.

"Why do we keep going to school to learn to add and subtract?" The Teacher asked. "Because it is part of learning. . .

"Your energy is a driving force and what it does is beyond your ability to see or understand right now. We can measure some waves. Sound waves. Light waves. But what about a thought wave in a dimension we have yet to discover? What about a wave that is created because you exist and you are moving and displacing forces you don't even know about? What about the compassion you show to another being, be it a thirsty plant, a hungry animal, a hurting human, and many infinite possibilities - where does that energy go? What does it drive, and to whom and where?"

"I don't know. I'd like to know." Tom whined.

"Everything in the Universe, everything that is, must have parameters, must have a set of laws that enable their existence. Not like the Adam and Eve story, but as one of pressure which we move against. Do we move against pain?" the Voice said sadly. "Perhaps the creation of all this could not exist at all without this law so compassion can exist and drive a pure energy we call love. . ."

"Pretty hard to move when a person is in pain, I'd guess," Tom said sarcastically.

Teacher ignored him. "What if your deeds and thoughts were a kind of food, an energy for your loved ones in another dimension? What would you say then?"

"I'd say that I would still want to fight against it, fight against pain!"

"Precisely Tom," A Voice said kindly. "You can fight against it. It is what we all need to do. There will come a time when the purpose for this horror no longer exists, when we no longer hurt each other and we have the answers to disease. . . and when that time arrives, you will no longer recognize us as human beings. . .we will have evolved."

The room froze. Time froze. And then it was happening again, that feeling and atmosphere that Tom loved so much. He recognized it and let everything in himself go, like when he stepped off the platform for the zip line, that feeling of letting go.

Then it was like a series of slides coming into focus. First, the colors became more vivid. Had they been diffuse and he hadn't realized it? They were like a grand kaleidoscope, but now they separated and became clear separate colors, each one sparkling with intense clarity. He observed them with such pleasure. And then the second slide called for his attention and it was one of contrast. The lights became lighter and the darks darker. He could climb into the depth of the inky dark and rest there and it was so amazingly beautiful, not scary at all, but containing all the colors tightly together. Then came a crystal-clear focus, and with this he knew he would always remember this instant of this so-called darkness, not entirely because it was too much to hold onto. It was too big for his human brain, but he knew he would keep enough of it to remember the happening, to know this instant of seeing things clearly from a very different view. He had become something like a particle, swimming in a sea of knowing, yet still being himself. He had been Tom, yet his form was gone, he was light and energy and . . .and. . . and he couldn't think. . of what. . .but he kept his identity. . . he had a consciousness. . . yet he had a connection with everything. . .and he understood. . .he knew he understood for a microsecond. . .he knew he had it. He had. He understood! Everything. What had he been? It was like a dream, except it was so natural, so perfect and complete.

Gradually the darkness turned to light and he was part of that process, but the darkness had been something so incredibly beautiful, he would never be able to find words for it. There were no words. Then the room became the room again, with a softness, a gentleness, like one would imagine coming out of a floating cloud in a slow-motion movie. Tom saw himself sitting at the table and then he was Tom at the table. He looked at the curtain in confusion, then in reverence.

"Numen," he said in awe. "Numeeeennnnn."

An old woman answered. "We are not without direction. Each of us has a purpose

MARSHA'S MOUTH

Marsha looked at the appointment book. It was Friday already, her favorite day. She never made appointments with possible clients on a Friday because she wanted to keep the day open to look in on conferences. It was always a busy day when meetings were either on-going or setting up - and she wanted to give organizers some personal attention. Today was no exception - according to the schedule she was looking at. Douglas & Tanaka, were first timers opening their sessions with a friendly sign-in table on the mezzanine.

She reached to assemble a couple of welcome baskets - pens, note pads, coffee mugs and glasses, napkins, a small linen towel (something the Japanese clients seemed to appreciate), a map, and chocolates - all with the hotel's insignia. Repeat business was critical.

It was Marsha's job to introduce new clients to the facilities and attract back previous ones, negotiate bookings, and plan numerous activities that dovetailed with their requirements. Her job involved big business. She was good at it. For this, she had a private office with a courtyard view, a dedicated secretary, a hospitality budget and a demanding travel schedule. She made it a point to visit the headquarters of several organizations, presenting them with the rewards they could have by having their conferences in her hotel.

Several businesses in town valued her - including the university. Her work brought in thousands of dollars from out of town companies. Airline companies, restaurants, real estate firms, other hotels, air B&Bs, and more, all knew who she was; and it was true, a conference attendee's first introduction to the university often resulted in new student enrollments. They all valued her.

It would not have surprised anyone to learn of a direct link between the university and the conference facilities. But there wasn't one.

Marsha usually worked late a couple of evenings so she could leave early on Fridays. This permitted her to have a standing appointment at Sally's Beauty Salon and Spa. She wished Carl could leave early too so they could have an evening of it, but Friday nights were always busy at the pizzeria. She hated that place. She often told Carl that the pizza shop was preventing her from pursuing her dreams, an inference that she had other thoughts for her life. She did, but not what he might have thought.

It wasn't that she wanted to quit working. She didn't. It wasn't that she wanted to start a family. She didn't. She only made comments like that so Carl would feel guilty. In fact, he was taking her more and more for granted, as if her monthly deposits into their joint checking account were more of an expectation rather than a joint effort coming from the two of them. It was true that Carl put in more than his share, but he never wanted to talk about how they were moving towards a joint goal, nor did he ever celebrate her abilities. Her end-of-the-year bonus was twice the amount she expected and actually much more than the amounts given to other managers, she was certain about that. She remembered how Carl had barely noticed it and it still rankled her.

It wasn't long ago that he asked her again if she'd decided what she was going to do with it.

"I'm thinking I might give some of it to momma," she said thoughtfully, curious about his response.

Carl smiled. "That would make her very happy."

"But on second thought, maybe I'll just buy some clothes." He hated the clothes thing. He never bought any for himself since all wore was a towel tied around his waist at the pizza joint or one of those coats he'd been fooling around with recently. They were a new thing. Those jackets. They were white with short sleeves and had a red stripe on them. They said "Carl's" above a front pocket and he had name tags for everyone. She noticed them one night when he came home. It was so funny. . . he never put anything in the laundry but suddenly he started sending out those stupid shop jackets. Now that was a new expense. She stopped for a minute and thought about that. She wondered why she had never paid any attention to that before. . .

What Carl hadn't realized, was that Marsha had not cashed the check yet, had not deposited it like she normally would have done. Every time she looked at it, she kicked herself for the mistake she'd made in getting married.

The next day during her lunch hour, Marsha took her bag lunch, climbed in the car and drove to Bank of America and opened a new account with her check. When she returned to work, she visited Donna in payroll.

"Can you deposit a portion of my check to one account and a portion to another?" she asked.

Donna said they didn't like doing it, but for a friend, she'd do it.

Marsha changed the amount she deposited in their joint account and started skimming off her check into her new account. She told Carl she had changed her tax deductions. In a couple of weeks, it became even easier when she was given a raise.

In the course of all this, Marsha decided to take a look at their account, to be certain everything was running smoothly; and she had a big surprise waiting for her. Their joint account had a LOT of money in it. It was so unexpected that she almost called Carl from the bank. Instead, she asked the bank to print out a duplicate of transactions for the last three months. She'd tried to get more, but the bank didn't want to do it. And there it all was, all accounted for, all that money - all coming in from the pizzeria. She thought she was going to faint.

No wonder Carl didn't care about her bonus. They had enough money in the bank to pay off their house!

Marsha's job involved a lot of paperwork. She was tired of accounting and money and paperwork, so at home, she left it up to Carl. After all, he was willing to do it. She'd had no idea why they had all this money. The first thing she thought of, was maybe he'd let things slide and the money had built up over time because he hadn't paid the bills. Because of this, she was agitated all afternoon. The first thing she did when she got home was look into the house payment and the bills. Everything had been neatly accounted for - and paid. On time! That was one thing about Carl, he was good at detail.

There on the desk were the receipts from the pizza shop. There were stacks of them. Stacks and stacks! Business was booming. It was clear that the money was coming in from the business. But why? He'd tried to tell her that it was those three guys, but that didn't make sense. No, it didn't.

That night, she asked Carl a few questions about the restaurant. He was only too happy to talk about it. "They're wonderful. You can't believe it. It is all this silliness going on - all these noises. They are like the three stooges and people are paying to see them. . . like comedians."

"Is it only when they are there?" Marsha asked carefully.

"Oh yes," Carl said. "It's them. Through and through!"

"What kind of difference are they making, Carl?" she asked, leaning over interested.

"Oh my gosh, people are standing in line for pizza. Every night is like a scene from a movie show - of people waiting in line to get their ticket, except it is to make their orders. It is amazing. And these guys - they love it. They really do. They like working for me." Carl nodded, happy to be talking about it, especially because Marsha wanted to know. She was never interested. He talked way into the night because she listened. She was very attentive, listening to every word. He was so happy. He couldn't remember the last time he'd been so happy. When he finally wound down, she was snuggling into him and he was ready for a night as good as any he had ever remembered with her.

As for Marsha, she was happy with the sex, but secretly visualized her partner was Robert at work. She would never risk having an affair, but there was no harm in fantasizing, was there?

She remembered how Carl had said the guys had turned down vacation time he offered them, paid time too. He had told them they could take off during finals week, but all three of them declined, saying they were prepared for their tests. She'd told Carl then that there was something fishy about that!

She still had not stopped in at the pizzeria - and she wasn't going to. She knew that something wasn't right at that place. She'd driven out of her way to go by there because she hadn't been that way in a long time and she'd noticed some crazy sign in the window about a Stampede. Carl had lost his mind.

It was that Friday at the beauty shop that Marsha commented about the pizzeria for the first time. It was unusual as Marsha usually talked about how great she was doing at her job. Sally had just finishing trimming her hair and had picked up a roller when Marsha asked, "Have you been down to the pizza restaurant recently?"

"I haven't. But I've heard that I should take the kids. It's great fun down there now. I guess Carl has made some fine changes." Sally rolled her first curl.

"I don't know what he's done and I'm worried about it."

"Oh? Why? Isn't it doing great? Judy was here a couple of days ago and said she'd gone down there, on a weeknight no less, and had to wait in a line at the counter to order her pizza. But I've heard you have to go on a Thursday. Imagine, waiting in line just to order. . .!"

Marsha coughed and Sally had to wait to continue working on her hair. "You must be so proud of your husband - having a business like that. . ."

Marsha nodded and then sat still. "He is a good guy, but I don't know about his employees, you know?"

"Ohhh?" Sally encouraged.

"Yeah. I mean, I really don't trust those guys. You know? They could be using my husband's place. . .well, I don't want to say anything. . ."

"What do you mean?" Sally hesitated, squinting at the mirror.

"Oh, I don't know. . ."

"You mean some kind of front for something. . .illegal?"

"I didn't say that." Marsha said too quickly.

"Drugs, or something like that?"

"No, I didn't say that." Marsha said raising her eyebrows. I would never say anything like that! Carl is absolutely ethical and straight. . .

"Well. . . I didn't think you were talking about Carl." Sally said yanking a little hard on a lock of hair.

"That's just it," Marsha continued. "He is such a good guy. I just don't want to see his business getting into anything that he isn't aware of. You know. . . he is kind of naive. I just worry about him. That's all. Please forget I ever said anything. I am a worry wart."

Sally kept humming along, working on her hair, thinking about how such a thing could happen to a business, wondering about that.

Marsha felt completely vindicated. At least she'd said something to somebody. Carl was dipping into a dangerous zone. He should know better! "I've noticed something has been different about him lately." Marsha said.

"Oh?" Sally raised the "Ohhh" up to a question.

"Not so stressed anymore. You know. About money."

Sally half laughed, the kind that said, I didn't know you had a question about money anyway, but covered the expression of her raised eyebrows quickly. Marsha obviously wasn't in any big financial hurt, not with the clothes she wore.

"Don't say anything to anybody," Marsha said quietly and contritely. "I'm just concerned, that's all. Let's keep this under wraps for now. Okay? I shouldn't have said anything. . ."

Marsha fluffed her hair, smiled at Sally, and gave her an extra-large tip, nodding. "I don't know anything yet. It's our little secret."

But Marsha knew Carl was up to no good and she would be the one hurt by him. She decided to increase her independence and to plan an escape from him. There was something not right going on.

She could feel it!

HAPPINESS

Tom's approach to doors was different now. He wanted to better comprehend what he could do and how to control it. He wasn't troubled by it anymore; in fact, he was happy about it. He understood that the environment of the room intensified some sort of power, or gift that he already possessed. He had tried many things at the door already. Now he wondered if he could just walk through it like an invisible man.

He tried.

Nope. That didn't work. But he could make the door invisible and then walk through it. He had tried to make himself invisible and that had been his folly. THAT was silly and stupid, he thought. Of course, I couldn't do that to myself! Next, he disintegrated the door and then waited for it to assemble back together again. It did, but it took a while. He wondered if he could hasten the re-assembly instead of just waiting, but he didn't know how. He tried it again, experimenting, thinking about the door coming back together again, as it originally was. Nothing. He guessed that was beyond anything he could do, since he had no idea of the make-up of the door to begin with. So, he just had to accept what he could do. Next, he wondered if he could disintegrate more than the door. Could he disintegrate an entire wall? Could he disintegrate the wall around the door and leave the door in place? He tried that.

Nope.

It seemed his ability only worked on doors. So, he decided he wanted to liquefy the door. He thought of water. He thought it would be so fun to turn the door into water and flow it down the hall. He wondered if he could turn the water into a particular color. He thought of clear golden water.

The door fell immediately to the ground and started flowing, like a small river toward the hall.

Tom jumped up and down in glee. He was so happy. Where the door had been was just an open space.

Tom trotted through the opening, not giving a second thought to the re-assembly of the liquid. That wasn't his problem. That was a problem of matter.

His vision was so natural and of course he was expecting it. It was one of his happiest moments. He remembered how the sun had shown so golden on the water, just like the color of the water he had just seen from the door.

The vision engulfed him immediately. He and Abbot were on their boat trying out their invention. They wanted to glide over the water to their favorite fishing hole. Neither boy had told anyone that they were ready for the trial. They were so tired of others meddling in their ideas - and they were tired of the trials that hadn't worked. They just wanted some moments to themselves to see if their latest brainstorming ideas were going to pan out.

They started their little motor and lowered the apparatus in the water. The boat turned and rocked into the pier instead of going straight. Tom pushed the boat out gently and the fins went to work quietly as he steered.
It was hard to steer it, but it was working! Abbot was feeding some of that crazy fuel into a small hopper.

He looked at his friend and the two of them let out a scream that could be heard all the way to the opposite shore.

"It's working!"

That day changed both of their lives. . .

Tom went over and sat in the side chair, something he had not done before. He had always sat in the roller chair at the table or stood. It seemed like he was more of a student when he did that, or at least more alert. But today he didn't feel like being a student.

"Hello Teacher," he said eyeing the door which now was completely intact.

"Hello Tom," The Teacher said in a soft voice. "How can I be of service today?"

"Why can I do that?" Tom asked gesturing toward the door.

"I don't know."

"Can any of the other's do that?"

"Uh. . .weell. . ." The Teacher didn't complete a sentence.

This was the first time Tom detected any discomfort in the Teacher.

"I'm sure I'm not the only one." Tom mused.

"What if you were?" the Teacher asked.

"I would want to know why. Why me? How come such a thing is happening to me? How come?" He swallowed. "Am I the only one?"

"I don't know," The Teacher said. "How would I know? I'm only seeing a small number of students here each week. Maybe there are others who can do it. . ."

"You're my Guide, right? You're some kind of soothsayer, a guru. Something like that. You're an - ALL SEER. I couldn't do any of this before I came to this room, this zimmer, this crazy place!"

"I wouldn't know. . ." The Guide said evenly., "what you were able to do before you came here. Maybe you were able to do a lot of things but you didn't feel safe enough to try. It's just. . .at this place you feel safe enough to . . .well. . .Let go.

"We don't know the differences we make." The Voice continued. "We often don't believe enough in ourselves, or we don't believe there is a reason. We can't see how we bring about conditions. . ."

"Why? Why does it matter if I believe it or not? I'm just one drop in a huge sea. Life is going to go on for everybody anyway."

"Yes, it will." The Teacher said. "The sun will set tonight, and it will come up tomorrow morning. It will be 58 degrees tonight, and you have no control over any of this. The moon will travel across the sky and as the night progresses, you will see the brightness of more stars in the dark sky. You will look up at it helplessly, and think about how very small you are. Infinitesimal.

"But you will keep changing every minute of every day none the less. You will say for the hundredth time, 'I don't know who or what I am or what I am supposed to be doing. What is all this about?' And you will listen, but there won't be any Voice booming down from the sky in answer to your questions, because God is not up there in the sky, God is in you. So, you will sit quietly on the grass and remember that God is in you, and you must go within for your answer. 'Who am I?' You will ask. 'Why am I here? If God is Everywhere and is all that IS and is in me, then there is an answer someplace *in me*. There must be a reason why I can do the things I do."

"That's right," Tom said. "I keep asking these questions, and I'm always sitting in here with the same questions, and while I'm here everything makes perfect sense, and then I leave. And you know what? I'm right back to where I was! Why do I do that?" He knew his melancholia was apparent even though he tried to hide it.

"Because you need to hear me say some things again and again." She said kindly, "Have you noticed that people go to church to hear the same messages again and again? Week after week?"

Tom thought about that and realized it was true. "Oh, I hadn't really thought about that," he said.

"There are a lot of distractions out there, Tom." She said. "Drugs, crime, school, tests, fights, liquor. . . and . . .women," she chuckled.

"I uh, I feel pulled in different directions." He said, not even smiling.

"Everybody does. But you are always where you are supposed to be, Tom." She said, seeming to know he was having difficulty expressing himself. "You have become self-actualized now."

"I am? What does that mean?"

"It means you know who/what you are. It means you are on a path and you have become aware of that."

"Oh." He sniffed. "I guess. Is there something different about me now?"

"Yes. There is. You can tap into your spiritual self now. You can tap into your abilities. . ."

"I can?"

"Yes. You are having lessons in new concepts and, like any course of study, it is always necessary to receive the information more than once.   What you are learning in this room is life changing and you are going through an assimilation process that takes more than one exposure. That's what learning is. You change in relationship to everything you learn.   Right?"

There was that silence. Tom let it float in the room while he let some of his raw nerves go away.

"Ah shit" He muttered. "Umm, yes. I guess. Why am I valuable? I'm just nothing!"

"Oh," The Teacher was now silent and Tom could sense she was thinking.

He repeated it, whining, "I understand, when I'm in here. But truly, I'm nothing."

"Okay, there's things we can do to help you. Okay?"

Tom nodded

"What is a favorite small object that you have handy, in your apartment, work or school?"

"I like my cell phone." He answered quickly pulling it out of his pocket.

"Okay, we'll do something about that today. But first, what exactly are you asking today, Tom?"

"I am asking. . . and I know you can't really answer this. . . How come I am not happy?" I met a girl I really, really like. I have a good friend and we took a fun trip! I have a job I like a lot!"

"But you are not happy?"

"NO! I am not happy. I am continually restless. . .so unsettled."

"What is happiness, Tom? I need to understand what you think happiness IS, so I know what you are expecting right now." The Teacher said kindly. "Perhaps you have been disrupted out of what you thought happiness is."

"Happiness is feeling like you want to touch the sky, like you want to dance around the trees and roll on the grass. It is feeling light-hearted and full of silliness and laughter and funny jokes. It is running around in a circle of joy and holding hands and skipping and kissing and . . . That's what I think it should be. . ."

"And what is it that you are experiencing instead?" A neutral Voice asked.

"Everything is so heavy on my shoulders - the weight of the world!" Tom mumbled.

"Yes. I can see it." The Teacher said. "You have made a definition of how you are supposed to feel. Like other definitions, it isn't real. You took away your joy by defining it."

"Wha. . .?" Tom was tired. He realized there was something to be learned today, but it was all tied up in so many words. He looked up at the ceiling. Then he felt a cool breeze in the room and it touched his face. He looked at his hands. "I'm so tired," he said again. "I feel so helpless."

"All of your definitions are physical, Tom. How can you feel like rolling in the grass when you are tired?" She asked in that same soft voice she used when something was especially difficult for Tom to understand.

She continued. "Joy is an experience. It is unique to you. When you buy into a definition, then you're disappointed when you don't have feelings according to that definition. You may have bought into a definition at one time. You thought it was hanging out with your friends drinking, doing some light drugs, womanizing and the like. Now you are working hard in school and your friends have changed. Your definition changed. Right?

"You might have bought into an image you saw on TV! People who sell products want you to believe what they are selling will make you happy. They are experts at this, you know. They show you happy images. Your brain is like a computer - it is your center that regulates your body, and more. You have an emotional center that your brain is reacting to and your brain doesn't necessarily control it, at least not always. For example, you may fall in love with a person that your brain tells you is not the person of your best choice, but you find yourself in love anyway. Have you heard of that happening to anyone?"

"All the time," he answered. "It happened to my buddy . . ."

"The brain doesn't control everything, unless you let it. The brain does not control the God in you and your brain does not control joy or happiness - unless you give it that power. You may have given it that power by not paying attention to what you are watching and then you gave it power over you. Or, your brain may be rebelling because you have changed your definition. Hmmm? When you give the power of definition to your brain over your emotional self you are relinquishing something. It is like the bird in the sunshine singing its song. The bird is not thinking, "I should enjoy the sunshine." No. It is simply enjoying the sunshine and doesn't have to be thinking about whether or not it is a happy moment, whether or not it should be enjoying the sunshine. It just is."

Tom listened. He gulped.

"Joy is perhaps beyond definition. It must be experienced."

"Oh, that is too much to think about." Tom said. "I'm not happy. I don't know about my brain. I'm just not happy."

"I want to help you." She said, a tinge of exasperation to her tone. "You have already said that you should be happy with all the things that are going on in your life. The problem is you don't FEEL happy.

"First, you must stop thinking about how you should feel when you are happy. Second, observe the happiness of other creatures. You are connected to them. Their happiness is your happiness. Connect to their joy. They will lift you up. Start watching the birds and other free-moving creatures and observe their joy. Look at a cat asleep in the sun, or a dog playing with a Frisbee."

"Okay." Tom said.

"The more you talk about happiness and what will bring you happiness, the less it will come to you. Framing the definition of happiness creates an expectation and makes you hunt for situations that will bring it to you, instead of just being in the moment. See? You have an expectation tied to a definition model from your brain, and then you start visualizing yourself tied to that definition and your own emotions may backfire and hurt you. You can visualize an end result, like getting a good score on a test, but to visualize an emotion, like love or joy is not the same thing. You can be very hurt by an emotional result that is supposed to happen and doesn't. Instead, ask the Universe to bring joy into your life, but maybe not visualize how. Only God in you knows what real joy is for you."

"I think I ought to know," he said, irritated.

"How would you know that? Do you know your destiny?" Numen asked.

"No." Tom said in a small voice.

"None of us really do, although we wish we did. It is part of the adventure of being here. We don't know the entire movie that is our life. It would ruin it, don't you think?"

Tom made some kind of noise that didn't mean anything.

"Concentrate on little things." She continued her explanation. "Big expectations can rob you. Dream big, but expect nothing."

"How do I separate the two?" He asked.

"You hope, you daydream, but you don't expect. It is playing the game of IF. Your emotional investment is small. It is a hope, or just a little dream, not an expectation, and certainly not an expectation of yourself. The ones that we put on ourselves can be very troubling, because if we don't deliver, then we translate that into failure."

"But Teacher, sometimes a person has to concentrate on a big goal in order to achieve it!" Tom said emphatically.

"Yes Tom. Sometimes it takes everything we've got in order to get to where we want to go. Then we must be very kind to ourselves because all our energy was expended on getting there - and we lose the happiness at achieving the goal. Temporarily. We used up our resources during the process of what it took to get to the result. Sometimes the reward we get at the goal line is far different than what we thought it was going to be. I think this has happened to you."

"Huh?" Tom was dumbfounded.

"You thought you were on a particular track with your education. Right? Now you tell me you are going to try and go for something else. Trying for Medical School is a long shot for you. Right? This was not your original goal."

"I don't have a chance," He said dejectedly.

"If you don't try you will never know."

"Okay. I am going to try."

"Are you thinking, if you don't get in that you won't be achieving your purpose?"

"THAT'S RIGHT!" He said too loud. "I'm so tired of all this and now I have such a burden."

Quietly, every so quietly, a sound interrupted the silence. It wasn't a he or a she or even an it. It was something else. It was Numen. "Once you have embarked on the path, you are always where you are supposed to be."

Silence.

"You have had bigger activities that have overridden little things that have been snuffing them out." He said, "Come to the table and write a list of little things that give you pleasure."

Tom had become surprisingly neat and organized, something that caused quite a stir in his family. "I never knew he was like that," his mother said to almost everybody she knew when he was home at Christmas time. "His room was like a cyclone growing up!" And maybe Tom had not been neat as part of his basic nature, but he was now. He placed his notebook carefully on the table with his pencil alongside.

"Happiness is not something that exists every moment of every day. There are highs and lows." Tom was having difficulty focusing on her words. She had too many words for him today. "It is the simple little things." She said more emphatically, seeming to know he was drifting.

"Please start writing down little things," she said.

He started a list, writing down little things, while the Teacher waited in silence.

"I'm sorry I am wasting your time," he said, writing faster. Morning coffee, teasing Jumping Jack Jake, work, adding cheese to pizza, walking to class, the pink flowers, talking politics to Susan, having a beer with Dad, watching Archer, calling mom, . . .

There was laughter in the room. First, it was the Teacher's laugh. Then it changed to a persona he thought of as IT. Then it was the Voice's laughter. "You are not wasting my time, Tom, or yours. You will refer to this list many times as you go forward in your life, refocusing on happiness.

"I see you singing to the stars at night and making a wish and dancing around the room for the very fun of it and smelling the grass. All these are images of joy. They are such small things, aren't they? They do not involve money or fame or anything except your heart and the joy that comes from being alive. It is important to know you have many little things," the Teacher had returned and said in a voice like his father and so familiar. "Concentrate on them."

Tom started to print more legibly.

"A big thing, like getting into medical school, can snuff out smaller things - like the wind blowing out candle flames. It takes a bigger effort to relight the smaller flames after a big effort because you were concentrating on the big one. The little ones seem insignificant in comparison. Sometimes you can prevent the wind from blowing out your happy moments from the start, other times you can't - it depends on whether or not the big vision was your goal or not. Sometimes a person buys into somebody else's goal for their life. Like getting a physics degree."

"OH." Tom sucked in his breath sharply.

"For example," Teacher continued, "It is like you are having a quiet time with your coffee, and you treasure that little space in the morning and then the phone rings and you answer it. The phone was the wind that blew out your candle, even if you liked what the caller had to say. You answered it. It was your choice; you didn't have to. You answered it during your ten minutes. If it was important, the caller would try again later and you could have your ten minutes. One time is no big deal, but add that ten more times and then another ten times with other things and soon you'd begin to feel that your life was not your own, you'd be out of control and you wouldn't know why, because it was so many little things that you lost. In fact, the things were so small that you didn't even notice they were disappearing.

"Soon you are not happy anymore and you don't know why. You must start back with the little things."

Tom had two pages written full of little things. He laid his pencil down and slumped.

"It doesn't do much good for me to be talking about all this, does it." Teacher said. "I think you still feel as though you have a big burden on your back. Are you still feeling that way?"

"Yes." He said miserably.

"You know," the Teacher said, "one small cell, one tiny cell in your body can end up making a change that will kill you. Small things are important. . .

"Tom?"

Tom was someplace else.

"Tom?"

Tom nodded. "Yes."

"It is a lie."

"What is?"

"Control your thought. Think a powerful thought, vocalize it or write it down. Then add to the power with a symbol to focus on. Make a new and unique physical action with it. The power is supersonic!"

But Tom was still off somewhere dark. He didn't want to do it.

"Supersonic!" Teacher repeated, laughing, trying to lighten Tom's mood, but Tom would have none of it.

"Would you like to try something supersonic to assist with your unhappiness today? Something simple you can take with you?" He asked, breaking through Tom's clouds.

"YES!" Tom said emphatically.

"Okay," the Teacher said. "Have an open mind. The exercise is not silly. It is important."

Tom knew from experience, that even when the Teacher's words were very, very simple, they were very, very important. "No, I won't think it is silly," he said.

"Okay. We'll do this. Go to the small cabinet in the corner and open it."

Tom had noticed the cabinet when he first came into the room, and then had stopped seeing it - it was just part of the scenery and unimportant. He went to the cabinet. It was shaped in a triangle mounted on the wall of the corner. It had one door. Inside were four shelves. Each one had labels: Drop, Rabbit, Infinity, Power. The Teacher directed him to the Drop shelf. There were four items; a box of large size eye droppers, a package of clear plastic cups and two framed images.

"Take out the items on the drop shelf and bring them to the table," Teacher told him. "Take a good photo of the framed image with the picture with your cell phone, then go out to the hall and fill one of the cups with water from the water fountain and come back."

Tom had a good phone and taking the photograph was easy. The symbol in the frame was very simple. The other frame didn't have an image - it was plain white.

Teacher had Tom arrange the two cups on the table side by side and had him set the two frames behind these. Each was about 8" square and had a kick stand behind it. The one with the image had a colored circle that was solid yellow-orange and in the middle was a blue image in the shape of a water drop. He was instructed to put them side by side vertically using their kick stands so they would act as a backdrop to the two cups.

"The one with the image should be directly behind the cup on the left. The other one, behind the cup on the right." Teacher said.

"This is what we're going to do. You're going to repeat after me and transfer the water from the cup on the left to the cup on the right in a logical way. Okay?"

"Unig," Tom made a noise that wasn't positive.

Teacher ignored him," Repeat after me, I am a drop."

"I am a drop." Tom said.

"I am not helpless."

"I am not helpless. Tom repeated.

"Small things are important."

"Small things are important."

"One drop falling to another. . . adds to the other." He said.

Then commanded:" Together."

Tom repeated the little ditty with him:" One drop falling to another. . . adds to the other."

Teacher continued," this is how the whole thing goes:

"One drop falling to another. . . adds to the other

Two drops together. . .attracts more to gather

Three, four and five. . .and it's alive. . .

A thousand or more than before

And it's a tower of power

Tom squirmed. He laughed and felt silly and stupid. "This is for little kids." He muttered.

"Again," he commanded, "Together now, three times:

One drop falling to another. . . adds to the other

Two drops together. . .attracts more to gather

Three, four and five. . .and it's alive. . .

A thousand or more than before

And it's a tower of power."

Tom repeated the words three times with his Teacher, and with each time the limerick was easier to remember.

"This is something like a mantra, "the Teacher said. "When you say it, it will bring you out of this helpless feeling you have."

The room took on a warm atmosphere, a strange phenomenon Tom had noticed before. He often wondered if it happened at this time of day because of the way the sun streamed in the windows.

"Okay, very good," the Teacher was saying, "and now you have an idea of what I'd like you to do. Umm?"

Tom sat in the chair and looked at the circle with the drop. He picked up the dropper. It was familiar as he often used one just like it for experiments in the lab for transferring substances. He fingered the second one, wondering about it.

"Ah, the second one is just in case the first one fails." The Teacher said. They aren't made very well."

"Oh." Tom said. "Yes."

The droppers were a bit larger than the small variety used for putting drops in one's eye.

"You will be surprised how fast you can transfer the water from one cup to the other using the dropper," the Teacher explained. "Place the cups directly in front of the framed symbol while you are making the transfer. There's no need to focus on it, because you will be looking at the dropper, but your mind will notice it in the background while you're doing it because it is there.

"While you are making the transfer, drop by drop, say the little ditty we just said. We can say it together, but you are the leader, instead of me. You decide the speed."

The Teacher's voice changed and was replaced by the neutral IT. It said: Please repeat your question and start the exercise. Your question was: "I am one drop in a huge sea. Why am I valuable?"

Tom looked at the exercise in front of him. He was going to do this childish thing with the water and that stupid ditty only because the entity behind the curtain was waiting. . .

"I am one drop in a huge sea," he said dejectedly, "Why am I valuable?" Then he started transferring the water drop by drop. As he spoke the limerick, a tune began in the background of the room. It was upbeat and went along with the dropping process. It was a musical melody he had not heard before.

"One drop falling to another. . . adds to the other. . .

Two drops together. . .attracts more to gather. . .

He started saying it rather slowly because some of the drops weren't matching the beats. He chuckled at this and then matched the beat. He came down to the last little bit in the cup and it seemed important to get that last bit of water, so he tipped the cup and sucked it dry with the dropper. He was silent for that space, and then finished his ditty midstream with. . . "it's alive" and thought to continue, but the voice behind the curtain had stopped too. The entire exercise only took a couple of minutes.

"That wasn't so bad, was it? Now, drink your cup of water and gaze intently at our symbol on the right."

The circle was a deep yellow, somewhere between yellow and orange, like the color the sun becomes when its hazy at sunset, when it gets that glow so you can look directly at it with the naked eye. Like the color of the water he turned the door into and that the lake was when he was there with Abbot. The drop of blue in the middle was intense and a bit towards lavender in shade, also like the color of the ocean or like a lake might become late in the day. The bluish water drop began to vibrate.

"Just keep looking at it Tom," the Voice said.

Tom drank his water and gazed at the symbol. Now, look at the blank picture on the left. The image of the drop appeared on the blank sheet. The drop was golden instead of blue and the background was now blue. "You were the drop of water." The Teacher said. "Now you are the sun."

Tom's face was hot. He felt like he did several years ago when he first blushed over a girl.

The exercise was so stupid and simple. Childish really. He sat there feeling like a little kid and he didn't like it. Tom knew about color and understood he was looking at a phenomenon caused by complimentary colors.

"I don't want you thinking of me like a child," he said to the Teacher.

"Why would I think that?" The Teacher asked.

"Weeelllll. . . ."

"Tom!" The Voice had a commanding tone that diminished the room. It was full and deep and almost like a song. "Do you think people who take communion on Sunday are acting like children?" The tone hung in the room vibrating.

Tom bowed his head in shame. "I'm so sorry!" He said.

"You will be shocked how important ritual is - how it governs our lives. At graduation, it is a robe and hat, a diploma, and our name being read. Everyone knows what the symbol of the hat means! It is a ritual. When we marry, it is a ritual, a ring, and vows. It is different for different cultures. It may be jumping over a broom! On Valentine's Day it is a red heart and chocolates. Can you imagine?. . .for a birthday. . . it is a cake - with candles! Stupid candles. . .and we do it until we are old, old, old! People take photos of these rituals. *They are important*. What you just did has tremendous power. You were a drop and you became the sun. You, Tom, are a powerful contributor. You are one drop that falls to another, and adds to the other and you become the sun! Is there anything that gives more energy to our world?"

Tom blinked steadily. It was time to go. He put the framed image away, but the droppers were his to keep.

"Tom, it will add to your well-being if you put the photograph of the image on your phone where you can see it often - maybe as a wallpaper." The Teacher said. "Also, I have sent you the tune you heard in the room today as a ringtone. If you like it, you might use it for notifications on your phone."

Tom actually jumped a little. He had always thought of the Teacher as some kind of wise man that wasn't up on today's technology. Now, he'd just gotten a ring tone on his phone! Who was this Teacher anyway? He had come to the conclusion that the figure was a genius of some standing, but he was probably disfigured or something like that.

He had asked him once about the drape and he answered that it was there so Tom wouldn't be distracted by things that didn't matter, and a person's appearance was one of them. So, he figured a detractor might be how the Teacher looked, although he saw a handsome middle-aged man in his mind - but not always. Sometimes he was a she about thirty years old and very beautiful. Other times he swore there was a very old man with a beard back there. Recently, an old woman seemed to have emerged.

Tom realized he was walking out the door with something, and that's what he had asked for. The Teacher always gave him what he asked for - answers to his questions. "Thank you, Teacher," he said, looking at his phone. "I think I will do that."

As he walked across the campus towards home, he fooled with his phone. Yes, there was the ringtone the Teacher had sent. He listened to it. It was the same beat and melody as what he'd heard in the room. He decided to try it out as his regular notification for incoming calls. He sat down on a cement wall next to pink flowers and made the change to his phone. He changed the image of his wallpaper to the photo he had taken in the room. It was too bold, too strong. He didn't like it but thought it wouldn't hurt to keep it for a day or two. He thought he could make it into a shortcut symbol and it would show up very nicely there in front and lead him to a page where he could look at it larger. He would experiment later with the thumbnail size.

He got up and looked at the pink flowers. He smiled. As he continued on his walk home, he didn't realize it, because he couldn't see himself, but something was missing from his back. He was walking straighter and his steps had a lift to them. He wasn't prodding along anymore. He didn't care that he could do some strange things, that maybe he was different. He said to himself, "I am different - we ALL are. It is an identity thing. I'm just me."

Later that night, Tom sat quietly in his living room, the little ditty going through his head. He wanted to be more than a drop. He still felt drained and dejected, but the Teacher's words made sense, as always, but they also didn't make sense. He looked at his notes. "Stop defining happiness." He had written. "Experience the small moments of joy." He underlined. "Watch the birds."

Tom had not been able to write everything down that the Teacher had said, but he remembered most of it. He added to his notebook:

Remember the coffee example, he wrote. Don't allow people to interrupt a special time.

"Sometimes people are unhappy and they DO know why." The Teacher had said. "Their partner is having an affair, they are having health problems, they lost their job and money is an issue, their children have gotten into drugs. All these things affect happiness. It is when a person says they are not happy anymore, that they are sick and tired and depressed, but they don't know why, that it is most often a loss of focus on the little things."

When people don't know why they are unhappy it is often a loss of the little things. He wrote.

Joy cannot be defined. He wrote that day. It must be experienced.

Happiness is not something that exists every moment of every day. Happiness is a grouping of simple little things, he wrote down, not big things, but the small appreciations of what life is. My desk, the light by my chair. He added to his list, writing many more things down. He wrote way into the night. There were so many things. He hadn't realized there could be so many things he was happy about. He loved his couch. He loved the wood on top of his desk. He always rubbed it while he studied. He rubbed it now. He loved his pencils, the neighbor's cat, his old car. He loved chocolate! My gosh, he loved everything.

As he drifted off to sleep that night, he was in that twilight space just before full sleep arrives, when something beautiful and happy came drifting by. He had a feeling of such joy. It was a smile that was coming from everywhere. He was bursting. He tried to see what it was that was making him have such a feeling, but couldn't quite make it out, and then he heard it, lightly spoken words that came tiptoeing across a landscape bathed in sunshine. The Sun. The water.

God is Everything. God is Everywhere.

SUMMERTIME

The school year finished uneventfully for Tom. He decided to stay and take two terms of summer school, much to Carl's relief as Tom's straight man routine was as important to his business's success as John's vocalizations and Jake's jumping. But Carl wasn't the only one so pleased. Chib, being a foreign student, had no place to go for the summer, and Susan was staying for summer school too.

Tom only had three meetings scheduled in the room during this time, but each one gave him something of value. He was always amazed by the experience. He and Chib endlessly discussed what they warmly termed, Numen Philosophy. Chib, always the scientist through and through, challenged every small detail of the happenings in the room, saying, "You gotta have evidence, Tom, evidence."

And Tom, completely and utterly transformed by the entire course of study in the room, would often challenge his friend. "How do you explain it? Do you have a better theory?"

The two young men, who no longer considered themselves "boys" since their bicycle trip, and resented anybody who did, talked endlessly about everything. Chib, unlike Tom, was visiting the room with the new summer schedule and found the whole experience "crazy fascinating." He even leapt across the table and yanked the drape aside.

"You did what!?" Tom looked at his friend wide-eyed as they were walking to the Quad for coffee after a morning seminar. "DO tell. I want to know."

Chib stopped, his face red. "Tom, you gotta believe me when I tell you this. Honest. I am telling you God's truth."

"I thought you didn't believe in God." Tom said, laughing at the euphemism. "Tell me what?"

"I don't, but. . ."

"But. . .?"

"When I pulled the drape aside, there was another drape, just like it. I pulled that aside too."

"Well . .?"

"Yeah. And I pulled the next one aside too and the next one and the next one. I don't know how many I pulled down. There was one drape after another, after another, after another. . ."

"Oh my gosh. No shit? You're shit'in me. Don't fuck with me, man. . ."

"I ain't fucking with you, Tom. . ."

Tom looked straight into Chib's eyes. "You're telling me there was just a bunch of drapes?"

"There wasn't just a bunch of drapes, Tom - there was an infinite number of drapes!"

"No lie?"

"No fucking LIE!"

"Ha ha ha ha ha! I told you. Ha ha ha ha. It's creepy. It's creepier than shit! Ha ha ha ha!" When Tom got his breath, he asked. "Then what happened?"

"The whole room disappeared and I was floating in a perfect vacuum. I know I was in a vacuum, because I was sucked in there with other objects and there wasn't any gravity or light or anything and it was very strange and something crazy was happening to me, and then, and then, it was orgasmic."

"You don't say."

"Yeah. It was better than bungee jumping, and my imploded body . . .it disappeared, I disappeared, down to less than a photon, I'm telling you I was less than a photon."

"How did you know that?"

"I dunno. Looked, I guess. I was viewing myself at the same time as being myself. Honest. I was looking through some kind of cosmic microscope. An electron microscope - with a boost. Ha ha ha."

"Ha ha ha."

"Then I exploded and became a Universe!"

"Holy shit! What a trip. Did you take something before you went in there?"

"Nah, you know I don't do drugs. If I got caught, my country would shoot me!"

"I told you. The room is better than drugs." Tom said matter of factly.

"When I landed back in the room, I was a puddle of jelly laying there. Numen told me, (from behind his drape) ha ha, 'you're connected to everything, EVERYTHING."

"HA HA HA HA. Told you. I wondered if you'd ever have a cosmic. . .supernatural experience in that room. I knew it!"

"Shit. What do you think is in that room?"

"Something bigger than us. Something that knows a lot more than we do. Do you believe in God now?" Tom asked.

"I believe in the devil. Ha ha ha ha." Chib couldn't stop laughing. Tom joined in and the two of them laughed all morning long. "The devil huh??"

"Yeah. The devil made me do it, made me pull that drape down. Ha ha ha. And I'm glad I did it. Ha ha ha! That trip will last me my whole life! Forever man. F-O-R-E-V-E-R!"

Later that day when Tom was sitting in class and should be concentrating, he was thinking about Chib's experience instead.

He could never have moved the drape aside like that, even though he had thought about it more than once. Doing such a thing was downright rude and against the rules set forth by being in the room; although the Teacher never once said that the drape couldn't be touched. Now he wished he'd been the one to have done it. Then he wondered if he could do it with his mind, the way he maneuvered a door. Was the drape like a door?

Of course, he could still do it, grab the drape with his hands, but he would never do such a rude thing!

Tom snapped back to the ongoing lecture about the neck. "When you are here," the teacher was saying, "this area is difficult to find, but you better pay attention to it, because a person's quality of life is at state."

The course was difficult. Here was lucky they let him take. Most students were at a more advanced level than him. Several of the students in pre-med were taking it for the second time. Tom was disgusted because he wasn't in pre-med, had not made up his mind that he was going to be, and his goal was to pull up his grade point average, not to bring it down with this fucking hard Gross Anatomy class! Chib had talked him into taking it. But he found he liked it and was doing well in spite of the difficult material and besides, the person teaching the course seemed to like him, singling him out occasionally as teacher's sometimes do when they want to point something out, so he probably would get his good grade after all, because it was uncanny. Every time the teacher did that, Tom just happened to know the answer, and that wasn't always the case. He didn't always know the answers, he only knew them when he was called upon!

He drew a picture of the neck and colored in the area under discussion. He had several of these drawings in his sketchbook. His drawings were different than the ones in the textbook and although they weren't to scale, they did have a degree of accuracy and were helpful. The more important an area was, the more intense Tom made the color to define it.

Later that day Tom worked at Carl's. During his dinner break he looked again at his drawing. He took a pencil and added an image of the devil over it so the horns were the ears. He laughed about it because certainly the devil was humankind! Of that he had no doubt at all. He knew the craziness of what he'd done would help him remember his diagram.

Carl was behind the counter and going back and forth boxing pizza while he and Jake were taking a break eating in back, when Tom glanced around the corner and noticed the line was getting longer. "Hey Jake, I'm going back to help - the line's too long." He said jumping up and sprinting out. "Carl's in trouble."

Jake couldn't follow. "I've had nothing to eat all day and I've got to call Lisa," he told Tom ravenously hungry. "The smell of the pizza has been driving me crazy!"

Carl moved over to the prep and boxing table with a look that Tom never forgot. There were already three pizza's waiting to be cut.

That night was the craziest Tom could remember.

John, who had already taken his break, was reaching exhaustion. All three levels of the pizza oven were constantly full. He started making his noise every two minutes so many pizzas were coming out.

A few people knew to ask Tom about his special, but many didn't know about it. Tom usually told everyone about the special, especially the new people, but he was so busy he hardly thought about it.

Sally from the beauty salon was in the line with her son, Frank. The kid had been begging to get a pizza there for weeks but she hadn't been motivated, not until her conversation with Marsha. Now Sally couldn't wait to go down herself and see the place. Frank was delighted.

Tom forgot to tell Sally about the special. She had overheard him mentioning it to other people - had heard the elephant, had seen the antics. It didn't really matter since Frank had arrived with something else in mind, a favorite that he wanted, so the special wasn't something they would have gotten anyway, only, Sally couldn't shake the innuendo she'd heard from Marsha.

Sally watched intently as people came and went. There were the Johnson's - they were told about the special. Oh yes. She had always suspected the Johnson's of something shady - from the get -go. Uh huh. And there was a couple she had never seen before; they had leathers on and arrived on a chopped motorcycle parked outside. The guy kept shifting his gaze. He was a real nut case. And what about the teenager with all the tattoos? She decided Marsha was right. Tom hadn't included her in his "code," at least that's the way she thought about it.

After they closed, when Carl went to his office with the night's receipts, he noticed a pizza sitting on the table in the break room. He stepped into the room. It was Tom's favorite - The Hawaiian, left uneaten.

The men soon filled the room. It had become normal for Tom to distribute his tips. He had a box that he kept under the counter in case his jar got too full so he could empty it under there. The box was heaping.

Carl went to his office and came back to thank the threesome.

He noticed Tom was eating a piece of cold pizza and counting out the tips. He sat down. "I'll not forget this night - ever."

The following week, there were a number of women having their hair done at Sally's and the gossip flowed. Sally didn't say much, but she opened the door for speculation - just as Marsha had.

There might not have been any harm done, but when Faye Diggs heard even a tidbit of gossip, there was no turning back. Carl's pizzeria and the three men were now part of a mafia ring pushing who knew what kind of drugs on unsuspecting youth.

And who was at the helm of all of it?

Tom.

THE ONLY SON OF GOD

Tom would never run out of questions. Why hadn't I thought of that?" He asked himself hundreds of times. But he knew this time the Teacher would not have an answer. It was something in the Bible he found troubling.

He stood at the door, impatient to go in. "Oh, just open up." He thought. It did.

He was standing in a row of kids in front of the church's congregation. He was happy and uncomfortable all at once. It was graduation time for his Sunday School Class.

His father had helped him dress in his first suit of clothes: white shirt, bow tie, matching trousers and pants. His mother took a photo of him standing with his dad outside before they left.

His Pastor went down the row to each child and said some special words, but Tom couldn't remember what they were. He had been too nervous to really hear them. He presented each child with their first Bible, shook their hand, the congregation stood, clapped, and they all sang a song.

Jesus love me this I know. . .

After the service, there were cookies shaped like people in long robes and cupcakes and punch. Many people came up and congratulated him.

As the vision vanished, Tom decided he would ask his parents to bring his Bible. They were coming for a visit soon. His parents said the Bible required faith, but Tom's argument with them was one of science.

Tom was an opinionated person, insistent about his position, something he inherited from his father and the two of them would tangle. So much so, his father had nicknamed him "Doggy" for being so dogmatic. But Teacher was changing this about him. Still, there were many things he found troubling about the Bible.

He asked the Teacher about it now. "Teacher," he said, "why does the Bible say, . . . 'God so loved the world that He gave His only Begotten Son. . .' His voice trailed off. "If Everything that is, is God, then why does the passage make this distinction? . . .That Jesus is the only son? The only son of God?"

There was no silence, no hesitation, as there sometimes was when the Teacher was thinking about how to answer Tom. But as he sometimes did, the Teacher answered a question with a question.

"Have you ever thought about how difficult it would be to try and put the entire ocean into a single glass of water?"

Tom looked at the curtain dumbfounded. "No," he squeaked.

"I think you may have noticed, in the Universe that there has been a compression that has taken place - movement and change that compresses huge amounts of shape, form, energy etc., into a very small space. The density and the gravity are tremendous. This is something you have observed in your physics studies. True?"

"Um. . .yeah."

"Okay," Numen continued. "Think about that. We are going to move away from the black hole of the Universe to the black hole in people. Here is the problem. God is ALL around you, but you cannot discern the fact. Why? God is everywhere, but man doesn't seem to recognize God in himself, in others and all around everywhere. Why not? Let us go back to an early idea. The cake. We use sugar in the cake. We have this huge sack of beautiful white sugar, but the person making the cake puts a pinch of sugar in the cake instead of a cup. So. . . you think there is no sugar in the cake. But there is. And there is sugar spread all around the kitchen, but because you cannot taste it in the cake, you don't believe in sugar. But if a cup of sugar is poured into a cup of water, you believe in sugar. It is *concentrated* or dense. You can taste it and see it, and feel its stickiness, and you distinguish it more easily. It is right there in front of you. Then you would argue with everyone about the presence of sugar. Right?"

Tom had an idea now where Numen was going with the thought. "Right," He said.

"There have been all kinds of definitions about what begotten means, and it means them all. We are all created by God, because we are all part of everything and everything is of God. But Jesus was a container that was able to hold more than the average human. Wouldn't you agree?"

"Yes. He was able to shine his spirit through his humanity, through his physicality."

"Most of us don't even know we have a spirit."

"True."

"Jesus was a container that held more of the ocean or like the example of the cake - he held lots of sugar. He held the sugar so you could see it and know the truth. Perhaps what he was saying to all of us was, believe in what I have, because you have it too.

"We are existing in a dimension that requires physical dominance, not spiritual dominance and therefore you and I can only tolerate a pinch not a cup of that spiritual essence (that I am likening to sugar).

"There have been many wonderful people throughout history that have been able to tolerate more than you and I, such as Joan of Arc or Mother Teresa, and still be human and still function under physical dominance. I'm afraid, though, that many people are intimidated by it. Many people are not able to hold much sugar. . ."

"You always say things so simply," Tom said. "I complicate them and yet your answer seems so clear. You explain so much about Jesus and what the Bible says. Do you think there were several that were containers like him?"

"No, I don't. We all are to a degree. There were others, yet perhaps not to the same degree. Jesus did not become physically ill so he was not pulled back into physical dominance by his being - that is - by being a human being. Other enlightened prophets, and there have been many wonderful ones, had an end to their physical bodies, like you and I. Some became sick before the end, and unfortunately people are believing more of what was said during their physical dominance rather than during the time that they were able to hold more spiritual essence in themselves. One can argue that this happened to Jesus too, by being crucified on the cross. But those who were there, have said differently. He left his body while he was enduring physical pain as a gift of love to us. Right? He probably did exit before His body failed. . .and that is why His body was so well preserved. . ."

"Ohhh, I see." Tom said quietly, "When we are able to control the physical better, then we will be able to bring about more spiritual dominance into this dimension. Do you think that?"

"Of course. Absolutely."

"Well, what do you think about the other part of that scriptural phrase. 'God so loved the world'. . .?"

"It is my belief, Tom, and certainly not the belief of others, that love, hate, and all the other emotional responses that we have, are confined to this level of existence. I'm just reminding you of this. We've spoken about it before. These are our definitions. God is the force of the Universe. God is Everything. God does not pick and choose. God does not say, this person is worthy to live and not drown in the flood, and this person's child is worthy to live etc. God does not do that. God is an all abiding force. It is within our spiritual family, our spiritual knowledge that love exists. It is important that we nurture it, because it belongs to us.

"It is our gift – it is like a parent who gives you a gift, because they want you to have it. It is a gift that was given to us, along with all the other gifts of emotions that comprise what we are; and Jesus wanted us to know that some of our physical emotional character we keep and take with us, and some of it we shed and leave here. Of course, God has created us along with everything else, and now we must understand that we are physical for only a short change while we experience many things, one of which is love. Can you imagine how many might want to come here for this gift. . .to take along with us forever? What an opportunity! We must learn to love ourselves and others the way Jesus taught! We might not be able to come here again Jesus loved the world - and showed us how to love. *We were given the gift of love.*"

"Take with us?"

"Yes, Tom. You will take with you all that you are and all that you have learned and all that you have become." Numen said.

"Genesis says we'll have dominion over the world," Tom said.

"Yes," Teacher said. "It's true. Dominance is physical. Dominion is our physical power, but that does not mean the power to disconnect ourselves from other creatures to be "better" than their creator - our creator, does it? Genesis does not say "Human" dominance. That is an egocentric assumption. Just like we don't want to believe in any kind of evolution." She laughed her beautiful tinkling light song. "God is change and evolution. We are connected to even the ugliest of creatures. Some of our own internal organs are not pretty to look at. . ." The room filled with her laughing essence. "We are connected to the snake. Yes, we can kill the snake, or the snake can kill us. So what? What then? The snake will not go away. What does go away are the physical things YOU created. They may turn into dust. Your painting does not have an identity address in the scheme of things. . .but the ingredients of the painting are all part of everything. . ."

And the room laughed.

Tom felt the tingle along the top of his shoulders.

"God so loved the world." Numen filled the room. "Love is our gift. We must love the world and all that is it."

The room dimmed. It didn't dim as when you dim a light, not like that. It dimmed as with a quiet, like when the cricket stops humming to listen to the night, or when the butterfly stops fluttering her wings for a second on a flower, or the tree branches are swaying ever so gently. It was a changing of the colors from the brightness that can sometimes seem artificial, to a softness that wraps a person in a hug of morning dawn. It was like when the players have finished a particularly difficult performance and are now taking a bow.

Tom felt himself lower his head, felt his hands open as if to receive something being poured into them. He sat there ever so still. He didn't know for how long because time became nothing. He was suspended. He didn't feel himself, his body, his heart beating or even his mind thinking. He just was. He loved this room and the Numen and the person he had become. He had changed. His life would never be the same.

Jesus loved the world. . . Jesus was our example. . .

As he arose, something in him was very quiet and very gentle. His words were soft, and as he said them, they had a quality that resonated from someplace deep, someplace special within him and now it was he that filled the room as he spoke.

"I love you Teacher."

THE CAT

Tom thought about Chelsea at odd times. One time it was because he was in the Quad and an advertisement came up on the wall TV about the dress shop where she worked part time. Another time it was while he was studying during his break and he remembered her saying, "I have to go now, Tom, I have to study." He teased her about it, saying that nobody was going to care about her grades when she went for job interviews.

"Have you ever heard of an interviewer asking for your grades?" He teased her. "The important thing," he remembers saying, "is to graduate without getting BAD grades that will get you on probation or getting into trouble. RIGHT?" Now here he was, really concerned about his own grades, but mostly it was because he had joined this study group and he didn't want to look bad and because he may decide, with a big maybe question mark, to continue on to graduate school and then they would matter.

Sometimes he wished he could go back and tidy up his transcripts, but he didn't think that very often. He had played too much! Chelsea used to say, "Tom, it isn't that anybody is going to ask me about my grades, it is about me asking myself about the job I did in school, about the people who believed in me and the money they gave me because they cared and they believed I cared too. I want to do a good job for them AND for myself. It is a matter of pride."

He remembered scoffing at her.   He had regrets over Chelsea, but they weren't about breaking up with her, they were about how he had done the deed of ending it and about himself, about his own shallowness. He regretted things about himself. One night he was sitting at his desk, studying Organic Chemistry, and he was thinking about this, when he thought about the power of thinking and about action. He had some 3 x 5 cards that he was using with his studies, and he picked one up and wrote on it. "I'm sorry Tom," he wrote to himself, "I didn't understand what a good person you really are."

He looked at it, thinking what a silly thing he had just done, and was about to tear it up, when he realized that was not a good idea. He laughed. He cried, he looked at it some more. He thought: This is crazy. Then he considered what he wrote. "I'm sorry Tom, I didn't realize what a good person you really are."

He nodded, and read it again. He had been doing an injustice to himself, he thought. But that is not what he had intended to write. It just came out. He was going to write something else.

"Oh well," he said to himself, taping it to the wall behind his desk. "I'll look at it for a while. I AM a good person."

He went back to studying organic chemistry. He needed a chemistry class, but it didn't have to be organic chemistry - which had a reputation for being harder than hard. He didn't know why he had signed up for it. It was one of those things he couldn't explain. It was Chib's fault.

He looked at the small clock he'd mounted near the back of his desk. It was 2 o'clock a.m. but he was going to study for a while longer before going to sleep, one of the hazards of his late job at Carl's. He would be meeting with the study group for coffee and he wasn't going to show up "foolish."

He had a hi-liter in his hand when his head fell against his chest. He slept like that dreaming of a large red barn filled with the scent of newly mown hay when something startled him awake. He couldn't be sure what. He listened. It was so soft, he could hardly hear it and he wondered why such a sound would awaken him, least of all cause him to startle awake? He went to his front door, opened it and looked outside, left and right. It was coming from his right, from his neighbor to the right.

A couple lived next door. Both were students, but they were happy, never fought and were graduate students looking forward to a future together when both of them were finished with school. He knew little about them. He tiptoed over and looked in the wide-open window. She was seated on the couch, sobbing into her hands, and then she seemed to feel his presence and looked up, tears streaming down her face. She nodded, got up and went to the door.

Tom looked down at himself, embarrassed. He was in T-shirt and sweatpants and was ruffled and unkempt.

"I'm sorry I bothered you," she said. "I didn't think I was being loud."

"No" he said. "I was just studying late and fell off for a few minutes."

"My cat," she said, "somebody hit my cat and just left him there - in the parking lot." She cried harder and couldn't talk.

If a person were to ask Tom later, during a particularly vulnerable moment, he might admit that he "felt" the kitty and its painful distress as he entered the room. He turned and met its eyes.

"He, uh, he, got out when I was carrying the laundry out and I didn't realize it until later." She said, "Then I looked for him and he wasn't here! I went outside and called him and he didn't come. I hunted and hunted for him and it was dark and he wasn't anywhere. I don't know what made me do it, but I crouched down and looked under the cars and he was lying down there, under a car!"

"How did you get him out?"

"I came up here and got our little sign board from the kitchen wall and went back down and slid it under him. He obviously was hit by a car!"

"Ohhhh." She cried, gesturing to her cat, now in a shallow box next to the door in the kitchen.

At first Tom thought to himself, "it is just a cat," and then the Teacher's words rang in his head, "we are all connected, we must respect all things. . . all life. . .everything."

The kitty was hurt, but alive.

"I don't know what to do," she said wringing her hands, crying. "Simeon is making a courier run and we don't have money for emergency vet bills. It is the middle of the night and I don't have a car!" She whined. "Oh, my poor kitty."

Tom crouched down next to the box. A gray kitty looked back at him through liquid eyes. He tried to move, but struggled and gave up.

"I have an idea," Tom said, looking back at his neighbor. "By the way, my name is Tom. I live next door."

"I know. I've seen you off and on. I'm Kate." She said, "My little cat is badly hurt and I can't do anything. . ."

"I have a car." Tom said simply.

"But it's the middle of the night. . .and I don't have any money. . .and. ."

"Let's try," Tom said. "Come on. Let's see if anybody is around the campus at the Vet Service building." He picked up the box, took the cat to his car and they drove on campus. It was deserted, but they went into the area where the graduate school was located.

"I came home from my late shift at E & Bs," she explained, "and I was so tired, but I thought I'd get to the laundry machines before they closed. I didn't realize Nibs had snuck out around the door. It was a couple of hours before I went to feed him. A couple of hours before I realized he wasn't in the apartment." She cried. "He has done this before but I always knew it. Tonight, I didn't catch him sneaking around me! It was so dark!"

"I found him in the parking lot, struggling to get up. He couldn't get up." She repeated again. "He couldn't get up!" She began rocking and sobbing harder. "It's my fault."

Tom said a silent prayer as he drove the quiet streets looking for signs at the various buildings. None of them had any lights on. He remembered seeing a sign about Veterinary services, or something like that when he had driven through the campus before. The University was large and complete with graduate schools in medicine, law, and veterinary medicine, but he seldom went into this area of the campus. There was a building ahead with lights on and a few people about, but it was the medical library, a 24-hour study facility and technical center. He parked. "I'm going in there." He said. "Do you want to stay with the cat?"

"Yes." She said hugging the box.

It was 3:30 am and he wondered why the place was open at all. There was a counter ahead manned by a person who could have been a student. "Hello," he said quietly. "How come you are open?" He asked.

"We're here twenty-four seven. We're a resource for the hospital. How can I help you?"

"I have a cat in the car that has been hurt. He was hit by a vehicle. I don't know where to take him. Do you have any ideas?"

The young man behind the counter locked his computer and looked around. "It is quiet, it won't hurt to give you five minutes. Are you parked close?"

"I'm right outside. I figured nobody would give me a ticket at 3:30 am."

"Oh, they will be around here," he said hurrying out the door. "They don't have anything else to do. I'm a veterinary student," he said. "In my last year."

Kate had tears rolling down her cheeks. She was hugging the box on her lap and was speaking quietly to Nibs when Tom opened her car door. The student looked at the box, looked at her, then at the box again, and said, "We better go inside, in the light." He took the box from her and turned to Tom. "You need to park your car somewhere else."

Tom didn't have a parking pass. "Where? Where can I go?" The student had moved away. Tom called out quietly, although he didn't know why since there wasn't anybody living around there. "I don't have a sticker. . ."

"Oh, uh. . .follow me. There's a loading space here. . ."

In minutes, Frank hunched over the box holding it close to his chest obviously worried the cat would jump out, a signal that he clearly had some experience with something like this in the past.

He disappeared behind the counter and unlocked his computer, "Have to do this first." He said looking up; then he was on the floor behind the counter examining the cat.

"We can't be sure without an x-ray," he said. "But I believe your cat's back leg has a couple of breaks from the tarsus down, which is a good thing, because it doesn't involve the hip. The hip seems to be okay. I think kitty was shocked but is going to be okay. We can't be sure without x-rays, but I don't think your cat has internal injuries. I think the injury is confined to his leg. We can set it tomorrow when the clinic opens. If you like, I can help you with that."

"I'm on a limited budget," she said.

"I understand, but I can use the experience. I know kitty is having some pain, but this is going to have to wait awhile. I believe your cat will live and we'll make it lots better for,. . um. . .?" He looked up questioningly.

"Nibs."

". . .better for Nibs in the morning. Okay?"

He was one of the kindest people Tom had ever met. He had been so used to his party buddies and now here was this person, so careful, so kind, looking over this small injured animal in such a loving way and speaking to his owner in a calm caring voice. He was to always remember how he asked the animal's name.

Tom went around the counter and reached into the box and pet the kitty, grateful he had been a part of the solution for the neighbor he hardly knew. At first, he had been scared the cat might try and bite him, but when he saw the student handle him and how the cat had reacted so favorably, he knew it was okay, that the cat knew people were trying to help him. He rubbed his finger under Nibs' cheeks and the injured kitty made a few purrs. Tom looked up surprised, "How can the kitty purr when he is in pain?" He asked.

"Because he senses he is being helped and that he is going to be alright," the vet student said. "Animals can sense kindness. . ." He said. "I'm sorry, but you cannot be behind here."

Tom and Kate left Nibs in Frank's hands and returned in the morning to learn what the x-rays had shown about the cat's injury. The feline had weathered through the rest of the morning without incident and Frank had transferred Nibs to an animal holding area in a small kennel. The kitty had been bruised and knocked silly but he was doing well.

"The news is positive," Frank said with pride at his initial diagnosis, "his permanent injury only involves his back leg." Later in the day, Tom and Kate were back in their apartments with Nibs who was hobbling around on a leg that was not cooperating - not in the way the cat would have liked. The lower part of the cat's leg was encased, almost like a human's would be, with an opening at the bottom for his toes.

When Simeon, Kate's husband, came back the next day, it was to a grateful Kate and to his beloved Nibs who had a good chance of healing - thanks to a student named Frank and his neighbor, Tom. Kate gave him all the details, sparing nothing, including the tears. Simeon, tired from a critical trip with a hand delivery for the hospital, had attended his morning class before coming home. His graduate studies in bioengineering were demanding and he didn't want any lost time from this particular class.

Simeon knocked on Tom's door, but he wasn't home. "He was so nice, Sim," she told him.

"I thought he was just a party boy," he said. "Guess I misunderstood him."

"I haven't heard anything lately," Kate said. "I never even hear music anymore. He was so nice, Sim. Our kitty is alive because of him."

Simeon crashed and was soon asleep. Both he and Kate worked at night, which was easier now that Tom was a quieter neighbor. Tom worked an evening shift too, but not as late as his neighbors and Tom hadn't needed daytime sleep in between classes - which hadn't interfered with the partying he used to have. It was loud and annoying behavior.

It was later when Simeon was in the parking lot, leaving for work that he heard his neighbor's door closing lightly above him. He looked up to see Tom coming out and called out to him. "Hey neighbor, got a few?"

Tom had never really met Simeon, but he knew who he was. He checked his watch, and said, "I got ten."

"So, do I," and the older student sprinted up the flight of steps to greet Tom, shaking his hand and following him into the apartment that Tom held open. "I want to thank you for what you did to help my cat - and especially that you noticed the distress coming from my wife. It is comforting to know I have a neighbor like you." He looked around Tom's apartment.

"Wow, you have a nice place here!"

And then he saw the stack on the desk.

"Hey, guy, what's ya studying for - the m-cats?" He laughed, referring to the exam student's take for entrance to medical school. "Nobody takes organic chemistry unless they have to." He gestured.

Tom shrugged, embarrassed, "Nah. . .I don't know why. . .I. . .uh. . .I. . ."

"That's how come you heard her," Simeon said knowingly, "My wife said she was sobbing quietly, but you came and asked about her at two am. She said you seemed to know there was something abnormally distressful about the situation. You were studying - that's why you heard her."

Tom glanced around his apartment. He felt vulnerable, like he wanted to hide, but there was no place to hide from the other guy. His study materials were out on the desk and dates were marked on his wall calendar; what had been private wasn't so private anymore. He felt a flush coming up his neck.

"That's uh. . .those are dates for my study group. It's just . . .the material is more difficult than I thought. Some of them are taking the m-cat test."

Simeon's eyes landed on the card that Tom had written and taped on the wall "I'm sorry Tom, I didn't realize what a good person you really are." Of course, he didn't know that Tom had written it himself, which added to Tom's embarrassment.

"You know, if you're taking Organic Chem, you ought to take the m-cats anyway," Simeon chuckled, "just for the hell of it."

Simeon's eyes went to the basket where Tom had the anatomy book from the summer's first session. "So, I see you studied some Gross Anatomy too? Was that for the fun of it too?"

"Well. . .I. . ."

"How did you do? It's a terrible class and nobody, but nobody ever leaves there with an A. If a person leaves there with a B they are top notch."

"Well I. . ."

"Did you take it from Tips the Terrible? He never, ever uses a fellow to help him teach. There's no chance with him, and from what I understand he's the only one who teaches the summer sessions."

"Yeah well, we got along okay."

"Really? What did you get?"

"I uh. . .I uh."

"Do tell, Tom. I got a "C" from him! He is a bastard, you know."

"Well, he seemed to like me. . .and I was lucky. He knew I wasn't going on to medical school so my grade didn't matter."

"No Tom. That isn't him. You can't convince me of that. Every grade matters to him and he doesn't give two cents of a care whether or not you go on to anything."

Tom remembered back to the day when T-T came by his desk, snooping around, looking to see what he was doing with his colored pencils. He thought he was playing. Tom had finished coloring in a portion of a diagram he'd drawn based on Tips lecture material.

"What's this?" T-T asked.

"That's the most important area - right here," Tom said tapping his pencil. "I color it in more intensely so I'll always remember what you explained. I want it to stand out."

Tom's diagram wasn't like the one in the book, but more closely resembled the Professor's explanation.

"Would you mind if I made a copy of that?" T-T asked. Of course, Tom gave it to him.

It was always like that. With T-T, Tom could do no wrong.

"Well, uh, it was probably because it didn't matter so much, but T-T gave me an A." He finally confessed to Simeon.

"That seals it Tom, you've got to take the m-cats. Getting an A from him will speak very, very highly of you on an application!"

"Taking the m-cats would be a waste of money," Tom laughed. "My overall grades aren't high enough. I could never consider such a thing. I wouldn't have the money to go to medical school anyway." He looked at his feet in embarrassment. "I have to go to class. I don't want to be late."

"Yeah," Simeon said, slapping him congenially on the back, "I gotta go too. Glad we had a couple of minutes to meet. Don't worry your secret's safe with me. If it is the right thing for you, Tom, then it will happen. It just will. You'll get high marks and it will fall into place. Best not to worry over it but just to do it. Right?"

Tom hadn't realized he'd been holding his breath until he exhaled. "Right" he said, hurrying out the door. He realized that Simeon hadn't believed a word he said. The truth was, Tom had told the truth. He had no intention of taking the m-cats. Why had Simeon said such a thing?

Tom thought back to the day when he signed up for that class in Organic Chemistry. He'd already taken the anatomy course and what a foolish thing that was. But he did get an A and that didn't hurt him. He'd heard he received the only "A" T-T had ever given.

Signing up for the worst, the most difficult, the most awful class known to a student - organic chemistry - was about his only stupidity. He needed some semester units in chemistry, simple chemistry - you know, just some lab work and fun stuff, but he had been putting it off, fooling around, having fun. But now his graduation was coming up and when he went to sign up for the simple chemistry class, they were all full. He couldn't believe it. He put himself on a waiting list. He was sure he'd get in at least one of the classes. Two of the listed classes created a conflict with other classes he needed. But he could juggle. He didn't worry about it for a few days, and even his advisor had been "overly confident." He could wait and get it in another term before graduation, but Tom was nervous about it. And then he met a classmate from anatomy who encouraged him.

In the end, Tom did it. He just cruised in and with the stroke of his silly pen put himself in organic chemistry. What had he done? He'd heard a few things about it, some comments in the grapevine, but he never paid much attention. It was like something blocked him from realizing what he was doing.

"We weed out the weeds in here." The professor had said. "All you guys are thinking about going to medical, dental or veterinary school? You better mean it with all you've got, because it will take all you've got just to pass this course. If you want good advice from me, you will form your study groups NOW."

Tom was invited into a study group that first day. He liked the time of their meetings and that they were going to assemble at the Quad, so he was "in." And it was the "in" group who knew how good a student he'd been in his previous class. They wanted Tom! Now, it seemed like all he did was study for the study group. The class consumed him.

Tom was busy that night working at Carl's. He didn't get a break and worked straight through until he left at 1:00 am. He had a big pot of tips again and excitedly took them back to his friends for the cut. It was a great night.

At closing time Carl came in just as they finished mopping up the counters. It wasn't Tom's job to help with the back-kitchen clean-up, but he'd started doing that lately. They all started helping one another with everything. "We're a team!" They said. More and more they worked that way and the public seemed to respond to the warm feeling that was present in the place. Tom had his pizza for the road - slices that he stacked so he could carry them easily, and was ready to head for home when Carl, the owner, sat down and started eating pizza with Jake and John causing Tom to hesitate. Carl never sat with them like that and it was nice, but he was tired and his pizza was wrapped and he looked forward to home.

"G'night," Tom said and sprinted for home.

Carl looked at Jake and John. "Hey," he said. "How are things?" They both nodded with mouths stuffed full. "You know, Tom is sharing with you guys. . .right? He doesn't have to do that." They nodded again.

Jake gulped. "It's making a difference for us," he said. "It isn't much, but it sure is nice. What a great guy!"

"Well" Carl said, "That nice guy," he gestured towards the door, is studying to take his m-cats. Did you know that?" They both shook their heads. They weren't up on what that meant.

"That's the examination for entrance to medical school." Carl said.

Jake choked. He had a coughing fit that lasted until he got up and drew some water and downed it. "No kidding," he managed. "Medical School costs a fortune!"

"No kidding," Carl said to Jake. "I saw him studying the materials. He has never talked about it. It is extremely hard to get into Medical School so I think he figures it's a long shot."

"Yeah, must be" They both nodded again.

"I just wanted you to know," Carl said, "That Tom is even a nicer guy than you thought."

That night, when Jake got home, he sat at the kitchen table and thought about Tom. His wife came in from her night shift at the hospital. She worked there as an RN, a good job, in fact, a great job. They were young and she was helping her husband through his last year of school. Life was good.

He told his wife about Tom.

"What do you think?" She asked.

"Well, he is different, and he does study a lot. . ."

"Did you notice anything about what kind of classes he is taking? What is he studying?"

"Yeah, he complains about organic chemistry."

"Oh yes," she said. "Carl is right! There is only one reason why a student takes organic chemistry. . ."

PAIN

That week Tom thought about a lot of things. Sometimes he just sat in his living room in silence and thought about the stuff the Teacher said. He thought about good and evil. He thought about things that were so far beyond explanation that he couldn't find the words to describe the thoughts, much less the questions that kept surfacing.

Finally, he pulled out his tablet. He wrote something down, crossed it out and wrote down other thoughts again. He tried to think clearly but one thought was being pushed out by other ones, toppling this way and that. He realized his thoughts were unfocused most of the time - that he didn't really know how to think. Was there such a thing as learning how to think? He was beginning to realize that his thoughts were more powerful than he had ever dreamed possible and that his questions could be important to his future.

He considered the animal in the trap when he was a kid. He thought about how everything in the world seemed to hurt everything else. Why was the system based on pain? He wrote down that question. Pain. Why was there so much pain? Susan had been in a lot of pain. He decided his next question would be about pain.

He understood he was part of a system. That made sense to him. It was the system itself that didn't make sense. He wrote down: Stupid System. But now, he couldn't think any more about it. He had school and work and his thoughts had to be about that. Oh well, he thought, I have my next question and right now that's what is important.

He had a quiz that week and a paper to write. He sat at his little desk and rubbed the finish on the top. It was smooth and nice. He was pleased that he found something so nice. It was a bargain, a price that he didn't believe possible. The desk looked new, not a scratch on it. He had a stack of papers neatly arranged and his laptop poised ready for work.

He started with his studies and although the work wasn't easy, he moved along at a good pace. He liked his school work. Soon he would be finished and looking for a real job. Who would hire a Physics major, he asked himself?

Tom never did write down any more questions that week. It seemed that the one question was very large and enough for his visit.

Tom forgot about the door and his visions, probably because of his change to a different day and the many things that had happened during the week. When he tried to push through the door, he bumped up hard against it. "Ouch!"

A couple of students had been walking down the hall and saw it, laughing uproariously. "Hey stupid," one of them called over, "You could've knocked!"

Tom glanced over at their backs and kicked the bottom of the door lightly. "Shit."

He stepped back and mentally created a huge beaker of a substance that he knew would disintegrate the metal door and leave it in a heap. What he didn't realize is that the two boys had stopped and were watching him from a distance, snickering and fueling their conversation with silly words about the guy trying to get into an office that was obviously CLOSED.

And then it happened. The door disintegrated.

"Hey!" One of them was screaming as they ran, "did you see that!" But as they arrived for a closer look, Tom was through the door and it had materialized once again.

"What was THAT?!"

The two boys pounded on the door

Tom could hear them on the other side. "Get lost ass holes." He said.

He could hear them trying the doorknob. He chuckled. "You'll never be able to enter here." Tom sniffed.

They stood outside the door for several minutes trying to figure out what they had seen.

"I know I saw that," one of them yelled. "Yeah. we saw it alright."

Finally, they left and Tom felt comfortable moving deeper into the room.

Tom knew the students had interfered with him receiving any kind of daydream or vision. He wasn't happy about it. But he shrugged it off and mentally flipped the bird to the two boys on the other side of the door.

The Teacher gasped.

Tom turned to the drape, grinning, "Why is our system based on pain?

"That's a big question and there's much to be said about that." The Teacher answered easily, as if expecting the question. First, I want to know what you mean regarding pain?"

"Why do we have to feel pain, physical pain?" Tom persisted. "One creature eats another. . ."

"Of course, you know pain helps keep us alive. It is a matter of understanding danger, but I don't think you mean that. Do you?"

"No, I don't mean that. I understand the flight or fright principle - it serves to keep us alive. But our bodies feel so much pain as they are giving out. Why not just give out when our time has come?"

"Without physical pain, we cannot understand one another within this system," the Teacher said easily. "It is one of our strong connecting links. It is part of belonging to a physical system. Love is not physical, joy is not physical, pleasure is not physical, unless of course it is sensory as in sex, but sex is not the same for all creatures. Pain is. We understand pain in a way that unites us. Pain is also a key to love."

"Huh?" Tom half laughed. "Pain and love?"

"Some say pain is the key to real love."

Tom sat still, very, very still. Something did not compute but he felt the tell-tell chill. Then he asked, "You mean it is pain that connects us and not love?"

"Yes."

"No." Tom shook his head vehemently.

"Yes. Consider this, "the Teacher said amicably, "It is through Jesus' ordeal on the cross that we love him and find truth in his words. Jesus could have said 'love one another' repeating it again and again like a parrot, but who would have listened? It was through his ordeal of pain that we listen."

Tom thought about this. The room was very quiet, as it usually was, when he heard something of great depth to think about. Then there was a faint hum, a song far in the distance, something about a hill, with words that had a kind of beauty, only he couldn't quite hear what was being said. He cleared his throat. "Teacher," he said, "do you hear that song?"

"I don't hear a song," the Teacher said. "Maybe it is your song."

Tom listened.

After a while, the Teacher spoke.

"Tom, when truth is spoken there is a ring to the truth. You've heard me say this before, but sometimes it can be more than that. When you know inside yourself that something is not only true but very important, there can be this little sound, this bit of vibration, like that of a bell going off someplace deep inside that can sometimes be like a song. Maybe you are hearing a song about truth? It is a wise person that learns what this vibration is. It is more than intuition, it is more than a hunch or a sound, it is your inner self, your being-ness. It is a knowing. It is telling you something with certainty - about truth and something more. . .that it is very important to you in your life."

Tom listened again. The song was gone.

"Humans in their superiority used to believe that other creatures couldn't feel compassion, or love or even have consciousness or self-awareness. We have devised all kinds of tests to measure these traits in animals, mainly so we could prove to ourselves how superior we are over them."

Tom heard something again. Actually, it was a perception. It was like he was hearing something being said, an imprint in his mind, but it was so sad and its pain so real. It was a cry, like that in his dream of the whale. His eyes welled up in response. "We have been so cruel with our experiments on animals," he said.

"Our presumption of superiority has cost us dearly. We are lonely. It has blocked us from better knowing our world! All creatures have their own set of being-ness and their own self-awareness of what they are. We presume to measure what they are when we don't even know what we are! We all have a stamp of identity for what our experience is here. All creatures have their right to exist and a purpose. An important lesson is not one of superiority, but one of respect, sameness, and connectedness. We may not understand what a dog's consciousness is, but we can understand the dog's pain and that the dog has a consciousness too. We can understand the heartbreak pain of a bird that has lost its mate, although we may not understand what its love for its mate actually was. It is through pain that compassion is built. We learn to love deeply through empathy - relating to another's experience."

Tom sat very still, breathing very shallowly, listening.

"The most common link, and the most understandable one, is the one of pain. It is important to allow yourself to feel both physical pain and emotional pain. Pain is the link to our fellow creatures. Our emotional pain is the unseen link to the spiritual system. It is one of the few crossovers we have. It is a kind of fuel that we give from the physical plane to the other dimension. They have a need for the fuel of love and compassion from us. It is important to feed this into the stream. . ."

"What?" Tom broke in. "What did you say? Did you say the stream needs fuel?"

"Last week we were talking about Hitler. Of course, the spiritual link to all the people Hitler hurt, still living after he died, is not physical now - but his identity is connected to all that emotional pain in this physical system. The spirit could not "feel" the physical pain inflicted, but emotional pain is the crossover. It exists in the physical plane AND in the stream - on the unseen plain and is felt even more so on that plane. The reconciliation is not physical. Do you understand?"

"Yes, I think so."

"Some people shut themselves off from emotional pain, others are thrown into major difficulties from it, and some have ways they manage it. Not much is known about this kind of pain. It can throw people into depression and other forms of mental difficulties that drag down a person's ability to lead productive lives. Some people find themselves wishing they were dead. Why? Because they are trying to connect spiritually. They are trying to connect spiritual links and cannot because it is somewhat one-way.

"It is a problem of feeling alone. We are in the process of evolving and eventually we may be able to manage these links more easily, but right now, most of us feel very alone in this regard. Actually, animals often feel this link more readily, as with your pet dog - who may understand your emotional pain and comes to you to comfort you. Yet, in the example of losing a parent, which in the natural way of life - and will happen to all of us, we link up from this dimension to the one they have entered through our grief and they can feel us, but sadly we still do not detect them. Do not misunderstand me - they can feel the link, most of us cannot. We are too involved with our physical existence - our physical plane, the system we are presently experiencing. We feel our physical loss deeply, but of course we haven't lost them at all - this is only a small portion of reality."

"Are you saying they can feel our pain from where they are? From their spiritual system?" Tom asked.

"It would seem so," The Voice answered. "Yes, it is a link . . ."

"For us, physical pain is often linked to our emotional pain. Yes? When one of our loved ones feels physical pain, we react with emotional empathy and compassion."

"I hate it." Tom said. "and I hate the way creatures eat each other. . . what an awful system. It makes me sick."

"How would you change the system?" The Voice asked.

"I would change that part of it!' Tom said fiercely. "I would eliminate pain!"

"That is you, Tom. The Human race has to change before the system can be changed. Right now, people are inflicting pain on each other, much worse than animals eating other animals to survive. Do you understand? One thing needs to be changed in order for another to change. Perhaps that is part of the experience."

"God did this, we didn't." Tom said.

"Is that what you think?" Teacher patiently said, "Really now. You are abdicating your part, the part of you that is God, but you can't do that, because of course you are part of God. You are connected to all of this." Tom felt the sweeping motion that took in far more than their room.

"Nooooo!" He cried.

The Teacher waited while the familiar wail died, like a distant echo.

"Have I answered your question of why our system is based upon pain?" Asked a soft and compassionate Voice. "The links with our spiritual community are love, respect, compassion, and yes, pain, which are unseen and understood in those other dimensions. In other words, our deceased parents can perceive our emotional pain, love or hate, but may not physically feel pain as when we cut ourselves.

"Every system has its laws, every dimension its divine rules of change. Everything is changing constantly. Everything, accordingly. If we want things to be different in this world, we are the change.

"Can we agree, Tom, you and I, that everything is in a constant state of change and everything changes at their own pace, a speed different than other things. Right? You are changing at a rapid pace, although you may not think about it.

"Your mind changes, your body changes. The system within your body changes so fast that it is almost beyond our ability to measure just how fast systems renew themselves. One thing renews another. One thing nourishes another. Remember, everything is connected. You seldom realize what happens within your body. You pay more attention to what happens *outside* your body, mostly, because of accessibility to your five senses. What happens in the next dimension is not accessible to your five senses so you don't know much about it, but something similar goes on there too. You are thinking in terms of death, but there is only continuation of everything. There is a consciousness guiding all that is."

"The God consciousness." Tom said. "The compassion generated from our understanding of pain generates movement into the next dimension?"

"Yes. Good. You got it. Something like that. And one part of it fuels another, in order to continue movement, that movement thing has to happen. Right? See? Here we have the birth of a little baby, its growth and all that it does, it fuels all that is around it - here in the physical plane. See. The unseen spiritual plane needs fuel too, like compassion. It is a system too, but it isn't physical and. . ."

"It's a crazy system," Tom said. "I don't have to like it. It seems so sad. All this killing. It is so sad,"

"Yes, it is." A different presence in the room said.

"Perhaps it will be good for you to understand." The Room continued, "that you are part of a grouping of 'travelers' - for want of a better term, who are striving for understanding, who are being educated. What then? Perhaps it is important to fuel compassion and love into another system. Didn't Jesus teach that?"

"Yes, but. . ." Then Tom looked at the curtain. He could see the outline of the figure sitting there. Sometimes the He or the She got up and even paced. The curtain took up a third of the room, and sometimes it seemed to take up half.

"Why are you behind that curtain?" Tom asked thoughtfully, his heart reaching out. "Are you disfigured?"

And then, for an instant, it was like the curtain wasn't there. He could see the wall that the curtain had been hiding, and there was a painting hanging there. It was a large oil painting of a field of flowers that could have been a Colorado mountain scene. There were children laughing and picking flowers. The sky was blue with fluffy clouds.

Below the painting was a small table with a cut glass vase of fresh flowers. The vase was catching a ray of sun that was coming in the window behind Tom and there were tiny rainbows from the prisms dancing around its area. Off to the side was a comfortable low-back office chair that had arms. It was upholstered in a soft gray material.

"Teacher," Tom whispered. "Where are you?"

"Everywhere," A soft Voice replied.

MARSHA'S FOLLY

Carl sat troubled at his desk in the back room. He'd overheard a nasty rumor while at the hardware store earlier. He was looking for some hooks to install by the time clock when he'd heard two people chatting the next aisle over. He hadn't intended to eavesdrop, but when he heard the name of his business, he strained.

"...yeah. ."a woman was saying,". . .it seems like the noises - they're some kind of signal you know? I guess it has to do with where the next drop is going to be, or something like that. . ."

Carl was stone cold still, like he'd been frozen to the ground and couldn't move. He stopped breathing. He was carved out of a brick of blue ice and an ice axe had carved down the middle of him and he'd been left alone to suffer in the wind, a relentless wind that made his eyes water to run rivulets down his cheeks. The wind against him was so cold that any words he might have spoken would be frozen to crack in the atmosphere and fall and break apart into nothingness. His mind was suspended somewhere between the deposit slip in his pocket and the reality that someone, some awful person had made up an ugly lie to not only ruin his business, but the three students working there, whom Carl was certain, did not have a bad bone in their bodies. He had grown to love them.

The couple, who were lingering over something near him, perhaps the colors of paint swatches, were chatting amicably, having a nothing conversation, like it could have been anything on any day. "Yes, I heard it from mother, and you know she is pretty good about what she hears."

A male voice interceded, "You should be careful about what you repeat."

"Oh, but this came from a reliable source - at least that is what mother said."

"How so?" He asked.

"Well Marsha. . ."

Carl moved, first a hand, and then a foot and then it was his torso that doubled over. He reached out and held onto the shelf and steadied himself as the icy chill ran its course. He didn't hear anything more, but he'd heard enough.

He had noticed business had waned the last couple of weeks and he'd wondered about it. He'd not been overly concerned. As with so many things new, the sparkle had probably worn off. Carl figured the business was settling into a more permanent groove.

But now he understood. He thought about it for days, sitting pensively at his desk, in his little room, smelling the pizza cooking. Then he decided he wouldn't be too badly hurt. College students weren't in the stream of that kind of gossip, and a good portion of his business came from students, but it was the idea that his own wife would have, could have, cooked up such a tale. At first, he was unbelieving. Then he was sick. Finally, he was angry. He felt an anger that turned whatever cold he'd felt that day in the hardware store into a white liquid fire. He was burning mad.

After that, Carl gathered information. He went to a new barbershop, hung out at a new place for a cold beer during happy hour and stopped in at a different branch for his Gym membership. He heard the gossip, and it wasn't good. Carl was made out to be the ringleader of a gang pushing drugs to college students and even kids! It wasn't just that his business could be hurt, but his employees were being implicated - Big John, Jake and Tom; and it could mean that Tom wouldn't get into medical school, and on top of it, it was that he, Carl, was losing his reputation. He realized that soon he would have authorities coming into his place, police detectives and who knew what kind of FBI or other type of investigators? Just having that kind of thing happen could mean death for his business.

Carl took his notes to an attorney. The lawyer explained he could not charge his wife with defamation of character, because she was his wife. And also, he had no way to ascertain the damage that had been done or to be certain that she was the one behind it. The attorney suggested he see a Public Relations person. He recommended Amy. "You have to hit this head on, Carl, and soon!"

Carl was prepared. Amy and the lawyer had suggested he have a document drawn up, just in case.

"You know Carl, finding this out now, about Marsha's character, may be a huge blessing for you. Imagine if the two of you already had children?" But Carl had defended her at first. It was just an informal meeting between him and the P. R. person and the lawyer. Carl was actually more worried about his three students than himself, but the implications to his personal reputation was huge. The lawyer explained how such a stain could follow him into his future. "This thing must be stamped out completely - and NOW."

"Carl," Amy entered into the conversation, "the difficult thing about this, is that Marsha never comes into the pizzeria. It is unconscionable what she has done. It is vindictive and hateful. After all, she is half owner in the restaurant. She wanted to personally hurt you and your friends." She drew a long breath.

"Did she really start this thing? Was it really Marsha?" He asked.

Amy's work in P.R. doubled slightly as an investigator and she was thorough and good at her job. "We have to find out. We need to know how widespread this problem has become - to know what kind of damage has been done, by whom and how to control it. Then we'll know what to suggest."

Amy started work on it while Carl waited. He stopped a couple of times to drop papers off for his lawyer and was glad he'd selected a person located in such a large complex. The law offices were in a business condominium configured almost like a mall. Carl could be visiting an accountant, a sandwich shop, gym or any number of other places located there.

In a week, Amy was ready with information and a meeting was arranged between the three of them. "Your lawyer needs to hear what I discovered," she told him.

"I traced the rumor in three directions." She began, after a few pleasantries were exchanged.

"I'm scared to find out." Carl said. "I didn't expect you to come back so soon!"

"You know, it's a funny thing. . .the truth takes a while to move around, but rumors spread like wildfire. I just don't understand the phenomena." She said.

Carl could feel the heat rising to his face.

"First, I traced it back, through a gossip chain, to where it began. There were two places I could identify - one was at Sally's Beauty Salon and the other was at the Cycles Gym. Are you familiar with Cycles?"

"Yes. My wife goes there. It's a gym - mostly for women, I believe." Carl said.

"Yes. It was the Cycles on 8th Street that I traced it to. There are two of them in town. Is that the one where your wife goes?"

"Yes. It's near her workplace."

"I did some very discreet digging and discovered your wife goes there on Thursday's after work. I don't know who started the rumor there, but I was able to do a fairly good job narrowing rumors to that place."

"Yeah, I go to a gym myself, and talk is cheap around those places," Carl said.

Amy continued. "The other place was Sally's Beauty Salon and Spa. I made an appointment for myself - that was easy to do without causing any kind of alert. While in the spa I chatted up the room, and then later, Sally herself gave me my haircut." The ladies there were only too happy to perpetuate what they'd heard. Sally told me, in confidence of course, that she'd gotten the story about Carl's Pizzeria from the horse's mouth."

Amy let the information fall for a short time, then continued gently. "The 'horse' being your wife, Carl."

Carl lurched sideways. He'd suspected that if Marsha had really thought such a thing could exist, she would never say such a thing publicly. In fact, he never thought she actually would believe it.

"The second thing," Amy was saying, "was I arranged an encounter with Marsha myself." Amy produced a small USB stick drive.

Carl winced.

"This is a small recording device." She said. "I just happened to have it on my person at the time of my encounter."

"Where. Huh. . .where did you meet up with her?"

"Strangely enough, it was at the coffee morning at the Chamber. That is certainly the most unlikely place where a person would or should defame a business in town, but I managed to sit next to her and she was all talk about it. She did, however, never let on that she was in any way associated with the pizzeria. In fact, I don't think anybody in the Chamber ever knew that she had ever been associated with it. She was there representing the hotel." Amy had a small notebook computer and she plugged in the USB. "Would you like me to play it?"

"This could never be used in a court of law," his attorney explained. It falls under 'entrapment' - and she could actually bring you up on charges about it. You must keep this, and remember   this is confidential - your ears only."

Carl nodded mutely.

The recording device was not of high quality, but it was good enough that the voices were clear and easily recognizable. It was almost as if Marsha enjoyed the story she had fabricated.

When Amy turned off the device, she immediately continued. The third portion of the investigation involves how wide spread the rumor has become, - in other words, how many people have heard it. "It is the talk of the town, Carl. I am surprised the police haven't been on your doorstep yet. We must hurry to deal with this."

Carl felt miserable. But he wasn't alone. Amy was there - and his lawyer too. A friend of Carl's had recommended him - and Carl was very glad he did. Now the lawyer was outlining his thoughts about the situation.

"Here is what I suggest," he said, already knowing that whatever marriage Carl had, it probably wasn't going to survive this. He outlined two scenarios. One involved a divorce and immediate signing of settlement papers. The other involved a situation should the marriage continue.

Then Amy took over. She was already ready with an idea that she thought could work. Amy had written a story; it was another one of her talents - that she could write. She was now asking Carl's permission to bring in one of the police officer's she knew from the local precinct (in uniform) to have an event with a group of children in his pizzeria.

She would hire a photographer, to accompany the story - after being assured the newspaper would print it, of course. The newspaper might even send their own writer.

She thought the story might make the community page. Amy had friends at the Daily. She'd let them know when the event could take place. "Can you set something up for earlier in the day with your team?" She asked.

Carl seldom showed emotion. He was a stand tall sort of guy, but when he was in Iraq, he'd cried in front of others for the first time. Nonetheless, he was glad he was sitting in a swivel chair. He turned away. He just couldn't speak.

Carl met with his team that night after the restaurant closed. It was like he thought - the rumor had not floated into their circles yet. None of them had heard it. First, they were shocked that anyone could have come up with such a thing. Then they were angry. Carl did not tell them of his personal heartache - that it was his own wife that had done the evil deed, that she had probably fabricated the story and spread it.

It was a scramble of coordination, but like Amy explained, time was crucial. They all agreed they could put it together in a week.

Amy sent the story over that same day. As a P.R. person, she was used to writing news releases, although sometimes she would write a feature story, leaving the bi-line off, because doing so encouraged the newspaper to print it and saved everybody time. She had done some free-lance writing for the Daily and was considered reliable, but she never wrote anything that was sensitive. When it arrived at the news desk, Linda was working it that day, pitch-hitting for Junior who'd called in sick. She thought the story charming, but didn't realize its significance until Amy called her.

"Did you have a chance to read my story?" Amy asked.

"Its' cute." She said.

"Yes," Amy said, relieved that Linda was the one answering the phone. "But it is a lot more than that. . ."

Linda had taken her kids to the pizzeria and loved it. When she heard about the appalling rumor, she sucked in her breath. "That's what newspapers are for. To get out the truth!"

She talked it over with the editor, went back to the processing room where Mark, their best photographer hung out, and found him leaning over the light table. She smiled. It was comical - that light table left over from the old days. It was a gathering place. There wasn't any reason for one anymore, but sometimes something came in from the archives and it was just plain handy to have it even though it was an overkill. Mark threw off his glasses in a very satisfying gesture. "I've been there with my kids." He exclaimed. "I know Big John. He has a heart of gold! We are going to nip this in the bud. Big Time! Big f--king Time!""

Not only did the newspaper send over a writer, they sent an entire team for the story. In the lead was their best photographer!

Mark got a choice close up of Big John making his funny face, the one where he pushed out his mouth, elongating it. It was the best photo he ever took. He also got one of John at rest - the handsome man who loved kids.

The newspaper crafted the story to get the most readership. The photo with the policeman was on the front page, with a huge headline: Pizzeria Selling Drugs to Children!

The other photos - the great human-interest ones, were a montage on the community page. There was Big John and Tom the Straight man, and Jake caught with his feet in the air. There were kids with huge smiles and Carl himself standing tall showing off his crisp white restaurant jacket with name tags.

This is how the story read:

Pizzeria Selling Drugs to Children

The town is buzzing about the drugs being sold at Carl Derby's Pizzeria. Some of the buzz claims the targets are kids, and if you've been there, you know it is true beyond any doubt, and more. The target is every person walking in their doors. The drugs don't come in syringes, or pills. They don't arrive in what the kids eat, in happy faces or in brightly colored costumes. They come in something so surprising that people are "stampeding" to experience a new kind of high - a high that comes from just being in the place. It is surprising - since most of us hate noise. The drug IS noise, and the noise is fun. It will make you smile; it will make you laugh; it will make you sing and maybe even be silly yourself. The kids are being drugged by noises - and adults don't mind because they are reminded of what it means to be a kid themselves.

It all started. . .

The story was a huge success.

Not only did the newspaper give it their front page, but they put it on their website too, along with a short video clip of the "noises."

The day the newspaper printed the story, by coincidence, was Friday. It was Marsha's day for gliding along. As fate would have it, she didn't have a hair appointment on that day and she ended up using her afternoon to catch up on correspondence at work. She grabbed the Daily on her way out, one that a room tenant had left on the chair by the side door. It was a mess, folded inside out, but no matter, she would read it when she got home.

She pulled into the garage and noticed Carl's Van was there. She wondered why. Then she reached over and collected her things from the passenger seat and the paper flopped open. She saw the uniformed police and the heading.

"Oh my God! Carl's in jail." She said under her breath, jumping out of the car. "That lousy man is in jail." She muttered in a hurry to get in the house. "He has ruined me!"

Her hands were full and she kicked the door open.

Carl was sitting in the kitchen. Her head jerked around. "Oh my gosh!" She said openly. "It's you!"

"Why wouldn't it be?"

"Oh, I thought. . ."

Carl looked around the room, then back at her. "Well here I am." He half laughed.

She walked over to the table, and threw her stuff down. "A mess you've made of it now." She said huffily.

Carl saw the newspaper in her hand, the things she was carrying and was confused. "I'm sorry you think so," he said.

"You should be! What's going to happen now!"

"I want a divorce." He said calmly, before losing his courage. "You're evil. I don't love you anymore."

"Yeah, but look at what you've done!" She screamed.

"And what is that?" He asked calmly.

She looked at him, her eyes fiery with a glare he'd never seen before. "Fuck you Carl. You and your dirty money! You come in here acting like you're some kind of saint." She screamed. "You are the worst kind - involving children in your fucking schemes! . . . A divorce? . . . and more! You'll end up in jail for the rest of your life!"

"Yes, My life has changed." He said sadly.

"Why are you even here?" She asked.

"I need to get some details in my life straightened out," He said, putting a paper down on the table, realizing that she'd only seen the front page of the newspaper.

"What's this?" She glared.

"It's an agreement. I used the money I made to pay off the house." He said. "I want to give it to you. It can be our divorce settlement. Is that okay with you? Nobody can take it from you."

"You don't have a pot to piss in - your pot if full of fucking SHIT, it doesn't even leave you room for all your shit!" She started screaming so loud that Carl knew the neighbors could hear her. She waved her phone at him. "You won't get a penny of my money, you fucker!" She screamed at the top of her lungs. "You ass hole!"

"It's in there. A release from your income, Marsha. . .?" He never raised his voice. But she was red with anger.

"It fucking better be!"

He passed the document over to her.

She sat down at the table. "I won't be responsible for anything, Carl. Not fucking anything. Anything." She was still screaming. "I won't have anything to do with what the authorities fucking do with your cesspool restaurant either. I want my name taken OFF OF IT. Now!"

"I understand." He said coughing, suppressing a surprise and pulled out title papers.

"Oh, thank God," she said, looking at her watch. "I hope we can get them filed today - you piece of shit!"

"I'll try. I can do it now." He said trying not to shake. He felt like something in him punctured and let out all the happy little things he had told himself about her and were leaving him empty, of all the carnations and roses and perfumes and smiles and stacks of cardboard nothingness that he had used to build his life. But he did have one thing - if he could pull this off.

He did have his pizzeria.

"We have to have a witness," he said," for the signatures on the title papers - to the house and the restaurant. Do you want to go over to Nancy's?" Nancy was a notary. He could only hope she hadn't read the newspaper yet.

Marsha nodded numbly. The entire transaction took less than an hour - from the time Marsha came home until all the papers were signed. Then they took them immediately to the county before they closed, and returned home. Carl was grateful they didn't meet anybody that he knew.

Carl was actually horrified at what he'd done. He had perpetrated a lie. He knew it. He realized Marsha had not read the newspaper - that she was under the misguided assumption that Carl was a guilty criminal, instead of one of the nicest guys in their community. She had read the headline, seen the photo partially and had assumed the worst - over the man she had married.

The divorce papers read that Carl had a month to clear his belongings out of the house, but he had already loaded the van with his most valuable belongings. He could never trust Marsha over anything ever again.

He took his copy of the papers and the title to his restaurant, said goodbye, and quietly left.

Marsha sat at the table and wondered why he was still on the loose. She guessed he had posted bail or something like that. She was glad because it meant that they got matters cleared up before he was nabbed, actually very easily. She was coming out so well. The house was paid for! Never mind that it was dirty money. It was hers. She could sell it and get something over on the Mockingbird Hill. She deserved far better than Carl.

She went to the bedroom to change her clothes and was mildly surprised to see that Carl had already moved out his personal belongings. She wondered how he could have done it so fast, then figured the big hurry was getting it done before going to prison. "Good riddance you son of a bitch," she screamed.

She danced to the fridge, got herself a cold beer and settled herself on the couch. She wanted to read the paper.

Two days later, Carl was contacted by the news team at the state's most influential news magazine. They wanted to cover the story about the restaurant.

It was just a couple of days later, that a struggling student, who hoped to have a career in journalism, expressed his dismay to the Teacher in the Room," Nobody reads anymore." He complained.

"Don't worry, the Numen told him," You'll find the niche that's right for you. Maybe it is in script writing. . ."

"But I like to write the truth."

"Some very good movies are true stories." Teacher said

"Do you think I could ever be good enough to write a movie script?" He asked.

"Oh yes." The Numen said, "There's a very interesting story going on right now. . ."

LANGUAGE

Tom had tried to make his door go away at his apartment, but he never could make it completely disappear, not for one second. He did succeed in making his door open routinely, however, even though it would just be ajar an inch or so. But that made it pretty nice for Tom to just push it open with his foot.

He had done that when his neighbor came out and observed him. "Wow," she said. "That's pretty nice the way your door opened. Can you make mine do that?"

Tom was half in the doorway when he froze. "Uh, yeah, uh. . .well. . .eh. . .maybe." he said, thinking fast." You gotta have really good internet."

"Oh, I'll ask Simeon about it," she said happily. "It's amazing what they're doing now - with the smart stuff!"

Tom thought about that now as he stood in front of that crazy gray door there at the school. Wouldn't she ever be surprised? He'd thought about it during the week. He decided he'd like to try and change the door into something else. He wondered if he could change the door into a drape, like the one inside the room, and then he could part the drape, or lift it, or something like that and get in that way. It would be cute if he could change it. Then he would have an idea if he could eliminate Numen's drape.

He stood there thinking about the drape.

Nothing.

He emptied his mind. He thought of his head like a container filled with water and that he needed to empty the water, so he visualized the water running out of his head/container - out through his mouth. THAT felt funny. He wasn't sure that he'd do that again. He drooled onto his shirt.

Pissed, he closed his mouth.

He saw the door as a blue fabric in his mind. Nothing.

Then he decided to try a different approach, because he didn't actually *see* the door as a drape. So, he looked at the door, gazing at it. He tried to superimpose a vision of the drape over it, to see it with his eyes.

It first was an image against his eyes, before it became a thought. He saw the door as a drape. Then the image became something in his mind. He stopped thinking of the door as a door and substituted it for a drape split in the middle. The door changed. He stepped forward and reached out to it.

It was soft in his hand.

He moved between it, examining it.

Then something awful happened. It started to change back and he wasn't all the way through. He felt the door hard against his sides.

He panicked.

It was closing in.

On *him*.

He looked to one side, then the other.

Metal was appearing on each side and moving fast trapping him in the middle.

"Oh God, NO!" He choked.

He realized, all within microseconds that he'd visualized the drape split in the middle, like the opening for the theater and now it was materializing back that way.

He couldn't move.

He was in a vice, and it was closing on him.

He could now only see to one side, not both as when he would stand in front of the door.

He looked at his right side, quickly gathered a thought, and visualized the drape. The metal gave way and was immediately replaced by blue fabric. He exited just as the metal from the left would have trapped him, and killed him.

He was shaking so bad that he had trouble walking and staggered to the table, mindless of any vision.

"How did that happen!?" He half asked and half exclaimed, hoping the Guide would have an answer.

"You stopped looking at the drape. The door was obeying your vision and you lost it. This was an important lesson. Emmm? It could have, and would have killed you. I sure would have had some explaining to do."

"How come you didn't stop it?" Tom accused.

"What makes you think I could stop it?"

"Well couldn't you?"

"No. That didn't come out of MY mind. It came out of *yours*. I can do many things, but I can't replace what is in your mind with my mind." The Guide was silent, then added. "I've been trying to understand how to help you better develop your. . .shall. . we. . .say . . .gift."

Tom had not come with a paper of questions. He had stopped doing that for every visit since becoming more familiar with the Teacher/Guide - whichever or whoever greeted him. He had so many questions that now he just asked whatever popped into his head.

But now he was so flabbergasted by his experience that he didn't know what he wanted to ask, so he looked around instead.

"Cat got your tongue?" A young girl asked amused.

"Oh." Tom said. "Not anymore." The sound of the girl caused him relief. "Why do we have to have audible language when there was a time in our evolution that we didn't communicate that way?"

"The cat took it." She laughed some more.

"No really. What happened to us?"

The Teacher replaced the young girl, and said, "It became important to communicate with the generations that would be following us. We were developing written language and we identified more with the physical in order to do this. We could have done both, but we had difficulty knowing how to pro-ject forward. . ."

And then he felt embarrassed because he hadn't even greeted his Teacher with a 'hello.' He felt a redness flush across his face.

"There is something to be gained by merging the physical dimension with the spiritual one," Teacher said in that special, patient tone. "Language is limiting. It has set us free, but it also binds us to our physical existence. As we change into a greater awareness, communication will change with us. But we won't see that in our lifetime."

"I'm sorry," Tom said, because he was clearly still distracted as he fidgeted.

"No need," The Guide said in answer to him. "You didn't need to say 'hello' - I heard you."

"You did? But I should've. . ."

"Yes, it's important to say what you are thinking," He said. "Not everyone can discern your thoughts."

"Why can you?" Tom asked, but he didn't get an answer. "Can other dimensions read our thoughts?"

"Not unless we want them to. You have always wanted me to. If you want a being of another dimension to understand you, it is best to invite them or say it audibly, to be sure. Other dimensions communicate with us all the time." He laughed. "But we are still physical and cannot receive them most of the time."

"They try to communicate with us?"

"Of course; we do receive what they send to us off and on, sometimes thinking of it as intuition. We just don't realize their communication fully, or we don't want to, because we are conditioned to believe otherwise. Plus, we are superstitious about ghosts and evil."

"What about between people?"

"Some people are on the same wavelength and have a line of communication between them that isn't audible. I know you have heard the expression about being on the 'same wavelength.' When one is hurt, the other knows it. There are thousands of documented cases of this."

"My mom and dad have this. She always knows things about him. Also about her mother."

"You have this with Susan, don't you?"

"How do you know these things if you can't read my thoughts?" Tom demanded.

The Teacher ignored him. Then the Guide seemed to step in. Tom wasn't sure how he knew this. "I can. I just can't change what you think. You have to do that."

"Oh. But I can stop you from . . .uh. . .reading my thoughts. I can, can't I? I mean, if I don't want you to know what I'm thinking, I can prevent you from seeing them, from knowing what I'm thinking. Right?"

"Yes. But you don't know how." The Guide laughed. And laughed. "Good luck, Tom." And laughed again, pointing to something hanging in the air next to Tom.

Tom was embarrassed. He tried to think back about things he'd thought in the room, some of which weren't very nice about the Teacher. And then about other stuff, maybe private things. . . like things about Chelsea and sex. . .and. . . then he tried not to think about what those might be, because by trying to remember, he was bringing up the thoughts and the Guide could read them. . .and. . .and. . ."

The Guide was laughing merrily.

"We sometimes are able to communicate strong emotions to animals - like compassion." The Teacher said. "Our animal friends understand we are helping them when they are hurt, even though we may be hurting them in the process! We are only, just now, beginning to understand some of these connections."

"I had a dog like that," Tom said, leaning back in his chair. "He always knew when I was on my way home, at least that's what everybody said. About ten minutes before I'd get there, Pix would go sit by the door. It was often at different times of day. My gosh, I loved that dog!"

"The thing to understand about language, is that it is like tools - it has a purpose. We used to have a hammer and nails, well, we still do, but now we have more ways of solving the same problem. We use an automatic nailer, I love mine, and I often use a screw gun. What used to be labor intensive now takes minutes. Pretty soon, we won't need to fasten things together at all, we will "print" them instead, or we will have better methods yet to be determined. It is all to be imagined. Who could imagine the 3-D printing of a body organ? Every tool has a purpose, and if its purpose isn't serving us well enough, well, we'll find a better way, another way will replace it. Change is the nature of our existence, as you realize." The Teacher's voice was almost hypnotic.

"Yes, it's true. I have changed just from knowing you." Tom said simply.

"But you had to be ready for it."

"Is that how it is with religion? That we have to be ready to understand God in a new and different way? Some people will think I have no religion." Tom squeaked. "That I am an atheist."

"Ah hah - but you're not. You do have a belief now about God. . ." The Voice said in its authoritative way. "What is religion? And worship? That sounds like bowing to a deity, of sorts, but that isn't what everything is all about. One thing is not better than another. We are ALL part of the God force, and so acceptance and love IS a slightly different philosophy of thought, rather than 'worship' per se. In that regard, no, you are no longer religious, you have belief in something so large, it is hard to encompass it in your brain. Maybe, by some definitions, you are an atheist."

Tom squirmed in his chair uncomfortably.

"Nobody changes what God IS. They change what they are." The Voice became the Teacher again. "Religion isn't always good, loving or kind. Is it?

"I feel human," Tom said. "So stinking, dirty, human!"

"ACCEPT WHAT YOU ARE!"

Tom didn't say anything. He stood up and looked at his hands, thinking about his original question about language. His questions always seemed to morph into other issues, but he wasn't sorry. There were always other questions that were answered in the answers. He asked himself why he couldn't move forward faster, why he continued to get so hung up on some of these issues.

"You must be kind to yourself, learning is a process. We don't learn big things with big steps, we learn by taking baby steps. Humanity is learning." And then it was like the figure behind the veil was right in front of him, leaning forward and speaking directly in his face. "You are part of humanity, and your acceptance of this choice will bring joy and peace in your life. You are part of a change that seems to be accelerating. It is happening at a rate we can actually see. We don't know the Big Plan for this, but there is rapid change nonetheless." And then like the pop of a bubble, the Teacher was back where he/she had always been.

Tom felt as if something light had fallen on his shoulders.

"The thing about language," The Teacher continued, "is, . . .it is a barrier. It gave us such wonderful skills in the beginning of the process here, and now it is getting in our way. We must understand that people are at different places in their development, or their education, and language is important. We must say what we think. We must write what we mean. Honesty is extremely important."

"I see." Tom said, as was usual for him to say, because he really felt like he needed to say something, but he really didn't "see."

"You will get beyond this barrier. This language barrier. "An old woman said conversationally. "It is like a wall that must be climbed, once we learn to climb it, there is the other side. Then we can lower the wall. It will take many tries before the wall will entirely disappear, but it eventually will."

"Yes," Tom said. "Yes." And with that simplicity, he slowly started from the room.

"Are you ready to leave now?" She asked.

"Yes, I think so," Tom said stopping at the door, and thought of the wall in his mind. He climbed to the top and sent a thought out to Her, his Teacher; his Guide. He thought of a smile that radiated throughout the room. He saw the feeling of 'thank you' in his mind and saw it reach out and fill every space with a light lavender glow that hugged the figure behind the veil. It didn't take any time at all, but it did take a special effort. As he turned, and opened the door, he heard a voice fill his head, but it wasn't really a voice, it was a color, a light amber glow that seemed to say, "my pleasure to help you understand." He held the door, startled, turned on his heel and looked back. He saw the figure nod, a nod that said "yes, I heard you, and you heard me."

"I saw you!" He exclaimed. "You are beautiful!"

FALL

Tom had selected the classes for his final year, and they weren't what he originally thought they'd be. He had his chemistry out of the way and he had thought he could cruise with some rather fun stuff in Physics, but instead he was taking some demanding courses in pre-med.

"Have you decided to try for Medical School?" His Academic Advisor asked with surprise as they met for his fall classes.

"I'm keeping my options open," Tom had replied.

"I see you've taken the two most difficult classes already, and honestly you've done so well in those that you could give it a try. Actually, Tom, I'm very surprised at this turn of events. Organic Chemistry separates. . ."he cleared his throat," uh. . .it truly weeds out the students who can't cut it in Medical School. Tom, you got an "A" in that class - and in Gross Anatomy too. Nobody does that! I thought you were interested in graduate school, but in Physics."

"What would I do in Physics?" Tom asked. "I never was particularly interested in pursuing that field."

"Oh? You were on a full-ride scholarship from this university!"

Tom nodded with appreciation. "I have really appreciated that."

"Your cumulative grade point average hasn't shown that, Tom. It's been disappointing to the board. It isn't the greatest. You never said anything about wanting to pursue anything in medicine. You'll be competing with. . ."

"I know. But it won't hurt me to take these classes, will it? I can still opt to go to Grad School in Physics. Right?"

"Well, we need to make some adjustments in your selections." He said, chewing a pencil. "Tom, It's expensive."

"It's all expensive." Tom said flatly. "I have no idea how I will pay for any of it! I'm sorry about my grade point average. It took me awhile to find myself. I really do want to make the university proud of me." He stopped and looked around. "I worked hard this summer. . ."

"I can see that!"

"I can pay it back." He said quickly.

"Oh no," The advisor said quickly. "That's not what I meant. . .but. . .uh. . .you were so promising. . .uh. . . and we wanted to see you go on and do something, uh, instrumental in the field. You know. . ."

"I don't think I have the right kind of mind for it," Tom said simply. "My thought process is different now."

"Oh?"

"Yeah."

"What has brought about this decision?"

Tom measured the man sitting across from him. He knew a letter from his advisor could be helpful - If he scored high enough on the m-cats; If he got an interview someplace, ff he managed to secure loans, If . . and. . .If. . and all the "If's" a person could think of.

"I was instrumental in saving a person's life." He looked at his hands. "Nothing like that ever happened to me before." Then he looked up and met the eyes of the man across from him. "And. . .and. . .I've been visiting with this guy." He said. "Going to this. . .uh. . zimmer. Uh room. Some of the students are calling this person. . .uh. . ." Tom cleared his throat and continued, "the Numen."

"Oh, I see." He said leaning back in his chair. "Nothing will ever be the same for you then."

Tom felt his face smarting, like he wanted to cry. He struggled. But the advisor seemed to understand and didn't say much after that.

All that fall semester Tom worked to bring up his grades and study for his m-cat test. He knew he couldn't bring up his GPA very far, but his two summer classes, which carried considerable semester hours, helped.

Tom took the m-cat test in January following Simeon's advice. He had wanted to take the April or May test, but Simeon pointed out that if he needed to retake the test, the later date would not give him enough time to do that and still make the application deadlines for Medical School. He would have liked the extra study time, but there was good sense in taking the test early and knowing more about the test itself. He had not expected to come out with a high score and went into it following Numen's advice: "Dream big," Numen had said, "but keep expectations low. . ." But afterwards? He felt like he'd done very well. He knew he had.

The day of the test was cool; cold in fact, and he was all set to drive to the test site. Simeon had said, "It will do you good to ride your bike over there, Tom. Leave early and peddle yourself and with every pedal you make on your bike you will think about how smooth it will be taking your test, and how surprised you'll be that the answers to the questions will be so accessible in your brain."

When the day arrived, Simeon was there giving him a small player and earphones to listen to on the way to the test site. "Here," he said, "this is for you my friend. There are some of the questions and answers that we covered on the flash cards as a final review on your way." Tom had taken the little player with shaking hands. He was anything but calm.

Simeon gave him a warm gel that they used at the hospital for injuries. "Hey," he'd said, "look at this," laughing. "We're going to put this inside your shirt and you're going to be warm, man, just nice and warm for your ride over! - and calm. Remember, calm."

He tucked the hot pack in Tom's shirt, and with that, they were out the door, hands raised with claps, thumbs up, and Tom was off.

The voice recording that Simeon had prepared took away Tom's butterflies and as it turned out, was right on target. In fact, it was uncanny.

When he got to the test site, he pulled his hands out of his gloves, warmed them against his toasty belly and walked into the room with a sense of calm he didn't know he had. Everything about that day had been right, except the ride back. When the test was over, he froze and couldn't stop shivering under a blanket on his couch.

What if my score is too low? He asked himself. What if I failed to do good enough?

What then?

MINIMIZING OTHERS/FAILURE

Tom didn't experiment with the door this time. He didn't "play" with it or try to do anything different. He just swung it open.

He ran through it as fast as he could.

Then he slowed, hoping there would be a vision. He missed it the last time.

It was a fiercely hot day and sweat was pouring down his forehead and behind his T-Shirt, but he was excited. He had a large piece of cardboard he was using to fan his sister, Cami. He stood with her behind a screen placed by the side of an open stage at the State Fair. There were fans on either side of the stage, but the air didn't reach them where they stood. There was a dancer doing a routine on the stage, but he felt sorry for the girl out there. It was so hot he could see her costume clinging to her little body. He sent a thought to her, wishing it to be easier.

"Look at that," a kid sitting below snickered pointing at her. "Stupid girl ain't worth shit!"

Tom glared at him, turned back to the stage and wished the girl a good finish.

Tom wondered how anyone could do well in that heat and looked at his sister struggling with her butterflies.

"I'm scared," She whispered, "That my fingers will slip on the keys."

Tom had always been her hero.

"You can do this, Cami." He told her. "Knock those judges dead and bring the audience to their feet!"

Cami was competing in the aged 9 - 13 talent category. She had reached the finals which was being televised on the local TV station.

The girl's act got better and she finished well. Tom's sister was next.

His heart soared when he heard the notes ringing out with her performance. It was flawless. She would be first. The dancer came in second.

It was a great day.

The table lamp was on in the room giving it the feeling of living space. Tom went in and sat down. "Hello Teacher," he said.

"Good afternoon. I hope you've had a good week. Susan told me you're a couple now."

"Yes. I am happy about that."

There was the usual interval of silence before he began. "What kind of a person minimizes another human being; thinks of them like a drink of whiskey?"

"Aren't you over that yet?"

"I wish."

"People who have little regard for themselves," Teacher said tiredly.

"Oh."

"They drink whiskey and see themselves like a useless drink. They are only useful to their friends as long as they have a glass to offer them. Such a person lets themselves be defined by their friends."

Tom thought about the friends he used to have. They dropped away when he stopped pouring their glasses and giving them free pot. He had started thinking of them as people who only wanted to lounge on his bean bag, smoke his pot, and sap him of his time. They didn't really care about him. They didn't even know him! He had been out of pot since the day he started coming to the Teacher - and they never bothered with him anymore. They only used him. Tom, the person, had meant nothing.

"Such a person," the Teacher went on to say, "has no feeling for others. We call that empathy. They don't know how to reach inside somebody else to try and feel what they might be feeling. Right?"

"I'm that person." Tom said.

"Are you?"

"Yes."

"But, not really. You only were for a short time, because you wanted to be accepted. You made a choice."

"Choice?"

"Yes. I spoke about this before. Perhaps you are understanding more about choice now. You are not alone when you make a choice. Others work with you. Right? I think you have seen some of that in action already, Ummm?"

"Yes. I have. I am making choices about my career. Maybe. I worry that I cannot do it, so I am reserving judgment. But I am going to try, I figure it can't hurt. And, I am making choices about my apartment and my friends and stuff like that, about how I spend my time."

"'As a man thinketh, so is he.' Truer words have never been spoken. As you think, so are you. You have complete control over how you think. You must learn to control your thoughts. It isn't just how others control you, it is how you control yourself."

290

"How so?"

"It is that choice I am talking about. We choose to become what we want to be. We don't have to accept what we are. We can change.

"If you find yourself thinking about another person in a minimal way, you can push that thought away and replace it with the way you'd like to think. After you do it a few times, it becomes natural. After you do it a few more times then it becomes you. Every time you find yourself seeing something in your mind that isn't the way you want it to be, just push it aside and replace it with the person you want to be. Remember, your mind is like a computer. Every time you think words or images that are not what you want them to be, you replace it with what you would like the thought to be - even if you do NOT feel that way. You can create a more forgiving person in yourself. Do you understand?"

"Yes, but. . ."

"It is hard, I know. Especially in the beginning. We like to float in our thoughts. We have not been taught to control how we think. We just accept how we think whatever we think, but how we think is something we have great power over. Power of thought. Imagine if Hitler had controlled his thoughts. He could have been somebody wonderful instead of somebody awful."

"Yes Teacher, I understand. But also, Hitler wanted his power. . ."

"Of course, Tom. You are absolutely correct in this, but consider, if Hitler had a different experience earlier in his life, would he have grown up to have been the Hitler he became? What if children, and everyone for that matter, were taught and understood the true importance of what they think. . .?"

Tom thought about himself and how little importance he ever put on anything he thought. Yes, he did think his actions had importance. But his thoughts? What if he had thought about Chelsea in a different manner, would he have treated her in a different way?

Tom sat there and thought about her. There was nothing about her that was like a glass of whiskey. She didn't even drink whiskey. He thought about the smell of her hair and how neatly groomed she always was.

"Chelsea is a good person," he said.

"That's right," a soft voice said. "When you see the good in others it is like a candle flame in darkness. It helps the good to grow in them as well as in you."

Tom said, "I regret what I did."

"What do you regret? The action, the thought, or both?"

"I regret the way I broke it off with her. I regret the way I thought about her."

"What are you going to do about it?" The Voice asked.

"I don't know."

"You can't go back and change it. What's done is done. But everything is always changing. Right? Make a change."

Tom wrote that down. He liked the sound of it. He thought about the Michael Jackson song - *Man in the Mirror.* He thought about what he could do right now involving Chelsea. He squirmed.

"Everything new feels uncomfortable." The Teacher said. "Be it the first day of school, the first time on a bicycle, - all firsts are uncomfortable, then it gets easier with time. Apologies get easier as we learn how to say 'I'm sorry.' They say human beings hate change, which is comical since we, ourselves, are changing constantly. We need to learn how to embrace change and be the change."

Tom crossed off the question in his mind and looked for another one. "What will happen to me if I fail my entrance examination?" He asked. "I am afraid."

"You will not fail." The teacher replied. "If you fail, you pick yourself up and take it again. The second time, you have an advantage, you'll know what to expect because you took it once before. Failure is a state of mind."

"No, it isn't," Tom said. "Failure is real. If I fail a class I can't get through school!"

"If you fail a class, you get a grade that says you didn't pass the class. It is you that translates that grade into a personal failure. You can take the class again and change the grade. Right?"

"Yes. But, but. . .it is my failure. Nobody else's."

"What are your criteria for failure? Because a student didn't do homework, a student didn't manage his or her time in order to pass that particular class or a person isn't smart enough to get a passing grade in that subject? Perhaps that subject is not part of that person's life's path. Maybe that so-called failure is really pointing to another path that is more important. You must be careful the criteria you use to judge failure in another or in yourself. If you do not score high enough on the exam, it may not be a failure, but instead a pointer for a different direction you are to take."

"I fail at a lot of things," Tom said. "I don't think I am a very good person."

"Failure is past tense." The Voice boomed.

Tom sat straight up - the Voice was so loud, it rocked the room, filling every inch of the space, of the air, the floor and walls and even of Tom himself. His eyes were wide. He gulped. His mind raced. "Failure is past tense." It rolled over in his head. It loomed bigger and bigger, like that Voice.

FAILURE IS PAST TENSE.

Gradually everything quieted down. Quieted? Had there been noise? Tom looked down at his hands. They were shaking. The moment. . . Had it been a moment? Or had it been seconds? He folded his hands, stroked his fingers, rubbed his legs.

"That is one of the big messages from Jesus, and one of them in Christianity today, Tom. It is called saving you from your sins. Another definition for sin is failure, isn't it? We keep hanging on to those things we've done or didn't do, they are things that wronged ourselves or wronged others in our lives and those things keep preventing us from doing better, from being better people, actually from being what we want to be.

"It doesn't matter what religion you are; we stack up failures and wear them, they become us, they are us. Sometimes they engulf us and terrible consequences result."

"But they matter, don't they?" Tom asked. "We can't just leave our wrongs behind, can we? There is a reckoning, isn't there? I mean if it doesn't matter then everybody would just do whatever they want to do to everybody else and that's part of the problem, isn't it? We just think what we do doesn't matter all that much!"

"What we do to somebody else, we do to ourselves. We are all connected."

"But I don't feel it!" Tom exclaimed.

"Oh, but you do. You just don't realize it. Yet. The physical part of our journey is very short, but our connectedness is forever. We can't sever that. Like I said, the soldier that kills his enemy is still attached to his enemy, and will be forever. That is the irony of it all - we cannot get away from any of this, as much as we try. We must learn an attitude of acceptance. Not of indifference or disregard, but one of cooperation. As we do more of this, our other senses will develop more. We have no enemies, we have instead a harmonious balance that is universal truth. We still have some distance to go before we see through the fog. But back to failure, because that is our topic for the day, is it not? - Dwelling on failure and our inability to deal with current challenges. The best way to deal with a current challenge is to deal with the perception of the past failure. Again, it is important to understand that failure is in the past and not the current condition. Let go. If it is a past failed relationship and you had a part in that, apologize, accept responsibility and go forward.

"Do not accept failure as your "now" condition. The "now" condition is a changed condition from the one of the perceived failures.

You can say, 'I won't do *THAT* again,' so you learned something from it and maybe actually gleaned some success from the failure of something you now know not to do again, so you can say: 'I will do something different with my now changed condition,' so a past perceived failure actually prepared you for a now success, or, 'I will ask for help this time,' which has actually given you a greater understanding of the importance of your connectedness."

"I still feel like a failure."

"Ahh, so you want to know what to do with your feelings? - Not with the failure, because you can't do anything about the failure, since it is past tense. You can only do something about how you think about it so you don't feel so miserable."

"Yes. I feel like a failure."

"Since failure is past tense, then thinking in those terms means you are not embracing change, which is actually your condition. You change constantly, don't you? Thinking failure keeps you in the past, keeps you from the change that belongs to you."

Tom shifted his weight. There was that thing about change again.

"It may be necessary to make simple and small changes, ones that replace feelings of failure," a female said congenially. "Please understand my words. This is something different for each of us and may require discovery and trial and error. Right? Conditions change as we change. What feels right for you today may change after you graduate. It has to do too with finding your niche. There is a place for everybody, but not everybody knows what that place is. But it is reachable. It is your right.

First: You feel happy when you are doing it. Second: You feel connected while you are doing it. For some people it may be as simple as being part of a prayer group, for others it may be picking up a hammer with Habitat for Humanity. For you, it may mean changing your major. Changes can be small or large. But it always, always involves change. The change may be just how we think about a thing - and it may require that we write out new ways of thinking so we can focus on the new thoughts. That is change too.

"We have been taught to rely on outer stimuli rather than inner stimuli to "make" us feel better. Our entire lives are built around exterior circumstances. It stands to reason that our feelings would then become controllable by outward things. We think it doesn't come from inside ourselves. Something good happens to us and we feel good, something bad happens and we feel bad, just like in the movies. Right? We are like a walking movie, only we are not. The majority of our lives, the majority of what we are, is what we are INSIDE not what we are OUTSIDE. We are first what we are inside, and we push that outside, not the reverse, but something happens and we allow changes to happen to us.

"The challenge is to try and change - inside out - in a way that is right for us. This can be especially difficult when we don't even realize what has happened - that we have relinquished something of ourselves to outside stimuli. We think that our connections to others happen through the outside - by our outward circumstances. We shake hands, say, 'hello, how are you,' but in truth, the connection to other beings is automatic and from within, it is in that warmth of intent BEFORE the, 'hello, how are you,' even takes place."

"Really now? How can I believe that?"

"It is important that you do. It is the truth of what we are."

Tom wrote down: Failure is always in the past.

"Simply remember: Failure = past /past failure. happiness = today's change.

Tom wrote it down that way.

"By placing guilt alongside the past failure, it is making the condition current, it is replaying the event and making the failure current. When you place guilt on a condition then it involves somebody else and your guilt holds them to your condition, then it becomes their failure too."

Tom wrote down: Guilt on past failures makes them current. Don't keep your failures active by assigning guilt to yourself or to somebody else. Cancel the guilt and go forward.

"Celebrate in your heart." Said the Voice suddenly. "Celebrate your thoughts about change and act upon them!"

"You came here to find your direction," The Teacher was back now. "You must believe that all things will work to the good of what you are supposed to be doing with your life. It is okay to feel fear. We all do when facing something new and considering we might fail. But that feeling isn't really 'fear' is it? It is a reaction in your body to something you're hanging onto.

"What did we learn about failure? It is past tense, so it cannot be something in the future, can it? You cannot fail doing something you have not tried doing."

Tom wrote that down too. Then he asked, "What is real fear then?"

"It is one of the conditions that connects us to other creatures." The Voice explained. "It develops compassion. It isn't what you think it is. When you see the deer running from the gun, it isn't with the feeling of failure, is it? It is fear of pain, death, trauma. It is important for us as spiritual beings to understand fear and to allow ourselves to fully develop empathy with our fellow creatures. It is a recognition of pain."

Tom could sense that his overall time was coming to an end. He didn't want it to. "I have more questions" he said.

"You will always have questions." The Voice said amicably. "By having questions, you will naturally become a seeker of truth."

Tears started coming down Tom's cheeks and he felt so utterly and completely vulnerable.

"I don't know who or what I am," he said.

"That is because you have been looking to others to define you and your ego has struggled for you to be separate. You are not."

"But. . .but. . .some people ARE better than other people. Some people do have better intellects, are more creative, are. . ."

"Some flowers are blue, some have a perfume that fills the air with the scent of rose or lavender, some can be ground into a medicine. Some people assist others to develop in ways beyond your ability to understand, others are gentle like rain, others hold babies when they cry. And you? You are connected to all of them and even to a drop of rain. You are correct, nobody is equal to another. Each person has their purpose and their value, but you cannot see the big picture to know what that is. Instead, they may be supplying the yeast for the bread to rise."

Tom gulped. "I'm sorry."

"It's okay. You are moving up in your education and each level has its tests. . ."

"Oh."

Tom gave himself a swift kick. When will I ever learn? He thought. I'm so stupid.

The entire room responded as one group of flowers, then another. They were blooms, large and magnificent falling from the ceiling and landing on the table and filling the room everywhere, like bubbles, only they were transparent flowers, all around him. Their aroma was light and pure and unlike anything he'd ever experienced. He reached out and cupped his hand under one of them. It was so different. Then it was like the bloom could communicate with him and said, "Yes, I am very different than you, but I am also just like you." And then it popped lightly just like a bubble and he felt so complete.

"Thank you." He said. "I will remember, Numen!"

As he left the room, he remembered the scent of the flowers in the room.

Tom found himself repeating four important words after he left, words that were to stay with him his entire life.

FAILURE IS PAST TENSE

THE BIRDS

Tom looked around as he walked along the campus, and yes, just like the Teacher had impressed upon him, he was walking in a wonderful garden every day. Of course, he was being distracted by a silly ol' snake and not *seeing* the garden around him! That was the way of the world. He smiled. Then he saw a little snake slithering between the bushes and he reached out with his mind and told the creature, "I'm happy to see you."

He was continuing to go to the zimmer to get grounded - a reminder to himself that he truly was living and observing the physical manifestation of God. He was in the middle of a garden of flowers and trees and animals and all kinds of miraculous things.

Someday I'll be a spirit and once again be able to see God, he thought. And then it was like something splashed him in the face and hit him hard. The thought had just entered his head without him *controlling* it. He stood there, in the middle of the sidewalk, realizing, probably for the first time in his life, that maybe, maybe, God would even be more difficult to *see* after his death For some reason he had been conditioned to think that God would become easier to see after he died, but maybe the opposite was true. He had to keep reminding himself that he was seeing God *now.* **NOW.**

The distractions are so many, he thought, that it is near impossible to focus on the true reality. He wondered Why. He smiled again and said out loud, "It's your fault, snake," and laughed, sending the little creature a hug, which he was sure was not appreciated.

"I am seeing God NOW." He said.

That is when the birds started to sing.

The day was overcast and cold but the birds started singing anyway!

At first Tom didn't think too much about it, but then more birds joined in and the sound became larger and grander and birds from everywhere were landing and there was more singing. They were in the trees and perched on the flowering bushes.

Students came to a standstill, just like Tom. Some of them started recording them on their cell phones and taking pictures. Tom did too.

Cyclists stopped and started walking their bikes so they could listen.

Tom quickly keyed in Susan's number. "You won't believe what's happening. You have to hurry. . .you have to come down here and observe this. I don't know how long it will last. Hurry!"

Tom didn't know why the birds were singing, but he was eager to tell her his theory, because she too, visited the Teacher. She would believe him. He sat on the rock wall and hugged himself against the chill of the day.

He allowed himself to drift with the sound of the birds, breathing deeply, thanking the birds, sending love to them, hugging them with his thoughts, with his heart, saying in the only way he knew how that he loved them.

"I am connected to you and I appreciate you and I am glad we are sharing this physical plane together, this garden!"

A Starling landed on the wall near him. Tom reached into his sack and brought out his sandwich and shared it with the bird. Some people didn't like the Starlings, some people didn't like people of another race, some people didn't like hound dogs, but Tom had grown beyond likes and dislikes. He knew he used to be a very opinionated person, but he wasn't anymore. He had changed. He went to church, but he believed differently, and yet the same somehow. He saw people there who claimed they were "saved." And yes, maybe Tom told himself, he had been saved too. By religion? He wondered. He knew it was by religion - kind of. It had been an unusual type of religion, one that was right for him, and it didn't conflict. He just understood things a little differently. He wasn't the same, he knew that. He believed in God.

"Yes, God." He breathed. "Yes, I do."

He knew Jesus was an extraordinary man who defied many things about the physical plane. He sat there and thanked Jesus. It was like He had learned to consciously create a bridge between the two dimensions, was in both dimensions all the time.

He didn't find the Bible conflicting in his life anymore - and he was learning to love the world, but there were many things he did NOT love about it; and it was humanity that headed that list. No, humanity was not nice! But right now, Tom was listening to the birds and he felt an outpouring of love for them.

Susan got there before the birds ceased their gathering and wonderful singing. The phenomena went on long enough that the campus news arrived with their cameras and microphones so they could photograph the clusters of birds. The little creatures were beautiful and amazing.

The Teacher had reminded Tom on several occasions, "sometimes there will be an occurrence to confirm a belief or a happening so you can remember it throughout your life. It will confirm that you have learned the absolute truth, because there can be no other way. Such a thing can be called a happening. It happens because it was a God thing. . ."

Tom's beliefs had jelled, but there was a passage that still bothered him in the Bible, one that the Pastor had read recently in church. Actually, he was surprised that over the past two years he had not asked the question.

When he thought about it, he was even more surprised that the Teacher had given him answers in the past that had satisfied him, because there were so many little things still nagging him about the Bible.

But right now, today, this moment, he was connecting to *Everything.*

GETTING ALONG WITH ONE ANOTHER

Tom continued to open the front door of his apartment. He liked opening it for himself and doing it didn't present any problems. The few people who saw him usually asked how he liked having 'smart devices' for his wifi. One night, Simeon asked him why he hadn't done his lights too.

"It's on my Christmas list for this year," Tom explained good naturedly. "Can't afford this stuff myself. You know. . ."

Inside his apartment, where nobody could see him, Tom practiced frequently. Every time he sat on the toilet, he experimented with the bathroom door. He kept trying to close it, to bring it back the way it was. Each time he tried inside his apartment, he "failed." He wanted to have full control over the phenomena. What had happened with the fabric door had scared him silly. He figured if he could do it, he could undo it. There was fallacy in that thinking - destroying a material object for a few seconds was far different than re-creating a material object the way it had been created in the first place. He knew nothing about its original creation. He never was able to bring any of his experiments back. They had to materialize back on their own.

Tom understood, as he looked back upon his life, that he was not alone. There was a presence that had been walking along with him forever. He never formally communicated with it, but Tom just "knew" things, like going and standing at that window at Carl's pizza. Something had compelled him to do that.

As he entered the room, his vision wasn't so far removed from him. He was back in Carl's Pizzeria. Big John had just made his first really big noise and Jake had done his first jump. Tom was standing there, his mind empty of anything, and then something just kind of compelled him to say his straight man words. He remembered how he slackened his face and stood like a board and the way he focused his eyes.

He heard those first merry laughs.

As the vision vanished, he realized that this too had happened for a reason. Nothing was by accident.

Then he wondered about the awful thing he'd witnessed of that woman driving over the flowers. . .

Tom sat down at his usual place at the table and opened his paper. "Why don't humans get along?" He asked.

"That's a silly question." Teacher said matter of factly.

"I don't understand," Tom said. "Why is it silly?"

"Because you are human and you should understand this. Right? What does it mean to be human, Tom?" Then he said it louder. "TOM! What does it mean to be human?"

"How in the hell do I know what it means to be human?" He said irritated, after his long silence of thinking about it. "That's what I've been trying to figure out! It means a lot of ugly stuff. Shit! It means I don't get along with my fellow man, I treat people like dirt, I hate myself, I don't believe in God, I kill people, I war with everybody - killing and shooting and raping and I'm lazy."

"You're having quite a day, aren't you Tom?"

"Well, it's true. Tell me it isn't true. We have great fun telling all kinds of stories about it all the time on the movies, on TV and in books. It is all we talk about. All the time. We're awful. Why are we so awful? It *is* because we are human. Tell me it isn't. We are more horrible than any other species. We do the most horrible things to our own kind. We even kill our children!" He took a breath, because he had to, not because he was out of words. "Couldn't God have made a better human being, a better species? Why us? Why all this horror?"

"There's that question of why again." A new sort of Voice said. "You are still focusing on the idea of God being involved with making human beings, "The Teacher said. "You are thinking of humans as being a begin all and end all - instead of God being the force of all the Universe, connecting all things to each other and you're just part of it all. There is a difference."

"Uh." Tom looked to one side and then the other, almost as if he were bored. He wasn't. It was just that he knew this story that the Teacher was telling. He was tired of it. It seemed that the Teacher was always harping about that change and movement thing. It didn't explain how come people didn't get along to Tom's satisfaction. No, it did **not**. "Uh-huh." He mouthed.

"Everything is in a state of change. Right?" The Teacher said. "Can we agree on that?" The Teacher waited patiently. "Everything is in a state of movement. Right?"

"Yes." Tom said tiredly, Impatiently, knowing what was next.

"Everything needs room to expand, to develop. To be." The Teacher explained. "It is part of position, direction and determination. You can't move unless there is a *space* to move into; then there is space left behind for what is coming up."

"Okay," Tom said guardedly, becoming more interested. It was the same as before, but it wasn't. The Teacher was spinning a new angle to it, a further explanation, he decided.

"So, when movement expands, then there is a push and something else fills the void. We are evolving and moving all the time, Tom, it is part of our position, our place right now. Not everyone is in the same place so there is conflict. Yes, it is imperfect. We are imperfect. We are supposed to be. Somewhere along the way, we got the idea that everything of God is perfect all the time. But it is *our* idea of perfect. There is no such thing!

"Oh." Tom said simply. "You told me all that."

"But you don't seem to be *getting* it. If we all got along with each other and we had no conflict, then the kind of evolvement, or what you hear me call movement, would not take place. We would be inert. We would not be pushing each other, would we?" The Teacher paused. "It is just evolvement of one species within the soup," He added. sensing that Tom was going in his mind to the begin all, end all of humanity again. "That's all. If we didn't move, what would happen to everything around us?"

Tom had jumped to the thought of why did humanity need to evolve, leaving out the step that everything was changing and moving and all that.

"Of course, the system, the Universe, and everything in it and all that IS, operates according to a perfect order, it must, it always will. It is the order that is perfect Tom. The order. It is the order of the Universe. Look around you. Isn't everything in order? The Oceans that support you, the forms of life within it, as it is within your own body. A system of order.

"There are imperfections all along the way. There are cells in your own body that become cancerous. But Tom, there *are* cells in your body. There is an order. And what about birth defects? They happen. All of this randomness happens within the ordered Universe. One thing will correct another. And so, it will always be. Nothing is perfect Tom, not even God. The most perfect thing we have been taught in our lives is an emotion, and it is something that cannot be measured, and even that is not perfect. Is it?

Tom frantically tried to think of what emotion the Numen was carrying on about. And then it became clear to him. Yes of course. **Love.**

"Why do you suppose we think of that emotion as the closest thing to perfect we know? Because it is forgiving and healing and accepting, and to us, to us humans and our specific needs - love is the perfect nourishment.

"God is love. That is certainly a human definition, isn't it?" The Teacher posed to the student in the room, and then continued. . .

"But if God is in you, that means you must love yourself, doesn't it? That love is not coming from an entity up there in the clouds. . . is it?" He chuckled, and then continued as a she.

"Perhaps if we understood this, and acknowledged the God within, and our connection with each other, we humans would get along." she said lightly.

"I see," Tom said, embarrassed that his mind had wandered away and that he kept asking what must seem like the same questions. At least most of his questions all seemed to roll back to the same basic explanation.

"We assigned perfection to God, because we wanted God to be perfect," She continued. "So, we have said God is love. God is perfect. But the truth is, God is Everything. God IS love and all other things, all kinds of imperfections and that child that is born with birth defects and that cell in your body that isn't perfect. It is *all* God."

"It makes sense." Tom said.

"Humanity, as we know it at this time is in a sad state of affairs. We give away responsibility to others all the time, every day in our lives. That's why we've made God separate. The Bible itself has made God separate as has other religions. "Our father, who art in heaven. . ." but it may be a matter of difficulty in translating the words, because I am certain that Jesus knew God was in him.

"We want God to be responsible, we want Jesus to be responsible, we want our parents and our teachers and our children, but what it all comes down to is ourselves, and that is hard to take. We are responsible to **one**. The power of one. We are accountable and must start answering to that big Voice, that *one* that is in ourselves, that voice that really is the big hurrah, that Voice that is the one we are born with and the one we die with. Our own. And that Voice is the God within. It is the one we are connected to. It is the Voice that speaks through Everything and from us to Everything. It is our reason for being. It is the development of our understanding and our awareness and our evolution. It is where we are in the movement of things, it is what is steering us in our positioning as we travel along in the direction of everything. It is a grand plan and we are not alone and a solitary entity. We are completely connected in all of this."

"Whew" Tom said thinking he'd never heard the Teacher go on such a tangent before. "It makes sense when I hear you say it, but sometimes when I am by myself, I lose it. It's like I can't grab hold of it, or that it isn't making sense anymore. It is like, you know, too much to think about and I can't think about it anymore and I give up," Tom said.

"That's okay," The Teacher said. "These things will come back to you when you need them and they will help you in your life. You are here because you are supposed to be here. So much will just be automatic in your life because you are on your path now. . ."

Tom sat in his chair. He felt the seat cushion under him and the seat back against him and how his legs pressed against the seat column. He rolled in slightly and his arms moved on the table top.

Those arms of his were connected to that table top, he thought, and that chair to the floor, and he was breathing air in the room and the sun was coming in the window and there was this aroma in the room like petals from a flower and he wondered where it was coming from. Was it coming from the Teacher? He had never touched the Teacher, yet this person was changing his life, was rocking his world, and all of this experience was making him into something he hadn't even known he could be, hadn't even thought was there, behind his thoughts, behind all those surface images in his brain. Was he connected to that person behind that gauzy curtain? And then IT spoke again.

"Yes," IT said. "You are connected to me. and to Everything that IS."

Tom was startled. The person behind the curtain had read his every thought. How could that have happened?

"Are you male or female?" Tom asked.

"Why do you care?" The Voice asked with that lilting quality, one that he hadn't heard for a while.

"Well, I am male."

"Yes, I believe you are." The Voice said amusingly. "So what?"

"Males think differently than females."

"Well, do you want to know just how females think or just how males think, or more about how the Universe thinks?" There was a silence, and then IT laughed, because how silly that sounded, how small and insignificant and petty.

Tom started to laugh, and then he had trouble stopping. "I am not complete by myself. . ." he said between breaths, "am I?" He laughed some more and said, "I am not complete without her and without the God within."

"Ah. . .wait a minute. You are not complete in this system without her, your parents, me, your fellow students, your teachers, and guess what? Everything. The "she" you are referring to is your close partner that is in this system with you to facilitate the physical laws of this system. She has a complete identity, neither male or female, just as you have. Sometimes I think you identify with the system beyond yourself. That is to say, your identity is based on the system around you instead of you - of what you really are. Everything comes into this system with an identity that is NOT based on this system. You were you before you entered this system, before you took on the form of a human being. Okay? It is as if you are playing a part in a game, like Baseball, for instance.

"Maybe you are playing the position as the Catcher in the game, but that is not who you are, it is just who you are during the game. There are other people playing in the game and you understand that their identities are not necessarily who they are when they are not playing in the game - like Joe the pitcher is a person totally separate outside of the game. Of course.

"The position of Pitcher facilitated the game, just as yours did, as Catcher. When the game is over, you go on as who you are, not as Catcher.

"Gender is needed by the role you are playing in this system," The Voice said. "We can call it the game of life."

"You mean I won't be a man anymore?" Tom voice rose a couple of notches.

"Why would you need to be?" The Teacher asked calmly. "Is there something I am missing?"

"Oh, to be a father to my children. To meet them on the other side. And other things." Tom said.

"Oh, the other things. . . like, in some religions, to have virgins on the other side?" the Teacher was a "He" and he had a lighthearted quality to his tone. "Sex of course is a physical attribute ascribed to this dimension. It is necessary, like eating and sleeping. As we evolve or change, we take with us those things we want to keep, like feelings and sensations. Perhaps some of what we have here will be easier to come by, or I should say - more accessible - in a different dimension, when not hampered by the physical confinements of this one." The Teacher laughed and laughed. "Perhaps we will connect with those sensations much more readily with our new understanding of our connections to All things. Now that's something to contemplate, isn't it? Think about *that* - and what it implies!"

And such laughter filled the room with a kind of joy and merriment that totally moved Tom into its space until his eyes were wide with excitement.

"Oh my gosh!" he said.

"Yes. Tom, your loved ones may take on recognizable forms initially to assist you with the crossover. It's a shock you know. One second you are here and the next someplace very different. It's like taking a step here and the next step there. But you know Tom, you are connected to the family you have here in other ways. But the blood thing stays here. It is part of this system. It isn't part of the next one."

Tom's laughter had quieted down. He thought about how truly funny we human beings are with our crazy thoughts! Yes, he had considered sex in the afterlife, but he had never considered being able to connect in several ways regarding the orgasmic affects, the sensations of sex, in multiple ways. Such a thought was titillating. He always wondered what it felt like, being a woman. .

The Teacher said, "I'd like to change the subject. It seems we have beaten the same question, just about to death now. How soon do you think you will be giving up your space here in the room to somebody else, Tom?"

Tom looked frantically about the room. "No" he said. "No, please. I'm not ready. I have more questions. I need more. . .uh. . . time. I'm sorry. I was a little bored today, but really, I'm not. I'm learning things, I am learning so much!"

A Voice filled with understanding and compassion answered him. "Of course." The Numen said. I understand.

But I hope you will have some new and interesting questions. . .

THE RESULTS

Tom's parents arrived on a sunny afternoon during spring break, his last break before graduation. Tom thought that traffic was going to be bad, but he didn't have any reason to be worried. There wasn't an influx of students coming into his town, but instead most of them left for other places promising beaches and party times, like Florida. The day before had seen a traffic jam of old cars getting away but today was quiet. His break took place in March, so the weather could have still been cold, but the day was as good as it gets for that time of year.

The sun streamed into the front windows of his apartment. He had neighbors on both sides. His kitchen was on the backside, and so was his bathroom. He had small windows in both rooms, and since his kitchen doubled as a place to eat (he would hardly call it a dining room), he was grateful for the light.

Two weeks ago, he received the email announcement that he could look up his m-cat test score. He felt sick inside. It was a big deal - the release day for the scores. He could have said he expected nothing, but that would have been a lie, he expected good results. He wanted good results. There was something riding on this, and he really wasn't sure what, but he knew it was a future that was life changing and very different from anything he had previously contemplated for himself. He waited fearfully to look up his scores. His hands were shaking just thinking about it.

He cleaned his bathroom

He called Susan, asked her to breakfast. Neither one of them had a morning class. They met at the Perkin's Restaurant near the highway, each riding along one of the many bike paths. He could have picked her up. He could have driven himself there. He had gas in his car. It would have been easier for her, easier for him. But she offered when he called, saying, "What a great day! It is finally getting warm. Let's ride our bikes!" It was like she had read his mind. It was like that with her. So often he would call, or she would call, and they both had the same thoughts, about the same things.

He loved her, he would always love her.

He liked the chain restaurant, although his former friends used to chide him about it - saying that it was an "old" person's kind of place. He liked it because it was light and airy and the service was fast.

He liked breakfast and a person could order it there all day long. He thought it was funny that the food for breakfast was in a category at most places, set aside only for a certain time of day. Food is food, he thought, either you liked it or you didn't and why did it matter when you ate it, anyway? He liked pancakes for dinner, and he would melt cheese on top of them if he could!

His eyes were bright as he walked in and saw her, standing by a booth at the window, pulling off her jacket. Yes, it was still cool outside, actually too cool for the ride over, but he needed that ride, to try and settle the butterflies that were dancing throughout his midsection. Susan took one look at him and knew. "I know," she said. "The test scores are out today. How did you do? Are we celebrating?"

"I don't know." He said.

She pretended it was no big deal, looking at her cell phone and fooling with it. She glanced up and then down at it. "Oh. Well, what are you going to order?"

"Pancakes."

"Of course."

"Hey, did you know Perkins has free wifi?" She said blandly." Look at this. . ." She had a funny video short of a silly dog running in circles.

"Yeah, I guess I knew that. . ."

She called up the test site. "Would you like me to look up your test scores and tell you how you did?"

"No," he said.

"Would you like me to call them up so *you* can see how you did?"

"Okay," he said in a small voice.

"What's your password?"

NEXT_OF_KIN2075

"What in the world do you have a password like that for?"

"I dunno," he said. "It was just easy for me to remember, I guess."

She didn't say anything more, but it took her awhile to enter it on her phone. She muttered having to do it twice. She navigated to the page of his scores and glanced at it slightly and realized she should not have peeked. She handed him the phone.

He gulped. It seemed better to be looking at them in a public place. He wouldn't cry in such a place. He wouldn't dance around the room and make a spectacle of himself either. He would just eat, or maybe not eat.

She knew though, and she waited. It wasn't just that he had good scores, not with what she thought she saw, it was that he had great scores.

He gulped again. "Are these right?" He said more than asked, looking at her and passing the phone over. Are these as good as I think they are?

She looked at the image on the phone, she squinted, and then screwed up her face in a mock "OH no!"

They both laughed hysterically.

"Oh my God," she said. "Are these for real? Are you kidding me?"

They both laughed hysterically.

Tom started eating his pancakes, but stopped and stared out the window.

"Tom," Susan said. "TOM! Are you listening to me?!"

"Huh? I'm sorry."

"With these scores," she was saying, "You can apply for scholarships. Do you realize what these mean? These scores are your ticket. . ."

But Tom had done research on it and Susan hadn't. Medical schools didn't give out scholarships. But there were some places he could apply. Unfortunately, Tom's undergraduate grade point average wasn't very competitive, unlike other pre-med students. His 2.9 would be going against pre-med students who had a 3.5 and higher in the pre-med field.

Tom's test scores were, in part, a fluke. He knew that. The luck of the draw. The game of chance. Simeon's drill on the way over had been questions he hadn't known the answers to, but it was as if Simeon had known what questions would be on the test. The answers were fresh in his mind and ready for quick recall, making for fast working time throughout the test. It was crazy - it was like a science fiction happening. He knew answers he would not have known without Simeon's help!

He kept thinking about it on the ride home after the test, about what he was going to tell Simeon. But it was later, much later, that Tom saw Simeon. He stayed up late, after his own work at the Pizza restaurant, to greet Simeon. But Simeon didn't show up at 3 o'clock, or 4 o'clock and Tom had a mixture of worry and fatigue and was getting nervous when he finally saw him pull up below.

Sim got out of his car quietly, like he always did. He was juggling bags of groceries. Tom met him down the stairs and took some of the load. "I like getting groceries this time of day," Sim said, "There's absolutely nobody in the store. How did you do?"

"I did well - because of you! How did you know?" Tom exclaimed. "It was so uncanny! Those questions. . . the ones you had on the recorder; they were on the test!"

"I didn't know," Simeon laughed. "I selected them at random. I just wanted to calm you and give you some focus. I don't even remember selecting them!"

Simeon opened the door. "I'll take these." He whispered." Kate's asleep. She has early duty tomorrow. I'm so happy the test is behind you and that you feel good about it. I hope you did well! You never know. . .if you did well enough," Simeon had said, "You might even be a candidate for some scholarships. . . ."

"I don't know how to thank you. You're the best friend ever!"

Tom stepped back into his place and wondered how he could ever repay his friend next door. He was glad the test was behind him.

That had been ten weeks ago. Now, Tom knew he'd be staying up late for Simeon again. This time to tell him his test scores.

Tom's parents were coming. Should he tell them? He hoped he could keep his apartment and go to the medical school right here, at this university, because he had a job, and an apartment, and Susan would be here. It was a long shot. It was one of those "dream big" things with "no expectations." He'd already filled out the application papers. But he had a dilemma. He might not get in anywhere. Med school was so competitive, he was applying at four schools just to be certain of his chances. Some places told him that having a different background, like his, in physics, was a plus. Others told him he didn't have a chance. He decided he would not tell them until he knew his status.

Tom's father had always wondered how he was going to get a job in Physics. It was a discussion they'd had more than once - trying to discover a strategy for Tom's future. His father would be shocked by Tom's decision.

Tom was ready for his parents' arrival. They had never stayed with him before. He had flowers in a little vase in the bedroom and empty hangers in the closet. He'd never owned a bedspread before, but Susan went with him to the Goodwill store and they found one that looked nice. She also found a painting for his wall, some decorative pillows to toss on top of the bed, which seemed like a girly thing to do, and some real glasses instead of the plastic things he'd been using.

Linda and Mike chatted the entire five-hour trip. They speculated about Tom's life and what they were going to find. Linda was certain they were going to end up at the nearby Comfort Inn, and in fact made back up reservations just in case. They brought pillows and a set of clean sheets with them. But Mike didn't think that was necessary - he was sure Tom's place was a makeover handled by a girlfriend. But it was Tom that had gone to the store and bought pillows, although they were cheap ones, because he wanted nice new pillows for his parents to sleep on and it was Tom who had purchased his own sheets.

By the time his parents arrived, he had made up his mind not to tell them about the m-cats and medical school. He asked Susan not to tell them. "I don't want to say anything," he'd said, "Until I know that I've been accepted someplace."

"I understand," she'd said. "I won't say a word.

But Tom had not counted on Simeon's wife, Kate. He intended to ask her to keep his endeavors quiet but he had not seen her. Simeon knew he didn't want anything to be said, but Kate wasn't in the loop. Kate and Simeon were going away for the break actually, so Tom wasn't concerned about either one of them.

Only their plans changed and the two of them gave up their flight for a nice cash deal offered to people willing to give up their seats for a day. They hadn't minded leaving a day later and gladly took the money and an extra ticket. What a deal, they'd happily said, and went back home. That is why they were going up to their apartment exactly at the same time as Tom's parents were going up to his.

Kate took one look at Tom's father and knew immediately who he was. "Oh, you are Tom's father!" She exclaimed. "You look just like him! Congratulations! You must be SO proud of Tom!"

"Well, yes, we are." Linda and Mike smiled, taken aback, thinking her remarks must be about Tom being in his last year of school, and perhaps about getting a good grade report. But Kate wasn't finished.

"We love having him as a neighbor," she said on the way up, leading them to his place. "He has worked so hard! He deserves something wonderful. We are very excited about his success!" She stopped on the stairs, turning toward them with the brightest of smiles. Simeon stood above her and touched her, the kind of touch that says, "Don't."

Kate realized aghast, that Tom probably was going to tell them as a surprise and she had ruined it. With eyes, huge in her face, she covered her mouth, "Oh." She said, and looked up at Simeon. "Oh no." She said again.

They all stopped on the stairs.

Kate looked back at them. "I'm sorry," she said. "I thought he would have told you."

Tom was at the window in the living room. He saw the whole thing. It gave him a chance to think. There was a time when he would have been furious, and actually he was, for a few seconds. The old Tom was livid. But he wasn't the old Tom anymore, and the new Tom stepped in. His dearest friends had spilled the news. He knew. He just knew. They weren't supposed to be there. But they were. He got those good scores *because* of Simeon.

Tom gathered himself, put a smile on his face, and ran out. He looked at Kate smiling, "Did you tell them, Kate?" He said encouragingly.

"No," she said, shaking her head, with a tear squeezing out and rolling down her face. "I'm sorry Tom. I'm so sorry. . . . I didn't. . ."

Tom raised a hand laughing. "Mom, dad, please meet my dearest friends, Simeon and Kate, and there isn't anybody in the whole world I'd rather have tell you my news, than them!" He was reaching out and trying to hug everyone he could reach.

"Kate, you've got to tell them!" He looked at her imploring and she would never have guessed that it had ever been any other way. "I'm so happy you are here. I thought you were going to be gone. Now look, here you are. . . you get to meet my mom and dad!"

Kate wiped her face and grinned. "Oh my gosh" she gushed, "I'm so happy too. I get to meet you." She exchanged hugs.

Tom nodded to her to come in and finish what she'd started.

"He has such great news. Oh oh oh! He should be the one to tell you, but I get to." She said quietly, then screamed, "He aced the M-CATS!"

Tom's mother, Linda, looked bewildered, but she didn't want to look stupid and tried to recover, smiling.

Mike didn't know either, but he guessed it was something important. He dropped the suitcases and reached out to shake Tom's hand. Linda, who was still trying to figure out what was happening moved to hug her son, her eyebrows raised as she looked over to Mike, who was equally bewildered. It was like the stop motion on a video, the way they were all standing in Tom's living room, the door still open, Linda looking at Mike and Mike trying not to stare off in space. Tom's bobbing head was in a lowered position trying not to laugh, and Kate had this disbelieving look on her face, as if there could be anybody in the world who would not know what the achievement meant. Then there was Simeon. There he stood, in the doorway, looking over the scene and evaluating all of it. That was his strength. Yes. Simeon was the person who could look at a thing and know what to do, know how to fix it or what was needed. He was one of the most respected people at the hospital, a go-to person when everything was bleak and all seemed hopeless. Nothing was hopeless when he was there. He always found a way, always made things better. It was his talent.

"Mr. and Mrs. Cross," He said in a serious tone, "There is a test, a very important test that is considered one of the most difficult tests there is. Many good students essentially fail this test or do poorly on it. It is called the M-CAT test. Maybe it is the most difficult test in the world today." He paused, letting the information sink in. "Students take this test when they want to get into medical school. . ." He stood there looking into their eyes while it registered that it was Tom he was speaking about, their Tom, Tom Cross, Thomas Michael Cross, the little boy who was always climbing trees and riding his scooter around the neighborhood, Thomas whose room was a cyclone, Thomas who smuggled beer into the garage one night and had an afterhours party when he thought they were gone. THAT Thomas. Tom. Tom who was standing there in his living room dancing from foot to foot. Their Thomas.

"This test," he continued, "determines whether or not a person can gain entrance into medical school. It goes on for eight hours of ass to the wall, detailed, most grueling test taking ever devised."

"Tom aced it," Kate said lightly flicking a hand toward him.

Tom nodded. He had no more decisions to make. "Thank you, Kate," He said, grinning happily, and taking a bow at the waste. He was happy. "These are my dearest friends," he said. "They made the difference for me!" He gestured to the apartment. "Come in everybody. I have goodies to eat and let's celebrate!"

The apartment was immaculate. Tom's mother was still in a state of disbelief as she stepped through his apartment, but his father was already building a swelling of pride in his chest.

There were enough places for everybody to sit, with the chair from the desk, which his father quickly grabbed. There was a magazine holder on the floor. It was filled with study materials - still. Mike picked up one and leafed through it. He shook his head. Stacked on the desk was Kaplan study guides.

"Tom studied for months," Simeon said simply gesturing to the stack.

"Simeon came over almost every day and drilled me with flash cards," Tom explained. "Now that's a really good friend! They live next door."

Tom had a buffet of eats set out on his table in the kitchen. He looked at it with surprise. There was enough for everyone. He wondered why he had put out so much, then shrugged and realized that there were many things in his life he couldn't explain.

"Tom saved our cat in the middle of the night!" Kate said.

Tom brought out his new glasses filled with the lemonade he had made earlier. His mother started to cry. "What's wrong mummy?" He asked, handing her a glass, but she just shook her head.

It was later at the Pizza Restaurant, that Linda turned to Mike and said in a low voice, "I don't know who he is," gesturing to Tom. "Who is that person?" Carl, the owner, had come over and treated them to the pizza of their choice, telling them how much he liked Tom and how his clientele had increased because people liked him so much. "Tom is the greatest," he said. "His generosity is amazing and his coworkers love him. He created a feeling here of the most incredible teamwork. We have turned into a family. Tom always shares his tips with the guys behind there," he told them in a low voice, "and now everybody benefits. His jar is always crammed with money that people put in there. The word has spread about our place, about how perfect our pizza is - the great crust, the sauce, everything. It is all because of these guys. They make it that way. I've owned this place for six years and I've never had anything like this happen. . ."

He sat with them. He told them about how Tom always studied during his break but always came back a few minutes early. Mike smiled and nodded to Linda with a look that said, see that's what I, Mike Cross, taught him.

"Have you met Susan yet?"

"Uh, no."

"That's his girlfriend. You will like her. A lot. She is the best there is. She is graduating this year too. She is also going to grad school - going into public health. She wants to work in disadvantaged areas." Carl looked from one face to the other wondering if he'd said too much. "Let me just tell you, everybody loves her too. Tom had never said, to any of us, that he wants to make anything permanent of it, but I hope he does. She's the best. I hope you will think so too." Carl excused himself thinking he probably had said too much and went back to the office where he ordered more mozzarella cheese. He loved Tom. He loved Susan. Heck, he hoped he could stay here for their advanced education plans. He made a few inquiries, but what he learned wasn't good news. "It is very seldom," he was told, "That a student goes to the same school as their undergraduate work." On the day he heard that, Carl started to pull every string he had, in the hopes that Tom would be accepted here. He didn't know many people, but he had a few friends at the golf club, and one or two at the gym.

He didn't know it, and nobody ever would, but Carl even mentioned it to the woman at the newspaper and to Amy. A person like that was not the kind of guy that was going into medicine for the money. Of course, Amy knew *everybody*.

That night, when Mike and Linda were laying in Tom's bed, on brand new pillows and nice clean sheets, they talked quietly into the night. Tom was asleep on the couch. "He is all grown up," she said, crying softly. "He is no longer a little boy. . ."

"Why are you crying about it?" Mike asked.

"He is so different," she said.

"Are you sorry?"

"No. It's just, it's just. . . my little boy. . .he's gone. . .

"Yes, He is all grown up. . ."

THE DERBY STAMPEDE

Carl's Pizzeria, Home of the Stampede, was packed. Spring Break was over, flowers were blooming everywhere, and Carl purchased small tables, each big enough for two that he placed on the front sidewalk. He blocked the side entrance by the parking lot, which he was sorry about because most people used that one, but by doing that he could provide more space inside and outside.

He made an agreement with Sam's next door to share a larger dumpster together in the back and that freed up more space for parking. When he finished reorganizing, he had Black Brothers redo his parking lot. He had five more parking spaces, a premium near the university. He installed a new flower planter along the parking and two more booths inside. He hung a cute sign directing people to the front entrance. Sam's next door was happy about the small renovation too. His place was a beer pub, and since Carl didn't serve beer, many of his customers floated over to Sam's, some even carrying their pizza along with them. Sam's had a few selections of finger food and popcorn, but Carl's was so valuable to him, that he put up table tents advertising the stampede next door, and suggested that customers bring their pizza back to his place.

Marsha drifted into the pizzeria one night when she knew Carl wouldn't be around. As usual, Carl went to the gym later on Thursdays; so he could meet Bob, a buddy of his, to play a game of Racquetball. Carl would have liked to play more often, but Bob didn't get off from his job at the university until 5:30 p.m. making their game at 6:00 p.m. Carl wouldn't arrive at the restaurant until after 7:30 p.m. - and all the activity with the three stooges started at seven.

Marsha wanted to know what all the fuss was about at his place. About now, she was beginning to get the idea that she'd been swindled. The "boys" didn't come on until 7:00 p.m. three nights a week - Thursday, Friday and Saturday. They also worked on Sunday during the day, but she didn't want a chance meeting with Carl on that day.

She arrived exactly at 7:00 p.m. to a crowd that had already formed. The line was almost out the door! By the time it was her turn, she was getting nervous. She'd already heard three orders come up finished. "How is that possible?" She commented to the guy next to her. "The place is already packed!"

"People get here early and place their orders so the pizza will be finished after seven. Ha ha ha!" he said. "That way they avoid the line and can be here for the fun!" Just then, Tom interrupted the order-taking to do his straight man routine. Then he started taking people's orders and ringing in their money. She didn't mind too much. The three of them really were fascinating to watch. By the time she left with her pizza twenty minutes later, she had to admit she'd forgotten about the troubles of her day at work. John was like the pied piper. He had a joyous way about him that reached out and caught a person up in the play. It was a play, a performance. How could it be? It was just pizza!

She walked out to the parking lot of a restaurant she no longer owned, got into a car that she'd just traded for, one that gave her shivers when she ran her hands over the seats, and one that would take a good portion of her salary, and revved the motor. She'd been cheated by that lying son-of-a-bitch husband! There wasn't one empty space in that parking lot and two cars were waiting for people to leave!

She'd gone to five different lawyers, on 'condition' of course, and not one of them would touch her case. She tried three in town and two out of town. By the time she went out of town, Carl's story, actually Tom's story, had aired nationwide. She had not been implicated as the "bad guy," but if she fought, it was bound to come out that she had been the culprit. Then Carl could sue her. He had never accused her of anything, and she wasn't even sure if he knew she'd been the wise guy who had started the horrible rumor. He never said why he wanted the divorce, only that he didn't love her anymore. His settlement was liberal, she thought, at the time. But in truth, it wasn't. The restaurant was worth hugely more than the house, plus she wasn't even sure how much he got from the exclusive 'expose' story about how a vicious rumor had been started against one of the nicest places in town.

Rumor had it that Tom received a check for $50,000 for the story from somebody! She'd also heard, at Sally's of course, that the three of them were being considered for other things, maybe even a movie. If that were to happen, then a person could only guess how much money was involved. The word was, they would have to be in the movie because nobody else could do their parts. After she saw them, she knew that was true. And of course, Carl would get a share of it all!

It was all because of that talk show host coming into the place incognito. Those crazy boys had given up their graduation parties, just like they had given up their time off during finals week! Humph! Who could believe anyone would do such a thing?

Sally said they even wore their graduation caps. They told people they did it because they didn't want visiting families to be disappointed. "I don't believe that at ALL," Marsha said to her hairdresser, "I think they must have had a tip somebody special was in town that would see them."

"Uh-huh," was all that anybody in the spa said about that. If any person had ever thought there was a problem with ethics, they surely didn't think so after they had visited the place especially after that program aired on talk television. "Why don't you put this one on a shelf Marsha. . ."

Marsha thought about that as she sat in the parking lot, sat there with that hot pizza on her lap, smelling the pepperoni and the cheese waft up and hearing again in her mind that trumpet sound signaling that her food was ready. The more she thought about it, the more she fumed.

"It was because of ME, you fuckers," she screamed, looking at the windows of Carl's Pizzeria and ramming a fist on her new steering wheel." ME!" She threw the pizza box over on the seat. "I'm the one who called attention to this place! Nobody else. Me. Nobody would have paid any attention to any of you," she pointed a finger at the place, "Not to any of you." She was shaking in anger, working herself into a frenzy. "If I hadn't pointed out what you were doing. Me. You were just a bunch of nobody's until I came along. Fucking nobody's!"

Behind her was a car waiting for her parking space. She didn't like the amount of space she had to back up. "Get out of the fucking way." She screamed. But the guy in the car behind her was talking on the phone. She rolled down her window. "Get the fuck out of the way." She screamed. He pulled the phone away from his ear and angrily motioned to the children in his car. "Bitch," he mouthed, not moving.

Marsha surveyed the surroundings and saw she could maneuver her car over the new planter, and that thought was quite agreeable. She revved the car again, threw him the bird, and steered directly over the newly placed stones. She aimed for the planter, drove directly over it and smashed the newly planted flowers flat, screaming out the window at the top of her lungs, "FUCK YOU! Fuck all of you!"

What she didn't realize, is only minutes before that, Tom went to the back room for his break, something he seldom did anymore, but one of those "compelling feelings" just came over him, that said, "take a little break, Tom." He turned to the other stooges, saying, "Hey, gonna take five. . .be back soon."

He ran to the back, not knowing why, and walked up to the window, cell phone in hand, thinking he would photograph the new landscaping Carl had just finished. He clicked his first photo just as a crazy woman came careening over all of Carl's work, screaming obscenities. . .

He kept taking the photos. He was further shocked later to see the driver had flipped off a car full of kids. . .

THE VOICE

Tom met Susan by a large tree in Middleburg Park. Both had finished their final exams and were celebrating the end of school. He had stopped and picked up lunches from Pic & Pie to celebrate. It was a perfectly warm and sunny day.

They sat on a blanket and leaned against the large tree trunk. "I can't believe I'm finished," she said.

"I know. Me too. I'll be having one more visit in the Room, and then that will be over too." He said with a note of nostalgia. "I'll miss the Teacher."

"Is it really true Tom, all the things she says?"

"Well, it sure seems so. The Teacher is really different, I know."

"I never told you what happened when I went home over the summer."

"Are you going to tell me now?"

"It makes me crazy when I think about it. It was so strange." She picked up a pine needle, twisted it and smelled its sweetness.

"I know. I've had lots of strange things happen since I started going to the room. You know? I can tell you but nobody else."

"Yeah, I know what you mean."

"I come from a really little town in the Midwest." She started saying.

"Yeah. I know that. How come you decided to go to a school so far away?"

"It's my dad's alma mater and I lived here with my aunt my last year of high school for in-state tuition. He really wanted me to come here. He wasn't doing well and things were hard on my mom. I thought I could help her, but then I discovered she wanted to take him to a place in Texas for treatment and having me around was going to make that difficult."

"Oh."

"The treatment didn't help him.

"I'm sorry."

"Me too."

"Anyway, I went home for spring break and his former club asked me to give a talk about how I used the scholarship they gave me. The membership is male, except they invited the Pastor from the local church to join them. And she did - the only female member. I don't know why they had her as a female member. Well, anyway, we sat together for dinner."

"What did you talk about?"

"That's just it. It's what we talked about - that minister and me."

"That minister told me a very disturbing story. And you know, Tom, I didn't even know her personally! It was a strange conversation."

"She told me about a little church from the town next door."

"Did you go to a small church like that growing up?" Tom asked.

"Not really. This place is even smaller than my town! I think they only have that one church.

"The church is the kind that chooses the pastors the them, you know, most congregations choose their own, but some denominations make the choice for them. It was a difficult choice for the town, but one that I thought would have been okay, but Midwest farm towns are not very diversified. They sent a Black female pastor!

"The entire town was mad about it and was ostracizing her. The congregation was all white and hated her. People were even burning stuff on her lawn! Can you imagine it? You know, Tom, the thing they hated the most, was she was preaching about accountability - just like the things we learn in the zimmer. . . "

"You mean they hated her because of her race? Or because of what she was preaching" Tom was surprised.

"Both. That's what I understood. The minister told people were burning crosses on her lawn and throwing bricks through her window."

"Oh my gosh, Susan. That's awful. I didn't know things like that were still going on, especially in places like our heartland!"

"Uh - huh."

"That congregation needs to meet the Teacher!

"Can you imagine? When I went back to my mom's house that night, Tom, I couldn't sleep. I was so distressed! I actually felt pain in my body for her. The next day Mom went to work and I was alone in the house. This is when it gets really interesting. It was like. . .uh. . .like. . uh. . . a voice, kinda, telling me to call that minister."

"Well, did you?"

"I couldn't help myself. I didn't want to. I didn't know her name, you know? But I had this feeling. I was compelled, like something was making me do it. So, I gave in. I looked up the number and called."

Tom held her hand and squeezed encouragingly. "What happened?"

"I was so relieved; I got an answering machine. The voice was a woman's voice, rich and full. You know? She sounded like Aretha Franklin. I was so relieved! I was literally off the hook! I hung up."

"Oh." Tom said disappointed.

"I'm getting there. That compelling voice wouldn't leave me alone. Honestly Tom, it wouldn't leave me alone! It was like the Teacher in my head! I started pacing the room. I can tell you I was uncomfortable. I remember talking to that voice, telling it to leave me alone, that I had called and nobody was there.

"It said I had to call again. I said NO. But it wouldn't leave me alone. It told me I would learn why later - that I *must* do it. I thought I was going crazy.

"So finally, I said, *okay* because I just couldn't stand that voice anymore. I called again and I got the answering machine again. I had no idea what to say."

"What did you do?"

"and then. . .and then. . . the voice took over. Honestly, I had no control at all. My voice was level and not shaking, or anything. It said: '***I just want you to know: 'I admire your* courage!**' Then I hung up. I sat there shaking. Honestly, I did. But I wasn't bothered anymore."

"That must have felt strange." Tom said.

"It did. But that's not all. The next day I was walking downtown to meet mom for lunch and that minister, the one who told me about her, passed me on the sidewalk. She stopped me and started talking about her. It was so strange! But she wanted to talk.

"She told me about a call she had just received – from that other minister. This is what she told me:

"You know, that horrible congregation I was telling you about? Well, they threw out their minister. It was awful. She had to go before a group of people calling themselves the *Church Betterment Committee*. She knew it was going to be terrible, like a type of lynching, but she told me strangest thing happened.

"She said she felt sick at heart and was shaking and she didn't know how she was going to face those awful people. *I went into my office to gather myself just before going in to face those people and saw a light on my answering machine but I didn't want to play it because I'd been getting such awful messages. Then it was like a voice told me to play that message! At first, I wasn't going to do it, but I was compelled to go over and play it. A voice made me do it.*

It was like a message from God. A woman was telling me how much she admired my courage! That message made the difference for me. I knew then, I was NOT meant to stay there and everything was going to be okay. I went into that committee with a sense of calm. They did kick me out, it was horrible, but I had been given courage.

"Then, Tom, she just turned and went on down the sidewalk!"

"Strange things are happening to me too," Tom said softly.

"I can't get over it! There are many smaller things too!"

The two of them sat there and talked about the things they'd been learning. Their experiences were different, yet the same.

"We are as infants in training, because we have been temporarily separated from purpose. Once we know what we are, we are extremely accountable." Tom said.

"When a person doesn't understand what *they* are, then we should have compassion and forgiveness for them. It was one of the last things Jesus said: Lord forgive them - they know not what they do."

"I would like to meet that that minister who had such courage." Tom said.

"Maybe some day we will," Susan said thoughtfully.

Tom sat looking at the green grass and the flower buds bobbing in the wind and leaned over and kissed her.

"I love you," He said. "I will love you forever."

WINDING DOWN

Tom flicked his hand up in the air, as if he were trying to get off a piece of sticky tape. The gesture was a bit much for the few leftover crumbs on his hand from the sandwich he had eaten on his way over.

The door responded by going somewhere straight up into the wall above it.

Tom hadn't thought anything about the door, but looked quickly around and went through the opening like a streak, still wondering exactly how he was controlling it.

He was standing in the middle of a tour group in a museum on their vacation trip. He was excited to be there. The Guide was talking about an important find of dinosaur bones. Tom looked wonderingly at a huge dinosaur robot.

Soon the family was outside in an area where they were allowed to dig. His dad had brought along a few implements for his kids to hunt for fossils. Tom had this "feeling" that he'd sometimes get, and went over to an undisturbed area and started fooling around with the topsoil. He made a circular trench and kept digging, like he knew exactly where he was going - and what he was looking for.

That's when Tom made the discovery of a perfectly preserved fossil right in the middle of his circle. He remembered his mother saying, "It's like that with Tom. He just seems to know things. . ."

He had that fossil now in his apartment. It had been the best vacation he could remember. . .

Tom took a deep breath. "So much has happened since I was here last." Tom told the presence behind the drape. He explained what had happened at Carl's and the deep sadness he was feeling for him. "We had something so happy and wonderful at the pizza shop. Why would his wife try to turn it into something ugly?"

"Maybe Carl is supposed to change direction in his life. "Numen answered, "Sometimes things are not what they seem."

"They just divorced. Carl says he wants to sell the restaurant after Big John and I leave. He is in so much pain."

"It won't be the same place after you leave, Tom." The Numen answered gently. "A change took place when the three of you became friends and started caring about Carl. A very big one. Perhaps there is something else meant for Carl. Maybe you guys were instruments to bring about a change that could only occur with your help. . ."

"I don't know. . ."

"But someday you will." The Numen said.

Tom was breathing easier and sighed. "What about his wife? I don't understand how she could turn on him like that. I don't understand anything about women..."

A soft tinkling laughter sounded around the room as if little fairy creatures were ringing little bells. "Who does?" And then the voice changed to a male. "Ahhh, the mysteries of the Universe, none are more apparent than those you find in the presence of a woman. Eh?"

Tom laughed. "Isn't that the truth!"

"The Bible is a mysterious Book, Tom. It has an interesting explanation, don't you think?"

"You mean Adam and Eve?" Tom blurted. "That's pretty crazy! Do you really think anybody believes that?"

"Why not?"

"Why not? Well, you're going to have to do a LOT of convincing to me about that one!"

Tom leaned back in his chair folding his hands, challenging the being behind the curtain, and relishing whatever was in store for the day's lesson.

"Push and pull, black and white, night and day, male and female. What a marvelous system. Well. . .let's get on with it. Tom, what is your definition of a garden?"

"Plants."

"Well, let's just say for the record, that early mankind didn't cultivate plants."

"Do you think we came from someplace else?" Tom asked innocently.

"Of course. We all, everything, has come from someplace else. Everything didn't just start spontaneously here. It was spawned. Even an idea comes from someplace. . ."

"But that's not material." Tom emphasized.

"According to. . . who. . . you? Physics. . .?" Tom recognized the tone of a divine entity, Numen.

Tom shook his head, trying to clear it, as if there was something fuzzy around him.

"The story of Adam and Eve tells you that you are part of God, as is everything - good and evil. Right?" Numen paused.

"For whatever reason, you found your way here, Tom, because you wanted to know more about this world - about God, about good and evil. Right?"

Tom answered in a small voice. "Yes, I guess."

"RIGHT?"

"Yes." Stronger now. "YES!"

"Okay. And since we're talking about Adam and Eve, we can say that all mothers are Eve, for all of us. Of course."

"I need to read it again." Tom said. "It is such a ridiculous story."

"The Bible is a fluid document, Tom. It is supposed to reach out to us at whatever level we are at the time we read it. It is important to have new insights in regards to where we have progressed. . ."

"Yeah. . .but. . .the Adam and Eve thing . . . that's not right. My mother has always hated it. I don't blame her. And not all women are mothers."

"But all mothers are women. Of course, she has hated it. The story has relegated her to supposedly being subservient, which is not true. She is alongside. Culture has separated her. Preposterous!

"What happens when you accept risk? Change?" The Guide stepped in. "It's not easy. It wasn't easy for the first of you to accept the challenges with the Earth plane. Especially the **split**. There will be a time when this is better understood."

"The split? You mean coming from the ethereal state into a physical one?"

"Well, yes of course, but more than that. Consider yourself in an ethereal state, having **one** identity - for a second of hypothesis - and then needing to enter a physical dimension requiring *two,* where reproduction is required to exist. And then entering the physical dimension and splitting in two: male and female. Other things can happen with your identity splitting in two. We should not be too hasty in judging."

"Huh. . ???"

"That's where the concept of soulmate come from." The Guide said. "We are connected to all creatures in different ways. Our human species, in our way. To do a disservice to any element of our species, or any other for that matter, is a disservice to oneself.

"The entire world, all religions, have a version of Adam and Eve." Numen said. "Again, there is an element that is not fully understood. The couple represents our split in two. It isn't that Eve was created from Adam's rib. . .no, it is that our identity had to split in order to survive *here.* We innately understand this.

Tom stood and focused on the drape. He breathed deeply and released three times. He relaxed his shoulders and his neck. He emptied his thoughts. Then from his central region he filed the space with a glow of light, raising it higher and higher, behind his eyes and then out towards his Teacher. He surrounded the other side of the scrim with appreciation.

He tried to think of what it would be like to have one identity. Then he tried to think of what it would be like to be merged with everything. He understood that he really was, but he couldn't quite understand how he could maintain he individuality and still be connected. . .

"Tom," The Numen said, "A cell in your body is individual, yet it still belongs to you, and to no other. That cell can divide. When a baby is first conceived, it does not have a gender at first.

"We follow a certain set of laws that we don't fully understand. We just must accept. The matter of gender is a matter of **ONE.** The laws of our dimension require a split. Before we enter, we are one, then split off into genders here. Here. It is a comical, paradoxical, oxymoron that any part of us is treated with any less respect, be it female or male."

"Oh, what about. . .what about. . .?"

"Tom, God does not judge, neither should you." Numen said simply, understanding the question of his thought. "If people love each other, they have a special connection. Can they have a connection to you, and to everything else? Well, they do, whether they know it or not."

Thank you.

Tom felt himself surrounded with a pale turquoise light. He would miss the Zimmer room, the Teacher, The Guide, The Numen. This would be his last session, he knew.

You're welcome.

As Tom left the room, there was one last message. It was sent and received in pure white light.

Welcome!

Tom turned back, confused. "Welcome? What do you mean?"

"Welcome"

THE INTERVIEW

Tom had an interview that morning that lasted twice as long as he'd expected. The Director of Admissions from the medical school - the only one left considering him, called unexpectedly with four questions, and although Tom felt he was ready for anything, he wasn't. The interview was over the telephone and Tom realized the normal give and take of an in-person interview gave clues that the telephone did not. He felt like he was floating in a vacuum. "When did you decide you wanted to be a medical doctor?" The person over the phone asked.

Tom decided truth was the best route. He replied that he hadn't wanted to be a medical doctor until recently; it wasn't a life-long dream, and his parents didn't even know about it. He spoke candidly about his first encounter in a medical environment, about how he had thought more along the lines of what it meant to help others and how he hadn't been a very good student because his future hadn't mattered that much. Until now. He hoped it wasn't too late.

He discussed his work to recover his grades and how he thought his physics background was useful.

The next question was: "Do you think you have what it takes to complete the many years of study necessary for the requirements to become a doctor?"

Tom explained that he couldn't look at it that way, that he needed to take one step at a time. "I'm not a person that visualizes the big picture very well," he said, "but I do well with the task at hand. I finish things and I don't procrastinate; but if I try to do everything all at the same time, to look at it all at once, then I have a tendency to feel overwhelmed. But people can rely on me. I'm steady. I'm not the fastest runner in the race, but I finish it. So, I just have to believe in myself and take a step at a time."

Then Tom went on to say that he probably could have said something more glowing about himself, but he wanted to be honest and that he really wanted to impress upon the people making the selection that he would take every step in the process very seriously and do his best. "If I confront an obstacle, I will overcome it." He said.

"I don't know how I will do this financially, but if I can stay here, I'm already finding ways to generate the funds I need." But it was the next question that really threw him.

"Looking back over your life, what one thing do you wish you had done differently?"

Tom was not prepared for that question. It hit him like a fire bolt to his solar plexus. There were a lot of things Tom could think of, but at this moment, there was one that stood out. He was a kid, after all, he'd had a good life, he hadn't had many things happen that he wished were different. But there was one. Yes, there was one.

Tom cleared his throat, but he still spoke softly. "It was something that happened a couple of years ago," he began. "You know. . ." He cleared his throat again, "I treated somebody with a. . .um. . .a. . . I don't know how to explain this. . .but. . a lack of dignity. I was callous. I didn't need to be - there was no reason for it. I have wished I would have done things differently and I have learned from it. I have wished many times that I could take back my actions. I wanted that person to know that her dignity really was important to me. . ."

"What did you do about it?" The interviewer asked.

"I apologized." Tom said simply. "It was heartfelt, and it was accepted. In Japan they have a custom called a 'sorry gift' and I gave a sorry gift."

The interviewer turned to the others in the room and nodded. There were three other people sitting in on the interview. Of all the things Tom said that day, this one thing was the most important. It was difficult to teach doctors the importance of a patient's dignity, and even more difficult how to empathize.

Tom was certain he'd blown it.

The last question was expected. "Why do you want to be a doctor?"

Tom thought he was prepared with the answer, but he was completely upended after the previous question. He was certain he had ruined any chance of entrance to the only medical school that was considering him.

He actually said something stupid about destiny, that he was supposed to be a doctor and then he wished he hadn't said that. He tried to cover up his words with some nonsense about teamwork and being part of something bigger than himself. After a while he realized he was rambling. He apologized, saying, "Excuse me, I don't know what I am saying. The truth is, I want to be a doctor because that is who I am inside - a compassionate person who has found a calling to help others with their physical maladies. That's all. I've discovered that I have a compassionate nature."

Tom was quite distressed by the interview.

He breathed deeply and reminded himself:

I am always where I am supposed to be.

GRADUATION

There's a reason why universities have graduation in June. Some of them even wish they could change it to July, but tradition is tradition, especially for Tom's school. Clouds were threatening over the East Hills and the smell of rain was in the air.

Tom's parents had arrived the day before and were watching a game show on the television while Tom showered.

"A five-year degree in Physics is something to be proud of," his father was saying. "That's not an easy course of study. He could have taken courses in pre-med, and guess what? If he didn't get into med school, then what could he do with *that* degree. At least with physics he has more options."

"He's going to get in, Mike." She said simply.

"That's not the half of it." He said. "It costs thousands upon thousands of dollars."

"Other people do it. Stop worrying. "She said lightly. "It's his graduation."

The town was packed. Tom had the good sense to buy a week's parking at The Art's Garage across town and have Susan bring him back several days ago, then his parents could park in his spot there at the apartment building, only two blocks from campus. In front of his place was a shuttle stop and the campus buses would be running all the time. The shuttle would be great for the three of them. Tom never used it, because he had his bicycle.

That night, Carl's Derby Stampede would be jammed with people. There would be kids, sisters and brothers of graduates, all wanting to experience the "Three Stooges." But Jake and John were graduating too, and their families would be in town as well. Carl couldn't ask them to work. He knew it would be a huge disappointment because there wasn't anybody else who could give their performance. After all, what they did was a performance, wasn't it? He arranged for other employees to cover for them. He made a happy sign: Congratulations to our Graduates: Jake, John and Tom.

The rain held off long enough and a big sigh went through the throng as hugs and handshakes took place. When all was said and done, there was quite a group between the four of them - they had thirty or more people meeting on the west lawn for introductions between families. All of their families were there – John's and Jake's and Susan's. Tom's sister was there too.

But when Tom looked over at John and John made a face back at him and uttered a familiar noise, it was like a signal had been made. Jake heard it and jerked his head in response. None of it was very apparent or very loud and nobody else noticed. Tom gestured toward the shuttle bus and the three men were off at a dead run.

It was Susan who stepped up to the plate. "They don't want to disappoint all those people or their employer. They're going to work." She said. "People are going to be streaming in all night to get pizza for their parties, but even more so - to see and hear them."

The group was bewildered. They milled around the lawn for a while, until it began to rain, and then, at Susan's instigation, headed for the Derby Stampede themselves.

The boys shed their robes on the way but kept on their hats. The sign stayed up. They weren't sure how long they would stay, or even if it was necessary.

It was necessary.

A line snaked down the block. outside of Carl's.

John never worked so hard. He was able to put another shelf in the pizza oven so he had four, each taking two pizzas at once plus the bottom. The three employees who were scheduled to take their places were needed. There were six people running, plus Carl. Normally, John worked the oven alone, in and out all from one side, but now he swung open the back. There was another person loading from the front and a runner taking the pizza to Jake for cutting. Sarah, the runner, also boxed after Jake did his jump. Poor Jake was really getting a work-out!

Big John got the Pizza out with a noise, making one noise after the other, then it was delivered to Jake who did his jump, then boxed and sent to the straight man, Tom, who called out the name and gave it to the customer. Another guy named Tom was taking orders and answering the phone. Carl was bussing the tables.

The three men thought that whatever people found funny about them was gone because they weren't working so tightly together. They couldn't get a feel for the crowd. The place was so crowded and buzzing so loud that even John's noises were being drowned out. All the fun was gone out of it.

It was Jake's mom who made the difference by running down to Walmart and getting portable mics for the three of them to wear. By then they were hot and tired and looked silly with their graduation hats on. What none of them realized, was sitting in the back of the room, next to her cameraman, was one of television's own award-winning hour-long television news-show hosts. She was well disguised with lightly tinted glasses, red-haired wig and dumpy clothes.

The video camera was an expensive unit held in a camera bag that looked innocent enough on this graduation day. Nobody would guess that the bag held a state-of-the-art video camera that was using the table like a tripod. Running alongside it, under place mats, were sensitive microphones. To the on-looker, it was just a normal camera bag filled with gear, taking up space on top of a table. After all, it was Graduation Day.

Everything came together when the boys had the mics on. As the evening wore on, and the crowd finally thinned, the extras went home. For the three of them, it had been a double shift. The three stooges had only a half hour before closing, but it was long enough to organize their work area back into the normal routine. Any person coming in now would see them as they normally carried out their duties. They were exhausted, but happy to be back into their synergistic patterns.

It was then that the woman in the back came forward to order her pizza. "Welcome to the stampede," Tom said, managing a smile. "Have I got a special for you tonight!"

"And have I got one for you," she said, taking her glasses off.

THE NOTICE

The hospital was located a five-hour drive outside Port au Prince on a good day, when the roads weren't flooded and too muddy for the drive. It was reached by driving on a paved road for an hour, then graded gravel stretches, and next a rutted lane that would be a poor excuse for a driveway in a developed country. It could take all the daylight hours to get there during the rainy season. Children would run out with vegetation to put over the mud, if it could be made passable, asking for a ten-cent toll. If not, travelers needed to wait for the muddy areas to drain off.

Seemingly located out in the bush, the hospital served a huge throng of people, severely in need, that made a long line for help every day at the hospital's gate. Most of them had walked miles to get there. Dr. Tom Cross, true to his word, and guided by the new revelations he had been given in the Room, had studied medicine. The cost had been easily covered by a movie about the three of them who'd worked at Carl's.

Presently, he and Susan were serving a one-year volunteer post at the hospital. Their assignment was drawing near a close and they'd soon be going back to the USA for a much-needed recovery from the difficulties of working in a bush environment.

Volunteers mostly came and went for two weeks at a time, because this was tough duty even for two weeks. The two doctors who were there for longer commitments found the revolving door difficult; but it was important for the short timers to be exposed to people in need, people who truly had nothing, people who had to walk a mile for a clean drink of water.

The hospital served the poorest country in the Western Hemisphere, and the participating doctors from Western countries learned sad lessons in patient care. It was often impossible to save a child dying from hunger. Although hunger was not unknown in America, Tom had never seen a case of kwashiorkor in the United States, that is, a child with an extended, or pot belly appearance having gaunt limbs and hair that had turned orange from starvation. Such a child is still "savable" but he was seeing children in the final stages of starvation when the entire body swells, an appearance that to the untrained eye may look somewhat healthier, but in fact precedes death. It is usually too late to bring the body back with food and nutrition. It has gone too long without it.

In Haiti Tom discovered that children still die easily from starvation and malnutrition. He almost specialized in pediatrics, but had chosen orthopedics instead, liking the more rugged hands-on approach and the opportunities to correct problems for people of all ages. He did have surgical rotations, but the majority of his practice was setting bones, evaluating arthritic problems, injecting swollen knees and solving dislocated shoulders and sports injuries. But now, in this bush environment, sometimes there wasn't an orthopedic surgeon and he was performing pins and other invasive placements for fractures. Complicated conditions where bones were crushed beyond his ability to repair, were sent to the overworked folks in Port au Prince. It was touchy for the people needing the care though, because money was an issue compared to the essentially free care provided at the hospital where he was located. Sadly, he wished he was more specialized to correct the cleft palates and the club feet. He was considering returning for a fellowship that would give him the surgical expertise to do the foot repairs. The cleft palates would be the purview of a maxillofacial surgeon, something that would take too many years for him to consider, but every time he saw one, he wished he had the expertise to do something about it. Once in a while, a doctor came to do those repairs. A precious two weeks. They scheduled every free minute and all personnel in support of the visiting doctors who volunteered to come and do those repairs. They prayed that something big would not happen that was life threatening to take away their two operating rooms. A club foot repair could not really be done in a makeshift surgical room, but they had been known to set up portable rooms for cleft palate work. They did things that would never be considered in more improved countries, but the risk to the patient was worth it. It was the only chance most of those patients would ever have of receiving medical care.

Susan had established a program of educating the local population on birth control, vaccinations and the importance of clean water.

Tom and Susan lived in a tiny house by the edge of the hospital. It was provided as part of their service at the hospital, because most of the population around the area lived in lean-to's made of cardboard boxes, or under bushes, without electricity or running water, in the hills or in conditions that were not acceptable to basic livability for a Western doctor. Also, security needed to be maintained for the few things Tom had brought with him, such as a stethoscope. One of the most important things Tom had brought, and the most valuable to him personally, was a solar cell. It was lightweight, almost a film, that was a portable unit he could put on his roof. It gave him and Susan enough power for their computers and an uplink to a satellite. They had little personal time and were often too tired to care, but they could watch a little news and catch up with friends and family.

In the morning they discussed their work. Before leaving for the day they always checked their email. It was on such a morning that two emails arrived, both with the subject: Urgent Notice. One was from the University and one was from a friend, but Tom had known the day before. It was always that way with Tom. He just knew. The Teacher had died.

A service was planned at the University. Tom was late to his clinic that morning. He could ask the volunteer at the hospital to help him with their tickets, but they had few resources to do it, and he was better equipped to find a flight.

When Tom and Susan arrived at the university on that fall morning, there was a chill to the air, but it was clear and sunny. The traffic was horrendous, almost as if there was a football game. The viewing of the Teacher was set up in the campus alumni assembly room. There were parking lots near this area, so he thought there would be parking available. He was wrong. Tom drove to an outer parking lot where they boarded a shuttle. They joined a crowd where students were circulating with obituaries and coffee. There were tables set up along the building that had homemade cakes and pastries.

Tom couldn't believe the numbers of people. "Are all of these people here for the service?" Susan asked. They were.

There was a tone in the background as people spoke softly about the person who had meant so much. "Of course, there'd be something nice to eat." They heard people saying." Yes, she would have wanted it that way." "I can still hear the Voice every day guiding me," said another. "I will always hear that Voice. There can be no tears when it is just a matter of change. . ." "Yes. Change." Tom heard the word, *change,* again and again. The Teacher had changed, had moved on, had become something else. "I wonder if his spirit is here," a woman said. "We are all connected to each other," another person said who still looked like a student."

He was looking around at the crown smiling. Many people heard him and nodded. Tom reached out to his arm. "Yes," he said to him, "we are!"

The student looked gratefully at him and asked, "What did you become?" "A medical doctor, An orthopedist, actually. What about you? What are you studying or doing? The student nodded. "I am studying veterinary medicine in terms of public health." Tom thought about the badly needed expertise, about the one overworked person in his region, trying to help the people with their livestock and vaccinations. "You are needed." He said.

"You know, I don't even know the Teacher's name," the student said. "I don't either," Tom said. Another person joined the conversation. They were now in a line moving closer to the door.

"I never saw her," The person in front of him said. "I know," Tom said. "I didn't either. I don't even know if the Teacher was a man or a woman. Although he most often spoke to me in a male voice." She laughed and smiled." She almost always spoke to me in a feminine voice. I think of her as female." Then two men spoke at one. "I think of him as male."

They all looked now at the obituary in their hands and read it. It was simple, only two paragraphs. The Teacher had been born in Poland and came to America when a small child with parents who immigrated. There was no reference to "he" or "she." It was like gender was carefully avoided. His/her name was Jean Oktober Kumiega. Jean held a PhD in Physics from the University of Illinois at Urbana-Champaign and another one in Guidance Counseling. The Teacher died at the age of 87 (and still working at the university) and passed from a heart event while asleep.

The Teacher's position at the University had been in Administration, helping students decide on their futures.

It took three hours to arrive at the casket. The aroma of flowers filled the room and a glow from a light filled the room. There were exclamations that could be heard as people entered the room. "Oh, it is so beautiful here. Look at the light!" But really nobody was surprised.

A small figure dressed in a light green robe lay in the casket. Above the casket was a simple quote. It read: "If I have helped one person find their true purpose in this life, then I have fulfilled my true purpose."

A serene face greeted each visitor as they said farewell to one of the most important people who had ever entered their lives.

There was nothing about the figure that gave you a clue about gender, and truly who cared? Some expected him to be large, but he was small. Others expected her to have strong features, but she was simply elderly and lovely in her way, and it was hard to tell if she had ever been beautiful once. But of course, she had been. She had always been beautiful! She is beautiful now. He was handsome in his own way. There was a strength to him. It was the first time any of them had ever seen the Teacher.

There were no tears shed by anyone who knew Jean, or it might be better to say by anyone that Jean knew, because who really knew her? It seemed like Jean had looked into every person there and had not only changed their life but the lives of all the people *they* touched. The ripple effect was beyond comprehension. That night there was a reunion, or more like a gathering of all those who had known the Teacher, a kind of alumni. It seemed like Tom didn't know anybody and then he knew everybody. It was just he had trouble recognizing people at first - other students from medical school and students from physics. There were so many people of all ages. The Teacher had been a Voice to so many for so long! "I didn't know you were seeing the Teacher" one would say to another. "Nor I" would be the answer. It just was something that none of them talked about.

"It was so private. I never told anybody the things we talked about. Oh, maybe snatches here and there in philosophical conversations, but I could never quite phrase things, or put them across in a manner that made sense the way the Teacher could."

"Imagine, a PhD in Physics, but I'm not really surprised. A counselor with an advanced degree in physics. . . "Yeah." "Oh Yes!" "My friend. A job well done. A life well lived."

"You fulfilled your purpose. You changed my life."

"I found my purpose."

In the thirty years that the Teacher had been with the University, there had been nine hundred and fifty-six people that had sat in the Numen Room. Many of them were there to say good-bye to the person who had changed their lives. It seemed that all these people had done whatever it took to get there and those that couldn't, because of flight delays or conditions beyond their control, had sent flowers and messages for the others to read. There was a simple buffet style meal organized in the large ballroom where they all gathered early that evening. They were all people, like Tom, that had come from all over the world. At the front of the room were three large panels. One of them said: *If I have helped you find your purpose, then I have fulfilled mine.* The middle one had a huge picture of a drop. The other side said:

One drop falling to another. . . adds to the other
Two drops together. . .attracts more to gather
Three, four and five. . .and it's alive. . .
A thousand or more than before
And it's a tower of power."

Tom and Susan found their places in the room. There were ten chairs at the round table. Tom & Susan, Chib & Cece, Carl & Chelsea, Big John and Julie, Jake and Janet were all at their table. Tom looked at Chelsea smiling, "It was you who originally told me about the Teacher, wasn't it?" She nodded.

At a few tables over, Tom saw somebody waving. It was Simeon and Kate! When everyone was finally seated, the President of the University, also a former student and alumnus of the Numen Room spoke: "In a few moments, students will be coming through with two containers, one will be an amber drink, and another that is empty. You will be given both. You notice, you each have two eye droppers at your place. There is nothing we can do to say our goodbye to this person, because there are no goodbye's. Right?" There was a murmur in the room. "The gift we received from the Teacher is beyond words, so we will do something together. It will take us only a few minutes or so, and some energy, to transfer our drink from the container to the other." She stopped with a grin and said," You won't get confused, because you'll notice that we borrowed beakers from the science department to have next to our glasses."

The silent group laughed.

"I had to justify the purchase of so many beakers," she added.

The group roared.

"We'll do this as a group together. You will be surprised how quickly we can do this."

She put her hand to her mouth, admitting and nodding, "I practiced first."

Now everybody was laughing knowing that was exactly what the Teacher would have wanted.

"When we are finished" she continued, "we'll make a toast to the Teacher and to each of us, especially for being able to transfer our drink, and we'll drink it! Please let the circulating students know if you are too young to drink alcohol or if you prefer plain juice because there will be enough in your glass for a hefty SHOT! She raised her empty glass to the group, and then suddenly her mood changed and she was pursing her lips in emotion and trying hard to keep herself from tearing up, but tears squeezed through her squinted eyelids anyway. She said shakily:

LET US BEGIN.

EPILOG

The Shrine was up a number of steps, 92 to be exact. It was a difficult climb to get to the top, so scattered escalators had been installed along the way. Once a person was there, they were often greeted by a Buddhist Monk who tended to the incense burners and insured all was in order. There were several paths on the way to this place. Along the backside of one of those paths was the entrance to a room that faced the ocean below. There was a table outside where visitors to this place signed their name before entering. Only a few people seemed to have appointments to enter.

It was rumored that sitting inside was a wise person . . .

In the Land of my ancestors, near the river that carves a narrow passage through the brown rocks, where my father's father, and his father before him, knew peace, but there hasn't been any for all of the generations since, there is a cave. It is well camouflaged by the trees and foliage, but if a person looks carefully, it is possible to see something almost hidden between the rock walls. It is an opening. It is said, there is a dweller inside that has answers. It is not easy to get to this place and only a few ever find it. Those that do will never be the same again.

In the marketplace, by the cardboard city, is a small hovel with a lone goat standing by the entrance to a lean-to shack. It looks like it couldn't withstand the next rain, that it couldn't possibly stay dry enough for the cardboard to keep its form, but none-the-less, there is a sheet hung over the entrance. Once a person ducts under the sheet, everything about their life will be transformed. . .

At the hospital there is a small room down corridor A at the corner where the windows meet. There is no label on the door, but there is a small table located next to it. There is a rumor about this room – that some people call the zimmer. Inside there is a person, a Teacher, a Guide. A Doctor. Some people called the presence, *Numen.*

Dr. Michael Cross exited behind the back door from the zimmer to do his evening rounds. He glanced back at the billowing drape and smiled once again, understanding the importance of his anonymity. He remembered his last visit with the Guide. . . his Teacher. . . .

Welcome! The voice had said.

Merriam-Webster:

numen

nu·men | \ ˈnü-mən , ˈnyü- \ plural numina\ˈnü-mə-nə, ˈnyü- \

: a spiritual force or influence often identified with a natural object, phenomenon, or place

(Wikipedia) Cicero writes of a"divine mind"(divina mens), a god"whose numen everything obeys,"and a"divine power"(vim divinam)"which pervades the lives of men."

"We choose ourselves"
The Numen

ABOUT THE AUTHOR

C. E. KELLY

Writing this book has been an exhaustive, solitary effort, but nothing of value is ever done alone. I am connected to everything.

A special thank you, to my sisters and my mother and to Numen.

I remain behind the drape, because after all, appearances are deceiving

May all your doors open for you
May you keep all the visions that lift your heart
May you find all your answers
May all your dreams come true

Blessings

http://www.thenumen.com